DEAD
SIMPLE

Other Books by Jon Land

The Alpha Deception
The Council of Ten
°Day of the Delphi
The Doomsday Spiral
The Eighth Trumpet
°The Fires of Midnight
The Gamma Option
°Kingdom of the Seven
Labyrinth
The Lucifer Directive
The Ninth Dominion
The Omega Command
The Omicron Legion
The Valhalla Testament
The Vengeance of the Tau
Vortex
°The Walls of Jericho

°Indicates a Forge Book

JON LAND

DEAD
SIMPLE

A TOM DOHERTY ASSOCIATES BOOK
NEW YORK

DEAD SIMPLE

Copyright © 1998 by Jon Land

This book is printed on acid-free paper.

A Forge Book
Published by Tom Doherty Associates, Inc.
175 Fifth Avenue
New York, NY 10010

Forge® is a registered trademark of Tom Doherty Associates, Inc.

Library of Congress Cataloging-in-Publication Data

Land, Jon.
    Dead simple   /   Jon Land.—1st ed.
      p.   cm.
    "A Tom Doherty Associates book."
    ISBN 0-312-86489-2 (acid-free paper)
    I. Title.
    PS3562.A469D4   1998
    813'.54—dc21   97-39737
                                                                     CIP

First Edition: April 1998

Printed in the United States of America

0 9 8 7 6 5 4 3 2 1

For my brother, who is brave

ACKNOWLEDGMENTS

In publishing, no man or woman is an island. Producing a book, from the birth of the idea to final publication, requires a myriad of people united toward a common goal. For me, the first of those people is Toni Mendez, as great a human being as she is an agent. Through eighteen books now, she has been joined by Ann Maurer in pushing me to make each the best it can possibly be.

We are joined by a group of publishing professionals who still care about their authors. The office doors of Tom Doherty, Linda Quinton, Yolanda Rodriguez, and Jennifer Marcus are always open. And my editor at Forge, Natalia Aponte, is always there for me, period.

For help on this one, I am also indebted to Michael Hussey and Katherine Vollen from the National Archives, Ross Allard, Skip Trahan, Steve Feinstein, John Rizzieri, Irv Schechter, Commander Paul Dow, and Matt Lerish.

My last and most special acknowledgment goes to Emery Pineo, who retains his title as the World's Smartest Man by solving no less than thirty technical problems on this book, many of them during sixth-grade lunch duty, outdoing even himself. Any mistakes you find are the result of questions I forgot to ask him.

PROLOGUE

OBLIVION

The huge truck lumbered through the night, headlights cutting a thin slice out of the storm raging around it.

"I think we're lost," Corporal Larry Kleinhurst muttered, straining to see through the tanker's windshield.

"We're following the map, Corporal," Captain Frank Hall said from behind the wheel. Hall kept playing with the lights in search of a beam level that could better reveal what lay ahead. But the storm gave little back, continuing to intensify the further they drew into Pennsylvania.

Another *thump* atop the ragged, unpaved road shook Hall and Kleinhurst in their seats. They had barely settled back down when a heftier jolt jarred the rig mightily to the left. Hall managed to right it with a hard twist of the wheel that squeezed the blood from his hands.

"Captain . . ."

"This is the route they gave us, Corporal."

Kleinhurst laid the map between them. "Not if I'm reading this right. With all due respect, sir, I believe we should turn back."

Hall cast him a condescending stare. "This your first Red Dog run?"

"Yes, sir, it is."

"When you're hauling a shipment like what we got, you don't turn back, no matter what. When they call us, it's because they never want to see the stuff again."

Kleinhurst's eyes darted to the radio. "What about calling in?"

"Radio silence, soldier. They don't hear a peep from us till we get where we're going."

Kleinhurst watched the rig's wipers slap at the pelting rain collecting on the windshield, only to have a fresh layer form the instant they had completed their sweep. "Even in an emergency?"

"Let me give it to you straight: the stuff we're hauling in that tank doesn't exist. That means we don't exist. That means we talk to nobody. Got it?"

"Yes, sir," Kleinhurst sighed.

"Good," said Hall. "The best we can hope for is to find shelter. But out here . . ." His voice drifted, as he stole a glance at the map.

Suddenly Kleinhurst leaned forward, squinting to peer through the windshield. "Jesus Christ, up there on the right!"

"What?"

"Can't you see *it*?"

"I can't see shit, Corporal."

"Slow down, for God's sake!"

Hall hit the brakes and the rig's tires locked up, sending the tanker into a vicious skid across the road. He tried to work the steering wheel, but it fought him every inch of the way, turning the skid into a spin through an empty wave of darkness.

"There!" Kleinhurst screamed.

"What in God's name," Hall rasped, still fighting to steer when a mouth opened out of the storm and the rig dropped helplessly toward it.

1

OLD DOGS

SIX MONTHS LATER

ONE

"This is as far as I can take ya," the sheriff said, stopping the old squad car where the dirt road ended. "And I only took ya this far on account of you being a friend of his."

Blaine McCracken nodded his thanks and started to climb out of the car. He took it slow, his hip stiff from the ride, focusing on the tangled growth of vegetation and the dark waters ahead.

"Ya need some help there?"

"I can manage."

"Don't forget your bag now," the sheriff reminded, shifting it across the back seat.

He was a dour man with a face marred by pits and furrows. The thickness of his southern accent seemed strange to Blaine, who didn't consider Florida to be part of the Deep South. Then again, this part of the state was new to him.

Blaine had flown into Miami and had a cab take him southwest to Flamingo. There the sheriff had offered to drive him to Condor Key, a swampy peninsula that jutted out into the northern tip of the Everglades. The only road sign he noticed on the way was faded and spotted with rust.

Blaine reached into the back seat and hoisted his duffel bag with his good arm, the bad one dangling limply by his side. He closed the door again and caught a glimpse of his face in the window. It was much thinner than he could ever recall, the cheekbones set high and jaw sunken beneath his close-cropped beard. His skin looked pale and furrowed, further exaggerating the thick scar that sliced through his left eyebrow where a bullet had left its mark years before. The sheriff made no motion to join him outside the car, pointed straight ahead through the windshield instead. "What ya wanna do now is walk out on that dock, far as you can. There'll be a boat coming to take ya the rest of the way 'fore too much longer."

"Thanks. I appreciate the lift."

The sheriff leaned a little across the seat. "I ask ya a question?"

"Yeah."

"Thing is, see, the man don't get many visitors. Fact is you the first I seen since he moved in, and that includes his family."

"You said you had a question."

"Does he know you're coming?"

"Depends if he reads his mail."

The sheriff nodded, not changing his expression. "I figured as much."

"Then why'd you drive me out here?" Blaine said through the window, dropping his duffel and leaning his hands on the door.

"Saw your ring, son." The sheriff cocked his gaze toward Blaine's ring finger. "He got one just like it, and I know enough 'bout such things to be sure there ain't many. You got that ring, way I see it you're a man he wouldn't mind seeing. He'll have my hide if I'm wrong."

"Yours and mine both."

The sheriff restarted the engine. "Give the ole boy my best. Tell him there's a meal waiting at the house whenever he gets it in his head to come into town."

He had to reverse his car a few times in the narrow roadway to manage the swing back around. With the sheriff gone, Blaine was left alone amidst the mangroves and black swamp waters that lay in every direction. The land was so flat, only a few inches above the water level and tangled with thick vegetation, he could see little beyond the worn dock. Blaine's shirt was already soaked through with sweat by the time he walked to the edge, the world around him alive with noise. Things shifted and plopped in the water. The mangroves rattled in the breeze.

Blaine sat down on the dock to take the pressure off his hip, felt the wood, moist with lapping waters and relentless humidity, soak through the seat of his pants. He slapped at the mosquitoes buzzing around his ears and fingered his ring, glad now he had worn it, tracing the two silver embossed letters amidst the black:

DS

It was a part of his past, dead and gone, but the past was what he needed now.

His mystical Indian friend, Johnny Wareagle, who knew him better than anyone, said men like the two of them walked with the spirits, their movements guided, protected. The last few years, Blaine had really started listening, because Wareagle's explanations made as much sense as any other. A small bullet could kill, just as a big bullet might not; it was all in where it hit you.

Johnny had spent many hours at the hospital over the past six months, strangely unmoved by the severity of McCracken's wounds or of what his prognosis might hold.

"Looks like your spirits deserted me, Indian," Blaine had said one night when the pain in his hip was especially bad.

"They are your spirits too, Blainey," came the seven-foot-tall Wareagle's placid reply. "The road you travel with them has taken a sharp turn, that is all."

"The end of it for me, maybe."

"You've been broken before, Blainey."

"Nothing a little gauze and antiseptic couldn't take care of. Small scars, relatively speaking."

"I was talking about your spirit, where the scars are never small. I was talking about years ago when both of us had withdrawn, accepting the emptiness."

"I came and got you."

"The years between that time and the Hellfire were merely a respite to convince us of the men we really are." Here Johnny had paused, his eyes seeming to light the room. "You still are that man."

"Not exactly."

Wareagle looked unfazed. "There is a legend among my people of a warrior who rode the plains through too many years to count. Entire tribes fell to his hand, if they dared attack his people. One night he slept by a calm stream, where he was attacked by a warrior who was his equal in every way. He had at last met his match, and the battle went on for hours. Others in the tribe found him bloodied and near death, and pointing at his attacker." Johnny's expression had fixed tightly on Blaine. "His own reflection in the stream, Blainey, come to take him in a nightmare."

"There a point to this, Indian?"

"Only one man can defeat you. The warrior of legend had bested every opponent, but he could not overcome himself when at last confronted. This is that confrontation for you, Blainey."

Blaine thought back to those words, fingering his ring again. It had been a gift to him and a select few others after the war in Vietnam. A gift from the man who had shaped him, pounded the folds of his being as if he were a sword and left him razor sharp.

DS . . .

Dead Simple, the motto of the elite unit Blaine had been a part of through those years. But the last few months had been anything but simple.

Lying in the hospital, listening to the grim pronouncements of specialists, fighting through the grueling hours of physical therapy—lower body first and then upper body, the dual regimens necessitated by his two equally debilitating wounds. Watching and hearing people marvel at his progress. A medical miracle. A triumph of will.

Yet he couldn't get out of a car without an old sheriff asking if he needed help. Couldn't use his left arm to lift a duffel bag that barely weighed twenty pounds.

So where was the miracle?

The doctors had proudly pronounced him capable of being able to lead a normal life. How could Blaine explain that wasn't good enough? When they said he would eventually get back ninety-five percent of his strength and mobility, how could he tell them it was that last five percent that mattered most, was responsible for the edge that made him what he was, at least had been?

They wouldn't understand, so he had come down here to Condor Key in search of the man who would.

Blaine saw a skiff pushing its way through the still water, slipping past the vegetation that stubbornly clawed at it. The skiff was unmanned, and he rose warily to his feet, hackles rising with that familiar and long-unfelt uneasiness that comes of sensing danger. A feeling of something not as it should be. The skiff could have broken away from another dock, of course, and drifted here with the currents. But a mangled hip and shoulder weren't enough to change the way he had learned to think: to accept nothing as innocent.

Blaine moved closer to the dock's edge so as to get a better view of the skiff. It rode high in the water, ruling out the possibility of a person lying down inside it on a surreptitious approach. He had let Sergeant Major Eugene "Buck" Torrey know he was coming but hadn't furnished a return address or phone number, not wanting to give Buck the opportunity to tell him not to bother.

The skiff slid closer to the dock, almost within reach. Blaine knelt, intending to pull it in toward him. He was reaching out to snare the small boat, when a hand rose from beneath the water and caught his ankle in an iron clutch. Before Blaine could respond, he felt himself being heaved off the dock. He took the impact against the surface on his bad shoulder and felt a shredding burst of agony in what passed for muscle now. He had twisted his body before striking the water as well, which made his hip feel like something was crunching around inside it.

The pain distracted Blaine long enough for a pair of powerful hands to grasp him round the head and throat. The hands dragged him further under as Blaine kicked and flailed. Then, just as quickly, he felt the same iron hands yank him to the surface and hoist him effortlessly back onto the dock. He squinted in the bright sunlight and gazed down at a grinning shape treading water just below him.

"I got your note, son," said Sergeant Major Buck Torrey. "Now tell me what the hell happened."

"*A*t *least you didn't waste much time," Blaine said to Hank Belgrade that day six months earlier at the Lincoln Memorial, where they always met.*

"Forty-eight hours to be exact," Belgrade told him. "I wanted you in on this while Red Dog's trail was still fresh. This is a bad one, MacNuts."

"So I figured when you asked me to bring Johnny along." And his gaze fell briefly on the shape of the huge Indian waiting patiently at the foot of the steps. Blaine waited for a pair of late-afternoon tourists to slide past them before he continued. "Who knows I'm here?"

Belgrade frowned. "You're looking at him."

"I'm sure you've got your reasons."

"Special Projects."

"The government's dirty tricks divisions. Doesn't officially exist."

"And another thing that doesn't officially exist is the research division Special Projects maintains at Brookhaven Labs. The latest phrase for deterrent there is active destabilization."

"I didn't know there was another kind of destabilization."

"Bear with me here. Active destabilization refers to isolating an enemy, cutting off his supply lines. Knocking out bridges, runways, command and control." The slump in Belgrade's shoulders deepened. "We set out to create something with one hundred percent effectiveness. And we did. It's called Devil's Brew. I named it myself. Trouble was it turned out to be considerably more effective than we expected or required. We're talking the biggest bang anywhere short of a nuke. Too big a downside if the wrong people found out it existed. So I decided to dump it."

"What happened?"

"Red Dog was transporting the shipment to be destroyed. Desolate roads away from major population centers, standard route through central Pennsylvania—you know the drill."

Blaine nodded.

"Then, all of a sudden, the rig vanished. Poof! Into thin air."

"You check the route?"

"Along with the entire surrounding area, with satellites, U-2 spy planes, ground sweeps, and full recon units. Utterly clean. No shrapnel, no evidence of any kind of a hijacking or of a crash. Storm that night washed away any tracks that might have helped us." Belgrade sighed. "Like I said, not a trace. Might as well have dropped off the face of the earth."

"What about the transponder?"

"*Died out suddenly.*"

"*Or was turned off.*"

"*There were two,*" Belgrade said, catching McCracken's meaning. "*The crew didn't know about the second.*"

"*Emergency beacon?*"

"*Never switched on.*"

"*Which makes this an awfully sophisticated piece of work if you're thinking hostile action from a source other than Red Dog's crew.*"

"*That's why I called you.*" Belgrade's expression became utterly flat and rigid. "*We can't let this stuff fall into the wrong hands, MacNuts. If Devil's Brew works even half as good as the preliminary testing indicated, there won't be a person in this country who'll be safe. And it'll be my goddamn fault, even though I took every conceivable precaution. It was a textbook operation.*"

"*Sometimes things happen you haven't got a chapter ready for.*"

Before Belgrade could respond, Blaine saw police cars tear onto the Mall and converge on the Washington Monument. In the distance, beyond the Reflecting Pool, tour patrons were scattering in all directions. Blaine stiffened, the hairs of his beard seeming to stand on end. From the foot of the Memorial, Johnny Wareagle turned and looked up at him.

"*Like I was saying,*" Blaine said.

"**All** right," Sam Kirkland, the FBI's assistant director in charge of counterterrorism informed McCracken thirty minutes after terrorists had seized the Washington Monument. "*This is what we know.*" Kirkland's expression was somewhere between a scowl and a sneer, and he didn't bother to disguise the reluctance in his voice. "*For starters,*" he continued inside the FBI's makeshift command post, where equipment was still being dragged in, "*we've got five perps armed with automatic weapons holding thirty-seven hostages on the observation deck. Our thermal scan was positive for explosives, most likely C-4, enough to blow the tip of the monument into orbit. The leader says he'll detonate in just under three hours if he doesn't receive twenty million dollars.*"

"*Any ID on the leader?*"

"*His voiceprint's not in our files.*"

"*What about photo reconnaissance?*"

"*He hasn't given us a clear look. He's bald, that's all I can tell you so far.*"

"*Not very much.*"

"*The money's twenty minutes away,*" Kirkland said, "*if it comes to that.*"

"*What about Hostage and Rescue?*"

"*Ten minutes away, with a response plan drawn up no more than one hour after that,*" Kirkland said, trying to sound confident.

"*Then they'd better draw up new specs for the Monument while they're* at it, Mr. Assistant Director. The observation deck windows are too thick to shoot or crash through, and my guess is the elevator has been disabled. Think your men can cover ninety flights of stairs and still take these bastards by surprise?"

Kirkland met McCracken's eyes for the first time, liquidy spheres that looked like miniature black holes. "You got a better idea?"

Blaine focused his gaze on the tip of the Monument. "Just one."

TWO

This the FBI *I* know we're talking about?" Buck asked disbelievingly, still treading water. "I can't see these keep-it-in-the-house sons of bitches opening up their doors to an outsider."

"Hank let a few people know I was on the scene; they took care of the rest."

"Too bad."

"Wrong place at the wrong time."

"Then or now?"

"Why don't you tell me?"

Buck finally pulled himself onto the dock and sat on its edge next to McCracken. His huge forearms pulsed slightly with exertion and his black t-shirt clung to his barrel chest like a glove. Blaine couldn't say Torrey was still muscular; he was just big—everywhere. His face was block square, his jawline so angular that it lent his expression a perpetual menacing glint. His jet-black hair showed some streaks of gray now and it was longer than Blaine had ever seen it. His face, though pitted and pockmarked, was strangely gentle, that of a man who could hug a person as easily as break him in half.

Buck Torrey's career had been that of a textbook hero until the relatively recent past. As sergeant major of the elite troop Blaine had been selected for in the early seventies, Torrey had designed the program that separated the good from the great among Special Forces personnel. This and subsequent work led to a steady rise for him through the Special Forces as it eventually became umbrellaed under the Special Operations Command based in Florida. Torrey, it was said, was being groomed to take over the post of Command Sergeant Major upon the retirement of the legendary Hank Luthie.

Everything changed on a single ragged morning in Somalia, when an army Ranger detachment was dispatched to "acquire" a Somali warlord. The operation went off without a hitch; the detachment was pulling out when one of its choppers was hit by an RPG. The chopper went down and the result was a pitched battle that rivaled any on record for ferocity and violence, ending with Ranger troops fighting with bayonets or hand-to-hand through an impossibly long night. The Rangers took three dozen casualties. The Somalis took over a thousand.

For Buck Torrey that was small consolation. He had written a half-dozen memos on the need of armored support for his men dispatched to that godforsaken country. Because they had gone unheeded, on-site Special Operations Command was helpless to mount a rescue or send in proper reinforcements. Torrey's men—and he saw them all as his men—had handled their end of things brilliantly, only to be fucked by an establishment that was balancing image and dollars instead of protecting lives. Torrey wrote one final memo, walked into the SOC commander's office, and broke his jaw with a single punch.

He accepted his discharge, took his pension, and dropped off the face of the earth, so far as most were concerned. But he couldn't escape the Special Forces network, which had a way of keeping track of its own, and that's how Blaine had tracked him down.

"I got to warn you that if you come down here looking for a place, there ain't no vacancies," Buck Torrey said, in a drawl that mixed both sides of the Mason-Dixon line.

"I came to see you."

"I talked with your doctors, son."

"You . . ." Blaine was unable to hide his surprise.

"They told me they put you back together."

"That's because I can walk without falling and shave without cutting myself. After that, things get tough."

"Not much of a life, walking and shaving."

"No."

Buck Torrey dangled his legs over the dock's side and shook some of the water from his clothes. "Now, you add fishing, son, and you got yourself something."

"I want you to train me again, Buck."

"Sure. Fly or cast, take your pick."

"I'm not talking about fishing."

Torrey looked at McCracken's *DS* ring, compared it to his own. "Looks nice on you."

"Thanks."

"When was the last time you had it on?"

"I don't remember."

"That would explain its mint condition." Torrey looked at Blaine closely. "You wear it today for me?"

"I hoped it would take me back."

"You can't go back, son. Forward's the one direction in a man's gearbox." Buck's eyes settled on Blaine's ring. "And everything you need to start shifting again is right there in those two letters."

"Dead Simple."

"Just words. You gotta look beyond them being our motto 'cause of how good we were at killing. Lots of boys can be good at killing. But to live to be old dogs like us, you got to be good at plenty more than that."

"Like you, maybe."

"I don't know. You're alive, ain't ya?"

"Not by much."

"It's a yes-or-no question, son."

"Yes."

"Then tell me the rest of the story."

The A-1000 Thunderhawk helicopter cruised through the sky in stealth mode, silent and invisible in the night. Blaine crouched in the doorway of its cramped rear bay, as the Washington Monument drew closer beneath him. When the tip was directly below, the Thunderhawk slowed to a hover and he eased out gracefully into the night sky, holding fast to the black line rigged to his harness. Camouflaged in black as well, Blaine knew he was invisible to even the trained eye.

All the equipment he had required had accompanied the FBI's elite Hostage and Rescue Team to the staging site set atop a baseball field in West Potomac Park. He left it to Kirkland to explain his role in the operation to the commandos, listening to the briefing as he buckled himself tightly into a climbing vest and carefully checked his supply of pitons and carabiners for wear and spring. Satisfied, he clipped or pocketed them in place and then went to work coiling the climbing rope so it would drape comfortably from his shoulder. Pulling the rope over him to get accustomed to its feel and weight, Blaine carefully eased the rest of what he needed into a pack, leaving inspection of the piton gun Kirkland had managed to obtain for him for last.

Now, twenty minutes later, three hours after the Monument had been seized, Blaine dropped his feet and angled his toes straight for the tip. The

wind pushed him slightly, and he learned fast how to compensate by twirl-
ing his lower legs to keep the tip of the Monument directly beneath him.

Touching down was a bit more jarring than he had expected. But Blaine
slid slightly down the precipice and leaned his torso against the base, legs
straddling it. His angle of descent had placed him down on the southern
side of the tip, since reconnaissance indicated that the hostages were con-
centrated along the other three walls. Several might be injured by the
explosives he had come up here to set. Since all were seated away from
the area where the blast's effects would be centered, their chances of sur-
vival were considerably better than if left to the whims of the terrorists.

Ready to go to work, Blaine pulled the piton gun from his vest and
inserted a piton eye-first into the barrel. Once fired, the sharp edge of the
piton would be driven deep into the marble face six feet below the Mon-
ument's tip. His biggest problem when he drew back to aim the piton gun
was the wind, because it forced the chopper to bob slightly in the air,
drawing him upward and keeping him from being able to steady the piton
gun long enough to shoot it.

Blaine shifted slightly to better his position. He got the piton gun level
and aimed, ready to fire it, when the chopper jerked him upward again.

Frustrated, Blaine settled back down against the smooth marble and
unclasped the support line from his harness. He waved the Thunderhawk
away as the line dangled free, leaving him clinging to the Monument's
south side with nothing to catch him if he fell.

His left arm wrapped tightly around the tip above him, Blaine fired the
piton into the Monument face even with his chest. After making sure it
was secure, he jammed the piton gun into his harness and flipped the start
of his climbing rope down from his shoulder. Taking it in his now free
hand, he threaded the line into the piton's exposed eye and then carefully
ran it through a trio of carabiners on his harness. He held the line tight,
testing it, and pushed off with his heels.

Two more rappels left him a few yards above the top of the observation
deck's windows. Blaine shifted his backpack around to the front and then
raised his legs as he lowered his head. Suspended upside down now, gazing
down the long white band of the Monument to the dark abyss of the
ground, he could feel the blood rushing to his head.

Awkwardly, he put some more slack in the line, lowering himself until he
could easily reach the top of the observation deck's twin windows. Next
Blaine pulled a rectangular mound of plastic explosives from inside his pack
and wedged it in place over the left side of the first window. Then he shim-
mied sideways and repeated the same process on the right, wedging a second
remote-controlled detonator into the mound. The charges had been packed
to ensure that not only the windows but also enough of the marble over them
would blow to create an accessible route in for the commandos.

By the time McCracken reached the second window, his movements had turned graceful, confidence coming from practice. The third and fourth explosive mounds took to the marble as if slots had been tailored for them. Blaine jammed the final detonator in place and gave it a hard twist to the right.

He regripped his line to ready his ascent back to the tip, flipping his feet and head again first. He felt better instantly, just dangled there while he waited for his blood to resettle.

"Mission accomplished, Kirkland," Blaine said into his headset. "Send your team in."

Less than two minutes later, after he had climbed to a safe distance above the charges, Blaine looked up at the sky and saw the Blackhawk soaring through the night, dead on line with the Monument. According to plan, he would hold here while the commandos finished the job, then join them in the observation deck.

"Eighteen, seventeen, sixteen . . ."

Kirkland's thirty-second countdown filled Blaine's ears until the approaching Blackhawk's rotor wash stole it. The downwind pressure made the line threaded precariously through the piton vibrate madly. It felt to Blaine like the vibrations made by a dentist's drill, the entire surface of the Monument seeming to tremble.

He could see the six Hostage and Rescue Team commandos leaning back-first out of the Blackhawk's bay now, heels touching only air as they held fast to the black cords fastening them to the chopper's tie-lines. They had angled themselves to swoop downward as soon as the charges detonated, creating their passage in.

Then the Blackhawk seemed to buckle in the air. It turned violently to the left, the Hostage and Rescue Team members left to cling to their tie-lines for dear life as the chopper began spinning.

The gear spur, Blaine realized.

He had seen it happen before, but never with the timing so bad. The gear spur controlled the spin of the tail rotor, and when it seized, the tail rotor sputtered and stalled. As he watched, the Blackhawk continued to spin wildly before flitting out of control, the pilot struggling with the throttle and control arm to gain it back. For now the chopper was lost in the night, soaring away, the attack aborted.

But the charges were still going to blow, leaving the rest of the operation in his and Johnny Wareagle's hands. Blaine took his SIG-Sauer nine-millimeter pistol in hand and readied his push off the marble face in the last moments before the windows erupted in a burst of smoke and flame.

The blast temporarily deafened McCracken but didn't stop him from swooping down toward the center of the chasm that had been blown in the Monument's observation deck. He came up a bit long and slammed into the blackened marble just beneath the jagged opening. Grabbing hold of the smoking, charred ledge, he hoisted himself upward, SIG-Sauer aimed through as soon as he cleared it.

The smoke and stubborn flames stole his vision and stung his eyes. There were shapes clustered about, most at least stirring, others crawling desperately away. More, undoubtedly, were blocked from his view by the elevator shaft, ten feet away in the center of the deck. He distinguished hostages rushing past it, some holding fast to the wounded or terrified, bravely trying to guide them toward the lone staircase on the north side, as a fire alarm wailed incessantly.

A pair of bleeding figures clinging to the wall for support raised submachine guns their way, fingers about to press tight to triggers, when Blaine poured the SIG's bullets at them. The multiple hits spun the gunmen around before dropping them, errant fire sent spraying in all directions.

McCracken started to hoist himself inside, when a burst of automatic fire greeted him. His bulletproof vest took most of the impact, but a few of the rounds sneaked beneath it and Blaine felt a series of hot jabbing stabs to his abdomen reaching toward his hip. His whole right side went numb, and he collapsed downward. A chunk of jagged marble sliced through his shoulder in a burst of fiery pain like none he had ever felt before. He screamed and lost his grasp on the SIG, watching it drop to the floor. He started to sink, and more hot agony drove through his shoulder, the sinewy flesh and muscle around it shredded and pouring blood.

A dark figure was angling for another shot, when the barricaded exit door on the deck's north side blew inward a breath ahead of Johnny Wareagle's charge through it. He held Heckler & Koch submachine guns in either hand, pummeling the figure with one even as he was turning the second on a fourth terrorist, who lurched behind the elevator shaft for cover. Wareagle darted to the left, blocked from Blaine's view by the elevator shaft, as he positioned himself between the terrorist and the sole exit door hostages continued desperately trying to reach.

Blaine felt himself slumping, holding on to the ledge for dear life, the pain numbing him toward unconsciousness, when he saw something shiny and metallic lying on the floor fifteen feet from him. A man had just crawled past the elevator shaft across the observation deck's rubble-strewn floor, heading toward the object, which had a red light flashing like a beacon in the night.

The detonator!

The realization shook Blaine alert an instant before he saw that the crawling figure was bald, the only thing Kirkland had been able to identify about the leader. Blaine heaved himself back over the edge of the chasm, feeling about his vest again as if his SIG-Sauer might have miraculously reappeared.

His hand brushed past the piton gun instead.

The bald man was almost to the detonator, starting to stretch a trembling hand determinedly outward.

Blaine yanked the piton gun free and loaded it.

The bald man raised a trembling hand over the button, even with the flashing red light on the detonator.

Blaine aimed the piton gun for the man's head, willed his hand steady.

The bald man's finger started down, as Blaine curled his inward. The piton shot out behind the familiar poof! But it wasn't made to fire at this distance, and Blaine sensed it veering from his intended target of the bald man's skull at the last.

He was already reaching for another when the piton pierced the back of the man's hand, plunging all the way through the palm. He screamed, and the reflexive jerk that followed sent the detonator sliding across the floor.

The bald man struggled to his feet and started to go after it, but a fresh swarm of hostages fleeing for the exit enveloped him. By the time he extricated himself, Blaine had the piton gun steadied on him yet again. There was a brief instant when they locked eyes, the bald man's as crazed and hateful as any Blaine had ever seen, before he fired. But the piton lodged in the elevator shaft eight feet away when the bald man ducked. He reversed his field and steered away from the lost detonator, bloody hand pressed limply against his side as he joined another surge of bodies groping for the stairwell.

Blaine fought again to heave himself all the way inside, but the pain exploded anew, even worse.

Rat-tat-tat . . .

Johnny Wareagle had taken the fourth terrorist out with a submachine gun burst that slammed the man against the east wall.

"Johnny!" Blaine called, and Wareagle rushed toward him, back pressed against the elevator shaft, with guns smoking and ready.

Blaine tried to cry out that the leader was escaping, turn Johnny's attention to the stairwell, which from this angle was blocked from his view. His words, though, were swallowed by a muffled gasp. And by the time Johnny reached him, Blaine couldn't speak at all. Consciousness slipped away one frame at a time, the last one centered on the bald man disappearing toward the exit amidst the fleeing crowd.

THREE

They ever find him?" Buck wondered.

"No."

"Ain't they never heard of a security net?"

"They were too busy evacuating the area."

"So a man runs out of the Monument with a goddamn piton through his hand, dripping blood everywhere, and nobody thinks to stop him?"

"I had the same question."

"God damn," said Buck, genuinely upset. "And I don't suppose anybody's heard from him again."

"Not yet."

"Smart boy."

"Won't be long, though: he hasn't gone far."

Buck narrowed his gaze. "I ask you something, son?"

"Sure."

"You fixing on going after him?"

Blaine remembered being carried from the Washington Monument on a stretcher, fighting to sit up as the paramedics worked on him and straining to see the faces of those he passed in the hope of spotting the bald man who had somehow slipped away. He had almost broken the hand of a paramedic who tried to hold him down.

"Soon as I leave here," Blaine said, leaving it at that. "One way or another."

"Yeah," Buck returned disapprovingly. "That's what I figured."

He looked Blaine over in the same disparaging way he had looked over the Operation Phoenix recruits the first day they had met, nearly thirty years before, and shook his head. Then he climbed back to his feet on the dock and stretched comfortably, gazing out at the waters like he owned them. "What do you say we find out how good you really are?"

Blaine stood up too, feeling better already. "Thanks, Buck."

Torrey flashed him a scolding look. "That's Sergeant Major to you, son. That's something you want to get straight 'fore we get started."

FOUR

iz Halprin sat in the car outside her son's elementary school with the cell phone pressed tight against her ear.

"Are you holding for Mr. Levine?" a receptionist broke in.

"Yes, I'm *still* holding."

Click.

Damn, Liz thought. She didn't want this call dragging on beyond the end of school, when Justin would appear with the other third graders at the front door of William T. Harris Elementary. The school was comfortably located on West Twenty-first Street between Eighth and Ninth Avenues. Thinking of how convenient it was to their apartment made Liz realize she might have to start looking for a new school for Justin to attend almost immediately. Somewhere in Virginia almost certainly, maybe even in the town of Quantico itself.

Just hours before, a call had come that she'd been waiting for for years. The man had identified himself as Rooker, calling from Quantico, Virginia, where the FBI's elite Hostage and Rescue Team was based. She had been scheduled for a final interview, having scored highest among all applicants wishing to join the squad. The final hurdle to achieving her greatest career goal was at last in reach.

The Hostage and Rescue Team . . .

Merely considering the possibility made her light-headed. The fact that the call had come the same day she had gotten a message from her lawyer,

Arthur Levine, was a twist of fate meant either to bring her back down to earth or to take her to even greater heights.

"Good afternoon, Liz," Levine's voice greeted finally.

"How good is it really, Arthur?"

"Your ex-husband has given up trying for joint custody. He'll settle for standard visitation rights, so long as you don't fight him on summer vacation. Can you live with that?"

Liz could barely contain her exuberance. "I'll force myself."

"Also, you accept the lower child support figure," Levine added tactfully.

"Done."

"You're making my job awfully easy, Liz."

"It's the least I can do."

"Congratulations."

"Thank you, Arthur. For everything."

Trembling slightly, Liz pressed END on her cell phone. She leaned back in the Volvo's driver's seat and took a deep breath. It had been a tumultuous two years since the separation, to say the least, her dream of joining Hostage and Rescue on hold while her personal life festered. Now she could put all that behind her. She didn't know which news she would share with Justin first: the fact that she would be moving to Quantico from New York City, or that he was now free to come with her. She turned toward the entrance to William T. Harris Elementary School, suddenly desperate for three o'clock to come so he would emerge.

Liz leaned forward in her seat. A man with long oily hair, wearing an army-green overcoat, was approaching the middle set of double doors, something all wrong about him. Never mind the fact that parents were prohibited from entering the building to pick up their children; this man didn't look like a father at all. His eyes darted about in squirrely fashion. He seemed to be breathing very hard, and his oily skin glowed with a fresh layer of sweat. As Liz watched, he reached under his overcoat and shifted something near his shoulder.

A gun! He's carrying a gun!

The man rushed up the stairs to reach the entrance before it closed in the wake of a woman who'd been buzzed in. Liz retrieved her cell phone and hit 911.

"911 Emergency."

"Response needed at P.S. 11, William T. Harris Elementary School, on West Twenty-first Street. Potential gunman has just entered the building."

"That's a potential gunman at—"

"How long?"

"Ma'am?"

"What's the patrol's ETA?"

"I don't—"

"I'm an FBI agent on scene now."

"Cars are already rolling. ETA three minutes."

Three minutes, Liz thought, an eternity. And her son was in the building. . . .

She was lunging out her door in the next instant, cell phone still clinging to her ear. "Please advise patrol en route that a female FBI agent has entered the building ahead of them and that I'm armed."

"Ma'am, I don't think I—"

"Just do it!"

Liz dropped the cell phone in her pocket and sprinted for the entrance. It was two fifty-seven, three minutes from the end of the school day and from the expected arrival of the police. At this point, though, she heard no sirens.

The front door clanged against the wall after she was buzzed in. The squirrely-looking man was nowhere to be seen. Liz swung right and headed toward the office. She charged in, nearly accosting a receptionist who had just finished stuffing teachers' mailboxes.

"A man in a long green coat—did you see him?"

"Excuse me?"

Liz flashed her ID. "He just entered the building! Did you see him!"

"I saw . . . someone."

"Where?"

"Through the window. Going down the hall that passes the office."

Liz twisted round for the door. Her mouth had gone bone dry and the pace of her heart had doubled. Back in the corridor, she drew the .380-caliber pistol from the holster concealed by her bulky sweater. She rushed down the hall, searching for some indication as to where the man had gone, eyes scanning each classroom she passed.

There was no sign of him.

Liz was beginning to wonder if she had overreacted. Maybe the squirrely man was just a custodian skulking back into the building after taking an illegal break, his long coat already off now and hanging in some closet to reveal his uniform. Still she kept moving, kept scanning.

The second-to-last door on the right was closed, while all the others on the hall had been open. Liz slowed, not wanting the echo of her heels to give her away. A colorful sign over the door announced this to be the room of Mr. Vaughn.

Her son Justin had a teacher named Vaughn.

Liz crept up to the door, the vertical glass slab covered up by some kid's drawing.

Damn it!

She pressed herself against the wood, trying to listen, pistol trembling a little in her hand. She could hear the sirens screaming toward the school now, hoped to God this would end in nothing worse than embarrassment.

Thump . . .

From inside the classroom, the sound out of place but maybe just a book toppling from a child's desk. Then silence again. The class could be taking a quiz, having quiet time. The possibilities were endless.

Liz's hand closed on the knob, stopping just short of yanking the door open. What if she was wrong? Burst in with gun raised and scare the hell out of a bunch of kids for nothing. Laugh about it later, let Justin tell everyone it was just show-and-tell.

Liz felt herself go cold. Justin had Mr. Vaughn for language arts *last period of the day!* He was in that room *now!*

She heard a sound: a sob, maybe a whimper. Then another thud. The roaring sirens masked everything, as Liz tightened her grasp on the doorknob, turning it, ready to pull.

"I said *shut up!*"

The scream from inside came an instant before the dismissal bell rang, hundreds of kids seconds away from spilling outside when Liz yanked the door open.

Her gun was raised and ready, clasped in both hands, as she burst into the classroom, barrel locking with her eyes on the squirrely man, who was holding Mr. Vaughn by the hair with one hand, a Mac-10 in the other.

A submachine gun! It was worse than she thought. . . .

"Drop it!" she screamed, .380 leveled on him.

She saw his eyes when he backpedaled, nearly stumbling. Wild, half-glazed eyes, mad with some drug.

"Fuck you!" he yelled back, shielding his body with the teacher's, Mac-10 barrel pressed against his head.

"Settle down. Just settle down," she said, trying to sound conciliatory, calming, but she didn't lower her pistol.

"*I'll blow his fucking brains out!*"

"Easy now. Take it easy."

"I'll blow *all* their fucking brains out!"

That's when Liz got her first glance at Justin, seated in the room's center, hands locked onto his desk for dear life. The sirens whined down, the police cars squealing to a halt as the elementary students began spilling into the playground and moved toward their waiting parents or the line of yellow school buses.

"You hear me, bitch? You hear me?"

The gunman snapped his Mac-10 away from Mr. Vaughn's head and twisted it toward the class as he spun round. The move put enough distance between the gunman and his hostage to create the space Liz had been waiting for. A tough shot she might never have taken if the Mac-10's barrel hadn't been sweeping toward Justin.

Liz fired the .380 and kept firing, her bullets punching the squirrely man backwards toward a window covered on the outside by a steel grate.

His gun hand jerked upward and emptied a burst into the ceiling and walls, which sent the children screaming and cowering.

"Down! Down!" Liz ordered, angling to put herself between the gunman and the kids. He seemed to be trying to resteady his Mac-10 on them when Liz fired again, spraying the gunman's blood this time against the window, an instant before he crashed through the glass. The force of his weight snapped the grate clean off and it tumbled with him to the cement playground below.

"Stay down!" Liz wailed, lunging toward the shattered glass, breathlessly relieved to see Justin lying safe on the floor, staring up at her, and all the other kids apparently okay.

But outside in the playground, the man sprayed bullets wildly in all directions as his own blood leaped out of him. High as he was on drugs, cocaine probably, the .380's bullets hadn't been enough to put him down. Liz hurdled through the window, to find the police frantically herding the panicked hordes of kids and parents to safety. Too many students were rushing past the gunman for the police to risk firing at him. Liz watched him dart through the open playground gates and rush toward the school buses double parked along the street. She gave chase as he lunged through the open door of the first one he came to.

Liz watched him fling the bus driver down the steps and opened fire through the glass of the nearest windows, trying to draw a bead on the gunman. The glass crackled and popped, but the bus drew away from the curb and hammered into the one parked immediately before it, pushing it aside.

From there the school bus smashed a number of cars parked on the north side of the street from its path, shoving them atop the sidewalk. Police return fire shattered the windshield, and in insane response, the squirrely man switched on the windshield wipers to sweep the broken glass aside.

Liz crossed behind the bus the gunman had slammed from his path and sprinted up even with him as he tried to pick up speed, grinding the gears. He had grasped his machine gun again an instant before Liz reached the still-open door. He jerked the Mac-10 toward her and fired.

Click.

The sound of the hammer closing on an empty chamber sounded just before Liz emptied her remaining four shots into the man's head and chest. He slumped over the wheel, and the bus ground to a halt against a long line of cars, crunching them together. The bus's flashers turned on, stop signs extending like limbs from its sides.

Liz watched it happen with the .380 still smoking in her hand. A swarm of people enclosed her. She realized a few of them were paramedics, asking if she was all right, suggesting that she sit down. Liz stopped long enough to see the blood staining her clothes. Her first thought was that the gunman had winged her with a bullet. Then she remembered the jagged window glass scraping at her clothes and flesh when she jumped through it.

Justin!

She turned and rushed off in the same motion, leaving the police and paramedics bewildered. She was out of breath, gasping, by the time she covered the short distance back into the playground, where police and parents were ushering the sobbing, terrified students away. All of them, thankfully, were alive and safe. Her desperate gamble had paid off.

"Mom!"

She swung toward the voice and saw Justin rushing to her across the asphalt. He struck Liz hard enough to stagger her, but she swallowed him in a hug nonetheless. He returned her grasp just as tightly, reluctant to let go.

Then she saw the gurney being rushed down the building's stairs, a pair of paramedics applying CPR to the man lying upon it.

Oh my God . . .

Liz eased Justin away, stiffening. The stretcher had passed close enough for her to get a good look at the bloodied form of the man lying upon it.

The man was Justin's language arts teacher, Mr. Vaughn.

And he'd been shot.

FIVE

ack Tyrell stood between a pair of trees, looking down at the grave site. He had found a shovel upon entering Crest Haven Memorial Park and was now leaning on it to make himself look like a work-man rather than one of the mourners. He was dressed for the part, in jeans and a denim shirt, and his long tangle of hair fell limply to his shoulders. Not a single gaze had met his since the cortege had pulled in. He was good at melting into a scene, invisible while standing out in the open; he'd had lots of practice.

Tyrell tightened his grip on the shovel's handle, his knees trembling a little. He was too far away to hear the minister's words and didn't much care. The size of the crowd impressed him: almost exclusively young peo-ple, their lives mostly untouched by death. Tyrell, whose life had been ruled by it for as long as he could remember, envied them today.

He wanted to get a better look at the front line of mourners seated in folding chairs by the grave site. He wondered who they were, what their connection was.

The sound of car doors slamming made him turn to the right. An in-nocuous-looking dark sedan had squeezed into the drive, double-parking along the row of the procession's cars. Two stiff-postured men had emerged and were making their way purposefully toward the crowd. They stopped just short of it and began scanning the faces of those gathered.

"Mr. Tyrell?"

Jack tensed, cursing himself for not paying more attention to his rear.

"Please turn around. Slowly. And keep your hands where we can see them."

Tyrell did as he was told, still clutching the shovel, and found himself facing a second pair of men. Both their suit jackets were unbuttoned, but only one of them had dropped his hand toward the holster concealed inside. They were young men, about the same age as most of those standing near the grave site.

"You'll have to come with us, sir."

"I'm going to wait until the funeral's over. You need to understand that's what I have to do."

"Now, sir. Please," the man said, an edge creeping into his voice.

"It's almost done. Just a few more minutes."

"We have our orders, sir."

"I'm going to ask you again for those minutes. You can come up here, stand right next to me, if you want."

Now both men had their hands inside their jackets. "I'm sorry, sir."

"Yeah, so am I," Tyrell said, and he started down the slight hill toward them.

The men fell in alongside him, not seeming to notice he was still holding the shovel. Tyrell stopped in the shadow of a great oak tree not far from a freshly dug grave.

"I'd really like to go back, stay to the end. I wouldn't ask if it wasn't important to me. You boys mind reconsidering?"

"Move," said the one who hadn't spoken yet, gun out of its holster now but still held beneath his suit jacket.

Tyrell obliged, taking one step and then another. He was halfway into the third step when he brought the shovel around, high and hard. It smashed into the skull of the man whose gun was drawn, pitching him sideways. The second man had just gotten his gun out when Tyrell thrust the shovel's blade into his throat, pinning him back against the tree and twisting so the steel would shred flesh. The young man's eyes gaped as he drew his fingers to the jagged wound. He staggered, his knees starting to buckle, while the first man crawled through the grass. His hands groped before him, feeling blindly for his gun. Tyrell drew the shovel overhead and finished him with two more blows. The other one was dead by then too, and he dumped both their bodies in the freshly dug grave near the oak tree.

Tyrell brushed his hands clean and started back up the hill. He got to the top just as the coffin was being lowered into the ground. A line of mourners had cast dirt upon it one at a time before the second pair of men noticed him and approached, looking about for the two who had accompanied them.

"They're down there," Jack said, waiting until the minister's final blessing had been given before he turned and followed the men down the hill, shovel in hand.

Jack Tyrell had been walking for hours, ever since he had gotten off the New Jersey Transit train that had brought him into Manhattan. He hadn't meant to stay this long in the open, where someone could recognize him at any time; for a man used to living his life in the shadows, the sunlit stares of others were something to be avoided at all costs. A casual glance, a smile or friendly gesture cast his way—these were the things that could give him away.

It wouldn't take a particularly smart person to recognize him, either. Just someone who knew a little bit about history, who read magazines, or who had seen his face on an FBI's Most Wanted poster, where it had been for seven years running a long time ago.

After the funeral, he took to the streets of New York City, figuring he'd do a block or two, get the lay of the land and the feel of what he should do now that he was back in the world, with four bodies left behind him. He had lots on his mind. It was time to work it out. He needed to get used to being part of the world again.

Horns made him stiffen. Don't Walk signs that kept him from moving in the direction he wished left his flesh crawling. He contemplated ducking back into the subway, where things were dark and people were afraid to look at anyone twice. But the next block passed more easily, and the one after that was easier still. By the sixth block, he had actually fallen into a rhythm. Letting his eyes roam. Taking things in, as he weighed his options.

He started meeting the faces of those he passed. Some of them looked familiar, stoking memories of friends, many of whom were gone forever. Friends he had gone to war with against a nation. Plans hatched in dingy basements and dark attics, life lived between the whispers, everyone full of ambition. The odds were impossible, but it never mattered to Jack Tyrell, although it probably should have.

He needed something to change the odds. He had dreams twenty-five years ago, and they kept him from seeing that. But he saw it now, because the dreams weren't in the way anymore.

Some people he passed carried giant radios they called boom boxes. Others passed him wearing headphones, walking to their own music with no idea what the beat of a different drummer sounded like. Deep thick drags off joints rolled thick as cigars. Cushiony dreams born of acid hits that made the sounds of the blasts clearer and the smell of blood sweeter. Wondrous things, these, but where had they gotten him? All the rubble he had left in his wake amounted to nothing when piled together.

This time it would be different.

He had gotten his start with the Weatherman movement, lasting until the rest of the leadership refused to back up in practice what they supported in philosophy. A bomb blast here and a kidnapping there, the group's biggest claim to fame having been to make a lot of smoke at New York City police headquarters in 1970. The movement went underground not long after that, but Jack Tyrell had unfinished business. Saw their withdrawal from the scene as a blessing, because it freed him to follow his own path by forming Midnight Run. He culled the best from the ranks of the Weatherman and Black Panther movements, lured them up from the underground with a promise that it was time to back up their words with deeds.

Jack found himself at Fifty-sixth and Lexington, his feet blessed with a mind of their own. He got chills as he came upon the corner across from the old Alexander's department store. A relic now, like him.

Standing there, gazing up the street, he couldn't believe his eyes. Last time he'd been here, there had been a parking lot where the Mercantile Bank building once stood. But now a sprawling, fifty-story office building rose toward the sky, swallowing even the alley he had made his escape through twenty-five years ago when things had gone bad in a hurry. Jack figured folks these days thought a little urban renewal was all it took to wipe out an age, an era.

He remembered guns going off when the Mercantile Bank building had been there; his people, the soldiers of Midnight Run, going down everywhere around him. The bearded countenance of one of his own men shouting instructions to the black-garbed gunmen, ordering them about. The goddamn son of a bitch was a plant, *a spy*! They'd been sold out!

"FBI!" the bearded man had yelled. "Freeze!"

Jack Tyrell had dived to the floor instead beneath a maelstrom of gunfire, crawling to his detonator. The charges hadn't all been set yet; some of his people were still in the process of planting them. But the wiring had been laid, ready to send the signal when Tyrell hit the button.

The Mercantile Bank building had erupted around him in a shower of stone and steel. How he loved that sound, loved the feel of the air getting sucked up around him and the hot wave that replaced it. He had let it swallow him that day, welcoming the end at long last. But instead of dying, he had awakened in an emergency triage unit set up on the street to treat those with wounds he had inflicted.

Jack had wiped the blood from his eyes and seen the police scouring the area, checking the wounded for a face that matched the description they'd been given. A description of a man who for two years had blazed a trail of terror across the country. For the past eighteen months, number one on the FBI's Most Wanted List. A man whom J. Edgar Hoover had sworn publicly to strap into the electric chair himself.

Jack turned away from the pigs coming toward him and watched a boy covered in a blood-soaked sheet die. He felt, not regret or guilt, but power. He had done this, he had *made* this. And in that instant he saw his escape.

He moved to the boy and collapsed over him, sobbing uncontrollably in a fit of hysteria. A father holding his dead boy's hand. The stuff of tragedy. Jack kept his face low, felt an arm on his shoulder.

The arm belonged to a man with an FBI ID badge pinned to his jacket, William something, it said. Jack wanted to ask him if he knew an agent with a beard, the rat-fuck bastard who had sold out Midnight Run. But instead he kept up his sobbing, and the FBI agent steered him toward a priest.

The priest drew him aside to offer comfort. Wrapped an arm around his shoulder, his narrow collar dripping with blood Jack had spilled. They walked together into a nearby alley. There Jack had killed the priest and used his clothes to make his escape. It took the FBI the rest of the day to realize that Jack was still at large.

He looked at that spanking-new building now and saw how easy it had been for them to wipe out his work, bury his impact beneath fresh layers of steel and glass. What he wanted so intensely was to make the kind of impact that wouldn't be forgotten quickly. Not just a building. Not just a single bomb people might miss learning about on the news if they channel-surfed. He wanted to destroy something there wasn't enough steel and glass in the world to fix.

Jack got a rush that felt like an acid hit, only smoother. He closed his eyes and saw it in his mind, the shape of things to come. He had to keep himself from laughing, feeling almost giddy. He imagined someone recognizing him now, Jack Tyrell looking like he had just told himself a joke.

Of course, he hadn't been called that in a long time now. On the posters displaying his face, and to the hordes of federal agents and police who had once made it their life's work to catch him, he had another name:

Jackie Terror.

The old warehouse looked abandoned from the outside, right down to the iron grate across its front entrance, secured by a rusted padlock. Jack Tyrell would have left if he weren't sure this was the correct address. He reached out to jiggle the padlock, and it came free in his hand. He slid the grate back enough to slide through and squeeze up against an old sliding door. The door opened with a ratchety clang and Tyrell stepped into a master's den.

The clutter of the place didn't surprise him so much as the source of it: shelf after shelf of electronics equipment in various states of disrepair. He could hear the sound from a dozen different televisions battling for attention, the dull glow emanating from their screens accounting for most of the huge room's light.

He continued through the junked stereos, hi-fis, and husks of major appliances until he came to a central worktable covered by what appeared to be an endless supply of cable TV boxes. A single bright bulb dangled from a ceiling wire. Beneath it a lone figure sat on a stool at the table, wearing a jerry-rigged light around the crown of his balding dome. Looked like a jockstrap with a bulb instead of a cock.

The figure appeared too enmeshed in his work to turn around. "Since you don't have an appointment," his raspy voice called out, "you got exactly three seconds to tell me who sent you here."

"You gonna shoot me if I take four, Marbles?"

The man on the stool stiffened, swung round in slow motion.

"You gotta be fucking kidding me," he said, squinting his eyes behind a pair of glasses with lenses as thick as old-fashioned Coke bottles.

Jack Tyrell started forward again, letting Marbles see the briefcase in his hand. "What are you, a goddamn TV repairman?"

Marbles kept squinting at Jack as though he couldn't believe his eyes. "Don't tell me you've come here because they finally wired your building for cable."

Jack reached the table, looked over the cluttered piles of descramblers.

"They're called black boxes," Marbles explained. "Plug them into the outlet and you get every premium channel for zip."

"Premium channels?"

"HBO, Showtime, Spice, pay-TV events—you know."

"No, I don't."

"Christ, where you been for the last twenty-five years, Jackie?"

The lamp attached to Marbles' skull followed Jack around the table like a spotlight.

"Here and there," Tyrell said. "How 'bout you?"

"You might say I've gone into the entertainment business."

Jack gave one of the boxes a closer look. "That the best you can do with your talents?"

"People on the up-and-up aren't racing to hire fugitives with a generation of paper following them. Anyway it lets me stay on the move and keeps me in cash. Enough to eat, work on my projects."

Jack liked the way Marbles said that, a man who still kept his real life hidden where no one could find it.

"I got lots of accounts," Marbles continued, "don't care where I work out of or what hours I keep, 'long as I make good on their orders. I got a new box I'm working on, lets you steal off the Internet."

"I read about that," said Jack.

"Pays well."

"That's what all this is about?"

"Times change," Marbles said unapologetically. "You want your techware updated, Jackie, you come to the right place. Otherwise . . ."

Jack laid his briefcase down just to Marbles' right, unsnapped it, and lifted the top. The hundred-dollar bills stacked and wrapped neatly inside were caught in the spill of his beam.

Tyrell could see Marbles' eyes bulge behind his thick glasses. "What the hell . . ."

"I've been busy the past twenty-five years."

"Okay, you got my attention," said Marbles.

"I need a wire man. Very elaborate setup. One-day gig."

Marbles looked up, his light suddenly angled on Jack again, stinging his eyes. "Twenty-five years go by and all of a sudden you flipped your switch back on?"

"It got flipped back on for me. I bought into something, but that's done and over now. There's nothing holding me to them anymore, and four of them got dead for being disrespectful."

That made Marbles straighten a little.

"You understand what I'm saying here, Marbles? I feel like the last twenty-five years never happened, like I'm picking up just where I left off, only this time I'm gonna make this country hurt in a big way. Where it counts. Make them stand up and take notice. Give them something they'll never forget."

"You expect me to just drop everything and come along?"

"Yup."

Marbles picked up one of the black boxes and let it crash to the floor. "Just tell me what it is we're going for. Tell me where we're gonna lay this hurt."

"A city," Jackie Terror told him.

"A *city*?"

"We're going to take a whole fucking city hostage."

SIX

Blaine lay on the porch of Buck Torrey's stilt house, the crickets and night birds singing around him. He had come outside so the breeze could cool his body, which was drenched in sweat even now, the air like a sauna from dawn to dusk and, after dark, a steam room inside Buck's stilt house. If his former sergeant major's plan was to make him forget about his shoulder and hip by making him hurt everywhere else, it was working. They'd been at it for three weeks now.

Three weeks . . .

But it felt like much longer. Blaine couldn't recall a time when he'd ever been this sore. His early years of training were certainly worse in terms of duress, but he'd been decades younger, which made the pain easier to swallow. No reprieves from training due to injury or hurt at that level, and with good reason.

You're in the jungle wounded, shot probably. Or maybe you got winged by a frag, or couldn't dance clear after hearing the *click* of the mine you triggered. Alone with your pain for company and the enemy on your tail, closing fast. Stop and you die. Nobody surrendered in the jungles where Blaine had spent his formative years. The Special Forces training he'd endured was meant to build tolerance, as well as character. If you couldn't take the pain in camp, you wouldn't be able to take it with a bullet in your leg, or an artery doing its damnedest to bleed out while you humped across twenty miles of jungle.

The door creaked open and Buck Torrey joined Blaine on the porch, settling his bulky frame on a patch of dry wood, a pair of beer bottles in hand.

"Woulda brought you one, son, but I know you and booze ain't exactly in bed together."

Blaine propped himself up gingerly on his elbows. "We were once."

"All of us were lots of things back then that fortunately got a way of changing, moving on. Life's not much more than that, from where I'm sitting. Going from one place to another. Packing up. You know how you can tell when an old dog like me's had enough?"

"No."

"He stops *un*packing. Just leaves the pieces of his life in boxes, so they'll be easier to move the next time." Buck Torrey took a hefty swig from his bottle. "Trouble is, you can't fit everything in boxes. Knew another guy never took nothing with him. Just bought everything new when he got where he was going, give himself a fresh start."

"You're talking about family, Buck."

Torrey's eyes turned to hot spheres of fire, hiding the wryness behind them.

"Sir," Blaine corrected, as he rose to a sitting position. No longer did he need to hold on to the porch railing to manage the effort. He casually stretched his bad arm toward the rail now and put some weight on it. The shoulder took all he gave it, complaining with a little stab of pain but holding fast.

Blaine watched as Buck drained a hefty portion of the bottle in a single breath, his stilt house like a moist wood shroud behind him. There were three small rooms, with a gasoline generator out back for electricity and propane tanks to make hot water. A cramped bathroom featuring a toilet that took a half day to fill and a galley kitchen with a stove Buck almost never used. He cooked virtually every meal out here on an old, rusted gas grill. Many of those meals consisted of fresh fish dropped off every few days by local fishermen. Shrimp was a staple, along with snapper and small, spiny lobster-like creatures called crayfish. Blaine didn't always like the taste of what came off Buck's grill, but he was so hungry by the end of the day it didn't seem to matter.

On a clear day Buck could glimpse a few of his neighbors' comparable dwellings, stretching up to a half mile away. At night and on foggy days, he might have been the only person living on Condor Key, a few flickering lights the only hint of others in this waterbound neighborhood.

The residents were all like Buck in one way or another. People who had come here because there was no place else they especially liked, but who took care of each other nonetheless. There wasn't a day went by that a neighbor didn't come up in his or her skiff just to check on things. And Torrey had taken Blaine out on several similar sojourns three or four times.

Folks around here looked after each other but didn't get in anyone's way. And the few times a stray boater had wandered into their stretch of water, it was a race to see which resident could motor out the fastest to turn him around. There would probably never be a time when everyone got together, yet they were a community all the same.

"I'm talking about family, all right," Buck was saying, the second bottle of beer cradled between his squat legs. "The one thing you were smart enough not to get yourself."

"I never wanted to settle down."

"You never wanted to give up being what I taught you to be. I see you on that dock three weeks ago from a distance, it was like '69 all over again. From that far away I swear you hadn't changed."

"I've changed. You know that now."

"Not enough to want that family."

"No."

"Not enough to want to hang up your guns and live off the world for a time instead of visa-versa."

"It's what I've got."

"And you come down here looking for me to make sure you could keep it." Buck went to work on his second beer, flipping off the top with a flick of his thumb as he squeezed the neck of the bottle. "Best thing I coulda done was send you on your way. Maybe told the sheriff not to bring you by in the first place. Shit, I thought about it. Figured I mighta been doing you a service."

"Why didn't you?"

Torrey leaned back against the stilt house. " 'Cause I wanted it to be like the old days. 'Cause maybe I figure you're the one who's got things right and I oughta be out there with you."

"So come with me when I'm ready to leave."

Torrey smiled, but he didn't look happy. "Can't teach an old dog new tricks, son. You come down here for one purpose, I come down here for another. When I got your note, I was hoping it was from my daughter."

"She ever visit?"

Torrey squeezed his beer bottle. "Never invited her. I haven't seen her since I popped that general in the face. Busted his jaw, you know. He was drinking his supper through a straw for six weeks."

"Well," Blaine said, "that's at least one new trick."

Blaine stayed awake for a while after Buck went back inside. He moved his shoulder up and down, back and forth. Stood up, grabbed the railing, and put all his weight on his bad leg. There was no pain, not even a throb. He let go of the railing.

They had started the day after Blaine's arrival, his khakis swapped for some old fatigues Buck insisted upon that made him hot but kept the bugs from eating him alive. They took the skiff past all the stilt houses, into the shallow muck that made Blaine remember this was the Everglades. The thickness of the vines that seemed to grow out of the water itself varied by the amount of light they got.

"All right," Sergeant Major Torrey ordered. "Climb out."

Blaine slid out of the skiff without question. The voice was the same one he remembered from a generation before, just a little more rasp to it, born of a thousand cartons of cigarettes. Blaine's boots touched the bottom only long enough for him to sink in up to his ankles.

"What now?" Blaine had asked eagerly.

"What now, *sir*," Buck Torrey corrected. "Now I start paddling and you start walking."

Blaine tried to budge his feet. "Walking?"

"You get a bullet in your hip or in your brain? Yeah, walking!"

Blaine pulled his good foot out first, felt it squishing around beneath him. He hesitated briefly before following with the second, finally gritted his teeth and lifted. His hip felt like someone was rubbing glass against it, but his foot broke free of the muck and sank back down. He stepped out with his good leg next and had repeated the process for ten steps each foot before the temptation to reach out for the skiff's side got to be almost too much.

By the twentieth step, it *was* too much. He went to grab hold of the boat and got an oar cracked against his knuckles for the effort.

"I say it was time to take a break, son?"

"No."

"*No* . . ."

"No, sir."

"Keep walking."

Blaine did as he was told. Occasionally he got lucky and the bottom hardened beneath him. But more often it stayed soft. Sometimes it swallowed his knees, taking every bit of strength and energy he had to negotiate his way through it. His bad hip felt numb by the time Sergeant Major Buck Torrey let him lean into the skiff for some water out of an ancient canteen, but it wasn't dragging any more than his good one.

"That's enough," Torrey had said, and snatched the canteen from his grasp.

"How far'd we go?"

"Well, let's see." Torrey turned around and gazed back dramatically, pointing his finger. "We left from there and now we're here. That far enough for you?"

"Yup."

"Good, son, 'cause now we're gonna walk back."

"You mean *I'm* gonna walk back."

Torrey snarled and hurled himself over the skiff's side.

"That's not necessary, sir."

"Yeah, old dog, it is, 'cause I want you to tow the skiff back with you this time."

It had been a long time since Blaine had taken this much pain willingly, but he liked it. Liked the way his dead-tired legs were dragging, each step feeling like his last, only to give way to the next.

The mosquitoes came out just after they started back, and Blaine had only his bad arm to keep them off. Torrey trudged along next to him, smiling as McCracken swatted at them, striking mostly air. The sergeant major seemed especially to enjoy when Blaine missed a bug and slapped himself hard instead, and that made Blaine swat even harder.

"Okay, switch," Torrey ordered, holding up.

Blaine figured Buck meant he was going to take the skiff now for a turn and extended the line toward him.

Torrey's eyes narrowed. "You fuckin' crazy, boy?"

"I thought—"

"No, you didn't think none. If you'd've thought, you'd know I got me something more important to carry."

He reached into the skiff, which was still in Blaine's hold, and fished a beer from his cooler. Popped the top off the bottle with a trademark flick of his thumb.

"See. Now, *switch!*"

Blaine's left arm had seemed a foot shorter than the right for months now. The wound from the Monument had healed clean, the doctors insisted, but left what they called adhesions—scars deep inside that were thicker and uglier than the single one that remained on the outside of his shoulder. Stretching them religiously would give him back his mobility, at least that dreaded ninety-five percent. Give it time, they'd said.

Blaine gave it Buck Torrey instead. The weight of the skiff dragging against the soupy current pushed his shoulder to its limits. He kept the arm crimped to keep the pressure off it at first, then gradually straightened it. The pain had started out bad and didn't get much better. But Blaine realized it wasn't a pain he should fear; it was like the throbbing ache that came with overexertion. He wasn't hurting himself more and began to realize that eventually he wouldn't hurt at all.

Buck Torrey walked ahead of him, coaxing him on the whole time. Despite the pain, the exhaustion that had long ago set in, and the bugs that were subletting space in his close-cropped beard, Blaine felt invigorated; even euphoric. The muck beneath him didn't feel as thick anymore. His feet churned through it like a plow, shoving it from his path. The sweat poured off him into the steamy water; even the snakes moved aside from his determined rush. Torrey set a faster pace, and Blaine resolved not to drop behind, dragged the skiff harder to keep up. His chest ached. His breath heaved.

He felt wonderful.

They stopped in almost the very place they had started, where the water level deepened and dropped, just beyond view of the stilt houses in Buck Torrey's neighborhood. Blaine found himself gasping.

"Not bad, son," the sergeant major said, climbing agilely back into the skiff. His forearms looked like slabs of flesh-tinted steel. "Not bad at all."

Blaine moved to follow him.

"The fuck you think you're doing? I don't remember saying we were finished."

"We're not finished?"

"I am, son. Think I'll rest a mite, take me a snooze. You remember the way home?"

"I can find it."

Buck Torrey stretched out inside the skiff, head resting against the padded seat. "Well, what are you waiting for?" he said, and tipped the bill of his cap low over his eyes.

Blaine knotted the line under his arms and around his chest, dragged it till they reached the deep water, and then began swimming forward, with the skiff's dead weight inching along behind him.

"I'm hungry, boy," Buck Torrey called to him. "Can't you go no faster?"

SEVEN

The two divers moved silently to the water's edge. A third man followed them to the softly lapping currents, pushing a cart that held equipment too bulky to carry even the short distance from the staging station slightly up the hill. The divers walked into the lake up to their ankles and then reached back to the cart for the last and most important parts of their gear.

A gunshot split the night, freezing them even before a bright floodlight caught them in its glare and a voice boomed out from a small motorboat fifty yards away.

"That's far enough, fellas," warned Liz Halprin. "The pool's closed for the evening."

She held the twelve-gauge Mossberg pump comfortably in one hand, aimed at nothing in particular. The floodlight was in the other, aimed straight at the divers. She shifted it slightly when a figure approached the shore from beyond the rise where she'd seen the divers climb into their wet suits. The man held up a hand to shield his eyes from the sudden wash of light, his olive-green suit seeming to shine in its glow.

Liz lifted a foot casually to the small craft's gunwale, and it wobbled beneath her. "Plan on taking a swim too, Max?"

Maxwell Rentz came as close to the water as his five-hundred-dollar Italian loafers would allow, still shielding his eyes. "You're in no position to tell me I can't, Ms. Halprin."

"No, right now I'm in a position to shoot you dead."

"And what would be your reason?"

"Trespassing."

"In my own lake?"

"I believe, Max, that is the item currently in dispute."

"Why don't we let my divers go down and see if they can find something to help resolve it?"

"I believe we agreed in court to accept the findings of an impartial underwater survey team."

"*You* agreed. I pointed out I couldn't afford a three- or four-week delay."

"That's what they make appeals for, Max. And the delay could be plenty longer than that, since it promises to be hard to find any diver from these parts who'll go down there." She rotated the floodlight from Rentz to his divers, then back again. "Wait a minute—I'll bet you didn't tell them what happened the last time somebody dove this lake, did you, Max?"

"He wasn't working for me."

"Good thing, or you'd owe him a ton of overtime—since he's still down there." In the beam of light, Liz could see Rentz's two divers look at each other.

"Rumors," Rentz said.

"Not according to his family. I'd make sure your men's insurance was paid up, if I were you, considering the legend."

Maxwell Rentz abandoned the pretext of conciliation and returned to his usual caustic tone. "If you were me, you wouldn't be planning to build the region's largest resort on this site, either. But I need this lake your farm just happens to abut."

"From where I'm sitting, the farms you've swallowed up just happen to abut my lake."

Rentz stepped closer, until the currents eddied around the soft leather of his shoes. "Either way, I need your farm to complete my project. And if I can prove you've got no claim to this lake, you'll have no choice but to sell it to me, because I'll rescind your water rights. That means no irrigation for your fields, Ms. Halprin. My offer's on the table until my divers tell me I don't need to be so generous."

Rentz nodded at his men, who exchanged a nervous glance before reaching toward the cart again for the last pieces of their equipment. Liz made sure they could see her turn the shotgun on them.

Rentz glanced up the hill. "Two Preston policemen are right up there watching everything, Ms. Halprin. I believe you're committing a flagrant firearms violation right now."

"Virginia law gives a person the right to defend her home."

"And when you prove this lake is part of your home, you can shoot to your heart's desire. Otherwise, as a federal officer . . ."

"*Ex*–federal officer," Liz corrected, wanting very much to turn the gun on Rentz and shoot him instead.

"Forgive me," Rentz taunted. "You got trigger-happy last month, didn't you? Cost a schoolteacher his life and cost you a career. I guess you always wanted to be a farmer anyway."

Liz cringed, felt her blood overheating. "You finished?"

"Actually, I'm also told that the incident led to your husband being granted custody of your son pending a hearing. Can you imagine the boy testifying in court about what it felt like when his mother almost shot him in the middle of class?"

"Too bad he's not here to see me shoot you."

"The police officers have their guns trained on you, Ms. Halprin. My men are going to dive. Let's see what they find down there."

"Or what finds them," Liz said, just loud enough for the divers to hear. In that moment all the legends of this lake she had heard since she was a little girl flashed through her mind. Her grandpa setting her on his knee and telling her of the ghosts that haunted the water. The ghosts of Yankee soldiers from the Civil War, he said, who died making sure something they were protecting stayed safe forever.

About those days and the farm Liz had always maintained the fondest of memories. There was plenty of sadness mixed in for good measure, like the time her mother sat her down on the dock and told her that her parents were splitting up.

Both her grandparents' wakes had been held on this farm, and it had been after the second one, shortly before Liz graduated college, that her mother broke the news that she was putting the farm up for sale. There was no one to run it anymore, no reason to keep it, and financially it was a losing proposition. Liz had argued against the sale vehemently, passionately, unwilling to let go of the last of her youth and the fading memories of the days when the family had been together. Since it was doubtful they'd so much as break even on the sale, her mother agreed to let Liz pay for the taxes and minimal upkeep. She had done that ever since, never really intending to move back to the farm but wanting the option nonetheless.

She had finally exercised it three weeks before, in the wake of the Bureau's response to the gunfight at her son's elementary school, which had claimed a teacher's life. Her bullet had been identified as the one that killed him, according to the forensics report leaked the day before her scheduled hearing. After Waco and Ruby Ridge, patience at the Bureau was low and tempers were high. She was given a choice of going through the disciplinary review process and being fired, or avoiding further complications by simply resigning.

Liz ran the events through her head over and over. What she could have done differently. How much longer she could have waited for the police to arrive. Liz knew, the day she walked out of the Hoover Building after accepting the review board's offer, that she would never work in law enforcement again. Lost her career and her kid the same day, and as her lawyers grimly informed her, getting Justin back under the circumstances was going to be as tough as regaining her badge.

So she had driven west out of Washington along Route 66 toward Preston, Virginia, located between Culpeper and Warrenton, where people still lived off the land and lived simply as a result. She needed simplicity now, needed to feel she belonged somewhere. She could make a home here for herself and Justin, once the courts came to their senses. She could rebuild her life on the very foundation where it had been built.

Liz had returned intending to do most of the touch-up work on the house herself, only to find it and everything else in worse disrepair than she could possibly have imagined. The idea of taking over the site of her strongest, and happiest, childhood memories was so appealing that she failed to consider seriously enough the task she was taking on.

What, after all, did she know about farming? Her two thousand acres of fields were run-down, the soil was exposed and superheated to a hardened clay instead of being the friable mixture she had spooned her fingers through as a little girl.

After only three weeks, the dollars spent were adding up, along with the hard work. She'd have to hire a couple of good hands, and that was assuming she could have the place up and running by next season. A task she looked forward to with excitement as well as trepidation, whatever doubts she was experiencing balanced by the security of feeling she was home.

Then millionaire developer Maxwell Rentz had shown up waving dollars, and she learned of his plans for building the region's largest resort. Disney had abandoned a similar notion in the area, opening the door for any number of entrepreneurs to capitalize on the same intention. Rentz had seized the opportunity first. He had somehow determined Preston to be the ideal site and had already bought the three farms adjoining hers. But he needed Liz's farm in order to stretch his visionary resort all the way to the highway, and thought finalizing its purchase was only a formality. It should have been a no-brainer; sell and cut her losses. Actually realize a sizable profit in the deal.

But Liz couldn't sell. There was a challenge here for her, and a challenge was what she needed to get rid of the bad taste from her mouth that her lost career at the FBI had left. Beyond that, she was home. No amount of money waved before her would be enough to change that. The more Rentz had increased the pressure, the more she found herself standing firm. She was going to get her son back and raise him here. That thought kept her fighting.

Maybe she would have weakened in time. Come to her senses about how best to remake her life. But then Rentz had brought in the courts.

Bunch of bullshit about water rights and declaring tacit ownership of the twenty-acre lake that formed in the winter of 1863, when Bull Run over-flowed and flooded the valley in the midst of a second raging storm in as many days. But whose land precisely had it flooded? Rentz claimed he was going to prove that none which lay beneath the water had ever been hers.

It was the disciplinary board all over again, men in suits she had no choice but to back down from. Take whatever they put on the table and go skulking off. She couldn't give in again, though. There was still fight left in her, but if she signed on Rentz's dotted line it would die right here on the land she had grown up on.

Liz was under no illusions. She knew full well that Rentz *owned* the courts in these parts. This was his county, more than one municipal build-ing and hospital wing bearing his father's name. Those kinds of favors gave him lots of political markers to call in.

But it felt good to fight him, fight for herself. This was the last dream she had left, and he was threatening it. It was either a shotgun or a pen, and right now buckshot made more sense to her than ink.

Liz gazed across to the shoreline opposite her farm, where Rentz's di-vers were just about finished readying their gear. One of them switched on a powerful halogen light array, capable of putting out a million candle-power underwater. The other dangled an air bazooka, rigged by long hose to a compressor on shore, from his shoulder and tested the weight of what looked like an elaborate metal detector. Not that she could say what good such a device would do them in trying to settle a boundary dispute.

At least the halogens made sense. A person couldn't see his arm if he stuck it in the water, never mind all the way down to the black bottom. She watched as Rentz's divers sank below the surface, a trail of air bubbles left in their wake.

The divers swam deep, slowing as they drew nearer the bottom. The halogen lights cleared barely any visible path in the black, silty water after they had passed twenty feet. Their field of vision had shrunk to less than a yard when the molecular frequency discriminator began to flash. Slowly at first, but then faster and faster.

On shore, Rentz heard a rhythmic beeping in his headset. He eased the microphone piece into place in front of his lips.

"What's going on?" he asked excitedly. "Can you see anything?"

"Not yet," returned the voice of one of the divers. "But there's definitely something down here."

"Metallic?"

The beeping grew blisteringly loud in Rentz's ears.

"No, wait a minute—this is a motion signal," the first diver told him. "There's something moving dead ahead."

"It's coming straight for us!" wailed the other diver, who was holding the halogen light array.

The beeping sounded like one continuous shrill whine by that point, reaching a fever pitch, when, suddenly, it was replaced by a gurgling, frothy rasp, like someone trying to scream underwater. The sound curdled Rentz's ears, as the currents lapped unnoticed over his shoes.

"Come in! Can you hear me? What's going on down there?"

Behind Rentz on shore, something tugged on the bazooka hose and tipped the compressor onto its side. The two policemen grabbed the hose and began to pull on it desperately, just managing to hold their own.

Still seated in her motorboat, Liz watched it all happening, the stories her grandfather had told her of ghosts or monsters that dwelled beneath the lake's depths no longer seeming so fanciful at all. She rose again and clutched her twelve-gauge tightly to her, as Rentz's frantic voice echoed through the night.

"Come in! Do you read me? Come in!"

The police officers were yanking the compressor hose up quickly now, falling into a desperate rhythm. Liz watched as a jagged, mangled end emerged from the water. The policemen drew it toward them in disbelief.

The thick rubber looked as though it had been bitten through.

The officers looked at each other and then at Rentz, whose gaze remained locked on the waters of the lake, which had gone calm once more.

EIGHT

Harrison Conroy turned off the motor of his Mercedes and listened to the smooth engine settle back, bedded down for the evening. He snatched his briefcase from the passenger seat and walked into the house through the garage entrance. Instinctively he turned to the alarm, but it had already been deactivated, by his son, Damon, probably, since his wife would be in foundation board meetings for the better part of the evening.

Conroy took his briefcase with him into the kitchen, leaving his jacket on as he mixed himself a Beefeater and tonic. He paused briefly before starting to sip, a small moment's pause to appreciate where he was, how far he'd come. A long, dark time buried behind him. Nothing but sunshine ahead in the beautiful town of Ridge, Long Island.

He heard splashing in the backyard pool and took a heftier gulp of his drink than he'd planned. His thirteen-year-old son was under strict instructions to stay out of the pool until his homework was done and not to swim alone. Conroy's watch read five-fifteen; no way Damon could have been to baseball practice and gotten his homework done by now. Well, there was going to be hell to pay. Kid might have grown up in the lap of luxury, but Conroy wanted it to mean something, wanted him to appreciate it. He'd told Damon often enough how it had been for him, always in general terms, with the specific dates sketched broadly, since there was a big chunk of years that Harrison Conroy had simply deleted from his life. They never happened, lost in a kind of willful amnesia.

He brought his drink with him out the French doors, across the lawn toward the pool.

"Damon, son, there better be a good reason why you're—"

Conroy stopped cold. The glass slipped from his hand and shattered against the asphalt. A man he wished he didn't recognize sat in an inflatable pool chair, his bulk making it sag into the water. The chlorinated water ran across his stomach, pooling near his navel. His shoulder-length hair was a wild, wet tangle, framing a face that looked too old for it. He was holding a tall glass full of something that looked like Hawaiian Punch, slurping it out of a party straw.

"You dropped your drink, Othell," greeted Jack Tyrell.

"I don't go by that name anymore."

Tyrell laughed, same way he had twenty-five years before, except a little hoarser. "No, you're Harrison Conroy now, assistant director of Special Projects at Brookhaven National Labs here on Long Island—what, maybe fifteen minutes away?"

Conroy stood there tensely, feeling a sudden chill in the late-afternoon breeze. "Ten," he answered.

"Even better, Mr. Conroy. But you'll always be Othell Vance to me. Hell of a job you've got for yourself."

"Thanks. How'd you find me?"

"You mean, since you didn't exactly bother to invite me over for Thanksgiving dinner and all. Answer is because I been keeping track. I take pleasure in an old friend making good. Was a time when a black man like yourself could only dream of snaring such a position. As I recall, that was of considerable concern to you once."

Harrison Conroy, who was born Othell Vance III, swallowed hard and wished he had his drink back.

"You put the fact that you were once a Black Panther on your résumé, Othell?"

"There were no questions about politics."

"I was thinking in terms of education. I mean, that's where you learned much of your trade, wasn't it? You might even say that I was the one who gave you your real start. Think you'd have that cushy job ten minutes away at Brookhaven, if it wasn't for me?"

"What do you want?"

"Have a swim and a drink, maybe that's all."

"Okay."

Jack Tyrell paddled the chair closer to his old friend. "We got some old times to catch up on. Why don't you change into some trunks and join me?"

"No, thanks."

"Why put a pool in if you don't use it?"

"It came with the house."

"Cold day, but the water's warm."

"It's heated."

Tyrell shook his head admiringly. "I'm beyond impressed. Big house with a pool, thanks to the folks at Brookhaven paying you to blow things up. Only difference between them and me is I never had to pay you, because you didn't do it for the money. I figure that's worth something, like I was your agent or something." He looked around him. "All this . . . I figure you owe me."

"You need money?"

Jack Tyrell slurped up some more of his drink, vodka mixed with the punch, Othell Vance figured, or maybe gin. "I ask you a question, Othell?"

"Sure."

"You go to restaurants a lot?"

"Yes. Of course."

"Big fancy places. Need a reservation to get you and your pretty wife, Jenny, a table, right?"

Othell nodded, a little uneasy that Jack Tyrell knew his wife's name. Funny thing how he would have died for this man a generation before but couldn't be more scared of anyone right now.

"How about movies? You like movies?"

"Once in a while."

"In those new theaters with the sound that shakes the whole building."

"Multiplexes," Othall elaborated. "Where's this going, Jack?" he asked, instantly regretting it.

Jack Tyrell flapped his arms through the water, coming right up to the side of the pool and hooking his legs over the edge to hold the inflatable chair in place. Water splashed onto Tyrell's sodden pants.

"I don't go to real restaurants much, haven't since the last time you saw me, at the Mercantile Bank, Othell. I go to the movies, but I got to show up late, after the movie starts and it's too dark for anyone to recognize me. I always miss the coming attractions. Used to be my favorite part."

Jack's gaze narrowed, his eyes seeming to darken. Othell knew the look well. So did the FBI: it was the expression they used on the poster when Jack Tyrell was America's most wanted man, when he was Jackie Terror. Othell stood there looking down at him, his skin gone clammy. In the next instant Tyrell seemed to shake Jackie Terror off his face.

"You know what this is about, Othell? You want to know what I want? I want what I got coming to me. I want a little payback. I want your fucking help."

Lots of comments ran through Othell's mind, most of them the kinds of things Harrison Conroy would say. Othell tried to keep who he was today front and center.

"I can't do nothing for you." *My God*, he thought, *I'm talking like I used to. . . .*

Jack smiled, ran his free hand through his tangled hair. "That's better. At least I recognize your voice now. But seriously, Othell, even though you didn't use me as a reference for Brookhaven, you're only here now 'cause of me."

"Those days are over, Jack."

"Not anymore. I decided to make a comeback. There's something that needs doing, Othell. I won't ask you to help me do it. I will ask for the required ordnance."

"Ordnance?"

"I need to blow something up. Something big. All the things you're into at Brookhaven, I figure there's got to be one that can help me."

"You want me to steal something from the lab?"

"I'd say borrow, but there's not really much chance of it being returned intact."

"You have any idea the kind of security we're talking about here?"

And then Othell shuddered, because Jack Tyrell melted into the sun and he found himself staring into the cold eyes of Jackie Terror again, and this time it didn't look like he was going away. "You have any idea where your son Damon is right now?"

Othell felt his knees wobble. "What, Jack, *what*?"

Tyrell took something from his shirt pocket and shook the water from it. "Let's play hide-and-seek. I hide your son and you seek him."

Othell came right up to the edge of the pool. He realized it was a prescription pill bottle that Tyrell was holding in his hand. "Where is he, Jack? What have you done?"

Tyrell popped the top off the pill bottle and it plopped into the pool. "I gave him some pills, Othell, quite a few pills. Shit, you might say I poisoned your boy."

"No, Jack! No!"

"Calm down, old friend, 'cause these pills I got here will counteract the others, like an antidote, if you're following me."

Jackie Terror shook the topless bottle, and Othell Vance watched the tiny white spheres bounce dangerously close to the rim, clacking against each other.

"Please, Jack, tell me where he is."

Jackie Terror took one of the pills out and flung it into the water. "I wouldn't squander too many of these if I were you, Othell."

"Jack, what you're asking me—I *can't* do it! I haven't got that kind of security clearance! *Nobody* has that kind of security clearance!"

"Too bad," Tyrell said, and dropped another pill into the pool.

Othell Vance snapped a hand out, as if trying to reach for it. "Hold on, there might be something. . . ."

"Now you're talking, old friend."

"But there's a problem: it's lost."

Tyrell poured a pile of pills into his palm. "You're trying my patience, Othell." And he extended his hand over the water, stopping just short of dropping them in.

"No, wait! I can help you find it. Get you every scrap of information in existence, in the goddamn world!"

Tyrell brought his hand back. "This stuff you lost, it's good?"

"If Satan sat down to shit, this is what would come out," Othell Vance said, in a voice that sounded like somebody else's, somebody he had done his best to forget.

Jackie Terror turned his palm sideways and let the bottle suck the pills back up. "Now we're getting somewhere. Tell me more."

"The stuff's called Devil's Brew. . . ."

NINE

"Whatcha think this is," Buck Torrey said, a foot prodding Blaine's shoulder, "a fucking hotel? Get your ass up!"

Blaine stirred and sat up in the first of the dawn light; Torrey's porch had become his permanent sleeping place. Took all the hours he could steal from the night just to cool down from the long hot days of training. Going on four weeks now, and the differences were striking.

Years of religious weight lifting had added rippling slabs of muscle to Blaine's frame. He had worked out obsessively, trying to cheat age and fool his muscles into thinking they were younger. But all those months in the hospital had taken both bulk and tone away, leaving soft layers of flab in their place. Now, after only a month with Buck, the flab was gone. He was thinner and leaner than he had been in years, trading muscle for speed while sacrificing only minimal strength in the process. The change was especially kind to his hip, since it was carrying twenty fewer pounds now than it had last year.

Blaine couldn't pinch fat anywhere on his body, and best of all, he could pinch with *two* hands. The restricted motion of his shoulder had vanished, the mobility back. He could pivot and twist now almost as well as ever, no longer doubting his hip could take the strain.

Blaine ducked under the porch railing and dove into the water, a daily ritual. Every morning he'd swim under Buck Torrey's stilt house and paddle around underwater as long as he could, trying to stretch the seconds each day.

"How'd I do?" he asked, heaving for air as he splashed back above the surface.

Torrey looked up from his watch. "Minute forty-five. Best yet, you son of a bitch, your new fucking record. But don't even think about leaving here until you top two minutes ten."

"Why two minutes ten?"

" 'Cause that's *my* record."

They had fallen into a routine that Torrey changed up or added to almost every day. Blaine hoped this morning they'd be taking to the trees that lay out in the swamp just beyond Torrey's stretch of water, where knotty tangles of drooping vines formed umbrella-like canopies. Trees that grew more out than up.

It had been agony at first for Blaine to climb those vines. Afraid to put too much weight on his shoulder, he overcompensated and had his face scratched to hell by the prickly ends. Once the shoulder began to shape up, he climbed easily at arms' distance, looking more like a monkey or a squirrel than a man.

Buck Torrey had him start moving from tree to tree up high, and when that became routine for Blaine, Buck outfitted him with a backpack a quarter full of rocks. Each visit to the swamp, Torrey added more, until Blaine was toting the equivalent of a fifty-pound army pack.

"Got a surprise for you today, son," Torrey said this morning as Blaine drooped a towel over his dripping frame. "Your first big test, see how close you are to being ready to leave me be." He checked his watch, then looked up at the sun. "We'd better get moving if we don't want to lose our chance."

They headed out on foot. The fact that Torrey wasn't carrying the back-pack into which he stuffed rocks was a giveaway that climbing was not on the agenda today, even before they trekked deeper into the swamp than they had gone before. Nearing the shallows, Blaine became conscious of shapes shifting about, dark blurs of motion sliding through the black water.

"Gators," Buck Torrey said softly, turning back to him.

"Oh."

"Remember the obstacle course at Bragg?"

"Live fire?"

"That's the one. You recall why we used live ammo, 'spite of the risks?"

Blaine continued to walk just behind Torrey along the thin trail of muck, careful to match his footprints as closely as possible. "Because if you know when and where the bullets are coming from and still can't handle them, you sure as hell won't be able to handle combat."

" 'Handle them,' " Torrey repeated. "I like the way you put it, 'cause that's the way it is. You get your fix on the first one and make sure you're somewhere else when the next one comes. Simple, but it keeps people alive."

"Dead Simple."

Torrey stopped and looked back at him. "My point exactly, son. The course was a prime way of cutting the fat off the bone. Every time through, we move the bullets a little closer. Take one on the course, you probably walk away wounded. Take one in the country somewhere, you don't walk away at all. So I get to thinking 'bout all we been doing this last month or so. I think I done everything you come down here for 'cept one, and that is to see if you're really ready for live fire again."

Blaine swallowed hard, having wondered the same thing himself.

"So I come up with a way to find out." He checked his watch for the third time that morning. "The time's just about right."

"For what?"

Torrey turned his gaze out over the swamp. "They're just waking up now, hungry like you wouldn't believe, and hungry makes them mean. Gator is mostly a lazy-ass creature. Sleep, shit, sun, and fuck's about all he does. Most times you got to step on his snout to make him move. Couple times a day—now and 'round dusk—they get ornery." He stuck his finger out and moved it in a narrow arc. "You can see 'em if you look close, all across there." He peered again at Blaine. "What I want you to do, son, is get to the other side of the swamp."

Blaine's reaction could have been one of many things, but what came surprised him as much as Buck: he smiled.

He let instinct fuel his pace. Started out slow as he cut into the heart of the swamp, leaving Torrey on the thin path. The water ranged from knee to waist deep, with islands of footing recognizable as slight splotches that reflected the sun differently. Blaine's plan was to dance from one to the other, never even stir a gator if he planned things right.

A twelve-footer slithered by with its mouth opened as Blaine leaped atop the first land pod. For a time his leaps from one land pod to the next became a frantic game of connect the dots. Initially he hit the soft patches too hard, drawing the death jaws of several gators uncomfortably close. Once, a grayish one had him dead to rights, when another gator's sudden leap knocked it aside. Then Blaine began to soften his landings, gliding through the air rather than lunging.

The problem was nature had not cooperated with his plan, putting increasing distance between the land patches the closer he got to the opposite shore. Blaine never once turned back toward Buck; this wasn't about Buck. This was about him. This was about fear and conquering it. Not of the gators; they were just an exercise tool. The fear of real danger, as opposed to pain.

With a third of the distance left to cover, he ran out of land; only water separated him now from the opposite shore. Blaine slid off the final land patch into knee-deep black water that quickly rose to his waist, alert for the sudden shifts in current indicating a gator had him in its sights and was coming fast. He got used to the feel of the water lapping around him, and when it lapped wrong he lunged to one side, a few times narrowly avoiding eager jaws, which snapped closed on nothing.

Suddenly he realized he could feel the presence of the gators even when the water did nothing to betray their location. He began to move more subtly, mixing with the currents instead of disturbing them. His first thought had been to grab a branch, a rock—some sort of weapon. But thought gave way to instinct before he had a chance to think again.

He learned to blend with the gators' movements, drift into the wakes left by their quick spurts through the water. Eventually they came to regard Blaine indifferently, or perhaps not regard him at all, even though they had him surrounded.

Blaine remembered other swamps, other jungles, in which the odds were the same and only the enemy was different, realizing then why Buck had waited until today to bring him here. Surviving required a mental edge as well as a physical one. This was Buck's way of saying the latter had been regained and it was time to check on the former. Give him back not just his muscle but also his mind-set.

Dead Simple . . .

That was how walking through the gators had felt. That was how thriving in another jungle had been.

Reaching the other shore, where Buck Torrey was now waiting, Blaine could have sworn a few of the gators lifted their snouts out of the water to give him a last look. They seemed confused, glad the stranger in their midst had gone before the day grew hot and they slipped back into the waters for a nap.

"Wanna come back for dinner tonight?" Torrey asked him with a wink.

"I'm gonna be gone for a time," Buck announced when Blaine got back from his distance swim that afternoon. "Some things I gotta attend to."

His voice held a somber tone Blaine didn't recognize from all the years they'd known each other. Torrey's eyes drooped, wide with worry.

"What's wrong?"

"Personal."

"So was me coming down here."

"This ain't your concern."

"You saying there's nothing I can do to help?"

"Nope. You can stay here and keep putting yourself back together so when I get home I can finally get rid of you once and for all." Torrey tried to force a smile, couldn't manage it.

"Why don't I come along?"

"Like I said—"

"I know: it's personal. Nothing's personal among old dogs like us. Sound familiar?"

"You're out of order, Private."

"I went out a captain, Sergeant Major."

"You went out an asshole who didn't know when to leave things be, and that's what got you in the fix you're in. I guess you're back to your old self, after all."

Blaine wasn't ready to give in. "You headed north?"

"It matter?"

"How about I call Johnny? He's a nice guy to have around." Blaine held the thought. "For company."

"I don't need no spooky giant Indian hanging around. What I got to do is simple shit, nothing up your alley or his. Bore the two of you to death, as a matter of fact. Family stuff is all."

"Family?"

Torrey's eyes shifted a little, like those of a man who realized he'd said too much. Blaine looked into them and saw he wasn't going to say any more.

"Something I got to do alone," Torrey explained. "You okay with that, or do I have to make it an order? Just leave me be to make up for some lost time."

"This about your daughter? Is she in trouble?"

Buck frowned. "Seems to be a run of it lately. I'm starting to feel like the Red Cross. I come down here to be alone, and now I'm helping people out left and right."

"You never wanted me to meet her."

"Never wanted *anyone* I trained to meet her. I know you boys too well."

"Afraid I'll break her heart or tear it out?"

A flash of pride showed in Torrey's eyes. "Try either and she just might gut you first."

"A true Torrey."

" 'Cept her name's Halprin now. Liz Halprin."

2

NEW TRICKS

TEN

em Trumble hoisted the gravestone from the ground and placed it gently across the front of the forklift. The night sky bled a little rain, but Lem didn't feel it as he shifted his massive shoulders and squeezed back into the forklift's cab. It was far too small to accommodate his vast bulk, and he had to sit sideways and shimmy himself around a little before driving off with one leg hanging outside.

Lem never complained about the size of the forklift cab, because he otherwise loved his work. This shift belonged to him and him alone. People didn't like him very much and never had. Ever since he was a kid, they considered him big and dumb. Well, they were half right. Lem stood closer to seven feet than six and was blessed with an incredibly muscular frame even though he had never lifted a weight in his life.

He pulled the forklift to a halt in front of the caretaker's workshop and carried the gravestone inside, laying it adroitly atop his table, ready with all the tools and supplies he would need to repair it. This Vermont cemetery was on the National Historic Register, which meant the stones had to be brought in for repair at the first sign of damage. The other workers could do the spot stuff themselves right at the grave site. But the larger, more complicated jobs were left for Lem. He would come in every night, check his board for the log of plot and grave numbers, then head the forklift out to the first one on the list.

He loved working with the marble and granite, took exquisite pride in making his patchwork meld perfectly with the structure as a whole. When finished, he would draw a line through that item on the log, return it to its place, and drive out to fetch another. There was an easy, simple rhythm to it all that Lem embraced, mostly because he could handle everything alone and at night. He didn't like the way people looked at him during the day, when he couldn't go out without applying thick makeup to cover the burn scars that corroded his face. There wasn't much the doctors had been able to do to put his face back together, but the important parts worked well enough. Only good thing was the face had kept everyone away from him in his twenty years hard time in a federal penitentiary. Bad thing was after the twenty were over he had to look at himself again.

In prison there weren't a lot of mirrors or glass. It was easy to forget what the heat of the blast had done to his flesh and hair. Once he got out, the mirrors and glass were everywhere he looked. On the night shift, though, he never saw anyone and nobody saw him. Work his magic with the decaying tombstones and take the check out of his box every other Friday. His hands looked like swollen slabs of meat, yet were delicate and adroit all the same. He could work them into any groove or crack in the granite, smooth in a patch so perfect nobody could notice once it dried.

His secret was making believe he was working on his own face, doing for the stones what the doctors couldn't do for him. Lost himself in the work, as now, smoothing out the inside of a chip so the patch would take better.

"Anybody I know?" a voice asked from the door.

Lem stiffened as he turned. A dark shape stood before him in the doorway, silhouetted against a shroud of light shed by the outdoor floods.

Lem squinted, couldn't believe what he thought he was seeing. "Jack?" His eyes bulged. "Is that you?"

"Hello, Tremble," Jack Tyrell greeted, using the pet name he always called Lem, since that's what people who saw him always did, and he closed the door behind him.

Lem was across the floor in an instant too fast to record, incredible for a man his size. He captured Tyrell in a bear hug and hoisted him happily off the ground.

"I knew I'd see you again someday, Jack! I just knew it!"

Tyrell waited for Lem to set him back down. "That day has come." He looked the giant over, not bothered by his ruined face.

Lem turned proudly to his worktable. "Got me a trade now. Wanna see?"

Jack followed him back to the gravestone. "And I prepared you well for it. Like your work, Lem?"

"Fuck, yeah."

"What if I was to say I needed you, Tremble, that it was time we went back to finish what we started?"

Lem stripped off his grubby work apron and dropped it to the floor. He couldn't smile anymore, since a good portion of his upper lip was burned away, but the look he gave Jack Tyrell was as close as he could come.

"I'd say I'm ready. I'd say I can't wait."

Jack reached out to touch the big man's shoulder, pet him like the loyal dog he was. "Neither can I."

ELEVEN

A ren't you going to ask me in?"

Liz Halprin found herself staring at her father through the screen door.

"Nice shotgun, by the way," Buck Torrey continued, gazing down at the Mossberg dangling from her left hand. "I guess you were expecting somebody else."

"Five years go by, I wasn't expecting you."

"Heard you had some trouble."

"Nothing I can't handle."

"With a shotgun?" Eyes on the Mossberg again.

"It's cheaper to feed than a dog," Liz said, as she finally eased open the screen door.

"Place looks pretty good," Buck said, and he slid past her into the kitchen.

"It looks like shit. Old; you know."

"The broken window in the living room's new."

"I see you've been looking around."

Buck plopped the duffel bag he was carrying down to the floor. Its contents clanked noisily on impact with the tile. "Bullet holes are easy to spot. Why don't we have a drink and you can tell me what's going on."

"If I wanted to tell you that, I'd have called."

"A tough chore, considering you don't have my phone number. Where are the glasses?" Buck asked, moving past his daughter to open a cupboard. "They used to be here."

"Next one over. And how'd you know *anything* was going on?"

He selected two rocks glasses and turned back toward her. "I got sources."

"You mean spies."

"Where's the whiskey?" Buck asked, working on another cabinet.

They talked for hours, bursts of conversation mixed with uneasy lapses of silence Buck Torrey filled with sips from the whiskey he had found on his own. Mostly, he wanted to know about the grandson he hadn't seen in five years, letting Liz tell in her own time what had happened that day at William T. Harris Elementary School.

"I'm proud of you," he said after she had finished. "The way you handled things: by the book, everything covered."

"An innocent man got killed. My bullet went straight through his skull."

"The way you tell it, if the suits at the J. Edgar Hoover Building knew a lick about combat, if any of them had ever seen a firefight, never mind been in one, they might realize you start your loss assessment by working backwards."

"This is the FBI, Dad, not the army."

"This is common sense, girl. That shooter, he was carrying . . ."

"A Mac-10," Liz completed.

"Stone age weapon. Absolute piece of shit. Three extra clips he had on him?"

"That's right."

"Okay, we say he manages to fire off two before somebody gets the balls to jump him. Sixty rounds in those kind of surroundings will give you twenty kills and twenty casualties. Twenty lives over and twenty fucked up forever *minimum*, instead of one. Makes *your* score a plus thirty-nine, which puts you at the top of my class. That's the way loss assessment works."

"Disciplinary board didn't see things that way. Said I should have waited for backup before moving in."

"How far away?"

"I could hear the sirens."

"A question of timing."

"That's what they said. They also said my presence precipitated the action."

"Precipitated?"

"That's how they phrased it in the final report."

Buck Torrey sneered. "Man goes into a school with a piece of shit Mac-10, and it's your fault he opens fire with it?"

"From their perspective, after Waco and Ruby Ridge, yes."

"They're full of crap."

Liz helped herself to a glass of whiskey, dulled it with a little ice and water. "You're telling me."

"Mac-10's a killing weapon—that's all it's good for. Spray it around and see what drops."

"It must have been a ricochet. I can account for all the bullets, while the perp was still holding the victim."

That set Buck thinking. "What were you carrying?"

"Smith and Wesson .380."

"Load?"

"Round-nosed hardball."

Buck shook his head. "No way that bullet exits the skull on a ricochet. Nine-millimeter's basically piss poor when it comes to stopping power."

"Anything else?"

"Yeah. Round-nosed hardball nines are standard ammo for the Mac-10."

"You think the FBI crime lab doesn't know that?"

"I'd like to take a look at the ballistics report. See how it was that crime lab was able to make a positive ID on your bullet based on what was left after a ricochet and a skull penetration."

Liz's superiors had shrugged that question off when she asked it, claiming the evidence was conclusive.

"I'll see what I can do."

Buck took a hearty sip from his whiskey. "Army sent me some of the new 4.5 millis to check out."

"The Beretta or the Heckler and Koch?"

Buck looked at his daughter with considerable surprise.

"I test-fired both of them last time I was down at Quantico," she told him.

"What'd you think?"

"Those thirty-shot clips have something to be said for them."

"My feeling is you accomplish the same thing by just training people to shoot twice as good with fifteen, know what I mean?"

"Where does it stop?"

"With people who score a plus thirty-nine." Buck Torrey raised his glass in the semblance of a toast. "My daughter . . . who can serve in my outfit anytime."

He took a sip. Liz joined him.

"Now tell me about this other problem we got before us."

Liz saw the truck pull onto the farm from an upstairs window first thing the next morning, three men squeezed into the cab.

"Dad," she said tensely, entering the kitchen to find Buck Torrey's coffee cooling and a huge plate of scrambled eggs only half eaten. *Of all the times to take a walk . . .*

One of the men knocked on the screen door's frame. Liz opened it casually.

"You must be Liz Halprin," greeted the first man to come through the door, a used car salesman's smile stitched from ear to ear. "I'm John Redding, head of the local Cattleman's Association." He extended his hand and Liz took it, squeezing only as hard as he did, then assessing the fat man and the short, barrel-chested one who had followed him inside. "Me and my fellow officers wanted to welcome you to the county. I knew your grandparents. Worked for them, in fact, for a couple summers."

"I hope they treated you well."

"That's why I'm here; to repay the favor." He looked to his two associates. "We heard you've been having some trouble, thought we might be able to help."

"Very kind of you."

"It's the least we can do. Been a long time since you been back, hasn't it?"

"Yes."

"Lots of changes. Different times than the ones you remember. The land's still the land, but what it's good for has changed."

Liz took a step back from him. "What exactly does a Cattleman's Association do, Mr. Redding?"

"Looks out for the best interests of its members, Miss Halprin."

"And what would those interests be?"

He tried to smile. "Why don't you tell us?"

"My only interest is in keeping my farm," Liz said, and moved to pour herself a cup of coffee.

"That's the problem," Redding said, approaching her once again.

Liz stopped before she got to the pot. "Whose problem? Since I have no intention of leaving, it's not mine. And since you're here to help me, it couldn't be yours. Who does that leave?"

"We wanted you to hear the town's perspective on things," Redding told her. "This county's running out of chances, Ms. Halprin. In fact, I'd say Maxwell Rentz's resort might be our last one. Now, we understand you got your reasons for holding out. If it's more money you want—"

"It's not."

"—the association will go to Mr. Rentz on your behalf. He needs the direct access your land allows to the main highway, and if he doesn't break ground on this soon, between you and me, he might throw in the towel and take his business elsewhere."

"You're worried about all those lost jobs, then."

"Yes, ma'am, I am."

"And you've got good reason to be . . . whether I sell or not. I've been reading up on the various holdings of Rentz Enterprises. This isn't the first time they've taken on a massive project; the only first would be if they hired locals to work on it."

Redding tugged at his collar.

"You see," Liz continued, "Rentz Enterprises is known for bringing in cheap, nonunion labor from wherever they can get it, usually after the local authorities grant them all kinds of tax breaks. You think it'll be any different here? You think the day Maxwell Rentz breaks ground on Disney World North, there will be a single local resident holding a shovel?"

Redding tried to look calm. "Well, Ms. Halprin, there's a lot of people in these parts who'd like the chance to find out. We've been holding them off as best we can, but I'm not sure we'll be able to much longer."

"Is that a threat?"

"Just relaying information. Now, we're aware there have been a few incidents already, and we're worried even we won't be able to prevent more." Redding paused, letting his eyes fall on a recent Polaroid of Liz and Justin held by a magnet to the refrigerator. The last one taken since he'd gone back to live with his father. "You planning on having your son join you here?"

The look in Redding's eyes got Liz's heart hammering. She felt pressure building in her head, and her mouth went dry. Before she could respond, the screen door rattled and Buck Torrey strode in. He had eased the door open with his foot, both his hands occupied behind his broad back.

"Morning, fellas," he greeted innocently. "Hey, that must be your truck parked outside. She's a beauty, lemme tell you."

Redding was trying very hard to see what Buck was holding. "I don't think we've met."

"Aw, I'm just the young lady's father. Retired now. Dividing my time amongst my children. You'll know what it's like soon enough."

Buck smiled broadly and Redding responded with a smile of his own.

"Hey, that truck parked outside—I was thinking about getting me one just like it. With all the traveling I do, I need a lot of space in the bed. So—I hope you don't mind—I checked yours out."

Something in Buck Torrey's expression changed at that point. Everyone in the kitchen noticed it, but only Liz sensed what was coming next.

He brought one of his hands from behind his back to reveal the pair of wire cutters he was holding. "Found this amongst the tools back there. I got to figure that one just like it was what cut my daughter's phone line last week." Buck laid the wire cutters on the counter and brought a shotgun with an elegant wooden stock from behind his back next. "Now, this is a beautiful piece of work. Twelve-gauge pump. Takes eight shells instead of your customary six. Accurate up to thirty yards, maybe." His eyes narrowed intently. "Funny thing. That's the distance from which I figure somebody shot up the bay window in my daughter's living room."

Buck Torrey was feeding on the air now, seeming to get larger as he stood there. He retraced his steps to the screen door and grabbed a 30.06 rifle he had leaned up against the frame just outside.

"And this piece of shit carries the same shell and load that killed one of the cows my daughter bought when she came back home." Buck's eyes bored into Redding's, daring him, daring all three of them, to make a move. "It takes a helluva man to shoot a dumb animal, let me tell you. Stand out in the open and take your time fixing your aim on something that's not about to shoot back."

In a blur of motion, Buck snapped the 30.06 up into his arms in a relaxed shooting position. Neither Redding nor his men moved an inch. Buck looked almost disappointed.

"An amateur might call this a marksman's rifle. A pro uses something with a lot more velocity and a lot less kick. Something he can control enough to paint a target up to a mile or more away. Think about that. You're driving in that nice blue truck of yours, minding your own business, and all of a sudden there's lead flying through the windshield, coming from so far away you never even hear the gunshots. You know any man like that?"

Redding didn't say a word. His two subordinates exchanged glances, warning each other off.

"Well," Buck Torrey said, "I do. I know plenty. Some pretty good friends of mine. Flushed the M-21 sniper system down the toilet in Nam for a modified M-16 with an infrared scope. Yup, they're good friends, all right."

Buck's face squared up, reddened a little. His chest blew outward to its true expanse. He looked taller, a breath away from springing, each of the men fearing it was going to be toward him.

"Now, I can almost let the shot-up window go by. Almost. And as far as shooting a dumb animal goes, well, that pretty well clinched things even *before* you mentioned my grandson. I figured then it was time I come in and introduce myself." Liz realized Buck was holding the 30.06 dead on Redding's gut. "I want you to go back to the rest of the members of your association and tell them this farm is not for sale. Tell them the issue is not negotiable. Mr. Rentz is just gonna have to use the old road across the way to access his condos, golf courses, and theme parks. Might make you a hero when you think about all those extra men he'll have to hire to level that land, lay that extra asphalt." The 30.06 rifle was still grasped in his hand like it weighed nothing. "I'd think about things from that perspective if I was you."

Buck Torrey backed away, showing them the door. They filed past him slowly, not bothering to ask for their guns and tool back.

"That the competition?" he asked Liz.

"So far."

Buck smirked. "I hope this Max Rentz can do better. I think maybe I'll pay him a visit and find out."

TWELVE

The Yost twins sat across from Jack Tyrell in the booth.

"It wasn't easy tracking you boys down," he told them.

"Well, we been moving around a lot," said Earl.

"Keeping to the roads," added his brother Weeb. "Real traveling men."

"Like the Allman Brothers song."

"That was 'Rambling Man,'" Jack corrected.

The whole time he'd been sitting there talking to them, Jack knew he might have had their attention, but not their eyes. Those two pairs of matching pinkish eyes seemed to move as one, studying everyone who entered the roadside diner. Following their steps from the parking lot after they parked their vehicles.

The twins had been with Jack for a good part of his run through the early seventies. They weren't very much committed to the times or the cause, though they claimed to be. They just enjoyed the violence. Tyrell saw right through them but didn't care much what motivated them, because they were very good at what they did. Hold guns on the hostages during a bank job or shoot a kidnap victim in the head when the ransom money didn't come through as promised. That kind of work didn't suit everybody.

Earl and Weeb were both rail-thin guys with skin wrapped tight over their bones, but they were the most terrifying men Jack had ever met up with. The measure of true fear was based on the extent to which a man was willing to go, and there was no extent too far for Earl and Weeb Yost. Absolutely nothing they wouldn't do. They placed no value whatsoever on human life, killing to them as natural as breathing.

"You like our car?" Earl asked suddenly.

"Green Caddy parked out there in the shade," added Weeb.

"Got killer air-conditioning."

"A must for the upcoming summer."

"You want us to get you one?" Earl posed, wanting to please like a puppy on its first day home, seeing Jack as probably the only man who appreciated their talents.

Jack looked at them across the booth. They'd been waiting when he arrived, having chosen the back booth because it was out of the sun. The sun hurt their eyes and burned their skin. The twins were albinos: faces that looked like they were smeared with talcum powder every morning and hair a tangle of sugar-coated thin spaghetti.

"How *did* you find us?" Earl asked, curious again.

"Why'd you bother is what I'm wondering," Weeb raised suspiciously.

As Jack peered at the brothers, deciding which to answer first, he noticed their eyes stray in eerie synchronicity to a Winnebago that had just pulled into the parking lot. The twins watched as a family of four piled out, looking road-weary and eager for any food that hadn't been cooked over a propane stove. The brothers turned toward each other, smiling.

"You were about to say how you found us," Earl picked up.

"No," Weeb disagreed. "He was going to tell us why he bothered."

"The how is easy," Jack told them. "The work you boys do leaves a distinctive signature. Couple newspapers, the TV news—you're not hard to keep track of for somebody who knows what to look for."

"It's a living," Earl offered, as the family from the Winnebago entered the diner.

"Doesn't amount to much from where I'm sitting."

"You got something better in mind?"

Jack aimed his words at Weeb this time. "That's why I'm here. Got some work for you, if you're interested."

The twins looked at each other again, not very excited. Weeb spoke. "And we're supposed to believe you can just pick up where you left off?"

"No. You're supposed to believe I'm gonna pick up a long way *beyond* where I left off."

"Fucking A," said Earl, tensing a little as the Winnebago family took a booth just two away from theirs.

Weeb slid a little closer to his brother. "I've seen people tow cars behind those Winnebagos."

"What's your point?" Earl asked him.

"I'm wondering if we can keep the Caddy, just for kicks. String it along behind us." Then, as quick as that, Weeb looked back at Jack. "What kind of job we talking about?"

"We're gonna take some hostages."

"Sounds easy enough," said Weeb.

"How many hostages?" asked Earl.

Jack Tyrell lifted his cup and sipped coffee through the steam. "Oh, five million, give or take a few."

THIRTEEN

Maxwell Rentz drove through his model community in a cart designed to haul a caravan of cars behind it, purchased back in the days when he envisioned hordes of potential buyers seeking tours of the property.

And why not?

It was a work of art, of perfection. From the time he announced his plans to build such a high-security, self-contained community eighteen months before, Rentz expected to be deluged with requests to reserve living accommodations. Enclosed by a high white stone wall, built upon the ruins of an inner-city Baltimore housing project off North Avenue, Paradise Village was perceived as not only a prototype for future neighborhoods but also a savior of urban America. People just couldn't escape crime anymore, no matter where they went or what they did. The alternative harked back to an old moats-and-gates philosophy: all that was bad kept out so that buyers would come in. Eventually, Rentz dreamed, the government would turn to his model for its vast projects, which would make Rentz a billionaire many times over.

To underscore the citadel idea, he had placed a guard tower in each corner to provide strategic viewpoints of the community's two dozen symmetrical, crisscrossing, immaculate streets. Nonobtrusive video surveillance via hidden cameras installed at numerous locations would give ample warning if anyone did manage to get through. A private security force would then swing into action, charged with protecting the community's thousand residents.

A mixture of villas, town houses, and eight-story buildings featuring four units per floor would serve as home to those residents. Each residence was wired to a central monitoring station. There was an elementary school, a pharmacy, a grocery store, an entertainment center featuring a first-run movie theater. Rentz boasted that a resident need never leave the confines of Paradise Village. It was a fortress built amidst a den of squalor and decadence, which rose as a monolith of hope for those the system had lost the ability to help.

Rentz imagined franchising Paradise Villages all over the world, gradually swallowing up the slums across the globe to provide good people with a safe place to live. Toward that end, he pumped the vast bulk of his dead father's resources into its construction, committed to having his working model up and running at the earliest possible time. He had even scheduled dozens of tours with foreign dignitaries, government officials, investors, and venture capitalists in advance of the completion date. When construction wrapped weeks ahead of schedule, he took this as a good omen and couldn't wait for the pitch meetings to begin, already counting the millions he would recoup for his efforts.

His father had always scoffed at his schemes. Rentz had blessed this opportunity to prove him wrong, at the same time he found it ironic that his father's death had given him the chance, and the capital, to do it. The accident had left him in charge of the business, millions of dollars to do with as he pleased.

And he had done so.

But the dozens of meetings, tours, and pitches that followed the completion of construction had not led to a single franchise request; not even a nibble. Paradise Village had become a great white elephant, with the monkey of a prohibitive operational budget riding its back. But Rentz couldn't cut that budget for fear of losing whatever hope he had of gaining some return on his investment. And if he shut down, Paradise Village would become nothing more than a hundred-million-dollar loss.

Rentz drove the streets in the carless train, marveling at how perfectly everything had turned out. Nothing had been skimped, no corners cut. He had started with a vision and refused to accept any suggestions that might have compromised that vision.

"Mr. Rentz." A call came over the car's dashboard speaker.

"Yes, Donovan."

"You're needed at your office, sir."

"Concerning what?"

"The Halprin farm."

"Did the crew find something?"

"You'd better see for yourself, sir."

Rentz returned at once. Donovan, his assistant, had just turned on the television and popped a tape into the VCR.

"This was just relayed from the site. Apparently there's been another incident."

The television screen filled with a grainy, poorly lit shot of the lake's dark depths. The picture came from a remote underwater vehicle Rentz had leased, outfitted with the most sophisticated underwater camera equipment known to man. It was piloted from the surface by a trained operator, who was receiving a thousand dollars per hour for his trouble. Rentz didn't believe for one moment that the lake he so desperately needed was haunted by a monster or ghosts lurking in its depths. But *something* had killed his two divers last week, and he'd be damned if he'd risk sending another man down there until he knew what.

Rentz watched the black lake come alive on-screen. He waited apprehensively for whatever had killed his divers to appear.

"Nothing yet," Donovan narrated.

"I can see that. How long has the ROV been down?"

"At this point, about ten minutes, sir."

Rentz moved closer to the screen. A black shape suddenly appeared before the ROV's cameras.

"What the hell . . ."

And immediately the screen turned to a blank, the signal gone.

"Rewind!" Rentz instructed. "Play it again in slow motion!"

Donovan did as he was told. But running the scene in slow motion made it no easier to discern anything.

"Again!" Rentz ordered.

He watched the last part of the tape five more times, reaching the same conclusion each run: something had snared the ROV in its grasp, something big enough to cover all the cameras at once.

"You can't go in there!"

Rentz was about to tell Donovan to rewind the tape again when he heard the protesting voice of his receptionist, followed by a light thud. Before he could even think of going for the security button, the door burst open and a tree trunk of a man with sun-weathered skin stormed through. Donovan moved to intercept him and was airborne in the next instant, smashing into the wall face-first and then slumping down along it.

The tree trunk of a man started across the room, glaring at Rentz.

"Time we had a talk," he said quite calmly.

Rentz slid back toward his desk. "Did we have an appointment I forgot?" he said, trying to cover his move for the security button. "Do I know you?"

"No, but you know my daughter—Liz Halprin," the tree trunk said. "My name's Buck Torrey. . . ."

FOURTEEN

Blaine felt lonely the moment Buck Torrey pulled away from the stilt house in his skiff. He was used to being alone; his whole life was based on solitude. He may not have moved to the woods like Johnny Wareagle, but he had left the regular world in spirit a long time ago. This, though, was different. The sounds along the water were suddenly magnified, the lack of anyone within shouting distance or simply passing casually by adding to his sense of isolation.

Two days passed, and he threw himself more and more into his training, hoping exhaustion would make him sleep every time he sat down to think. But he was worried about Buck; the feeling of unease nagged at him like an itch he couldn't reach.

As soon as he heard the outboard chugging his way, Blaine sensed something bad had happened. He saw a small motorboat coming and in the fading light recognized the sheriff who had driven him to Condor Key a month earlier, being ferried through the water. A local deposited him on Torrey's dock and tipped a sweat-soaked cap up to Blaine.

The sheriff climbed the ladder leading to the porch, his face like sun-dried paper ready to rip. Blaine didn't like the look on the man's face when he swung off the top rung.

"What's wrong?" Blaine asked him.

"It's about Buck," the sheriff said, holding his hat in his hands. "He's missing."

✽   ✽   ✽

Blaine sat on the porch well into the evening, the birds and crickets making welcome company, Buck's cell phone never far from his reach. He fingered the ring on his hand and let himself hope that this was only his next exercise, another game Buck was playing with him to make sure he was ready for the world again.

But he knew it wasn't. Buck had gone up to Virginia to help his daughter, and something had happened to him there. The sheriff had given him the number of a man who was expecting Blaine's call.

Expecting his call . . .

Because Buck had provided Blaine's name for the man to contact if something went wrong. And Buck never would have involved Blaine unless he was certain Blaine was ready to handle whatever was waiting. Trusting him with the safety of his daughter. Trusting him with uncovering whatever had happened.

Blaine drew the cellular phone to him, pressed out a number different from the one belonging to the man up in Preston, Virginia, who was waiting for his call.

"Yeah?" a raspy, cranky voice greeted.

"It's me, Sal."

The voice perked up instantly. "You still enjoying all that fun in the sun, boss?"

"I'm coming home."

" 'Bout fucking time," said Sal Belamo.

"Buck Torrey's missing."

"Uh-oh . . ."

"I'll give you what I know. Details need to be sorted out."

"Already on it. Anything else?"

"Yes." Blaine gazed down at the ring again, the essence of the Dead Simple motto hitting him hard and fast. "Call Johnny. Tell him to pack his bags."

FIFTEEN

Queen Mary concentrated on the card the woman was holding tight against her chest.

"Okay, what is it?"

"A heart," Mary answered.

The woman with whom she was sharing the lockup shook her head as she flung another dollar toward her. "That's eight in a row right. How you do that?"

"What card is it?" another woman in the cell, with bad teeth and a rank smell, yelled out, grabbing Mary's wrist before she could snatch the bill from the floor.

"I said I could tell the suit, not the card."

The woman wasn't letting up. "Come on, bitch, show us what you really got. What card she holding?"

"Eight of hearts," Mary answered.

The inmate holding the card dropped it faceup on the floor: ten of hearts.

"Pay up," the one with bad teeth ordered.

"You don't want to do this."

"I don't?"

"You've got enough problems."

"I do?"

"Killed your own kid, didn't you?"

The woman with bad teeth froze up. "What the fu—"

"He OD'd on your drugs. Little ten-year-old going into the bathroom to shoot up like his mama."

The woman let go of Mary's wrist and started to move away, but Mary followed her across the floor.

"You found him, the needle was still in his arm. Was he already dead or did he die later? That's the one thing I can't see."

The woman screamed.

Jack Tyrell walked into the Akron, Ohio, police department looking fresh and neat in his newly pressed clothes, his hair combed and clubbed back with a rubber band.

"Excuse me," he said to the clerk inside the thick glass directly before him.

Another man was in there with the clerk, manning the radio. Four more cops were milling about within; two of them had just sat down at their desks after refilling their coffee mugs.

"What can I do for you, sir?"

"I understand you're holding a prisoner here for transfer . . ." Jack checked the man's name tag. "Sergeant. Friend of mine named Mary Raffa."

"Transfer?"

"To county jail tomorrow. Thirty-day stretch for petty larceny, I think it was. She was sentenced yesterday."

"That all?"

"Well, like I said, she's a friend of mine, and I'd like to see if I can pay the fine on her behalf, set things right."

"Now? It's almost midnight."

"No better time than the present."

The sergeant didn't know whether to take him seriously or not. "Look, this is something you need to take up in court with a judge."

"Tomorrow?" asked a disappointed Jack Tyrell.

"Best I can do."

"You sure?"

"Sorry."

Tyrell turned and walked back through the door dejectedly. The sergeant had gone back to his paperwork when the roar of an engine made him look up.

The Winnebago's lights were off, so he didn't actually see anything until Lem Trumble crashed the vehicle through the entrance and slammed into the glass security wall, collapsing it. Earl Yost was the first one out, quickly followed by Weeb, both of them wielding submachine guns they fired nonstop until none of the six cops inside was moving.

✵   ✵   ✵

"You've lost your mind, Jackie! This time you've really gone and done it!" Mary yelled at him as he led her down the hall just beyond the lockup.

They had met during the Second Battle of Chicago, in the fall of 1969, a Weatherman action that had deeply disappointed Tyrell when the twenty thousand expected to show up turned out to be less than a tenth of that. Then, even worse, the leadership had distributed clubs instead of guns. Mary was with the movement's women's militia, and at one point during the second night of rioting she and Jack found themselves fighting, quite literally, back-to-back against the Chicago police. The first time Tyrell looked into her eyes, he could tell she was enjoying it as much as he was. They slept out together that night in a park, nursing their wounds and dreaming about the way things could be.

The first time he saw her gift in action, what she called a "quickening," was a few days later when they prepared to board a bus out of the city. Mary had clamped a hand onto his arm the instant he was starting up the steps.

"Don't get on," she ordered in a voice that left no room for argument.

Jack looked into her eyes, which had suddenly glassed over, and figured there was something wrong with her. It was only later, after a pair of Illinois State Police cruisers had run the bus off the road, killing two and injuring thirty, that he realized what Mary's gift was all about.

He didn't make a single move without consulting Mary from that point on. And to this day Tyrell believed that if she had been around for the Mercantile Bank action, it would have gone off altogether differently. He often played it out, pretending she'd been there. Wondered how his life would have been.

Tyrell stopped when they came to the main floor of the building, where the Yost brothers stood guard over a half-dozen dead cops, and smiled at her. "I rescue you out of jail and that's what you say to me? After twenty-five years you can't come up with a nicer greeting?"

Mary looked around and shuddered. "Oh God, Jackie, what have you gone and done?"

"Nothing, compared to what I'm going to do."

"You went through all this to get me out? You did this for me?"

"Thing is, babe," Jack told her, "I need you to find something for me."

SIXTEEN

Will Thatch poured himself another scotch, hand trembling so much he spilled some on the newspaper that lay atop his table, open to page five. A headline halfway down the page, next to an underwear ad, jumped out at him again:

SIX DIE IN JAIL BREAK

The article had an Akron, Ohio, log line. According to the account, last night four men had driven a stolen Winnebago into a police station and killed all officers present, to free a single female prisoner slated to be transferred to the county jail today. On his first read, Will hadn't gotten any further than the grainy still shot salvaged from a damaged security camera that pictured a pair of shapes moving toward a wall pockmarked with bullet holes. The blurriness didn't prevent Will from recognizing who they were; he'd know them anywhere, could almost smell them through the newsprint.

The Yost brothers.

Thatch had their pictures hanging right here on his memory wall, among two dozen others who formed the nucleus of Midnight Run. He lifted his eyes to that wall now, past his eight-by-tens of Jack Tyrell and Lem Trumble and the Yost brothers, to those of Othell Vance and Mary Raffa, better known as "Queen Mary," or "Mary Mary Quite Contrary," since she was responsible for planting six men in their graves, half of them cops. That's how her garden grew.

Will had started on the scotch right about then, dipped into an alcohol-induced fog, hoping things would settle in his mind. Kept drinking but couldn't stop shaking, even after putting on his thick bathrobe, with the threads hanging down from the bottom.

For twenty-five years he'd known this day would come. A piece of the past reaching out to drag him from the present. He sat now with his scotch, gazing at the article until his vision blurred, trying to remember where he had left his glasses.

As well as pictures, his memory wall was lined with newspaper articles, some of them of the FBI agents assigned to track down Jack Tyrell and Midnight Run. One of these agents was a handsome young man identified as Special Agent William Thatch. The last article in the row included pictures shot in the aftermath of Midnight Run's final act of terrorism, one of which showed William Thatch administering CPR to a wounded man on a smoky New York City street.

That was the day an FBI plant in Midnight Run had finally provided the opportunity to nail the entire gang at the Mercantile Bank building. The task force showed up along with a heavy complement of New York police and shot it out with gang members in the minutes before the bomb exploded.

Despite killing a number of the gang, the FBI task force had let Jack Tyrell and several of his soldiers, including the Yost brothers and Othell Vance, slip from their clutches that day. But Will bore the dubious distinction of having had Tyrell himself dead in his sights, only to look away.

A *father covered in blood, grieving over his dying son . . .*

Will had actually comforted the man, given him a towel, and brought him to a priest, who was found dead in his underwear twenty minutes later.

Jack Tyrell had disappeared after that, avoiding all attempts by Will and others to track him down. The difference between Will and those others was that he never gave up, not even after it cost him his job and his family. By the time it was clear Tyrell was gone for good, each day began and ended for Will the same way, the middle not much different. After being fired, he spent another three years squandering his pension on his own personal pursuit of his quarry.

When that failed he fell into the bottle, and he hadn't come up much since, except to study newspapers. At the New York Public Library mostly, as many out-of-town papers as he could scrutinize page by page until his eyes got blurry. If Jackie Terror ever came back, Will knew that's where he would find him. He kept his now ancient .38-caliber Smith & Wesson snub-nosed hidden under the mattress in case that day should come, tempted on numerous occasions to use it on himself in the meantime.

How ironic that when he saw Jack Tyrell again for the first time in twenty-five years, it wasn't in the library but at a newsstand, on the back page of the *New York Post* a month before. A black-and-white composite sketch of a man wanted for questioning in the murders of four unidentified men at Crest Haven Memorial Park, a cemetery in Clifton, New Jersey. Will bought the paper and stood there on the sidewalk studying the sketch for a very long time, the *Post* trembling in his liver-spotted hands.

The more he looked at the face, though, the less convinced he became it belonged to Jackie Tyrell. He brought it back to his room and studied it until his head throbbed. Before long the face could have been anyone's.

He'd been reading all the New York papers every day ever since. But strangely, that one edition of the *Post* contained the only mention of the cemetery murders. There wasn't a single follow-up story anywhere to be found, and if he hadn't tacked the article to his memory wall, Will might have doubted they ever happened.

Then the article about the Akron killings had run in the late edition of today's *New York Times*, along with the shot of the Yost brothers lifted off the surveillance camera and picturing a third figure in dim view from the side. The dim view was enough for Will.

He could recognize Jack Tyrell from any angle, and as it turned out, the composite sketch reproduced in the *Post* a month earlier wasn't such a bad likeness, after all.

Will poured the last of his scotch into the glass and guzzled it down. His throat burned and his stomach felt as if somebody was stoking logs inside it. He ran his eyes along the various pictures tacked to his memory wall, wondering how many other Midnight Run members old Jack had managed to contact. Tyrell never did anything without a firm purpose behind it, and now something had triggered him into rallying the troops again. What exactly that was Will didn't yet know, but there were a few things he was sure of:

Jackie Terror was back in business.

And, this time, Will was going to stop him.

SEVENTEEN

When was the last time you saw your father, Ms. Halprin?" Chief Lanning asked Liz.

"Day before yesterday."

Lanning noted that on the report form in front of him. "And you have no idea where he was going?"

"He had some business with Maxwell Rentz."

Lanning glanced up at that. "What kind of business?"

"He wanted to discuss Mr. Rentz's last offer for the family farm."

"What does your father do for a living?"

"He's retired."

"Retired from what?"

"Is that important?"

"Routine."

"Does the routine include questioning Mr. Rentz?"

"What was your father retired from, ma'am?"

"The army."

Lanning's eyebrows flickered. "And he went to see Mr. Rentz to discuss an offer for your farm."

"Why don't you ask Mr. Rentz, Chief?"

"I'd like to know first why your father came here to Virginia."

Liz felt her frustration begin to simmer over. "And I'd like to know what two of your officers were doing in the company of Maxwell Rentz last week."

"I thought we'd been over this before. On the phone."

"Not to my satisfaction."

"They were off duty at the time. Mr. Rentz retained them on a per-hire basis to secure a work area."

"What's there to secure around a lake, Chief? Was Mr. Rentz expecting them to direct traffic a half mile from the nearest road?"

"I don't know, Ms. Halprin. What I do know is if I'd've been the one at the lake that night, I would have arrested you for unlawful discharge of a weapon and maybe felonious assault." Lanning dropped his pen and leaned forward. "The thing is, you come in here asking me to do something about Mr. Rentz, when he has a hell of a lot more call to come in and ask me to do something about you."

"Then why hasn't he?"

Lanning looked unmoved by her comment. "Maybe he's trying to handle things in a gentlemanly fashion."

"Rentz doesn't know the meaning of the word."

"Don't ask me to take sides, Ms. Halprin."

"I'm asking you to do what's right."

"Right now, in the eyes of the town, that would be to arrest you. Maxwell Rentz is a powerful man, and he's planning to build a theme park that will bring this town to life again, put people back to work."

"Like the ones from the Cattleman's Association who paid me a visit, Chief?"

"This county hasn't had a Cattleman's Association in a long time, Ms. Halprin."

"Man named John Redding?"

"Never heard of him."

"Then he must have been one of those people who are looking for work."

Liz hadn't come to the police station expecting help so much as to put the town and county on notice that she wasn't going to give in easily. If they wanted a fight, she intended to give it to them; in fact, that was what she wanted now too. She would never have called her father, would never have involved him in this after so many years of estrangement. He hadn't even told her exactly how he had found out what was going on; Liz guessed it was his old army network, someone keeping an eye on her, with orders to call if there was a problem.

She didn't believe for one second that Maxwell Rentz, and any number of goons he could muster, were any match for her father. Buck Torrey was like a wall of granite it had taken the first twenty-six years of her life to find a crack in. That had been five years ago, when Buck discharged himself from the world and his family, along with the army. Moved to some godforsaken place in the middle of nowhere you couldn't reach, if you could find it. Liz didn't even have his address for almost a year, sent letters care of Fort Bragg and had no evidence he ever received them.

He finally wrote back, giving her a post office box address, to which she wrote frequently. She told him about the dissolution of her marriage, certain he took some pleasure in the fact that he had insisted from the beginning that her ex was a bastard. She kept him up-to-date on Justin's progress in school and sports and on the travails of her own career, centering on her pursuit of a long-sought-after position on the Hostage and Rescue Team.

Liz didn't stop writing, even if his infrequent replies were cursory at best. Every time she was ready to give up, memories flooded back: rich, warm, and uniquely Buck. Liz was his only child. She never once thought he would have been happier to have a son, because Buck was nothing if not totally fair about such things. Boy or girl—it mattered not at all to one of his upbringing. Buck wanted to raise a person, not a girl or a boy, the rituals for either not varying.

They did everything together, even after the divorce. Liz knew he had given up the farm in the money settlement because she loved it so much; her first thought upon returning to find it so run-down was of him. They played catch, went to movies, fished, and hunted. Well, not hunted exactly, because they never actually killed anything. Just slid through the woods tracking animals and seeing how close they could get before the animals scampered away.

Sometimes Buck would take her deep into the woods, where he would find and destroy traps laid by poachers. The only time he had ever killed anything was when they came upon a fox caught in one. Buck hadn't let her watch.

He taught her to shoot, and Liz loved that best of all. Her twelfth-birthday present was a camping trip to the mountains, where Buck lay in wait for some hunters who were illegally killing bears, leaving a trail of orphaned cubs in their wake. They had come upon the hunters' camp at night, and this time Buck did let Liz watch as he dealt with them. It had been the defining experience of their relationship, the moment in her life when Liz loved her father most, at the same time she found herself as terrified of him as were the men she was certain would never hurt an animal again.

Buck Torrey loved people in his own unique way, but he didn't believe you could love someone you didn't respect too. Liz could look back on those days now and see not only how important it was that she respect him, but also that he show how much he respected her. That was why he had let her watch him that night with the hunters. She was old enough at that point to be initiated into his world, see her father for what he really was.

It was strange how she had chosen to marry a man who was the exact opposite of Buck. Liz wondered if she had been overreacting to the fear that she would never be able to find a man who could measure up to her father, so why bother trying? Instead she had settled, perhaps worried she would grow consumed by her career down the road and wake up one morning in her forties with the realization that there would be no kid to take on overnights to the mountains. Teach how to spring traps and what to do to hunters who orphaned bear cubs.

Justin was almost nine now, and they hadn't done much of that. And if the return of Buck into her life was cause for any regret, it was how much her son had lost these last five years by his grandfather's withdrawal. Maybe she hadn't felt unequivocally happy to see her father because she feared that once this problem was resolved, he'd be gone again. More years sliding by as she checked the mail eagerly every day, only to be disappointed.

The Jeep coasted along at sixty, the road black and empty before her. A river blossomed on her right, making her think of the lake that kept the secrets of her property. The old law was vague but plain on this subject: if Maxwell Rentz could prove she had no claim to the lake, thus denying her water rights, his county contacts could order her land condemned and quit-deed it over to him.

She drove on, making out a wish list of what she would need if the county decided to condemn her land. Some claymore mines would be nice, a few fragmentation grenades, an M-16 with plenty of ammo. Maybe find them in the duffel her father had stowed in the front hall closet before he left. Hunker down and hold Rentz off long enough to make the press aware of his tactics, maybe take him out with her.

Liz didn't see the truck until it loomed as a huge shape in her rearview mirror, drawing up so fast it seemed to swallow the Jeep. She braced for impact, then realized the truck had sliced across the center line at the last instant, speeding up alongside her. She recognized its royal-blue color from the visit paid her by John Redding's nonexistent local Cattleman's Association.

The blue truck swerved suddenly and sideswiped her Jeep. Liz felt the passenger side grating against the guardrail, powerless to do anything but hold tight to the wheel. Slam the brakes and she'd be sent into a wild spin across the road, causing a horrific accident almost certain to take more lives than her own.

Thump!

The truck smashed her Jeep again, Redding's two cohorts from the other morning recognizable in the raised cab, sneering down at her. The barrel-chested one was driving, the fat one strapped into the passenger seat.

Liz shot them the finger, continued to battle the truck, the guardrail, and her own steering wheel. A trail of sparks flew in her wake. Cars whizzed by through the impossibly narrow gap left beyond the tandem width of her Jeep and the blue truck. It seemed to shoot out ahead of her, tiring of this game, she thought, then it slowed and swerved back, clipping her front fender on an angle that sent her up and over the guardrail toward the river below.

The Jeep struck the surface hard on an angle that turned it onto its side. The air bag did not deploy, and Liz's skull cracked against the roof in spite of her shoulder harness.

The world darkened before her. Her eyes fluttered, then closed. Liz felt only an immense weariness. A few minutes' rest and then she'd wake up, tend to her chores. She had never felt more relaxed.

The thud of the Jeep settling on the river bottom jarred her alert again. Around her, cold water was rushing in. The Jeep had landed on its passenger side, and she could see the surface shimmering thirty feet above through the window. Easy to reach it, but first she had to extricate herself from the vehicle. For the moment she had air, but the water would swallow it before much longer.

Fighting back panic, Liz pressed the emergency release button on her harness, freeing her to try to escape. But the Jeep had no sunroof and the closed windows were electric. That meant her only hope of escaping was to break one of them.

The water had reached her chest, leaving Liz still enough time to hammer at the glass of her window with an elbow. But her angle was all wrong and the water already covered too much of the glass. Before she could consider an alternative, the water swept over her face and left panic reaching for her as she tried the door latch, sucking in a final deep breath. Liz felt the latch give and pushed her shoulder against the door. But the water pressure outside refused to let it budge, and she had lost valuable seconds in the process. No, the window held her only hope for survival.

Feeling the breath beginning to burn in her lungs, Liz yanked off a boot and used its heel as a ram. Again, though, her angle and the water betrayed her, and she failed to even crack the glass. She didn't actually feel herself weaken until the boot slipped from her grasp. She was left holding only water, knowing it was going to pour into her lungs any second and consume her just as it had consumed the Jeep. But she turned back to the window, determined to give escape one last try.

The devil looked down through the glass at her. With black eyes, hair whipped crazy by the swirling waters, and a short beard that made his flesh look black too, he had to be the devil. Liz looked hopelessly into those eyes in the instant before the glass shattered behind his thrust.

Why the devil? How did I go that wrong?

She felt something jabbing at her, grabbing hold, and then she was being dragged upward. The world brightened briefly before she slipped into an even deeper void, where she forgot how to breathe and everything turned as cold as the devil's black eyes.

EIGHTEEN

'll be the only one in the place sitting in a chair on wheels," Jay Don Reed, the man who had contacted the sheriff in Condor Key, advised McCracken before he came north.

Blaine met him later that day at a diner in the center of Preston, Virginia, across from the small police station. His wheelchair tucked beneath a table, Reed waved to Blaine as soon as he entered.

"Act like you know me," he said when McCracken got there. "We're old friends, maybe served together. Some shit like that. Don't want the locals to think different right now."

Blaine smiled and clapped Reed on the shoulder before sitting down across from him.

"Food's not bad here, if you're hungry," Reed told him.

"I'm not."

"You don't order, you're giving people more cause for notice."

Blaine picked up a menu and opened it. "You serve with Buck?"

Reed closed both hands on his cup of coffee before raising it. "Gunnery school a thousand years ago. Different career paths after that." He looked at his chair. "Different results."

"You were checking on his daughter for him."

"Keeping an eye on her is the way I prefer to put it. I called him when it became clear she was in trouble. Just like I called you."

"Buck's orders."

"He gave me a number. First time he misses a six-hour check-in, I'm supposed to start dialing." Reed gazed across the table, sizing Blaine up. "And here you are."

Blaine caught the edge in his voice. "Something bother you about that?"

"I made some calls, asked around a little about you."

"What'd you hear?"

"My sources musta been mistaken: told me Blaine McCracken was a memory."

"Wishful thinking on their part."

"You walk in that door, I'm looking at a ghost."

"I was . . . until I went to see Buck."

"He made a lot of men in his time."

"And remade at least one."

Reed gave his useless legs a long look. "I was a little beyond his help."

"Where?"

"Nam. One tour too many."

"You were a sniper."

Reed's cup of coffee clamored back to its saucer, spilling a little over the side. "How the hell you know that?"

The truth was Blaine couldn't say exactly, but his eyes stayed focused on the way Reed's finger looped through the coffee cup's handle, treating it like a trigger.

"I think Buck may have mentioned your name," he lied.

The waitress came and poured Blaine a cup of coffee, got her order pad ready. Reed told her to give them a little more time.

"What happened after you let him know his daughter was in trouble?" Blaine continued.

"He asked me to get the intel together on the opposition. Real estate developer named Maxwell Rentz, who's planning to build the Disney World of the north up here. Trouble is he can't do it without the Torrey family farm. The daughter—Liz—isn't about to sell."

"Sounds like a Torrey."

"I made the call when Rentz brought in some hired hands, if you get my drift. I saw these boys nosing around, up to no good. Bad things start happening, I get Buck on the line. Asked if he wanted me to handle things myself." Reed pulled his hand away from the cup. "Don't need my legs to sight them in my crosshairs. He told me to stand down and wait for him. Put some supplies together for him in a duffel bag."

"What happened yesterday?"

"He didn't call in. I waited a few hours before making the call. I shouldn't have, but I did."

"But you don't know what he was up to, why he figured there was a chance he might not be coming back."

Reed shrugged.

"Then I better go introduce myself to his daughter. What can you tell me about her?"

Reed fixed his gaze through the diner's plate-glass window, which bore a HOME COOKED MEALS sign. "For starters, that's her just driving away now."

Blaine had caught the Jeep in his sights again just before the blue truck riding its driver's side shoved it over the guardrail. He watched it turn onto its side in the air, hitting the river with a thud that sent up plumes of water.

Blaine gunned the engine of his rental car, the Jeep long gone from the river's surface by the time he tore down the bank and plunged into the water. When he reached the Jeep, Blaine blessed the long underwater swims beneath the stilt house. He pried a rock from the river bottom and slammed it through the window on the first blow. Smashed the glass aside and yanked Liz Halprin out of her seat.

She wasn't breathing when he got her back to the surface, and Blaine struggled to remember how to apply CPR. Strangely, he had never performed it before. It was magical to watch, considerably more desperate to practice, especially on someone he feared might be beyond saving by his unpracticed technique.

But this was the daughter of Sergeant Major Buck Torrey, and if blood meant anything at all, she wouldn't die without a fight. Blaine continued to push breath through Liz Halprin's pursed blue lips, moving to compress her chest at regular intervals while hoping he recalled the counts correctly.

He was exhausted and almost out of breath himself when Liz finally twitched, stirred, and then coughed up a stream of water into his face. Hacking away as he held her by the shoulders.

Buck Torrey's daughter stared into his dark eyes resiliently. "Just tell me I'm not dead."

"You're not dead."

"That means you're not the devil."

"Close enough," Blaine told her with a grin.

Shortly after a pair of officers had pulled up, Chief Lanning arrived, looking disinterested as he joined them in walking about the scene. A tow truck with winch capacity was already in place, awaiting only a diver to hook the sunken Jeep up to haul it out of the water. Lanning followed the skid marks from the road to the smashed-in guardrail, measuring off the distance to the water in his mind.

"The nonexistent Cattleman's Association again," he heard Liz Halprin say from behind him.

Lanning turned to find her standing there, surprised since he was sure, based on initial reports from the scene, that a rescue squad would already have carted her off to the hospital. She had a blanket draped around her shoulders, and there was a man standing next to her, whom Lanning didn't recognize.

"You'll find the blue paint from their truck all over my Jeep," the woman continued, pestering him. "Shouldn't be too hard to find it in town now, Chief, I imagine."

But Lanning's attention was rooted on McCracken. "I know you?" he asked finally.

"No," replied Blaine McCracken. "You don't."

"Thanks for your help. You can be on your way, lemme take care of the lady here. She's safe now."

Blaine made no move to oblige or even acknowledge him, sliding a little closer to Liz. "That's right. She is."

"You hear what I just said?"

"You want to be writing this down," Blaine told him. "Maybe take some pictures."

"Her car will tell me everything I need to know, once we get it hauled up."

"I don't see anyone taking statements from the people who pulled over to help before they leave, in case they saw something."

"Would that include you?"

"No. I got here late."

"Just happened to be passing through?"

"Not at all," Blaine told him.

"I told you," Lanning repeated to Maxwell Rentz, "I don't know who he is."

"But he didn't just happen to be driving by at the time."

"No. He made that pretty plain."

"A friend of Halprin's father, you think?"

"I hope not."

"So do I," said Rentz.

"Where do you want me to take you?" McCracken asked Liz when she was seated next to him in the rental car's passenger seat.

"Nowhere until I know who I'm riding with," she said, still trembling from the shock of her ordeal.

Blaine started the engine, switched on the heat to keep her warm. "You sound like the chief."

"You told him you didn't just happen to be driving by."

"I'm a friend of your father's."

She looked down. "How'd you find out he was missing?"

"Same guy who let him know you were in trouble called me when he disappeared yesterday."

"Wheelchair?"

"That's right."

"I saw him watching me in town a few times. There's a certain look. . . ."

Blaine stopped short of telling her he knew all about that.

"And what about you?" Liz asked.

"Your father and I go back a ways."

"Operation Phoenix."

"Nice guess."

She glanced down at his ring. "Not a guess at all. He ever tell you what DS meant, Dead Simple?"

"Not in so many words. It seemed pretty straightforward. We were good at what we did over there. It came easy to us."

"You're talking about killing."

"Mostly."

"Dead Simple," Liz repeated. "Pretty straightforward."

"Except now I think I had it wrong. Buck told me as much in Condor Key. Made me think I'd missed the whole point."

"But he didn't elaborate."

Blaine shook his head. "There are some things you've got to figure out for yourself. Buck knows that, and even a man like him can only take you so far. If you can't get the rest of the way on your own, you picked the wrong ride."

"And deep down, those who stay on it until the end are all the same. Don't get me wrong, but I thought your kind, men like my father, had gone extinct with the dinosaurs."

"Not all of us have yet."

"What brought you to Condor Key, then?"

"Long story. It's more important that I hear yours first."

"Why?"

"Because I'm not the one somebody's trying to kill."

Back at the farmhouse, Liz pulled out the bottle of whiskey she and her father had done their best to polish off a few nights before. She brought two glasses, filled hers and took a hearty sip, while Blaine's remained empty when he declined a drink.

"I wish he'd never come up here," she said, turning the glass around in her hand.

"He wanted to help."

"He didn't have the right. Five years he's a stranger. Five years I don't see him, and then he pops back in, out of nowhere."

"Because you needed him."

"I didn't need something to happen to him!"

Blaine gazed across the table at the hard set of her jaw, the thrust of her chin, the way her eyes could ride way back in her head. The sight almost chilled him. This wasn't Buck Torrey's daughter; this was Buck Torrey all over again.

"He leave you with a duffel?"

"How'd you know about . . . ?"

"You thinking about checking the contents yourself?"

"It crossed my mind."

"After the swim?"

"Even before. I was going to look as soon as I got home. Like opening the presents on Christmas morning. See what Santa left behind." She smiled mirthlessly and refilled her glass with the last of the whiskey.

"What would your father think?"

"Not very much, or he wouldn't have had his friend ready to contact you."

"Maybe you should trust his judgment."

Liz held the whiskey but didn't drink it. "It's a shooting war now."

"Meaning . . . ?"

"That maybe I'm glad to have you with me."

"Maybe?"

"Relax, soldier. We can open Dad's duffel together."

"Let's talk about where your father was going before he disappeared."

"To meet Maxwell Rentz."

"Friendly little chat?"

"I think he said something like that."

"What about?"

"He never told me." Liz paused. "Not in so many words."

"Go on."

"He kept disappearing after he got here. I saw him down by the lake a few times and heard him rummaging around in the attic."

"He say anything about what he was looking for?"

"No."

"What did you tell him when he first got here?"

Liz thought for an instant. "The lake. A little over a week ago, Rentz sent divers down there at night to—"

Blaine was studying Liz's face intently when the red beam crossed it. He thought at first it must be a trick of the light. But a second sweep circling toward her forehead sent him lunging across the table, taking her down beneath him an instant before the kitchen window exploded.

NINETEEN

Glass showered them as more gunshots peppered the house.
"Stay down!" Blaine ordered Liz, and began to edge away from her.
"The hell I will!" she blared, crawling on her elbows after him.
"Like father, like daughter," he said when she had caught up.
"This is my house, soldier!"
"Yes, ma'am. Now, where's your father's duffel?"
"Front hall closet," Liz told him, and Blaine gave her the lead, staying just behind her with pistol in hand now, Buck Torrey's Glock nine.

Neither gave any thought to trying the phone, because even if the line hadn't been cut, they both knew that by the time help arrived it would be too late to do them any good, especially coming from Chief Lanning. This was their fight alone.

Automatic fire blew out another pair of windows in twin staccato bursts that ripped into the walls and dumped picture frames to the floor. More shattered glass sprayed them, and they picked up their pace, reaching the hall as shapes dipped and darted just beyond the front door, briefly visible through a worn sheer curtain.

"We're about to have company," Blaine warned.

Liz had the closet door open by then, but her eyes turned back toward him, as empty as her hands.

"The duffel's gone. They were in my house, goddamn it! *They were in my house!*"

A pair of shapes lunged up the outside front steps, straddling either side of the door, ready to come crashing through. Blaine opened up with a barrage that blew out the vertical slabs of glass on either side of the door, scattering the intruders the instant they had spun to burst through.

"You should have waited until they were inside!" Liz snapped. "Didn't my father teach you anything?"

"They were carrying submachine guns. You want to face that in close with a single pistol?"

"I've got a twelve-gauge and a pistol upstairs."

Blaine started to slide away. "I'm going outside after them."

"Around the rear?"

He nodded.

"Looks like my father taught you something, after all, soldier. I'll head upstairs, find a window to cover you from."

Blaine left Liz moving in a crouch for the shattered front windows. He hurried to the rear of the house, staying low beneath the sight line of all windows he passed. Back in the kitchen, he slid across the tile floor and shimmied to the rear door on his stomach. Its top half was glass, covered by open miniblinds. He rose only enough to reach the knob and yanked the door open.

He dropped out down the back steps, careful not to let the door slam before he sank to the grass. Trees rimmed the yard, offering plenty of cover, the farm's fields invisible from this vantage point. Blaine clung to the house, keeping to the deepest shadows as he worked his way around to the front. Felt his heart thudding hard against his chest and calmed himself with a few deep breaths as he reached the front yard, which sloped down into a rolling meadow. The lake lay beyond that meadow, plenty of cover from trees and low shrubs for any man who needed it.

They were probably dealing with three to five well-armed men, decent shots but far from experts. The problem was picking out their positions in the night. Time and firepower were both in the opposition's favor, and they knew it. A pistol in these conditions was good up to fifty, maybe sixty yards; a rifle, two to three hundred. And the gunmen had come equipped with laser sights. Blaine needed to determine where they were, swing the odds a little in his favor.

Think!

The Glock felt foreign in his grasp. Six months without holding a weapon, and they all become strangers. But this wasn't Condor Key anymore and he didn't have time to learn to shoot all over again. He had eight shots left, another full clip in the car if he wanted to risk a dash to it.

Blaine pressed his back against the house, his insides tightening briefly until a sense of exhilaration began to spread through him. He remembered the feeling of negotiating his way past the gators, the mind-set, and felt it fill him again. A familiar chalky taste spread from the back of his mouth, and Blaine knew he was back in his world.

His rental car was diagonally across from him, parked between the house and the barn under partial cover. He focused on it, judging distance and darkness, planning his next move.

It was time to flush the bastards out and take them as they came.

Liz had been keeping the loaded Mossberg twelve-gauge in the corner of her bedroom, and her .380-caliber Smith & Wesson in the top drawer of her night table. She reached the second floor and padded softly down the hall. Started to ease the door open.

A burst of breeze caught it from the other end of the hall and pushed the door all the way ajar. A breeze meant an open window, a realization that drove her to the floor below the first burst of submachine-gun fire from down the hall. She kicked the door closed behind her and scurried for the shotgun as more gunfire tore chunks from the old wood.

She grabbed the Mossberg by the butt and drew it down. Shoulders pressed against the wall, she leveled it and fired through the door. Pumped and fired again, watching another huge chasm appear at chest level in the wood. She heard a grunt, followed by the sound of something heavy hitting the floor. Liz chambered a third round and moved across the room toward the ruined door. Her ears stung from the roar of the shotgun's blasts, feeling as though they needed to pop. Almost to the door, she brought the shotgun to waist level, preparing a quick burst through.

She heard the thump of heavy footsteps an instant before the door was torn from its hinges and slammed back into her, the intruder she had shot screaming as they both tumbled to the floor with the door between them.

His upper body angled awkwardly over the driver's seat, Blaine got the rental car started and gunned the engine. He slid his feet backward against the ground and shifted into drive with one hand while he kept the brake pedal depressed with the other. The final touch was to place a rock over the accelerator. As soon as he took his hand away, it would hold the pedal down, freeing the car to shoot across the field in an apparently desperate escape attempt.

He released the rock and the brake pedal at the same time, had all he could do to lurch out of the car and get the door closed before it dragged him away with it. He sprawled to the ground as the car picked up speed with a grinding screech that sprayed mud backward.

The car shot across the field, drawing fire just as he expected it would. Blaine was hidden in the darkness of the low grass before the first of the bullets chewed into its frame and coughed glass in all directions. More rapid fire blew out both driver's-side tires, sending the car into an uncontrolled spin.

Blaine traced the sources of the barrage, memorizing the positions of the gunmen. Certain they weren't watching anything but the car, he stepped out and steadied his pistol in both hands. When the next muzzle flashes came, Blaine fired toward the two nearest shooters, sighting down the line of what he expected was their bores.

He was in motion again before he could tell if his bullets had found their mark, rushing low across the meadow with his gun poised for its next target.

Liz's breath was knocked out of her on impact with the floor. She maintained enough presence of mind to try and right her shotgun, but it lay pinned between the door and her body.

A pair of bloodied hands groped for her throat. She finally looked up at the intruder and gasped, screaming.

The left side of his face had been blown away, the flesh hanging in huge clumps, the eye gone, part of his skull visible. Blood dripped from his mouth with each labored breath, the smell of it sickening as he loomed over her.

Liz had only one arm free, and she jammed it under his chin to keep him off her. The intruder's breath turned wet and gurgly, but his hands found her throat and began to squeeze.

Liz fought to extract her other arm, maybe free the shotgun in the process, but it was no use. She felt the life being pressed out of her, the pressure in her head already incredible as she fought for breath, writhing, kicking with her feet.

Her free hand flailed backward, trying to reach the night table and the .380 Smith & Wesson inside the top drawer. Coming up empty, she heaved herself backward and felt her back grinding against the bedroom's bare floor.

The intruder stayed right with her, the door dragged between them.

Liz heard herself gasping, felt her eyesight begin to dim as her free hand smacked the drawer. She located the drawer pull and yanked with all her might. The drawer popped out, banged to the floor, and spilled its contents all around her.

The intruder seemed not to notice, his remaining eye fixed with hateful intensity on her face, as if he didn't care if he died right now so long as he could take her with him.

Liz's hand was shaking as it whipped desperately across the floor, feeling for the .380. A finger brushed steel and then her palm found the pistol's butt. Her hand closed around it as the man with half a face rose further over her to better his angle.

Her eyes had started to mist over when she brought the .380 upward. Aiming it from behind her own head. Firing blind.

The gunshots sent sharp needles digging into her eardrums, the pain dizzying as she continued to fire. One bullet caught the man under the chin, another just over the top of his nose. Liz felt more blood shower over her when impact lifted the man upward and dumped him off, freeing her to breathe again.

She drank in the air, not even trying to move, eyes and gun fixed on the corpse whose blood was spreading across her floor, as she waited for him to stir again.

Blaine moved in a well-practiced zigzag. He dared the gunmen to turn their bullets upon him so the flashes would give their positions away. He offered return fire each time there was a flash of gunfire, counting his shots to make the most of his final clip, salvaged from the rental car.

He could feel the automatic fire burning the air close enough for him to catch the sparks, extinguished like candles blown out one at a time as he continued his jagged charge. Then he heard the soft crunch of grass and brush underfoot as men rushed to get away.

He had them! They were trying to flee!

But where were they? When darkness or camouflage denies sight, the trick is to aim at sound; at least use it to pick out shadows that would otherwise go unnoticed.

Blaine hunkered low, closing like a predator on its prey when he reached the line of trees that separated Liz's house from the rolling meadow leading down to the lake. He placed a hand on the ground to brace himself and felt something wet and sticky coating the grass. Blood.

Blaine brought his fingers to eye level, trying to see the blood through the darkness. He followed the blood trail along the tree line until it vanished near the road. The gunmen had made it off the property, had run away with their tails between their legs.

Blaine turned and sped back toward the house and Liz.

Chief Lanning gazed up from the sheet that covered the body of the man Liz had killed in her bedroom.

"So, Ms. Halprin, was this one of the men driving the truck that forced you off the road, or wasn't it?"

"There's not enough of his face left to be sure."

"Uh-huh." The chief stood up, looked back and forth from Liz to Blaine. "I'm gonna have to close this room off for the state police crime people."

"I wouldn't have slept in it tonight anyway."

"Got a call in to them now. Detectives should be here within the hour."

"I know the procedure."

"Oh, I'm sure you do, Ms. Halprin." Lanning peered back down at the body. "Just like I'm sure you know how to use a gun. Couple different kinds, in fact."

"She comes upstairs," Blaine interjected, "finds an intruder. She supposed to think he's here selling magazine subscriptions?"

"Where were you?"

"Out looking for my dog."

"Didn't notice one in your car earlier today."

"That's why I was out looking for him, Chief."

Lanning's face reddened. "I don't think I got your name this afternoon."

"It's tough to spell. I'll write it down for you."

" 'Cause what I'm thinking is that maybe you're the kind of man gets called in to solve other people's problems for them. Woman with Ms. Halprin's background would know where to look to find one."

"And what kind of background is that, Chief?" Liz snapped at him. "Maybe you're forgetting who the victims here were."

Lanning's expression tightened some more. "Maybe I'll check the rest of the property. See what I find."

"Why don't you call Rentz first?" Liz shot at him. "See if he approves."

Lanning squared his shoulders and flashed her a look. "You implying something?"

"Let's leave the chief to his work," Blaine said, drawing Liz's rigid frame away and positioning himself between her and Lanning. He glanced down at the bloodied sheet, a man with his face mostly missing beneath it. "Maybe he'll want to interrogate the victim."

They sat on the porch outside, waiting for the state police detectives to come. Blaine cradled Liz's shotgun in his lap, back against a boarded-up window.

"You know what set my father off, don't you?" she asked him.

"You're in my light," Blaine said. "And, yes, I think I do."

Liz moved out of the way.

"Well, that wasn't any underwater survey team you watched dive and never come back up last week, I can tell you that much. You were describing top-of-the-line *salvage* equipment."

"Then what do you think Maxwell Rentz was looking for under that lake?"

"That's what I'm going to find out tomorrow."

Liz's features tightened. "The lake's not as easy a dive as it looks."

"And why is that?"

"Because it's haunted."

Liz told him the story as her grandfather had recounted it to her a hundred times. Blaine did not interrupt once.

"Civil War soldiers?" he asked when she was finished.

"Their ghosts. Protecting some kind of treasure. That's what the legend says."

"And you believe this legend?"

"Not until last week. Not until what happened to Rentz's divers." Blaine started to shake his head, but she continued. "And they weren't the only ones, either: five more have disappeared in the past twenty years, along with a local boy who went in for a swim. His body turned up on shore a few days later, all ripped to shreds."

"We talking about ghosts or sea monsters here?"

Liz was unmoved. "You weren't here last week. Something had ahold of Rentz's divers, I'm telling you, and when the men on shore yanked up the compressor line to their air bazooka, nothing followed."

"Liz—"

"Then the day before my father disappeared, Rentz sent down an unmanned submersible. It never came back up, either."

"Ghosts got the sub too?"

"Legend says they were Union soldiers stranded here in a storm during the Civil War. They froze and then were buried forever when Bull Run flooded."

Blaine gazed over at the lake. "And you think that's what I'm going to find down there tomorrow."

"We'll see."

TWENTY

The thing is, Jack, well, I thought we had a deal," Othell Vance said across the table, summoning his courage.

"How's your boy, Othell?"

"Fine."

"I kept my word, didn't I? Gave you the pills he needed, as soon as you said you'd help me."

"And I did. I did help you."

"And now I'm doing you a favor, letting you tag along. Rediscover your youth, the fire that was your very defining essence." Jack Tyrell shoved the Big Mac into his mouth as far as it would go, talking as he chewed. "How's your burger, Othell?"

"Huh?"

"Your burger. You're not eating it. It's what you asked me to get you."

"I'm not hungry."

They had the table to themselves. Jack had asked Mary, the Yost brothers, and Lem Trumble to give them a little space. So they had taken a table on the other side of the McDonald's; at this time of night, the six of them were the only ones inside, though the drive-through was still doing a brisk business.

Tyrell checked out Othell's supply of fries. "Can I have those?"

Othell shoved them across the table.

"I eat in places like this a lot."

Othell looked at him quizzically.

"Oh yeah. Fast-food joints. Places where nobody pays much attention to anyone else and mostly keep to themselves. The kind of people who would know my face aren't likely to come in. Most important, it doesn't take long to eat. You follow me?"

"Doesn't take long to eat, yes."

"There's another reason why I like McDonald's especially. Can you guess what?"

Othell Vance tried futilely for comfort in the stiff chair, desperately wanting to go back to being Harrison Conroy. "Do we have to talk about this?"

"Yes," Tyrell said, and chomped off some more of the Big Mac. "Yes, we do. The past is all I've got, Othell. I like talking about it. Come on . . . McDonald's, remember? What was it, '70?"

"No, '71."

Jack Tyrell looked pleased with him. "See, you *do* remember. Okay, help me out here. We go in at lunch hour, busiest time of the day. Place is packed. We're carrying those bags with us. What do you call them?"

"Backpacks."

"Yeah, backpacks. I see kids carrying them all the time now. We had your homemade C-4 packed inside them, as I recall. That shit was the work of genius, right down to the way we just peeled back the tape and stuck the mounds under the tables. Gobble up our food so we could get out of there and the next people could take our place. I was holding the detonator. We move ourselves to a safe distance, everything ready to go. Then the school bus showed up."

Othell Vance felt suddenly sick.

"Where were they coming from, again?"

"A museum," Othell said. "The Smithsonian, I think."

Vance looked around him, and suddenly the McDonald's seemed to change. Golden arches sprouted where they'd been missing for years. The prices on the menu board lowered dramatically.

"You freaked," Jack Tyrell continued. "You tried to get the detonator from me, and when you couldn't you made a run for the restaurant. Am I remembering this correctly?"

Othell Vance couldn't even manage a nod, he was shaking so hard. Right before him, the man on the other side of the booth was changing too, morphing into someone else. Jack's hair was suddenly held back by a bandanna, his face tanned instead of almost sickly pale. It was '71, alive and well and totally fucked up. An acid trip that wouldn't end.

A bad flashback, that's what today felt like.

"Remember what happened next, Othell?"

More silence.

"Come on, give it a try. We're playing here."

"You . . ."

"Yeah?"

"You made me press the detonator."

Jackie Terror glowed with pride across from him. "Not before the bus emptied out, I didn't. It was your indoctrination into the world of Midnight Run, man. I helped you define your essence. And over the years you proved me right. Don't prove me wrong now, Othell. I came back to do a job, but this is the nineties. Everything's bigger. People are used to buildings blowing up, big jets dropping out of the sky. So my job's got to be appropriate for the times, big enough to make my point. And to do that I need you." He settled back again. "Hey, thanks for the fries."

Othell Vance figured he might as well get it over with. "You remember I told you we lost the stuff, a whole shipment of what was called Devil's Brew?"

"Something like that."

"I thought the story was bullshit. A hoax so we could keep the stuff while everybody thinks we lost it. I figure I dig around a little, I find where we're really hiding it."

"You telling me you figured wrong, Othell?"

"The story wasn't bullshit at all, Jack, it's the truth. A tanker carrying the Devil's Brew up and vanished into thin air about seven months ago, just like I told you."

"Somebody beat us to it, that what you're saying?"

"It's a possibility. But I don't think so. See, the tanker had a built-in transponder so it could be located easily if something like this happened. The thing is the signal died right around the time the tanker vanished. Search teams scoured the area fifty miles in all directions, then expanded it to a hundred. Didn't leave an inch uncovered."

"But nobody found it."

"No."

"You bring a map?"

"What's the difference? I checked and double-checked, did everything I could. The Devil's Brew is gone."

Tyrell glanced across the restaurant at Mary, picking at her chef's salad. "Just give me that map."

They rented four rooms in a cheap motel from a clerk in a bathrobe who didn't ask questions. Jack was looking forward to his first night with Mary in longer than he cared to think about. Busting her out the night before had gotten the old juices flowing, and they celebrated in their room with more blasts from the past. Toked on some great hashish, which made them cough, and did some hits of acid, which made them dizzy. It almost felt like their bodies had forgotten what it was supposed to feel like. Jack shrugged it off and blamed the age thing again, those missing twenty-five years.

The Yost twins, meanwhile, had found a couple of college girls fixing a flat tire and brought them along for the ride. Had them in their room three doors down now, Tyrell certain they'd be done with them well before morning. He wasn't a squeamish man, far from it, but he was glad the Yosts' room wasn't next to his.

Jack Tyrell got out the map Othell had come up with, creased by lines made by numerous refoldings, and spread it over the bed for Mary to look at.

"It's no good, Jackie. I haven't got the feeling yet," Mary said, snuggling up to him and wrapping her arm around his shoulder.

Jack cradled her against him. "You will, baby. Of that I have no doubt whatsoever."

"You know how the vision thing is with me. The quickenings come and go. Always have, since I was a little girl."

"You weren't much more than that when I first met you."

"And you always appreciated me."

"You had the right answers, more often than not."

Mary looked sad. "Less so as I've gotten older. Like the gift dries up with time. Makes me worry."

"About what?"

She looked at him with those dark puppy-dog eyes that hadn't changed since she was seventeen. A few wrinkles, the first toes of crow's-feet, and a few strands of hair starting to go gray—that was all Queen Mary had to show for the twenty-five years they'd been apart.

"That when it dries up altogether there'll be nothing to appreciate about me anymore."

"You think the gift is the only reason I came back for you?"

Mary shrugged. "It's been a long time."

"Not that long."

She cuddled tighter against him. "I know why you came back, Jackie." Mary felt him stiffen. "I saw it one of my good days a few weeks back. The whole thing."

"It hurt."

"I saw that too. I can feel it now."

"You remember what I told you about pain?"

"It's a good thing, you said."

"Why?"

"You keep going until the ache goes away. You turn it around and make other people hurt just as bad."

"I never had this much pain before, baby. Passion but not pain. Difference being I never knew who I was doing it all for. Now I do."

"I understand, Jackie."

He eased her away from him. "We got to do this, Mary. We got to do this because the world got so fucked up so slowly that nobody seemed to notice. They let it happen and look what we got. Twelve-year-old kids with machine guns. Old ladies' skulls bashed in for their grocery money." Tyrell felt his emotions wobbling and summoned the pain back. "They hunted us like dogs twenty-five years ago, because we were fighting what they were and all the shit they stood for. Beating them was all we ever wanted, and we came lots closer than most realize. Control—that's what it comes down to. Control and power. They were afraid of losing it, of us taking it away from them."

He paused and stared into space. His face hardened.

"Now, all these years later, they've lost control and don't realize it. Difference is they've lost it to people who don't give a shit. I look out there and see everything we worked for doing a slow crash and burn. The old enemies are too pathetic to hate. They're just going through the motions. They're not gonna be ready for us this time. We're a whole new species, far as they're concerned."

"You're angry, Jackie," Mary said, and hugged him tighter. "You were never angry the last time we went to war."

"Maybe that's why we lost. But this time's gonna be different. Find Othell's missing shit—that's all it's gonna take. This time we're gonna win."

Mary took a deep breath. Jack Tyrell felt her stiffen in his arms briefly before she began to shake. He was sure she was having a seizure, ready for the eyeballs to roll up in her head. He cursed the drugs they'd bought on the street.

Mary started to slump. Jack tried to bring her against him, but she slipped away and reached for his spread-out map with an index finger. He watched the finger plop down and quickly replaced his over it before he lost the spot.

"Well, I'll be damned. . . ."

Then Mary was hugging him again, tighter than before, tighter than ever. Jack kept his finger glued to a point in the Valley and Ridge region of central Pennsylvania she had marked.

"Did I do good, Jackie, did I do good?"

"You did fine, baby," he replied. "You did just fine."

TWENTY-ONE

I don't know exactly what I can tell you that I didn't tell the other fellas who were here," the head groundskeeper at Crest Haven Memorial Park told Will Thatch.

"You were the only one who got a look at the killer," Will said. "Am I right?"

"Apparently. But that was over a month ago now. I don't see why I got to go through it again," the man said impatiently. His name was Sunderwick, and his gaze kept drifting over the grave sites, eager to get to the day's work. Will wondered if funerals were being held up on his account.

"Just routine."

"I see your ID again?"

Will produced it from his pocket and forced himself not to look away, not to do anything that might betray the sham that had started when he retrieved his old FBI identification and badge from a dresser drawer in his hotel room.

The picture inside had made him gasp. He'd forgotten what he looked like all those years before when he still believed in hope and justice. Losing that belief was what had torn him away from his career and deposited him in a bottle. And the bottle had conspired with the years to turn his face into a patchwork quilt, slabs of flesh separated from each other by valleys deep enough for birds to roost in. His face had the lived-in look of a man about to move.

He'd had a passport-size picture of that face taken at the Kinko's around the corner from his hotel. Then he trimmed it to the proper specifications and glued it over the face of the man he'd forgotten a long time ago. He worked on the ID's issue date next with a Bic fine-line marker, trembling hands preventing him from getting the job done as fast as he would have liked, but it looked decent when he was finished. Good enough to fool anyone who didn't take a second look, like Sunderwick. The only thing the disguise lacked was a gun; Will thought it a good idea to leave his old .38 under the mattress, where it wouldn't do anyone any harm.

The groundskeeper handed the ID back to him. "Not the same as the other guys who were here."

"Well, the FBI's got lots of departments."

"I say they were from the FBI?"

"No. I just assumed . . . Who were they from?"

"Somewhere I never heard of. Don't remember the initials. They were official enough, though."

"Sure," Will said, his curiosity piqued. "And they wanted to know about the killings?"

"They came for the bodies. I practically had to force them to listen to what I knew."

Will pulled a copy of the composite sketch from the newspaper out of his jacket. "You told them this was the man you saw do the killing."

"No. I saw the man. Saw the bodies. I made the connection for myself later on."

"Get a good look at the bodies?"

Sunderwick almost laughed. "You kidding?"

"How'd you know they were dead?"

Sunderwick looked at Will as if he had missed the punch line of a joke. "They were dead, all right."

"And the killer . . ."

"I wouldn't have given him a second look if he wasn't holding one of my shovels. Since he doesn't work here, that's a problem. I'm about to head over and make my point, when I get called away. I check to see if he's still hanging around later, I find the bodies."

"And these men who came to pick the bodies up, they didn't ask you anything?"

"Didn't care what I had to say, either. Just wanted to get out of here as soon as possible."

"The man you saw," Will started. "What do you think he was doing?"

"Doing?"

"With the shovel."

"Leaning on it."

"Besides that."

"You mean, in the cemetery?"

"Yes."

Sunderwick frowned. "What do people come to cemeteries for?"

Will nodded, the man's point taken. "How many funerals were there that morning?"

"Seven or eight, I think. We were busy. The murders really messed up the afternoon schedule. We had to hold the Masterson funeral at a temporary site."

"Why?"

Sunderwick leaned in closer to Will. "Because that man with the shovel, he buried the four men he killed in their plot."

TWENTY-TWO

You come very well recommended, Mr. Dobbler," Rentz greeted. The man whom Donovan had escorted into his office first thing that morning was built like a fireplug and looked extremely uncomfortable in a suit. He was sweating heavily, and Rentz could see the material straining as he shifted his shoulders.

"Thank you, sir," Dobbler responded.

"I have a problem."

"You wouldn't have called me if you didn't, sir."

"A *different* one than that which led me to seek out your services initially."

Dobbler cocked his square head to the side like a confused dog.

Rentz cleared his throat. "This is a very delicate matter. Last night some men I retained failed completely to perform what should have been a simple task—"

"I understand."

"I haven't finished explaining."

"It's not necessary, sir. There's usually only one thing I'm called on to do. Normally I don't work for strangers and almost never involve myself in personal squabbles." Dobbler leaned forward. "But, sir, you come very well recommended too."

Rentz nodded. "Someone else showed up on the farm yesterday, someone my information leads me to believe will require someone of your . . .

expertise to deal with," he explained, thinking of the man Chief Lanning had run into twice the day before, who on both occasions thwarted Rentz's plans for Liz Halprin.

Dobbler removed a thick, folded wad of papers from his inside suit pocket and rose stiffly to hand it across the desk. "My complete file, sir."

Rentz started reading. "You were dishonorably discharged from the army?"

"Yes, sir, I was. The only officer to be so disciplined after the Gulf War. I served eighteen months in the stockade."

Rentz flipped one page, then another, looking up as he read. "You turned a flamethrower on the inhabitants of an Iraqi village?"

"Yes, sir."

Rentz just skimmed the rest. "Why do you want me to know all this?"

"I like my potential employers to be aware of exactly what they're getting."

Rentz considered the prospects. "I'll need a few bodyguards as well; say, three. The best men you can get on short notice. Price is not an object."

"Not a problem, sir."

"And you can start right away?"

"I always carry everything I need with me."

Rentz stood up. "Then I'll let Mr. Donovan fill you in on the specifics of the assignment."

Dobbler stood up, almost to attention.

"One more thing," Rentz said, as Dobbler started to turn around.

"Sir?"

"These Iraqi civilians you burned . . ."

"Their village was hiding Scud missile launchers. I wasn't leaving until I found them."

"And?"

Dobbler's expression was utterly flat. "I left, didn't I?"

TWENTY-THREE

Blaine was waiting outside when Sal Belamo pulled his cranky old sedan to a halt in front of Liz's house just before eight A.M. "Welcome back, boss." Sal greeted him matter-of-factly, moving around to the trunk.

"What have you got for me, Sal?"

"Some new toys to play with. Christmas came early this year." He reached for the trunk but looked over at Blaine again before opening it. "Best present may be the dope I dug up on this Maxwell Rentz." Sal frowned. "I ask you a question?"

"Sure."

"He the one behind Buck Torrey's disappearance?"

"There's a good chance of that, yeah."

Sal's eyes narrowed. "Glad you called."

In many ways Sal Belamo was a twin of his car: scuffed and scarred on the surface, but sharp and tight as ever underneath. As a boxer, he'd fought Carlos Monzon twice for the middleweight championship of the world and had his nose busted each time for the effort. That nose still dominated an angular face that looked like a neat wedge carved out of weathered granite. His hair had begun to gray, but beyond that Sal Belamo seemed ageless.

Sal had saved Blaine's life the first time they met, over a decade before, something of a change for a man who had served the government as a contract assassin following two tours in Korea. He had more sources and contacts than any man Blaine had ever known and, just as important, a deep reserve of favors to call in when needed. Pushing sixty now, Sal had become as adept with a keyboard as he was with a gun, and Blaine made sure he got plenty of opportunity to use both.

He started to rummage around the trunk, shifting equipment about. "I picked this stuff up at the SEAL training facility outside Washington. Guy in ordnance is ex-intel. I told him who it was for, and he laughed. Said he heard you were dead."

"I was."

"This is a funny world, boss. People judge you on how good you were yesterday, and yesterday was a long time ago for you." Sal stood up again. "It's like this. You got lots of enemies always wanted to take that shot at you who were scared off by what they knew and heard. Now they're hearing different shit. You ask me, there's plenty of young bucks out there like nothing better than to make their bones by taking you out. And plenty of important types you pissed off over the years like nothing better than to give them the okay."

"You worried they'll be coming?"

"Fuck, I know they'll be coming. I'm worried about what you'll do when they show up."

Blaine saw something unfamiliar flicker in Sal's eyes before he looked down into the trunk again. Doubt, maybe; hesitation. Belamo's surly cockiness was gone; he, too, didn't see Blaine the same way anymore. Blaine wanted to tell him not to worry, that all one hundred percent of him was standing here right now thanks to the magic Buck Torrey had worked in Condor Key.

As Sal carefully removed the first of the SEAL ordnance from the trunk, Blaine thought back to Liz's insistence that ghosts, or monsters, or *something*, lurked beneath the lake. He hoped she was right, couldn't wait to dive. Face the monster and kill it.

Make Sal Belamo look at him the old way.

"It's like this," Sal said to Blaine and Liz at the kitchen table over coffee. "Maxwell Rentz ain't everything he's cracked up to be. He's lost his shirt on a bunch of bad investments and he's facing more foreclosures than Reese's got pieces. He's in debt up to his eyebrows, leveraged to the absolute max. Everything he owns is mortgaged out, and from what I hear, he's got maybe a couple months to make good on some short-term notes or he's a memory."

"What about the financing to cover the resort he's planning to build up here?" Liz wondered.

"That's the kicker, 'cause I couldn't track any down. Just a paper trail leading to the farms that used to belong to your neighbors. Rentz squeezed them all into his portfolio with low-interest six-month balloon notes. Means he doesn't plan on holding on to them long, or he's expecting some sort of windfall. Don't ask me from where, though."

"But I've seen the plans!" Liz insisted, befuddled. "There's a scale model of the resort on display in the town hall."

"About as much of it as Rentz can afford to build, probably. This guy's got himself so overextended you could knock him down with a sneeze."

"Then what's he doing here? What's he want my land for?"

Blaine stood up. "I think it's time we had a look at that lake."

"**W**ireless underwater communicators?" Liz asked incredulously, after Sal Belamo had handed her a headset forty minutes later.

"Only the best," McCracken told her, fitting his into place.

"Forgetting something, though, aren't you?"

"Am I?"

"I don't see any of those high-tech halogens around, like Rentz's divers used."

"Didn't help them much, now did it? I don't want to be lugging anything bulky around once I'm under. Besides, artificial light only works until something gets in its way. Much better to make use of whatever light is already down there."

"You're talking night vision."

"Exactly," Blaine said, and lifted an oversize diving mask from the supply bag, complete with shaded recessed lenses at eye level in the opaque plastic. "Won't even need a flashlight with this baby on."

Blaine rose and accepted a portable air bazooka from Sal Belamo; no compressor hose to worry about dragging. His diving belt had a huge knife cloaked in a sheath that extended well below his hip. He wore a second knife strapped to an ankle.

"What about that metal detector Rentz's divers brought down with them?"

"Based on your description, I'd say it was a state-of-the-art spectron magnometer," Blaine told her, "used by salvage teams and treasure hunters to find precious metals; not by underwater surveyors."

Liz gazed out over the water. "The legend says the soldiers down there died protecting something."

"Now let's find out what."

Dobbler lowered the binoculars to the ground beside him and lifted a camera to his eye in their place. It didn't look like a camera really, more like a flat four-inch-square slab with the controls painted on. The lens was recessed until Dobbler focused on the big, bearded man strapping on his flippers. He heard a mechanical whine and felt the thing extend outward, making Dobbler think of a dick going hard.

The camera took a digital impression, not a picture, which would be decoded by a special machine made by the same manufacturer. All Dobbler had to do was slip back to his nearby car, slide the thin plate out, and send it via the fax machine the car came equipped with.

"Test one, two. Test one, two," Blaine said into his headset, after wading out past his waist.

"Got ya, boss," Sal Belamo said, from Liz's small outboard floating in the middle of the lake.

"Loud and clear," Liz followed, loud enough to make Blaine flinch.

"My ears weren't one of the things that got wounded," he reminded.

"My father would have fixed them, too, if they had been, soldier."

Blaine gazed toward the outboard and flashed Sal a thumbs-up sign. Belamo had also obtained from the SEALs a sophisticated range finder based on passive sonar. He had rigged the sensors to the bottom of the outboard and was monitoring the grid that encompassed the better part of the lake's center, where the disappearances had all taken place. If anything bigger than a trout so much as breathed, Sal would know it.

Blaine took one final deep breath, secured his mask over his face, and dropped into the water.

Maxwell Rentz held the digitized picture at arm's length before him, cellular phone in his other hand.

"It's definitely the man described to me yesterday, Mr. Dobbler. Now I'll see if we can get him identified. . . ."

"Don't bother, sir," Dobbler said, the words emerging through clenched teeth. "I know who he is."

The waters darkened almost instantly, the lake's black bottom discouraging most light from coming down. Blaine swam slowly, falling into an easy rhythm as he kicked with his flippers, angling himself for the bottom. His high-tech mask gave the black waters an almost translucent greenish glow. The lake was known to be forty feet at its deepest point, and Blaine had covered about half that before he spoke into the microphone squeezed inside his mask.

"I'm down twenty-five feet. Nothing so far."

"How's the view, boss?" Sal asked, voice marred a little by static.

"Crystal clear. How's yours?"

"Zero. Zip. Nada. Only thing moving down there on my scope is you."

"You should see something now," Liz said nervously. "There should be something in view."

"Not— Wait a minute . . . !"

"What? What is it?"

Silence.

"Blaine, can you hear me?"

It seemed for an instant that Blaine wasn't there anymore. Then his voice returned, a bit shaky.

"You're not going to believe this. . . ."

TWENTY-FOUR

Blaine watched as a ghost world appeared before his eyes. The high-tech underwater mask not only gave the scene an eerie backlight but also eliminated the distortion normally caused by water, creating the illusion that he wasn't diving so much as floating over land.

The remains of a farm had appeared directly beneath him. He could see enough wood frame to recognize a barn long collapsed by the weight of the water, a pair of ancient rusted plows resting in the berths they'd occupied the day the land was flooded. Well beyond the barn's remnants stood the remains of a split-rail fence: just a few posts set a dozen feet apart in the lake's bottom. Lying near the posts were the skeletons of what must have been livestock, horses or cows, probably; Blaine was too far away to be sure.

"Blaine," Liz said, her voice sounding strong and resonant through his headset. "Can you hear me?"

"Yes."

"What's down there? What do you see?"

"Parts of somebody's farm that got swallowed up in the flood. What was the year again?"

"Early 1863. Winter."

One hundred and thirty-five years, Blaine calculated. The degree of decomposition and decay fit perfectly.

"I'm heading down," he reported.

"Be careful."

"Don't worry, boss," Sal Belamo reported from the outboard. "You still got the lake to yourself."

Blaine reached the bottom and tested it with his gloved hand. His hand plunged through the black grainy silt, the bottom firm but false. The water table must have fluctuated in these parts, changing the lake's depth by the year, or even the month, and shifting its secrets about.

"Anything, Sal?" he asked.

"All clear, boss."

"You there, Liz?"

"What is it?" she returned eagerly.

"Been a stormy spring, has it?"

"Worst in years, decades. How'd you know?"

"I think a lot of what's down here has been stirred up in the relatively recent past. That would explain why no one would have charted any of this stuff before."

Blaine freed the air bazooka from his shoulder and switched it on, aiming its barrel at the black bottom. The silt fled from the stream of air, creating deep furrows that widened as he shifted the bazooka slowly from side to side, watching for anything that was uncovered. He grew impatient quickly and switched the bazooka's power up a notch.

The furrows deepened, became caverns forged out of the bottom amidst black clouds of disturbed silt. He could see a pale object sharpening into view, thought it was a rock until the bazooka coughed it up into the current.

It was a human skull.

Blaine snatched at it with his free hand, caught the skull on the third try and drew it to him. It grinned toothily back at him, remarkably well preserved by the silt and the frigid aquifer that must have passed beneath the property. Blaine recalled the legend of Civil War soldiers lost here in a storm. Defending their last patch of land from all interlopers—that's how Liz said her grandfather explained the legend of this lake.

Blaine gave the bazooka's trigger pressure again, and more bones floated up from the bottom. He kicked his flippers to move out deeper, toward the center of the lake, aiming the barrel down and ahead as he swept it from side to side.

"Check your air, boss," Sal Belamo warned.

"I'm okay for now."

The water grew noticeably colder and blacker as Blaine approached the center. But his slow, angular sweeps with the bazooka yielded nothing but black funnel bursts kicked up from the bottom. Based on the water table, Blaine figured there were probably pockets and chambers down here hidden by the silt and holding the true, ever shifting secrets of the lake.

The bazooka coughed another wave of silt from the bottom, but this time a solid object was pushed out with it. Blaine groped for it with his hand, watched it flee with the currents the bazooka had kicked up. He swam after the object fast, afraid of losing it again to the darkness, closing on the lake's center.

He managed to snatch the object when it dropped back to the bottom, stowed it in the diving pouch secured on his belt after shaking the silt from his glove. Something else came free of the glove, floated down through the water. Blaine caught it and drew it up to his mask, eyes widening at the sight:

It was a gold coin.

Half expecting the lake's legendary ghosts to pop up and snatch it from him, he dropped back to the bottom and worked his air bazooka about. Several more coins, identical to the first, fluttered upward, rousted from their resting place. Blaine tried to catch them, but the currents steered the coins away from him.

Treasure, he thought. *No wonder Rentz had equipped his dive team with a spectron magnometer . . .*

"Boss," Sal Belamo said suddenly, filling his ears. "I think we got something."

"What?" Blaine responded, still swimming after the elusive coins.

On the surface, Belamo watched a white mass flashing on the motion grid, picked up by the machine's sensors. "There's something moving, coming straight for you."

Blaine, swimming slowly toward the escaping coins, rotated his gaze on the black waters dead ahead. "There's nothing there."

Belamo worked some knobs. "According to this, there is."

"Come up, Blaine!" Liz called. "Now!"

But the coins were almost within his grasp. One last surge and he caught some of them. Blaine managed to snare five in all, stowing them in his diving pouch as well.

"It's right on top of you, boss!" Sal Belamo warned.

Blaine unsnapped the sheath and drew his knife into his hand. The waters before him had all at once turned utterly black, the silt floating everywhere. His high-tech goggles could give him only a yard or so. The silt crept toward him in a dark cloud.

"Boss, can't you see it? Jesus Christ," Belamo resumed, panic edging into his voice.

"Blaine!" Liz cried desperately.

McCracken had started back-kicking with his flippers when the thick cloud of silt enveloped him like nightfall. He had let himself think that Sal Belamo's machine had registered nothing more dangerous than this mud-thick shroud, when a set of gleaming teeth burst out of the darkness.

✿   ✿   ✿

"**B**laine!" Liz's scream buckled her own eardrums. "*Blaine, can you hear me?*"

When there was still no reply, she grabbed the spare air tank. She pulled her arms through the straps, then fished another high-tech mask from the dive bag Sal had brought along.

Liz barely had time to tighten her regulator into place and bite down on the rubber mouth guard before charging into the water and dropping under the surface.

Blaine felt claws raking at him, digging ever deeper the harder he tried to pull free. Barely any of the air from his tank was reaching his lungs, indicating his hose had been nicked, even punctured. An impact a moment before had cracked his mask and it had begun to leak, his vision stolen. The resulting blackness kept him from seeing what had grabbed hold of him. Blaine felt as though he were being reeled in, imagined some great mouth open behind him. He tried to twist around but felt something dig into his shoulders, agony seering through him, while all his air bubbled away.

Liz swam downward, the SEAL night-vision mask giving life to this underwater world. She bypassed the area where Blaine had sighted his initial finds and continued rapidly on. She felt the pressure of the deepening waters in her head, spreading from ear to ear. It had been a long time since she had dived; thirty feet felt like three hundred.

She came up on what looked like a black empty hole at the lake's bottom. She dropped closer toward it and felt the water suddenly begin to shift angrily about. Her foot snared on something and she yanked it free, had stretched herself forward again when a shape lunged out of the black. Liz backed off, screaming into her mask.

The thing veered, then came to a complete halt, as if drawn back by a leash. Liz stopped and held her position, recognizing twin sets of flippers first and then a second, almost identical shape just behind the first. She hadn't gotten a good look at the two of them that night over a week before, but she was certain these were Rentz's divers, caught and sliced apart by what looked like a thick tangle of barbed wire. Rentz's expensive robotic submersible lay on its side not too far away, trapped as well. It looked almost like a spider's web, everything that ventured near caught in its traces.

Liz pushed herself backward and twisted her mask about the churning mess, swimming on, searching for McCracken.

A hand grasped her ankle. Panicked, Liz kicked away desperately, then looked down. Blaine was directly beneath her, bubbles from his severed hose churning up the muck and stirring the blackness. Another section of the barbed wire that had killed Rentz's divers had snared him as well.

Liz dropped down and pushed her regulator into his mouth. He drank the air in gratefully, his breathing returning to normal as she began carefully to extract him from the tangle of steel. Her eyes wandered slightly and made out the remains of more bodies, some little more than skeletons, caught by the wire and blanketed by silt. The barbed wire waited like a great basking monster. Once snared, there was almost nothing a diver could do to free himself, especially if his air hose was punctured. Panic, inevitably, would follow, and a legend was born. She imagined what a person would feel dying that way and shuddered, as she worked Blaine free of the final prongs.

When McCracken was finally freed, he and Liz started upward, steering over the deadly entrapment of wire that seemed to occupy the whole center of the lake's floor. Only a few feet beyond it, and already the tangle of silt and rusted metal was invisible again, ready to sink back into the bottom to await the next unlucky victim.

They exchanged breaths from her mouthpiece on the way up and broke the surface together ten yards from Sal Belamo's outboard.

"I guess this makes us even," Liz told him as they treaded water facing each other.

"Not exactly," Blaine corrected. "You haven't given me mouth-to-mouth yet."

"I saw Rentz's divers down there," she said, recalling their severed air hoses and wet suits marred by puncture wounds. "Some of the others too. It was the barbed wire that killed them, not a monster."

"You sound relieved."

"I am."

"Don't be," Blaine warned. "That barbed wire was sprung off some kind of trap."

"A trap?"

"Pretty simple process: just a few springs and pulleys, and very easy to disguise with all the silt down there."

"Sprung by trip wires?"

"You know your stuff."

"Not really; I thought I felt one just before the barbed wire snapped out at me."

"There you go." Blaine nodded.

"The question is why. What's down there that somebody doesn't want found?"

Blaine fingered the diving pouch on his waist. "I'll show you when we get inside."

They had barely reached shore when Liz happened to look up and caught a glimpse of a figure in the swirling mist on the rise on the western side of the lake. A broad-shouldered man with very strong features that included a gaunt face and what looked like a thick handlebar mustache visible under a wide-brimmed hat. Liz glanced down to get her footing, and when she looked up again the figure had disappeared.

"What is it?" Blaine asked, noticing her stiffen.

"I thought I saw a man watching us from up there."

"A man?"

"Well, not exactly. More like a . . ."

Blaine followed her line of vision with no result. "A what?" he prodded.

"A ghost." Liz shrugged and started on again.

TWENTY-FIVE

Will Thatch left Crest Haven Memorial Park with a list of the eight funerals that had taken place the morning Jack Tyrell paid his visit. He took a New Jersey Transit local back to the city and walked to the main branch of the New York Public Library on Fifth Avenue to find the obituaries.

Some of the newspapers were being transferred onto microfilm and took a while to track down, lengthening what should have been a short process. Normally Will wouldn't have minded, having nothing but time. But today he was impatient, because he had a job to do. And why not? He'd waited twenty-five years for this opportunity and couldn't even be sure the obituaries would provide any clue at all. Maybe Jack Tyrell had come to the cemetery just to meet with the four men he had ultimately murdered.

No, Will decided, meeting in the open didn't fit his style at all, even if it was in a cemetery. Tyrell hadn't been expecting the four men to appear any more than they had been expecting to die.

The setting was convenient, if nothing else.

The thing that kept nagging at Will was the men with official-looking IDs who had shown up at Crest Haven later the day of the murders and left with the bodies in tow. They didn't care what Sunderwick had to say because there was nothing he could tell them that they didn't already know. That much was clear.

What wasn't clear was who they were and what their connection to Jack

Tyrell was. If they had been on his trail, if those were their men he had buried, why did the whole incident suddenly become hands-off to the media?

Will didn't know what was going on here, but it had to lie somewhere in the obituaries for those buried that morning just over a month ago. He made photostats and studied them in the library for what seemed like and then became hours. None of the three women and five men had been members of Midnight Run; Will felt certain of that much. Four had died of old age, two from illness; one had been in a car accident and one had been shot to death.

What was he missing?

Will checked their ages again, remembering a picture that hung on his memory wall, as faded and curled as all the rest of them.

What if . . .

The thought had crossed his mind a long time ago, dismissed because it had no foundation. Now he started to wonder.

Will gathered up the photostats and rushed for the exit. Get back to his room, tear the picture from the wall, and see if his suspicions had any foundation. If they did, oh boy, things were going to be even worse than he originally thought.

He jogged almost the whole way back to the hotel, panting and sweating as he pounded up the stairs. Opened up his door intending to head straight to his memory wall.

There was a man already hovering before it, another standing by the window. Both well dressed, with holster bulges just inside their hips.

"Close the door, please," the one by the window said.

Will did as he was told, trying to remember if Sunderwick had described the men who had come for the bodies.

"Nice collection," the man near his memory wall said.

"Mean anything to you?" Will wondered.

"Should it?" the one near the window, the bigger one, asked him.

Will shrugged. "It's just that if you're thieves, I think you're going to be disappointed."

"We want to talk to you about Jack Tyrell," said the smaller man.

"Go ahead."

"You seem to have quite an interest in him."

"With good reason."

"Really?"

"I let him get away."

The two men looked at each other.

"Third row from the right, fourth picture down," Will said.

The man at the wall shuffled sideways and looked closely at the yellowed tear sheet. "This is you?"

"That's me."

"You're shitting me, right?"

"Had him right in my hand and let him get away." Will tried to make himself laugh. "You boys come all this way without knowing who I am?"

"We knew you were FBI," the bigger one said.

"We didn't know you had a connection to Tyrell," added the smaller one. "Your interest in him makes sense now."

"So now that you know my connection, how about telling me yours?"

The man by the wall moved toward Will. "What we want to know is where you went after you left the cemetery this morning."

"It really matter to you?"

"Who else you might have spoken with on this subject," elaborated the larger man.

Will looked past the smaller man toward the picture he had been thinking of at the library. Couldn't get a close enough look at it from this far away. He turned toward the bed, the blue-steel .38 tucked neatly beneath the mattress.

"You mind if I sit down first? I'm a little tired."

"Go ahead," the smaller man said.

Will moved to the bed and sat down with his legs straddling the .38's position. "I've got to figure we're colleagues on this. I mean, you guys must be looking for Tyrell too, right?"

"Sure."

"The four guys he buried in Crest Haven were your people. They got close but must have underestimated him. Easy mistake to make. Am I figuring this right?"

"Who else did you speak to after you left the cemetery?" the smaller one asked.

"You boys mind telling me who you work for?"

"We're colleagues, remember?"

"But you're not Bureau. Hell, if you were Bureau you probably would have knocked instead of letting yourselves in."

Will knew they were going to kill him. Find out everything he knew and then make it look like an accident. He inched his hand toward the mattress.

"Thing is, if you're looking for Tyrell, I can help you. I can help you find him."

"What makes you think we're trying to find him?" the bigger man asked.

"How'd you find me?"

"It wasn't hard. We can find anyone."

"Nice to be good at something."

The smaller man came a little closer. "Who else knows you went to the cemetery?"

"Maybe the Bureau's on the case now."

"You haven't been there."

"Maybe I called. One of those anonymous tips. Give up the man who left four bodies in the ground. Tell them Jackie Terror's back."

"It's not their jurisdiction."

"Making it yours," Will said, just a snatch and grab from the .38 now. "What I'm still wondering is who you are."

The smaller man poured some scotch into a dirty glass and brought it over to Will. "Why don't you have a drink?"

Will took the glass. It wasn't hard to make his hands tremble. "Thanks."

He guzzled it down, but it tasted terrible. Last thing in the world he wanted in his gut right now, for the first time in longer than he could remember.

Will held the empty glass upward. " 'Nother be nice."

The smaller man took it. "Who else knows Tyrell was in that cemetery?"

"You're protecting him, aren't you?"

"You're making this hard," said the bigger man. "It doesn't have to be."

"We want to find him as much as you."

"In that case, you wouldn't be wasting your time here with me now."

The smaller man poured Will some more scotch and started to bring it over, the bigger man following his movements. One not watching, the other with a hand tied up with a glass.

Will went for the .38.

He yanked it from under the mattress in a motion too awkward to be threatening. The men didn't realize what was happening until he brought it up, intending to do no more than hold them at bay. But the larger man went for his gun and the smaller man let the glass crash to the hotel room floor to go for his.

Will started firing. There was no real discretion to his aim, but at this distance there didn't have to be. Instinct took over, and before he could think or breathe, both men were going down, blood spurting in all directions. They hit the floor as the .38's hammer clicked on an empty chamber.

Will realized only then that he was still sitting on the bed. He rose with considerable effort, backed away, and moved to his memory wall. He stripped off the picture he'd remembered in the library and stuffed it into his pocket with the photocopied obituaries, as pushpins clattered across the floor.

The two men had stopped moving altogether by the time he started for the door. Blood spread in pools beneath them, mixing with the scotch near the smaller one. Will saw it had splattered against the wall behind the bigger man, barely visible amidst the mold and mildew.

✧   ✧   ✧

Outside, Will didn't leave the area, not right away. Dressed as he was in nondescript clothes, it was easy for him to blend into the scene, walk about the block without anyone giving him a second look.

From a corner pay phone, he made an anonymous call about hearing gunshots coming out of the National Hotel. The police were on the scene five minutes later, but that's not who Will was waiting for.

They didn't appear for another hour: a pair of well-dressed men in a sedan much shinier than police issue. They flashed their IDs to the officers who had cordoned off the scene and were passed straight through.

Will thought of Sunderwick telling his story to similar men at Crest Haven Memorial Park, only to have it ignored. He ventured close enough to copy down the license plate on their sedan. He still had friends, acquaintances at least, in law enforcement. The kind of people who could trace a plate for him. Maybe help Will figure out who was trying so hard to make sure Jackie Terror wasn't caught at all.

3

STRATTON'S FOLLY

TWENTY-SIX

Why would someone want to keep people out of the lake?" Liz asked Blaine when they were back inside the house, Sal Belamo standing guard outside in case whoever Liz had seen watching them from the hillside returned.

"To keep anyone from finding out what's down there would be my guess." With her help, he had just finished dressing the wounds inflicted by the barbed wire; nothing very deep, but painful all the same.

"Leaving us where?"

"With this for starters."

Blaine laid the jagged piece of wood he'd snatched from the water on the kitchen table.

Liz studied it closely. "There's something carved into it. . . ."

Blaine lifted the piece of wood up and moved to the counter. He found some vinegar and worked it around through the old grooves to reveal letters forming a name followed by a date:

H. CULBERTSON
January 1863

"It looks like some kind of plaque," Liz said, as Blaine scrutinized the letters more closely.

"A mounting plaque," Blaine acknowledged. "This must be the name of the builder and the date he delivered whatever it was mounted onto."

"So what's this have to do with my father?"

"I think he figured out what Rentz was up to. This might help us figure out the same thing."

"Not alone it won't."

"I also found these," Blaine said, and he produced the gold coins his bazooka had stirred up from the bottom.

Liz's eyes bulged. "So there really is treasure under that lake. . . ."

Blaine joined her in gazing down at them. "Let's find out."

"The entrance is on the other side," Liz said, when Blaine led her down Pennsylvania Avenue toward the rear of the National Archives building ninety minutes later.

"For tourists only," Blaine told her. "You want to do some research, this is where you go."

"Really?"

"Surprised?"

"Most of the men my father trained don't have much use for research."

"Hobby of mine," Blaine quipped. "On weekends."

"Most of the men my father trained have other ways to spend their weekends."

Inside, after signing in, they went straight to the eleventh floor, where the military archives were housed. There Blaine explained to an archivist that they were looking for any reference to a master carpenter named H. Culbertson, circa 1862. The man didn't look terribly optimistic about the prospects, explaining it would take some time to come up with all the required records, until Blaine produced a nondescript ID that looked like a library card. The archivist gave him a longer look, straightened his shoulders, and took his leave.

"Let's go," Blaine said, taking Liz's arm gently.

"Where?"

"Central Reading Room, to wait for our material."

"Man said it could take a while."

"Half hour at most."

"Because of that card you flashed him?"

"It tends to quicken the process. Standard government issue."

"There's nothing standard or government about you."

"I've got friends."

"After six months away?"

"Cards like that don't come with an expiration date."

The archivist delivered a wheeled cart to them in the spacious, wood-lined Central Reading Room forty minutes later. The cart contained a dozen sleeved containers called Hollinger boxes, packed with Northern military manifests from the Civil War listing the various orders and shipments produced to advance the war effort. The archivist had flagged a trio of instances where the name of H. Culbertson, a master carpenter on retainer to the North, came up. But none were from the time that fit the mounting plaque.

Blaine and Liz spent the next two hours seated across from each other at a long wooden desk, paging through the manifests in search of a delivery close to the January 1863 date. Blaine was halfway through his third book when he found it.

"A dozen heavy-load wagons," he said suddenly, tightening his gaze at the manifest open in the shallow light before him. "According to this, Culbertson produced a dozen heavy-load wagons for a work order dated October 1862 and delivered them in January 1863 to a Colonel William Henry Stratton."

Liz leaned closer and turned the book toward her. "Looks like Colonel Stratton took delivery of something else on the very same day," she said.

"Four keg chests," McCracken read.

"Keg chests?"

"Large strongboxes."

"Perfect for carrying gold coins—is that what you're thinking?"

"Especially since I saw what looked to be the remains of one of those keg chests on the bottom of your lake."

On the second floor, they ordered the military records of William Henry Stratton from an archivist in the Microfilm Research Room. Once again the material was delivered to the Central Reading Room; only a single Hollinger box this time, twenty minutes later. But the results were considerably less impressive.

"Maybe there's more," Liz said when she finished studying the records on the chance Blaine had missed something.

"If there was, we'd be reading it," he returned, massaging his eyes. "There's no record of this Colonel William Stratton commanding any mission in early 1863. In fact, there's no record of Colonel William Henry Stratton at all after late 1862."

"Could he have died?"

"That there'd be a record of."

"You don't look surprised."

"Because I don't believe Stratton existed after early 1863." He slid his chair closer to hers. "Let's put together what we know. According to the manifests, Stratton took delivery of those wagons and keg chests on January 11, 1863. Assume whatever unlogged mission he was on took him into Virginia."

"A Union brigade heading south with heavy cargo?"

"Say they were taking a back route in the hope they wouldn't run into anyone from either side. Problem was the regiment ran smack into the teeth of that legendary blizzard instead and sought refuge in the nearest shelter they could find." Blaine stopped and looked at her. "In a barn, maybe."

"The one you found remnants of under the lake . . ."

"A lake that didn't exist until Bull Run flooded the valley the day after the storm stranded them."

Liz nodded. "Swallowing up the troops, and whatever they were carrying, forever. Stratton never completes his mission, but since there was never any record of it . . ."

"History pays no attention," Blaine completed.

"Until Maxwell Rentz, up to his eyeballs in debt and facing bankruptcy, somehow figured out the same thing we just did. Then he concocts a story about plans to build a resort and buys up all the land around the lake to keep anyone from realizing what he is really up to."

"But then his plans ran into a snag, didn't they?"

"Me," said Liz.

"And then Buck. Only problem is that Colonel Stratton wouldn't need twelve heavy-load wagons to transport four keg chests full of gold coins."

"Meaning . . . ?"

"Meaning he must have been carrying something else too."

Liz flipped absently through the last pages of Stratton's military record, coming upon a grainy, tattered photograph of a powerful-looking man in a sharply pressed Union officer's uniform. She lifted it closer to her tentatively, the color washing out of her face as she traced the line of the handlebar mustache that curled over Stratton's upper lip.

"You look like you recognize him," Blaine said.

"I do." Liz finally looked up again, expressionless. "Maybe I did see a ghost, after all: it was Stratton who was watching us from that hill this morning."

TWENTY-SEVEN

W e had some FBI men here a few days ago," the highway patrol detective named Huggins told Will Thatch outside the police station in Akron, Ohio, where the massacre had taken place. "Down from the Cleveland office," Will said, thinking fast. "I'm in from Washington."

The detective looked him over. "By yourself?"

"That's right."

Huggins studied him closer, then just shrugged.

Two hours after jotting down the license plate on the car belonging to the two men who had shown up at his hotel, Will had met with a man named Bob Snelling on a bench in Gramercy Park. He had gone through the Academy with Snelling a lifetime ago, and the two of them had come into the Bureau together. Snelling, the only person Will had any contact with from his former life, ran a successful security firm now. He had lent Will money a few times, which Will had never paid back, and on a few other occasions had kept tabs on Will's family for him.

Will had phoned Snelling and asked him to run a trace on the license plate. Ninety minutes later, Snelling had requested this meeting—on the other side of the city from his office.

Approaching his old friend seated on the park bench, Will thought he had the look of a man already eager to leave.

"Sit down, Will," Snelling greeted, not bothering to rise or extend a hand.

"What is it?"

"This some kind of joke?"

"God, no."

"Then are you sure you wrote the numbers on the license plate down right?"

Well, Will thought, he hadn't been wearing his glasses, but he'd gotten close enough to the plate to touch it.

"Yes. I am."

Snelling looked jittery. "The combination makes it a government plate; I've been around enough to know that. And it's not hard to track down the specific branch; I've been around enough to know that too. FBI, Justice, ATF—you name it. Each has its own distinct register for accounting purposes." Snelling looked a little pale. "I made some calls, ran your plate through the system to see who it belonged to."

"And?"

Snelling stopped fidgeting. "Nobody, Will. The plate doesn't exist."

"You just said—"

"I know what I said. It's a government plate, but it doesn't belong to anyone I can access, and I can gain access to *everyone*."

"What are you saying?"

"These people you're mixed up with are buried deep. You know how it works."

"Not really."

"The deeper they're buried, the less people have access. Sometimes *nobody* has access."

Why would someone like that be protecting Jack Tyrell?

"You say something, Will?" Snelling asked him.

"Just thinking out loud."

"I'd do it quieter, if I were you, and I'd lay low for a while." Snelling finally stood up, looking relieved.

Will stood up too. "Wait a minute, you haven't even asked me what this is about."

"Because I don't want to know."

Will rummaged through his coat for the folded copies of the obituaries he'd accumulated in the library. "But I've got something else to show you."

Snelling started to walk off. "Maybe you didn't hear me. I'm not interested."

Will caught up with him. "It's Jackie Terror, Bob. He's back. You've got to help me find out why."

Snelling laid a forceful hand on Will's shoulders and pushed him from his path. "No, I don't."

"Someone's protecting him. I don't know how, but the answers are in these somehow," Will insisted, flapping the obituaries before him. "I can't find them alone."

Snelling stopped and swung around. "Then don't look."

"Bob—"

"And don't call me anymore. People like the ones who own those cars tend to know when you're looking into them. That means they've probably already got tabs on me. I let things cool down, maybe they figure it was an innocent mistake."

"I'm sorry."

"Drop this, Will. Whatever it is, drop it."

This time Will had let Bob Snelling walk off without a fight. He thought of him again as he faced Detective Huggins. Will had had a thousand dollars to his name at the start of today, a significant chunk of which went to pay for his plane ticket to Cleveland and the rental car that had gotten him to Akron.

"I thought you boys traveled in teams," the detective said now, an edge of suspicion creeping into his voice.

"Task forces, you mean."

"Yeah."

"I'm advance. We've got some leads. If they play out, you'll get your task force and then some." Saying just enough to make Huggins figure there was more on his mind.

Satisfied, the detective moved toward a padlocked door erected as part of a temporary repair job on the ruined front of the police station. Will breathed easier when Huggins fished a key from his pocket and popped the lock open.

"I got the case file in my car," the detective said. "Photos too. We moved all the prisoners. Sons of bitches are the only witnesses we got left alive. Bastards that did this killed six cops for no reason. I been over the security tapes a dozen times. You can't see much, but you can tell they were smiling the whole time."

Will didn't know what he expected to find here. Not revelations certainly, nor clues as to where Jackie Terror headed off with Mary Raffa in tow, ready to get their garden of death going. He was looking for a feeling, a scent. Something to follow after all these years away.

The inside of the station had been cleaned up for the most part, but there were still plenty of bulletholes dug in the walls. The glass security wall hadn't been replaced, and the desks looked as though they hadn't been touched since the massacre; turned sideways or spilled over by men seeking cover desperately.

"Here's the file."

Will hadn't noticed Huggins enter. He took the manila folder from him and drew out the eight-by-ten still photos that had been produced from the security tape.

By all accounts Jack Tyrell had proceeded to the cells alone, leaving the Yost brothers to finish up the slaughter. The still shots caught them only from behind, but that was enough for Will to recognize Earl and Weeb in different poses, leaning over the desks where the outgunned cops had hidden. A few of the pictures showed the twins with submachine guns in their hands. At least two showed a smoke trail burning from their muzzles, the slight blur caused by the motion of the barrel firing.

Will suddenly stopped amidst the toppled and turned desks, having involuntarily retraced what must have been the Yost brothers' murderous path.

It's your fault, you dumb son of a bitch! All this happened because you let Jackie Terror get away. . . .

He felt the old hate welling in him, self-loathing as much as detestation for Jack Tyrell. Will was dead too; nobody had gotten around to burying him yet, though. All chewed up inside, the world eating away at him. Will blessed at last with his chance to bite back.

"You got an office I can use?" he said suddenly to Huggins.

"Yes."

"Computer?"

"Sure."

Will Thatch made for the door, shoulders high, suit no longer looking like an old sack draped over his frame. "Then let's get going."

TWENTY-EIGHT

From the Archives, Blaine and Liz went straight to the Bureau of Engraving and Printing, specifically the annex building across Fourteenth Street from the sprawling complex commonly known as the "Money Factory," where all paper currency in the country is printed. Since they didn't have an appointment, the receptionist was adamant in refusing to send them upstairs in search of someone who could help them identify the origins of a specific rare coin. All such requests, they were told, needed to be filed in writing, with a tracing included in lieu of the coin itself. A response, or certificate of authenticity, could be expected within three to four weeks.

"Maybe I can help," a collegiate-looking young man, who must have overheard their conversation on his way out of the building, said from behind them. "My name's Evan Reed. I'm an intern in the Records Department."

"Congratulations, Evan," said Liz.

"I'm also writing my graduate thesis on rare coins."

"How are you on the Civil War era?" Blaine asked him, while the receptionist shook her head in dismay.

"Depends on the minting. What have you got?"

"Why don't you tell me?" Blaine said, and produced one of the gold pieces he'd found under the lake.

Evan's eyes widened. He took the coin and handled it gently, checking one side and then the other. "Where'd you get this?"

"The bottom of my piggy bank."

"Is this some kind of joke?" Evan asked both of them, clearly not amused.

"If it is," Liz told him, "it's on us."

"It's just that . . ."

"What?" Blaine prodded.

"Let's go upstairs to my office," said Evan, steering them toward the elevator.

"You'll have to sign in first," the receptionist snapped before they could leave, and shoved the registry across the counter toward Blaine and Liz.

The office to which Evan referred was more like a lab, shared by a number of interns, the others of whom had left for the day. He inspected the coin under a binocular microscope, rummaged through some books, and then scanned some files on a computer.

"Just as I thought," he said finally.

"What?" Blaine asked him.

"Simply stated, this coin doesn't exist."

"You saying it's a forgery?"

"No, I'm almost certain it's real, but there's no record I can find of a coin like this ever being minted." Evan adjusted a large magnifying glass set on a swivel, so Blaine and Liz could get a better look at the coin. "At first glance, or to the novice, this is an ordinary ten-dollar gold piece. On the head side here we have the goddess Liberty." He flipped the coin over in his fingers. "And on the tail we have the eagle."

"Sounds familiar," Blaine said.

"Only on the surface. Notice anything missing on the tail?"

"No."

"How about 'United States of America' in a rim here?" And he traced the empty space with his finger. "It's on every coin ever minted by the Treasury, which means whoever made the mold on this one must have screwed up."

"Is that possible?"

"A mistake that big? Not if the coins ever got out of here, no."

"Is there any way to find out for sure?" Liz asked him.

Evan thought briefly. "Maybe."

Only elevators reserved for staff use could reach The Tombs. The three of them emerged on a dimly lit basement hallway. Evan led the way down it to a solid wood door he opened with a key.

"Coins aren't minted in Washington anymore," he explained, ushering

Blaine and Liz in ahead of him. "But all records have been consolidated here for years. Not that anybody cares. Most of them aren't even important enough to be transferred onto a database or microfilm."

The Tombs was actually a series of rooms, each cavernous and lined with shelves. The wooden desks and chairs placed amidst the shelves were all heavy and dull. The books stacked carefully around them looked like massive ledgers with broken and tattered bindings. The rooms smelled of paper, antiseptic, and stale, untouched air.

"The date of the issue is 1862, according to what's imprinted on the coin, and the lack of an identifying letter means that they were minted here in the capital," Evan explained. "Is there any way you can narrow it down further?"

"Try December," Liz said, recalling that William Henry Stratton had taken delivery of the keg chests and wagons on January 11.

Evan located the proper logbook for the Washington Mint on the shelf and lugged it over to the heavy wooden table. He began turning the pages rapidly, scanning the precise inventory of which coins were minted when and in what quantity. He stopped suddenly and flipped back to a page he had already checked, obviously perplexed.

"I guess the records weren't as complete as I thought," he announced. "There must be a page missing."

He spun the book around for Blaine and Liz to look at.

"See?" Evan resumed. "The bottom of this page ends on December 15. But the next page picks up with December 27."

"Maybe they closed for Christmas," Liz suggested.

"Let's find out," said Evan.

He moved to a different section of the storage shelves and brought another book back with him.

"These are the inventory logs listing shipments both incoming and outgoing. Let's see what it has to say. . . ."

He worked the tattered pages carefully, afraid of tearing or crinkling them. He seemed to find something that interested him, studying a number of entries before speaking again.

"Major gold shipments from San Francisco were logged in on December 14, 17, and 21."

"I guess they stayed open, after all," noted Liz.

"How much gold?" Blaine wondered.

"Roughly, I'd say enough to mint as many as a quarter million of your mysterious gold pieces."

"Enough to fill about four keg chests," Blaine calculated. "What would their value be today?"

"Impossible to calculate," Evan explained, "because you can't factor in collector's value. We're talking about a huge minting of coins in perfect condition, never placed in circulation. But without an actual history to lend authentication, you're looking at a substantially deflated price if you intend to sell."

"And if such a history existed?"

"Wow. Then we could be talking in the range of twenty thousand dollars per coin."

"That's five hundred million dollars!" Liz noted disbelievingly.

"That's right," said Evan.

"So what was Stratton doing with them?" Liz wondered out loud. "Where was he going?"

Evan came slowly out of his chair. "Stratton? *William Henry Stratton?*"

Blaine and Liz looked at each other. "You mean you've *heard* of him?" Blaine asked.

"You mean you *haven't?* Stratton's Folly doesn't mean anything to you?" Together, they shook their heads.

"How much do the two of you know about the Civil War?"

"The North won," Blaine quipped.

"Not for the first two years," Evan responded. "The fact is we were getting our butts kicked right up until mid-1863, to the point where Lincoln was under a lot of pressure from Northern industrialists to cut his losses and accede."

"Where does Stratton's Folly come in?" Liz asked.

"After northern losses at Vicksburg and Fredericksburg, with the South moving on Washington, Lincoln ordered the North's gold reserves moved from the capital. Legend has it that he sent the gold in a heavily armed convoy by train to Mexico for safekeeping until after the war."

"Under the command of Colonel William Henry Stratton," Liz surmised. "What happened?"

The snow had been falling for hours, a white blanket growing beneath the convoy as it trudged through the valley.

"Hold up," Colonel William Henry Stratton called to his men when he saw the rider approaching along a narrow trail that cut between the hillsides.

"We're running behind, Colonel."

Annoyed, Stratton turned on his horse and glared at the civilian who had ridden up alongside him from the rear of the convoy. "I'm aware of that, Mr. Tyler."

"You should also be aware that we have a schedule to keep. Our cargo must reach the rendezvous site on time. Am I making myself clear?"

Stratton gazed over Tyler's shoulder at the twelve heavy-load wagons containing that cargo. The wagons were being pulled by oxen, huge, lumbering beasts that exuded raw power as their hooves pounded the frozen ground. The weather had been deteriorating fast ever since they set out nearly six hours before. Stratton's two dozen troops looked chilled to the bone, his only consolation being that Tyler's small detachment of civilians looked far worse.

"Quite, sir," the colonel replied.

"Well," demanded Tyler when Stratton made no move, "what are you waiting for?"

"To find out what's ahead of us," Stratton said. "You wouldn't want to lose your cargo to an ambush, Mr. Tyler, now would you?"

Tyler frowned, as the scout Stratton had sent on ahead of the regiment drew even. Stratton had ridden with Billy Red Bear from the beginning of the Civil War and intended never to stray far from his side for its duration, having come to see the Indian as the one person who could guide him through hell.

Red Bear ignored the civilian and saluted.

"As you were, Sergeant," said Stratton.

Red Bear's leathery face was creased with concern. "No one ahead of us or to the sides, sir."

"What's wrong, then?"

"The storm, Colonel." Red Bear seemed to be sniffing the air, his eyes rising to the smoke-colored sky. "It's turning into a big one."

"Recommendation?"

"We should find shelter, sir. Fast."

Tyler drew his horse up closer, forging his way between the two soldiers. "The hell we will! I'm in charge of this mission, Colonel, and I order you to continue on the route as planned. Is that clear?"

Stratton nodded and reached almost imperceptibly beneath his great-coat. "Very clear, Mr. Tyler."

The colonel raised his pistol and, without any hesitation at all, shot Tyler in the face. Taking that as their signal, Stratton's troops turned their guns on the members of Tyler's civilian detachment and opened fire as well.

The shooting seemed to go on for a very long time, when it was actually over very fast. Stratton blamed the illusion on the echoes of gunfire lingering shrilly in the wind. Even after those sounds had subsided, clouds of gray gunsmoke continued to sift through the air, visible amidst the falling snow.

Colonel Stratton climbed down off his horse and crouched over Tyler's body. He reached into the civilian's coat pocket and extracted a leather pouch, which he quickly stuffed into his Union-blue greatcoat.

"Better find us that shelter, Sergeant," he said to Red Bear as he remounted his horse, the snow becoming a blinding white barrier before them. "Better find it fast."

"So the gold shipment never made it to Mexico," Blaine said, when Evan had finished.

The young man nodded. "And that's where the legend really takes off. Stratton had to be an extremely loyal and reliable officer to be entrusted with such a mission. But the temptation posed by the gold must have been too much for him; neither he, his men, nor the gold was ever seen again."

"Gold packed in twelve heavy-load wagons built by someone named Culbertson," Blaine said, putting the pieces together. "How much exactly are we talking about?"

"The Northern reserves would have been enough to fill all twelve of those wagons," said Evan. "Be worth about seven hundred fifty million dollars in today's market."

Blaine looked at Liz. "Over a billion when our mysterious coins are added in. Think that would be enough to get Rentz out of the hole?"

"What does the legend say happened to the gold?" Liz asked Evan.

"That something went wrong after Stratton stole it. Maybe he was ambushed or betrayed by his men. Maybe Indians wiped out the brigade as it headed west. The only evidence ever found were the bodies of a civilian detachment that was riding along with the convoy."

Blaine slid one of the strange coins across the table. "And where do you think this fits into the story?"

Evan took the coin in his hand. "It doesn't. Why would Lincoln order a special secret minting of such an unusual coin just to be hidden until the war was over? And why would Stratton be transporting them? It doesn't make any sense." Evan paused and looked the coin over again. "Whether they stole the gold or not, though, it's like Stratton and his regiment just fell off the face of the earth."

TWENTY-NINE

W e're not anywhere near the route I mapped out for you," Othell Vance protested again.

"Maybe that's why you never found your tanker, Othell," Jack Tyrell snapped back, as their stolen Jimmy thumped over the road. "Bad weather that night, right?"

"I told you that from the beginning."

"So maybe they took a wrong turn."

"And ended up *here*?"

The route Mary had set them on cut through Pennsylvania coal country into the heart of the Valley and Ridge region northwest of Harrisburg. About as mean as land could get. Roads mostly forgotten by even the locals.

"I can feel it close by." Mary spoke defensively from the passenger seat. "Like we're . . ."

"Yeah?" Tyrell prodded.

She looked across the seat at him like a hurt child. "You giving up on me, Jackie?"

"I say that?"

" 'Cause I don't know how I'd take it if you did. You believing in me is what kept me going all these years, what held me together."

"Why'd you think I came back?"

"I'm just afraid of letting you down, that's all."

Jack Tyrell relaxed a little behind the wheel. "We've been over these roads all day. We'll keep going over them until we—"

"Stop the car," Mary said suddenly, stiffening. "Stop it now!"

Tyrell jammed on the brakes, feeling the Jimmy fishtail on the rocky road surface. It wasn't strictly a road at all, so much as a path between the ridges. They'd been struggling across different stretches of it through the brutally long day, Tyrell uncertain whether they had actually covered this patch before. The road surfaces had been gritty and granular, full of washouts and covered with masses of loose stones. For the better part of the day they had bumped and ground their way over debris that looked to have been shoveled on by some mad road crew. Tyrell had never felt anything like it, coaxing the vehicle's tires to keep churning the whole way, as Othell Vance bounced around in the back seat. The Yost brothers and Tremble were driving behind them in a stolen pickup. Night had fallen hours before, and the darkness slowed their speed to a jogger's pace, the world extending no farther than what their headlights showed them.

Mary was out of the truck before Tyrell had brought it to a complete stop. She sank to her knees and spooned the road dirt through her hand like she was mixing a cake. Her eyes had gotten that dreamy, faraway look Jack Tyrell had remembered for twenty-five years.

"What do you see?" Jack asked her.

Mary cradled herself tightly. "It's underground. That's where we'll find—"

Tyrell saw her start to shake and move into that staticky field that seemed to encompass her when one of her quickenings overtook her. He tried to embrace her, but she pulled away.

"You didn't tell me, Jackie," she said sadly. But then her expression turned mean, emotions changing as fast as heartbeats. "He was *ours*. You should have told me. I had a right to know."

And Jack realized where her mind had drifted, what it had found when it got there. "I didn't see the point."

"It's my pain too, Jack, *that's* the point. Why should you bear it alone? Others deserve to feel it too, something you shouldn't deny, especially to me. How could you, damn it, how could you?"

She was on her feet by then, pounding at his chest. Tyrell barely felt the blows, letting her wear herself out. When she was spent, on the verge of crumpling, he took her in his arms.

"It's all right, babe. I'm right here."

Mary pulled away enough to find his eyes. "For how long this time? Don't you see that it doesn't matter if I can't trust you? I couldn't trust you all those years ago and I can't trust you now. How do I know you won't leave again when all this is over?"

"Because it's not gonna be over," Tyrell said softly. "Because what this stuff is going to do for us is only the first step. You follow the news?"

"Bits and pieces."

"Oklahoma City, the World Trade Center, Flight 800, the Unabomber—you see what I'm getting at?"

"No."

"It's a different world now, Mary, the kind of world we were meant for, where one crazy can threaten to stick a bomb on a plane and ground all flights. We make a call like that twenty-five years ago, the best we can hope for is to get our dime back when it's finished. People have learned how to be scared. All these boys, they're just bad imitators of what we did, but they got more people paying attention, and that's what we want." His expression tensed in determination. "Yeah, people have learned how to be scared now, and we're gonna keep scaring them again and again. We're gonna make them scared to leave their homes, make them scared to send their kids to school. And then, just for fun, maybe we'll bring the whole country to a screeching halt. But we need the Devil's Brew to make it happen, Mary. Best minds in the country couldn't find it, but here we are now, thanks to you. You're mad because I didn't let you share my pain. Well, there's something a lot bigger you can share with me now."

He watched Mary nod, a slow, determined motion, the two of them standing there as though the missing years had never happened. The others all held their distance, knowing how it was when Mary got one of her quickenings.

"Up there," she said, cocking her gaze toward the foothills enclosing them, dotted with the open mouths of caves and openings to long-abandoned anthracite mines that had stripped the land clean.

"I thought you said underground."

"The way in's *up there*. Follow me."

She set a torrid pace over the rough, uneven ground. Jack did his best to keep up but kept slipping and sliding along with the others in the darkness. She moved like something was pulling her on, not letting go. Jack Tyrell's breath was long gone when he saw what looked like the mouth of a cave gaping in the middle of absolutely nowhere. Mary had picked up her pace again when he lunged forward to grab her.

"Lemme go!" she roared, stiff under his grasp. "You wanted me to take you to it. We're almost—"

"Shhhhhhhhhhhhhhh," Tyrell said, covering her mouth, signaling back to the others to hold their positions. Then he gestured toward the cave. "There's a light on inside there."

THIRTY

Buck Torrey nursed the fire, willing it to stay lit. He still had plenty of matches, but the thought of venturing outside on his broken ankle in search of more wood was enough to keep him blowing and stoking the flames all night. Buck watched them lick at the air, smoke rising in small wisps that quickly grew into warm clouds blowing over him. He shivered and shifted closer to the fire, dragging his splinted leg in both hands, as near to the warmth as he dared.

His first-aid kit had perished with his truck, the second thing to have gone terribly wrong with this trip. The first, his cell phone battery going dead, had seemed routine enough. He'd planned to recharge it on the next leg of the drive, but the storm had intervened and left him peering out a windshield blanketed by rain that fell in black sheets. Being the only vehicle on what passed for a back road was all that allowed him to keep going until the road vanished before his determined headlights.

He experienced a moment of panic when it seemed he had driven off the edge of a mountain and was plunging to his death. His bowels turned to jelly and he squeezed the steering wheel hard enough to bend it in the long moment before he felt the jarring impact on all four wheels. Buck rolled down the window and gazed out.

He had driven into some kind of long, deep sinkhole where he was certain the road had been just seconds before; the windshield wipers had cleared enough of the rain away to show him the scattered rocks and debris. Buck might have spent more time trying to figure out what had happened, if the hole hadn't begun to close up around him almost as quickly as it had appeared. The walls were caving in, the floor of the pit seeming to rise as wet mud.

Fearful of being buried alive, Buck climbed atop the truck's hood and then the cab, still a hefty leap from the nearest side of the quickly closing hole but offering the only chance he had for escape. He had come up just short with his first leap and crashed back down, his leg buckling on the curvature of the roof. He heard *and* felt his ankle snap, had all he could do just to keep from sliding off into the collapsing pool of muck that was intent on entombing both him and Jay Don Reed's truck.

Numbness had set in, allowing him to stand on the roof again and put a slight amount of pressure on the ankle. Buck knew he would get only one more shot at climbing out, anything that passed for a wall certain to be gone before he could mount another try, assuming his ankle could handle it. No way he could manage the reach with only one leg pushing off. He needed to use his broken one for balance and thrust, which meant giving it most of his weight.

Buck knew the pain was coming, but it was worse than anything he had imagined; his entire ankle felt like shattered glass as he leaped outward for the edge, wailing at the top of his lungs. This time he managed to catch both hands on the rapidly disintegrating surface, dirt and mud running through his fingers even as he desperately clawed to pull himself up. He kicked with his good leg and then his bad one, regained the surface coughing dirt from his mouth. No trace of Reed's truck remained, the whole of it swallowed up in the freak cave-in.

Buck wondered if he had taken a wrong turn somewhere and ended up in the Bermuda Triangle. That might figure. Lend credence to what he had begun to put together after his meeting with Maxwell Rentz.

As a boy, Buck spent many an hour down by the lake with his grandfather, listening to the old man spin tales of the secret Northern mission that had crossed their farm in the middle of the Civil War. His grandfather claimed even to have seen the soldiers through the raging blizzard that had stranded them. But he also claimed there was no use looking for the treasure, because they left with it before morning, before the flood that accompanied an even more powerful storm a day later and carved out the lake.

Still, Buck had spent his formative years as a teenage diver exploring every inch of that lake bottom. Feeling about blindly through the utter blackness. Teaching himself never to be scared by the black silt kicked up over his mask. As the years passed he began to dismiss his grandfather's yarns as tall tales meant to entertain a young boy and nothing else. No treasure had ever left the Torrey family farm, because no treasure had ever been there in the first place.

But Maxwell Rentz had proved Buck wrong and his grandfather right. The only thing Rentz had wrong was the belief that the treasure was still under the lake. Buck's grandfather claimed Stratton's men had not frozen to death in the blizzard, because he had seen them leave well before the valley was flooded. Of course no one, including Buck, had ever paid him much heed, since the old man was known to cuddle up with a bottle more nights than not. If he was right about that part of the story, though, maybe his insistence that Stratton had headed north into Pennsylvania was right too. Even showed young Buck a tattered map he claimed the soldiers had left behind.

How Buck could have used that map three days ago, after his little talk with Maxwell Rentz confirmed he was on the right track. He knew that following what he suspected was Stratton's trail would have to wait now. His truck was gone, the first-aid kit buried under a ton of dirt with it, and his cell phone was dead. First on the agenda was finding a way to splint his leg, immobilizing it so he could move, then look for some shelter. All he had on his person was a nine-millimeter pistol he would gladly have traded for an air cast or a good chug of whiskey.

Buck Torrey had taught good men how to survive under similar circumstances and had himself done so on at least one occasion. His wound at that time was a bullet to the shoulder, the rest of his scout team wiped out, and five miles to cover before morning gave him up. He'd managed then with a hundred Cong soldiers scouring the brush for him. He'd manage now with no one prowling about, but no one waiting beyond the fire line to extract him, either.

That was last night, and the splint he had fashioned from branches and vines was still in place, albeit with fresh vines from that morning. He'd spent today limping along the roadside, hoping for a vehicle that never came. He had found this cave just before dusk. Its warmth promised a limited salvation, a respite to get him into another day, when a vehicle might come by.

He should have told somebody exactly where he was, what he was up to, damn it! Pushing sixty and he was still playing games, figuring that keeping his body rock hard was enough to cheat the years. Except this was no recon mission and he had no relief beyond the next ridge. He could do nothing about the swelling of his ankle, and the feeling of bones shifting about just below the skin was getting worse instead of better.

He wanted to believe he was doing this for Liz, leave her one thing to make up for the missing years. But deep inside he knew the truth was he longed for one last great adventure. He had run to Condor Key, trying to turn his back on the man he was, and thought he'd pulled it off until Blaine McCracken arrived, dragging the past with him. In training McCracken again, Buck realized he was training himself, learning that what Blaine was desperately striving to get back he had lost as well, though in a different way. He actually welcomed the call from Jay Don Reed, because it gave him the excuse he needed to go back to being who he really wanted to be.

Buck dozed off and on through the night, waking on occasion certain he had heard vehicles in the not too far off distance. Sounds, though, were tricky in these parts; the wind made plenty of them up and pushed the rest a long way, bouncing them in all directions.

But the wind had no part in the footsteps and voices he heard approaching the cave from below; they must have been campers attracted by the blessed fire he had tended so obsessively through the first part of the night.

Buck had dragged himself up and was almost to the doorway, propped on his makeshift crutch, ready to wave gratefully to the approaching party, when he saw the car thumping down the unpaved road. He couldn't make out anything at first beyond a dust cloud moving behind bright headlights. As it drew closer he saw on the roof the light bubble of a Pennsylvania Highway Patrol car.

The small group approaching the cave stopped on the hillside, as the patrol car slid to a bumpy halt. The driver's door snapped open and a big trooper climbed out, straightening his cap as he started up the slope after them.

"You folks mind telling me what you're doing out in these parts?"

The big cop wasn't holding a gun, but Jack Tyrell could tell he was thinking hard about his police-issue Beretta, the restraining snap open over its holster.

"Hiking, sir," Jack said, feeling Mary stiffen at his side, hoping the others would follow his lead.

"Not a good idea at night, sir," the trooper warned, advancing. "Matter of fact, I'd say it's a lousy idea in these parts anytime."

"We're being careful."

The cop stopped, sizing them all up cautiously. "You mind if I ask you a few questions?"

"Not at all," said Jack.

"We been on the lookout for a stolen GMC Jimmy all day."

"Is that a fact?"

"Occupants been reported missing too," the trooper said. "Couple of college girls. None of you folks would recall seeing them or their Jimmy, would ya?"

Jack looked at the others, shook his head on their collective behalf. "Sorry, Officer."

"See, the reason I ask is that I came upon just such a vehicle back down the hill. Different plates, of course, but I still had to check it out."

"Like I said—" Jack started, but the cop wasn't finished yet.

"I got a description of the missing girls too."

"Haven't seen them," Jack said.

"Got a pretty complete rundown of what they were last seen wearing, including Timberland hiking boots," the trooper continued. "Just like the one lady's size seven I found a couple miles back down the road." His hand flirted with the Beretta, maybe hoping for an excuse to draw it, but holding them in his flashlight beam instead. "You folks might just wanna come down so I can ask a few questions and . . ."

"*. . . get a few things straight.*"

As he shrank further inside against the cave entrance, Buck found his own motions mirroring the cop's, thinking about the pistol he had left back by the fire. Kind of man he had walked into battle with often enough to know the type. But it was a type that should have known not to prance straight into trouble, outmanned and outgunned. Buck figured another couple of cars must be streaming in after him, except they still hadn't showed when the impossible happened.

It must have surprised the big cop as well, because he barely managed to free his gun from its holster before the bullets tore into him. The first took him in the throat, spouting a geyser of blood that washed down over his uniform top as the next three or four shots thumped into his chest. It was a head shot cracking into his skull, spewing bone and brain matter into the air, that finally spilled the cop over several feet from where a gun he hadn't fired had fallen.

Buck saw that the group was now moving toward the cave again, gun smoke still fluttering from their barrels. Whoever they were, they were good, especially the pair of pale-skinned men who even together didn't seem full-framed enough to make a single man.

Buck retreated, anxious not to make the same mistake the trooper had made. The familiar heat of battle surged up his spine, but the dry, sour taste in his mouth was that of fear. He'd known it a few times before, but this was as bad as any.

He scooped up his pistol and hobbled toward the back depths of the cave, out of view of the meager spill of light from the flames when the enemy reached the entrance.

THIRTY-ONE

Blaine turned the delivery van off Fourteenth Street onto the ramp accessing the National Museum of American History's after-hours underground entrance. He and Liz were both aware of the surveillance camera that followed them as they passed inside the complex through a garage-size door, along with the metal detectors waiting inside, which had led Blaine to stow his pistol under the seat.

"Nervous?" he asked her, working a wad of gum around in his mouth and holding a well-wrapped package under one arm.

"This uniform is way too tight." Liz had pinned her hair into a bun, so she could fit the delivery service's required cap over it.

"Best I could do on short notice."

Blaine tipped his cap lower over his eyes and drew the van to a halt just beyond the service entrance. With Liz at his side, he rang the buzzer and pretended to wait nonchalantly for it to be answered. A buzz sounded and then a click, as the door snapped unlocked. Blaine pulled it open and trailed Liz inside, clutching the box tightly. They moved through the metal detector toward a desk where a security guard eyed them with disinterest.

"Got some more additions for the new Lincoln Archives." It had been Evan who informed them about the recent discovery of bundles of correspondence to and from Lincoln hidden amidst boxed documents from that era.

"That a sign only?" the guard asked.

Blaine shook his head. "Sorry. Vault placement." Evan had educated him on that procedure too.

"Shit." The guard lumbered out of his chair. "You know the routine?"

"My first time."

"Sign here."

He handed a clipboard over. Blaine's was the first signature of the night.

The guard fished the proper key from his belt. "Now let's go pop your cherry," he said, paying no attention to Liz.

The guard keyed in the code to open the steel door behind his desk, then watched as Blaine and Liz passed through ahead of him. He resealed the door and then led the way to an elevator door with a key slot. The guard worked a strangely shaped key around until it seated, turned it left and then right.

The elevator opened.

Evan had told them that the National Museum of American History maintains a climate-controlled underground repository to retard deterioration of stored documents. Many of the documents, already in varying states of disrepair, are slated for restoration or analysis to reconstruct their contents. Others are placed on display and then returned to the stable air of the subbasement storage levels at closing time. According to Evan, the Lincoln documents might not be made public for years, until restoration was complete.

The elevator whisked them down quickly, the door opening to reveal a depository that was the antithesis of the ancient Tombs at the Bureau of Engraving and Printing. Everything was bright and sleek, the floors polished tile and the walls dull steel. The air had an antiseptic scent to it. The humidity-free confines made it seem colder than it was, and the touch of the air made Blaine's skin feel clammy.

The guard reached a set of steel doors and keyed a combination into the pad, turning back toward them when the door opened with a *whoooooooosh.* "This is the overnight storage—"

Blaine yanked the guard's pistol from its holster and spun him back around.

The guard's eyes bulged incredulously. "You're kidding, right?"

"We want to see the stacks."

"The new Lincoln Archives," Liz added.

The guard looked at the gun, shaking his head. "What is this, a robbery?"

"Lead on," Blaine said.

The guard started moving. "Because if you take this stuff back to the surface, most of it will be dust before you can sell a single page."

"We just want to do a little reading," Liz told him.

The guard led the way to an airtight, vacuum-sealed door labeled MAIN DEPOSITORY. A keypad rested just to the left of it.

"I hope you don't think I've got the combo to this one."

Liz reached past him and keyed in the same code he had used to access the overnight holding room. The door to the Main Depository slid softly open.

The door closed automatically after all three of them had entered the gymnasium-size, partitioned facility, lined with steel drawers that were built into the walls.

Blaine stuck the guard's gun in his own belt. "Keep leading."

"This way," the man relented.

The brief walk ended at a vaultlike door that opened with a simple latch.

"You want me to go in, give you a hand finding what you want?"

"I think we can handle things from here," Blaine said. "Gonna have to tie you up while we're inside."

The guard extended his wrists. "Just observe the handling rules inside. There's a checklist on the wall."

"We'll be careful."

They were searching through the boxes lifted out of cabinets vacuum-sealed to keep unwanted air away from them, when Liz spotted a neat stack of eight pieces of correspondence clipped together. "That's strange. These were in the January 1863 drawer, but they're from October of '62."

"That must have been when Lincoln sent them."

She scanned the letters as quickly as she could, given the clumsiness of the powdery surgical gloves they wore in keeping with document-handling procedure. "No, they're letters *to* Lincoln, not from him. The authors are expressing their satisfaction with Lincoln's acceptance of their suggestions pertaining to the war effort."

"When was the meeting held?"

"Let me see . . . October 6."

"Interesting," Blaine said, as he gingerly grasped the stack and began to page through them gently.

"Why?"

"It would take about two months to ship gold from San Francisco to Washington by water, the most viable route in those days by far. Remember when the gold shipments used in our mysterious coins arrived at the mint?"

"Not exact—"

"The fourteenth, seventeenth, and twenty-first of December. Do the math."

"Are you drawing a connection between this meeting Lincoln held in October and the coins that went missing with the rest of Stratton's convoy?"

"Absolutely."

"Care to tell me why?"

Blaine tapped the pile of letters. "If we researched the men who signed these, I'll bet we'd find they were from the pool of Northern industrialists who wanted the war effort ended there and then—October 1862."

"So they go to Lincoln, leave satisfied, and then he orders the minting of a coin no one's ever heard of."

"He had his reasons."

"Like what?"

Blaine checked his watch. "Later. Let's put this stuff away."

Blaine and Liz left the guard bound in the stacks, gun back in his holster, and rode the elevator up to the ground floor. The door had just started to open when Blaine glimpsed the shadows looming in the hallway beyond. He shoved Liz behind him and pressed the Close Door and Up buttons in the same instant. As the doors closed again, a volley of shots poured through the slit between them. Blaine and Liz twisted together against the compartment's side wall to avoid a stitch of bullets that tore into the rear of the elevator's cab.

Bullets were still slamming into the elevator after it sealed tight and the compartment began to rise. They dashed out when the doors slid open again on the third floor, sped beneath a sign patriotically proclaiming a "We the People" exhibit and into the museum's military wing. Together, they slammed and locked a set of double doors to buy time.

"What now?" Liz asked.

Escape was still a possibility via a set of stalled escalators near the rear of the wing's foyer, which had been embellished with Civil War memorabilia. Paintings of famous men and battles hung from the walls. A huge selection of ordnance and weaponry and lifelike models wearing full uniforms were on display in glass cases. A pair of cannon faced them from opposite sides of the room, bracketing a Gatling gun that had been set back behind them. Unlike the cannon, the Gatling looked to be in operational condition, except for the empty slot in the top of the shaft, meant for a rectangular magazine of cartridges.

Blaine moved to one of the cases and broke the glass with his elbow, then reached in and snatched a full clip of .58-caliber rimfire cartridges for the Gatling from the display. He eased the clip into the gun's slot until it clicked home. Liz readied the hand crank, but it flopped around in her grasp.

"We need a pin to attach this to the shaft," she said.

"Not anymore," Blaine told her, plucking one of the bobby pins that held her hair up, as the first of the gunfire slammed into the doors before them.

THIRTY-TWO

Buck Torrey hobbled through the cave, gun in hand, and listened for the murderous group that was in pursuit. He was certain at least one of them had noticed him in the cave door before the state trooper's arrival.

Buck could judge a person lots of different ways, but no way was better than how that person handled a gun. These men had done so with cold, brutal efficiency rather than practiced precision, the trooper's life clearly meaning no more to them than a cardboard target. These were killers, all right, though not men who made their living from it. It was just something they did when they needed to and would not hesitate to do again. The trooper might have been a tad slow, yet he was a pro, and still they had cut him down like a rank amateur.

And now they were coming after Buck, even more intent to find him since he was a witness to a cold-blooded murder. In ironic counterpoint, Buck figured, the trooper had likely saved him from the identical fate.

He continued on through the darkness of the cave, a key-chain penlight providing the only breaks in the blackness, and then only occasionally, so he wouldn't give his position away. The trail sloped downward for a time, the passageway narrowing and shrinking, his descent underground measured by the drop in air temperature.

He had sixteen bullets to use on them, and a bum leg guaranteed to cut down dramatically on his mobility. That against a force of six, five men and a woman. His best bet under the circumstances might be to lay an ambush. Wait for them to pass and come out blasting. But Buck had the feeling these men were too good to fall for that.

So he limped on, using the wall for support now, hoping to find a route through the cave back to ground level. Put as much distance between them and him, and then—

The ground dropped away, and Buck went tumbling. He tried to relax into the fall as he thumped down what felt like a straight drop, engulfed by darkness, until he at last struck bottom. His bad leg had been bent beneath him, doubling his agony and stitching a grimace across his face. He willed himself not to cry out.

He lay there gasping for air and trying to get past the pain. After what felt like a few seconds—though Buck was too disoriented to be sure—he rose in wobbly fashion, needing desperately to get his bearings, switched on his penlight, and shone it about.

He found himself in a symmetrical underground chamber, which must have been an old coal mine carved out of a mountain. There were piles of debris and rocks everywhere, clumps that looked like mounds in the ground's surface.

Lots of hiding places, Buck thought, turning his penlight off when he heard voices approaching.

"Stay back!" Jack Tyrell had ordered Mary at the entrance they had found to the mine.

"No!" she resisted adamantly. "It's *here*, in this mine! I've got to show you!"

He planted his hands against her shoulders. "We'll find it!"

"You believe me, don't you?"

"Never doubted you for an instant," he assured, which wasn't enough to keep Mary from following slightly behind them along the trail.

"I'll stay back with her," Othell Vance offered.

"Sorry. We'll need you when we get there, tell us if it's the Devil's Brew or not that's waiting."

"Jesus," Vance returned fearfully. "How could it have ended up in a goddamn mine?"

"Left for safekeeping, maybe," Jack Tyrell suggested. "Somebody beating us to the punch."

"No! I'm telling you it wasn't like that! And who was that guy we saw?"

"A witness—that's all that matters."

And then the gunfire began blazing at them.

Buck fired into the advancing streams of light, hoping he'd get lucky. The return fire came almost immediately, kicking up dust in all directions. Buck grabbed his pistol and rolled, ignoring the raging pain in his leg and firing back into the darkness with only muzzle flashes to indicate his targets.

He fired judiciously, trying to conserve his bullets, until he found cover behind one of the raised mounds of dirt, the result of a miner's hard labors long ago. Eight bullets left now, which he had to make enough.

"Is anyone hit?" Jack Tyrell whispered hoarsely. "Is everyone all right? Mary!"

"I'm okay, I'm okay!"

"Who is this guy, Jack?" Othell Vance whined. "Who the fuck is he?"

Jack knew the man was good, something special, even. About as far from the yokel cop they had cut down as it got.

"Othell, you told me the government pulled its people out, gave up the search."

"You think he's one of ours? Jesus, our guys carry metal detectors, not guns."

Jack shrugged. In the darkness he couldn't see Tremble or the twins, but he could feel them nearby all the same; they'd closed protectively around him at the first sign of fire. Then he sensed Mary coming up close against him, could hear her rapid breathing and smell the lilac scent of her hair.

"We should leave, Jackie. We should go." Mary tugged at him, pulling in the direction of the path she had found that led down here.

"I thought you said we were close."

"We are."

"Then what—"

A second burst of gunshots sent Jack diving to the ground, taking Mary down under him.

Buck had aimed this time at the sounds of muttering drifting out from the darkness, four irreplaceable bullets expended toward very uncertain results. He had burrowed under the dirt and debris to get closer to the grouping of voices, stifling his urge to cough and contriving to leave himself the widest possible escape route.

The walls and the ceiling were shedding veils of dust and dirt. He could feel it stinging his eyes and lodging in his scalp before he started pulling himself through the camouflage.

Buck remembered the tunnels of Vietnam, remembered the way scout teams known as "tunnel rats" described how it looked like nothing was holding those tunnels up and the feeling when small-arms fire made one collapse. The dirt piling up, burying you alive.

He continued to move slowly, barely ruffling even the dirt beneath him when the anguished scream pierced the silence of the cave.

✿   ✿   ✿

"**O**thell!" Jack Tyrell wailed. "Othell, where the fuck are you?"

Unable to still his shaking, Othell Vance shuffled out from behind the dirt mound he was using for cover and moved toward the flashlight that had suddenly switched on.

"Mary's hurt, Othell! Mary's hurt bad!"

Othell wanted to ask him what he was supposed to do, since all he knew about medicine came from a couple of biology courses way back in college. But that would be pointless now, and Jack in his panicked state might well kill him if he said anything at all.

Othell Vance reached Tyrell as he lowered Mary gingerly to the ground. Even in the near darkness Othell could see the desperate plea in his eyes.

"Do something! You've got to do something!"

Othell lowered his ear against the woman's chest. There was no movement, no breath sounds.

"Give me your flashlight."

Jack Tyrell handed it over. "She wanted to leave. She told me we should go. She must have seen this."

Othell was cocking Mary's head upward to check her pupils when he felt the thin ooze of blood near her temple.

Tyrell had sunk to his knees, as helpless as a baby. "Why didn't I listen to her? *Why didn't I goddamn listen!*"

"There's nothing we can do, Jackie," Othell said, trying to sound more compassionate than terrified.

But Jack Tyrell had already gotten that mad look in his eyes, brushing the long stringy hair from his face as if to clear a path for his stare to reach outward in the darkness. Jackie Terror.

"Yes, there is."

Buck Torrey figured one of the rounds he got off had been fatal, and that was enough to make him stop and rethink what he was doing, sensing the sudden advantage that had swung his way. Chaos had replaced the certainty of the enemy's stand. They would be expecting him to flee now, figured they could buy themselves some time. Buck decided to cross them up. Circle round the enemy's rear flank and take out the man farthest out at the earliest possible opportunity. Then appropriate his weapon to change the odds. Defense to offense. When in doubt, attack.

But Buck didn't rush things. Even as the chaos continued, he clung to the darkness, closing ever so slowly. The circuitous route took him briefly out of view of the enemy camp, and when it returned to eyeshot, he couldn't tell how many of the small group remained.

A shape moved briefly nearby, the target he had been waiting for. He glimpsed it again and resisted the temptation to fire, the target too obscure for him to risk any shot with only four bullets left.

Buck crawled away on his stomach, pulling himself past the piles of rocks and dirt that looked to have fallen in on themselves. He could almost reach out and touch the shape's ankle, gazed up to see a face whiter than death itself, oblivious to his presence. He could take this one with his knife, save himself the bullet.

Something crunched behind him.

Buck knew then he had crawled straight into a trap, the other rail-thin ghost closing while this one served as bait. Buck spun onto his back and clacked off two of his last bullets. He hauled himself to his feet, ignoring the searing pain in the leg that had hobbled him.

The staccato burst of submachine-gun fire traced him as he stumbled away. He dove toward the ground to avoid the spray, but something like hot metal touched his side, a match flame against the skin. Buck fell, instantly dizzy and disoriented, yet he maintained the sense to pull himself on. He knew he'd been hit, the warm soak of blood already creeping through his shirt. But his legs and arms were still working, and that was the best he could hope for.

He turned onto his side in the hope of bettering his pace, the angle allowing a glimpse of one of the two ghosts darting through the darkness. Buck pulled the trigger twice more before he heard the *click*. He watched the ghost spin viciously around, howling in agony as he collapsed. The second ghost-man rushed up and grabbed the first, dragging him backward.

If only I had another bullet . . .

Disgusted, he abandoned his pistol and pushed himself on. Still moving silently and ceaselessly, he was able to pick up speed as wild shots trailed him through the darkness. He'd been here before, at least a place much like it.

Medic!

Buck had to stop himself from shouting the word as he collapsed, imagining he was back in the jungle, rolling through the mud with an M-16 hot against his chest. He took a deep easy breath and closed his eyes, hearing the distant whine of a chopper coming to haul him out.

Come on, he urged them, *hurry up. . . .*

He raised his head when they didn't show, found a huge black hulk fashioned from steel, and crawled toward the cover it promised.

Weeb was the twin who'd been shot, a mean wound that had left a bullet high in his shoulder amidst ruined shards of bone. It was bleeding profusely.

"Jackie," Othell Vance pleaded, having no idea how to bandage it or even stanch the blood, "we got to get ourselves outta here."

Tyrell was still cradling Mary in his lap, Tremble hovering protectively nearby, watching the air like a guard dog. "And leave that bastard free to escape?"

"I got him," Earl insisted from his brother's side. "I'm telling you I got him."

"Sure about that, are you?"

"I saw him go down. Put a stitch right in his spine. I don't need to see the body to know the man's dead out there."

"Man shot your brother, killed my Mary."

Earl snarled, something like a low growl rising in his throat. "Don't you think I know that?"

"Takes a lot to kill a man like that. He's not some state trooper or FBI agent. Man like this you gotta drive a stake through his heart before turning your back." Jackie Terror got to his feet. "Now Tremble and I are going after him. Finish this, one way or another. You come or not, I don't really give a shit."

Buck Torrey knew they would be coming. Crawling under the huge black tanker truck that had appeared out of nowhere wouldn't do him any good at all; not without a weapon anyway. Best thing he could do was hunker low, bury himself, and strike with his knife when they drew close enough.

Unless . . .

Buck stayed low and ducked under the truck, after all. Felt his way about until he found the gas tank. His knife was made to puncture steel, but it had trouble with the tank, ultimately bending under the strain of poking a decent-size hole. The gasoline spilled out and soaked the ground, splashing everywhere.

Buck pulled himself under the tanker, toward the cab. He could feel his wounded side stiffening, to add to the problem of his hobbled leg. He'd have to stand up when he reached the cab, and the prospect of that scared him as much as anything until he heard the enemy approaching.

"**O**thell!" yelled Tyrell. "Othell, get the fuck up here!"

"Holy shit," Vance muttered when he drew even with Tyrell, finding himself facing the tanker of Devil's Brew that had been missing for seven months now.

"This is it, isn't it?"

Vance couldn't believe his eyes. "I don't believe . . ."

"Mary found it. She was right all along, right up until the end."

Tyrell moved on ahead, Tremble and Othell Vance just behind him. Suddenly Othell stopped, sniffing the air.

"Jesus, Jackie, I think I smell—"

A figure shifted in the darkness on the far side of the tanker, its faint outline just out of range of Tyrell's flashlight. A glimpse was all he needed to raise his pistol and aim. In that instant he wanted more than anything to kill the man who had shot his Mary, so much so that he failed to hear Othell's desperate shout of warning.

"Noooooooooooooooooo!"

Jackie Terror's bullets ignited the gasoline still soaking into the ground, and instantly raging flames surrounded him. Tremble screamed, lurching back from the same kind of fire that had stolen his face. Still wailing, he whirled wildly through the mine, slapping at himself to make sure none of the flames had gotten him this time.

Jack Tyrell could feel their heat licking at his skin, trapped in the middle and not caring in the least, because Mary's killer was burning up before him. Snared by one of his bullets and now turning into a charred husk on the mine floor as Jackie watched.

It didn't bother him that he himself was going to die. He was ready, certain Mary would be waiting on the other side.

Then, suddenly, the tanker rumbled, and a white frosty mist sprayed out from nozzles hidden all along its sides. Tyrell stood stark still and the mist enveloped him, chasing the flames away with its cold, smothering them. It felt like ocean spray on his skin, and he watched while the raging fire shrank away to nothing.

"Jackie!" Othell Vance called, advancing toward him tentatively across the scorched ground. "Jackie, you all right?"

Tyrell's eyes were locked on the tanker. The fire-extinguishing spray coated it in a thin blanket of white. Made it look so pristine, he could almost forget the tanker was carrying the deadliest explosive known to man.

He turned to Vance. "We got work to do, Othell."

THIRTY-THREE

Liz held the wheeled carriage called a limber steady while Blaine worked the doubled-over bobby pin into place, attaching the crank to the Gatling gun's shaft. This time, when he turned the handle crank on the gun's right-hand side, an audible *click* sounded, indicating it was now ready to fire. Prior to being exhibited, the gun had obviously been restored to prime condition. Now, once he began turning the handle again, gravity would feed the bullets into the firing chamber, the gun firing as fast as he could churn. Its weight was balanced in the rear by a long wooden trail attached to the limber. The quickest way to rotate the gun would be to hoist the trail up, and Liz positioned herself behind Blaine in case that became necessary.

They were ready when the first of the gunmen crashed through the double doors. Blaine started turning the handle, and the Gatling's six barrels spun in a smooth rhythm, belching smoke and fire with each shell, clacking in a loud staccato. The first two gunmen through the door never knew what hit them, while the next pair managed to slide belly-down across the floor, searching futilely for cover as they tried to steady their weapons.

Blaine rotated the limber slightly to trace them with the Gatling's fire, his hand never leaving the handle. Wax dummies, glass display cases, and their contents fell to his onslaught as he sought a bead on the remaining gunmen by shifting the heavy gun to the right with Liz's help behind him.

The two who had scampered off that way opened up with submachine guns. Without sufficient cover, though, they were no match for the old rimfire cartridges, which spilled the men over one at a time. And none too soon, as Blaine's next churn coughed the jerry-rigged bobby pin out of the shaft, the crank going limp in his grasp.

McCracken took his hand off the crank and was turning toward Liz when a man shaped like a fireplug hurtled over the escalator rail and grabbed her in a single motion. He yanked her brutally backward and pressed a pistol against her head.

"Don't!" Blaine ordered, turning the Gatling on the man and thrusting his hand back onto the crank, hoping the ruse would work. He still had a third of the magazine showing, enough to be intimidating.

The man smiled and drew Liz closer against him. She looked weightless in his bulky arms. "I been waiting for this kind of opportunity for a long time. Something certain to drive my price up."

"I know you?"

"No, but I know *you*." The man's squat, muscular shape was further exaggerated by his bulbous neck and military crew cut. "Name's Dobbler."

"You working for Rentz?"

"He pays pretty well."

Blaine kept his hand steady. "He pay you enough to die?"

"I see that crank start to move again, I'll kill her, McCracken."

"Let her go, Dobbler, and you can spend what you've earned so far."

"Step away from the gun, and I let her go, McCracken. Leave this between just you and me."

Blaine met Liz's gaze and for an instant saw Buck Torrey's eyes look back, telling him she was ready.

"You said you knew me."

"That's right."

"Not very well, apparently." And Blaine made sure Dobbler could see his hand tighten on the Gatling's handle.

Something changed in Dobbler's expression, his focus redirected in the moment before Liz slammed her heel down on the instep of his nearest foot. He howled in pain and lashed her across the head with his pistol. Liz crumpled, as Blaine lifted the trail and shoved the wheeled carriage forward fast across the freshly waxed floor.

The Gatling gun was upon Dobbler before he could resteady his pistol on McCracken. His eyes bulged when Blaine rammed the barrel into his midsection and drove him backwards. Dobbler's back crashed through a glass display case, sending a host of Civil War saber swords tumbling to the floor. His gun dropped and skittered across the tile, as he fought for his footing and his breath.

The sudden burst of motion, though, had weakened one of the carriage's wheels enough for impact to strip it off. The entire carriage toppled and the clamoring Gatling staggered McCracken, freeing Dobbler to burst through the jagged remnants of the display case's glass.

Sneering, Dobbler grabbed a shiny saber off the floor. Blaine snatched a similar sword, which had fallen between the trail and the spilled Gatling, in time to block Dobbler's furious downward stroke and throw him off balance.

Blaine pushed Dobbler away and shoved him backwards. They faced off against each other blade-to-blade, tips crossed as Dobbler sidestepped. He kept his legs close together, feigning lunge after lunge to gauge McCracken's reaction.

Blaine missed with a swipe, slicing the head off a mannequin outfitted as a Union sergeant. He darted behind it as Dobbler lurched out with a thrust, the mannequin's midsection taking the impact instead of Blaine's own. Dobbler yanked the blade out before Blaine could move on him again, sweeping it around instantly in a long cutting motion. The blow at first appeared lumbering and awkward, but it picked up deadly speed after it crossed the midpoint of its diagonal slice. Blaine just managed to dodge sideways and deflected it with his own blade, trying a counter which Dobbler blocked effortlessly.

The two men pirouetted across the room, twisting and turning. Blaine assumed Dobbler's men must have disabled the museum's nighttime security force and disconnected the security system while they'd been waiting upstairs, meaning no help would be coming from either quarter.

Blaine ducked under Dobbler's next strike, and a painting brilliantly recreating a Northern field hospital was lost to his slice. Dobbler twisted inside Blaine's retaliatory thrust, toppling a glass display case full of letters home from Southern soldiers. Blaine surged over the shattered glass, feeling it crunch underfoot, but Dobbler parried a quick pair of McCracken's blows, which left the two men locked up at the hilt. Eye-to-eye now, both searched for the slightest opening that would end one of their lives.

Dobbler whirled away and Blaine darted sideways to follow him, nearly blinded by one of several spotlights aimed at a collection of interconnected paintings making up a wall mural on the foyer's western side. He pretended to slip, drawing Dobbler toward him to launch an expected diagonal slice for his throat.

Blaine waited until the last possible instant before knocking it aside, darting in at Dobbler to force him to turn into the spotlight's spill. Blinded for an instant, the smaller man's eyes narrowed, and Blaine thrust his saber out low and hard, the blade digging deep into the fleshy part of Dobbler's thigh.

Dobbler screeched in agony and tried to lash an overhead slice downward, slipping as the blood gushed out from his leg wound. Blaine twisted to avoid the strike and thrust his blade through Dobbler's shoulder. The razor-sharp tip shredded flesh and muscle. Blaine felt it nick some bone as he pushed harder on the sword and shoved Dobbler backward.

The blade emerged through the back of his shoulder and embedded itself into the wall. Dobbler tried once to pull free and wailed horribly, pinned to the paneling.

His screams were still echoing through the third floor of the museum when Blaine reached Liz.

"Are you all right?" Blaine asked.

She sat up woozily with his help. "I . . . think so," she managed. She had a nasty gash across the side of her head, near the temple. Blood dripped from it down her cheek.

Blaine eased her upright, supporting her weight. "Lean against me. We're getting out of here."

He retrieved Dobbler's pistol from the floor and held it in his free hand as they retreated out the shattered white doors and retraced their steps through the "We the People" exhibit. Liz recovered quickly and was walking almost on her own by the time they reached an emergency exit. She needed only minimal support to manage the flights of stairs down to the ground floor. Blaine quickly found a door leading back outside and tensed briefly before bursting out into the night on the Fourteenth Street side of the building.

"The van," Liz remembered.

McCracken jammed the pistol into his belt. "Never mind. We'll find another vehicle and—"

"Don't move!" a voice blared from behind them, emerging from a nest of bushes. "Don't turn around!"

Blaine and Liz froze.

"Drop the gun!"

Blaine lifted Dobbler's pistol lightly from his belt and let it plop to the soft ground.

"Now turn around. Slowly. Both of you."

They swung together, eyes widening at the sight of the figure holding an ancient Colt .44-caliber, single-action percussion revolver in his hand.

It couldn't be!

Blaine recognized the figure's thick handlebar mustache and deep-set brooding eyes from Liz's description of the ghostlike specter who had watched them from the hillside, the same face he had seen later on a picture in the Central Reading Room of the National Archives.

It was Colonel William Henry Stratton!

THIRTY-FOUR

B y late afternoon the lure of the bottle had beckoned Will Thatch
from inside the cheap motel room. He sat wearing his t-shirt, the
one suit he still owned laid neatly across the room's single bed,
the darkness broken only by the splotchy flashing of a neon sign
missing half its bulbs.

God, he needed a drink.

He had returned to Huggins' office and taken up residence behind his
desk at his keyboard, Will's files on Jack Tyrell's former soldiers pulled
from his mind instead of his memory wall. It was time to find out where
the former soldiers of Midnight Run were and who among them Tyrell
might already have contacted. Will had committed twenty-six names to
memory long before, for which he was able to track down eighteen firm
addresses. Of these an even dozen could not be found. They had quit their
jobs suddenly according to their bosses; or abandoned their apartments
according to their landlords; had their phones disconnected or simply
weren't around to answer.

They were disappearing, and it had started *four weeks ago*, right after
the funeral that had cost four men their lives in a New Jersey cemetery.

Jack Tyrell was putting his Midnight Run crew back together, the most
lunatic of the lunatic fringe, by Will's reckoning. Those who had stewed
in the underground or rotted away in prison for a while, along with a few
others, who had managed to slide into normal lives they were ready to

abandon in an instant. And that didn't even account for the fugitives so-ciety—and Will—had long lost track of.

The list lay before Will on the motel room table, aglow every time the sign flashed. He buried his face in his hands, traced each wrinkle and furrow as if he were following a map. Sooner or later some authentic FBI agent would realize who they were dealing with here, but Jack Tyrell wasn't a name that leaped to mind anymore. For now, the truth lay solely with Will Thatch, and he had no plans to disclose it just yet, not until he took a crack at picking up Tyrell's trail by himself.

But how? He had nothing to go on, besides the cold certainty that Tyrell had a lot of catching up to do and had a plan to manage just that.

It had come to Will in the early hours of the evening. Huggins thought he was crazy when he laid it out.

"You want *what*?"

Will repeated himself authoritatively.

"Why don't you just get it from your own people?"

"Because the information I want only goes back two days, to the mas-sacre. Local authorities—highway patrols and state police especially—will have much more complete reports that won't have reached Washington databases yet."

"That's gonna take some time," Huggins sighed.

"I can wait," Will had said.

The waiting would have been easier with a bottle. Will sat at the table long past sunset, imagining those first sips going hot down his throat, warming his insides. To still the trembling and the fear. Take hold of the memories and blur them a bit so the edges wouldn't be sharp enough to cut.

One bottle would take care of things. Oh yeah, just fine.

Will gazed at the phone instead, thinking of all the times over the years he'd dialed up the family the booze had stolen from him. Never said a word. Just listened to the voice and then the click. Eventually the numbers got changed.

Occasionally, when Bob Snelling tracked them down again for him, Will would dial up the new numbers. Or take a rental car out to one of his grown-up kids' homes, hoping to steal a look at his grandchildren. He never stayed long enough, though, seldom even stopped the car. Just cruised up and down the street a dozen or so times before driving off, hoping no one had seen him.

Maybe he should give Bob Snelling another call. Get the latest names and addresses, so he could tell his wife and kids what he was doing.

He had actually started to reach for the receiver, when the phone rang.

Detective Huggins hadn't been happy about meeting Will Thatch in his office at such a late hour. To his credit, the detective had assembled on a single disk all the crime reports from a dozen states that had occurred over the past forty-eight hours since the massacre at the Akron, Ohio, police station.

Thatch sorted all the domestic-type and petty crimes first and deleted them. He was looking for the kind of crimes Jack Tyrell and his soldiers had been known for the last time they'd made their presence known: unexplained disappearances, missing persons reports, kidnappings.

In the end, Will was left with three reported incidents that fit Tyrell and his people to a T:

The family of four whose Winnebago had been used to smash through the Akron, Ohio, jail were found dumped off the road just outside Cleveland.

Two trucks carrying circus animals had been commandeered, the animals released and the drivers forced to walk through the outskirts of Pittsburgh in bare feet, chained to each other.

A pair of girls driving back to college from spring break had been reported missing in central Pennsylvania. Girls meeting that description had last been seen yesterday struggling to change a tire on their GMC Jimmy. The Jimmy was missing too.

Three incidents that were right chronologically as well as geographically, occurring over a twenty-four-hour period. Will imagined Jack Tyrell heading southeast from Ohio. Continuing the same line in his mind, he found no other police reports that fit Tyrell's style at all. So with any luck at all, he hadn't left central Pennsylvania yet.

And with a little more, Tyrell would still be there when Will Thatch arrived.

THIRTY-FIVE

said don't move or I'll kill you right here! Stop you from telling the world!"

"Telling the world *what*?" Blaine asked the man who was the exact image of William Henry Stratton.

"The gold! You're bringing it all back, doing everything you can to destroy my family name!"

"Who are you?" Liz demanded.

"I won't let you," the man said, instead of responding. "I've worked too hard to bury the past to let anyone dig it up now!"

"The traps!" Blaine realized. "The barbed wire under the lake—it was *you* who planted it!"

"And it worked! For years it kept everyone from pulling up the treasure! . . . Until you showed up."

"You wasted your time: there's no treasure under that lake."

"Bullshit! It's there, and if someone finds it—"

"They're not going to find it, because William Henry Stratton and his convoy got away," Blaine said, as much to Liz as to the stranger.

"No! He was never heard from again! He stole the gold and died on that farm!"

"He didn't steal the gold at all," Blaine insisted, "and I can prove it."

✧ ✧ ✧

"**Y**ou, drive!" Stratton's replica ordered Liz when they reached the corner of Fourteenth Street and Constitution Avenue, where his car was parked. Then he gestured for Blaine to join him in the back seat, his old Colt .44 still aimed dead-on.

Liz waited for both doors to close behind her before starting the engine and shifting into gear. She pulled out into the street and then jammed on the brake in the same instant Blaine's right hand knocked the pistol aside. The Colt roared and a flash illuminated the interior. The window behind the stranger exploded as Blaine cracked his free hand into the man's face, catching him in the nose. Before the man could respond, Blaine snatched the revolver from his grasp.

The man's watering eyes regarded it fearfully.

"All right," McCracken said, dropping the Colt into the front seat next to Liz. "Who are you?"

The man was holding his nose, his fingers red with blood. "Farley Stratton," he said in a nasal tone. "The colonel's great-great-grandson."

"Okay, Farley, what would you say if I told you I could clear the colonel's name?"

The man pulled his hands from his nose and let the blood drop freely. "That you're crazy. My family has lived with the disgrace of Stratton's Folly for a hundred and thirty-five years. The legend nearly destroyed us, but so long as it stayed a legend we could at least live in peace."

"That's why you booby-trapped the lake," Liz said from the driver's seat.

"Yes! Where the gold ended up after he stole it."

"Wrong," said McCracken. "Everything William Henry Stratton did complied with the orders of President Lincoln himself."

"Lincoln *ordered* him to steal the gold?"

"No. Lincoln *gave* him the gold as a settlement he was supposed to deliver to representatives from the South."

"What kind of settlement?" Liz asked before Stratton had a chance to.

"The kind you make when you're suing for peace, ready to accede to your enemy's demands."

"Lincoln was *surrendering*?" Stratton asked incredulously.

"He ordered a quarter-million gold coins minted in secret just days after a meeting with representatives of the Northern industrialists who were actually running the war effort. Ten-dollar gold pieces missing the 'United States of America' on their tail because they had been minted *for the Confederacy*. As a *payoff*, since the gold in the Northern treasury must not have been enough. That gold was loaded in its own strong boxes in the heavy load wagons, along with the four keg chests containing the freshly minted coins." Blaine tightened his gaze, looking at Liz briefly before turning back toward Stratton. "Your great-great-grandfather was sent to deliver the gold and the coins, along with the official surrender documents, to representatives of the South."

"What's the difference? He still stole it!"

"No, he didn't. Stratton's Folly was all a ruse, a plot hatched by Lincoln to get the Northern business leaders off his back. Your ancestor was never supposed to make that rendezvous in the South at all. His orders were to make it seem like he had stolen the treasure, so Lincoln would have no choice but to continue the war effort. Those orders included murdering the civilian detachment that was bringing along the accession papers."

Farley Stratton's mouth had dropped in shock. He was trembling slightly. "Prove it."

"Help me."

"How?"

"The route he was supposed to take. You must know *something*."

"It doesn't matter. He never got there. He never left that farm."

"He did, I tell you. The convoy—and the treasure—were lost somewhere else."

Stratton blinked his eyes rapidly. "But I don't know where he could have gone! The storm would have made him change his route, deviate from the original plans."

"Give me a ballpark destination."

"Pennsylvania," Farley Stratton said, after a pause. "He planned on heading north through Pennsylvania. It was in a letter he wrote. Just that much."

"Good."

"What now?"

"Get out."

"But—"

"Do as I say!" Blaine ordered, reaching across Stratton to throw open the door.

Stratton slipped out reluctantly, still holding his nose.

"If I'm right," Blaine told him, "there'll be proof, and I'll bring it to you."

"How will you find—"

"Don't worry." Blaine swung back toward Liz. "Go!"

She screeched away from the curb. "Where we going?"

"To pick up my friend Johnny. Then to have a talk with the last man your father saw before he disappeared."

4

DEVIL'S BREW

THIRTY-SIX

"We'd like you to move away from the window, sir," one of his bodyguards told Maxwell Rentz as he surveyed the view of Paradise Village from his penthouse apartment.

But Rentz had more important things on his mind than worrying about his safety.

"Still nothing from Dobbler?" he asked a second bodyguard, trying to hide his concern when the man shook his head.

Rentz had come to think of the three bodyguards Dobbler had hired to supplement his own security force as the Three Bears. He had secured himself with them in the high-tech confines of Paradise Village. Until he could make more permanent arrangements tomorrow, holing up here was the best he could come up with. He even began to think he might be writing the best commercial for the facility yet: based on what he had learned in the past day, if these walls could keep Blaine McCracken out, then maybe there was hope for him to revitalize the project. The irony was striking. Even his father would have approved of his grit. Refusing to give up in the face of utter failure.

It all came down to how far you were willing to go to get what you wanted. After Dobbler finished with McCracken, the plan was for him to "borrow" Liz Halprin's son for as long as it took the woman to come to her senses. Now Rentz was beginning to fear that it was McCracken who had finished Dobbler, in which case he had come to the right place to get through the night.

Rentz had managed to get twenty men to Paradise Village, a combination of the private force that patrolled the facility and the company that handled security for his office building. Additionally, all gates had been sealed, Paradise Village closed off behind the ten-foot brick-and-cobblestone wall that enclosed it. Electronic surveillance kept a constant watch on every inch of space, alerted by any stray movement. Armed patrols crisscrossed the streets in Jeeps, their firepower increased for the night.

Rentz had chosen for himself and the Three Bears an eighth-floor, fully furnished model penthouse where he could look out over half the community. The steel-core doors were outfitted with cobalt locks programmed for keypad entry only. The windows could withstand anything up to a shotgun shell and, with the hurricane shutters in place, a forty-millimeter grenade.

Since this had always been intended as his personal residence, the king living amongst his people, the penthouse was also equipped with a miniature version of the main security deck: a converted closet containing a built-in console featuring three closed-circuit monitor screens that provided a rotating view of the grounds. Rentz had stationed one of the Bears behind the console to be his eyes as the long evening wound down.

In spite of the other Bear's warning, he remained by the window, gazing out over his domain, refusing to concede anything within its confines.

Come and get me, he urged McCracken, as he stared out into the night. *Just try it. . . .*

Bear Number One swung from behind the monitoring station. "Security reports a couple of vagrants just outside the main entrance."

Rentz headed over. "Bring it up on-screen."

The middle screen of the three built into the console showed the vagrants seated against the high wall, their clothes tattered and stiff with soil.

"Get them out of here. Last thing we need tonight is distractions."

"Yes, sir."

"And after you've done that, run another status check. Anything seems out of place, no matter how small, I want to know about it."

Rentz moved back to the window, reviewing his options if Dobbler had been removed from the picture for good. The Three Bears were good men, certainly capable enough to handle the simple kidnapping of a child. But Rentz questioned if they were good enough to deal with McCracken.

"Mr. Rentz!" Bear Number One called a few minutes later. "There's a problem in sector one."

"What is it?" Rentz asked, hustling over.

"An intrusion of some kind, but I've got nothing on my screen."

"Small animals set the motion sensors off sometimes. That's probably it."

The man touched a hand to his headpiece. "Wait a minute—we got a report of a man down."

"Where?"

"Same sector."

"Find it, goddamn it!"

Rentz grabbed a second headset and fitted it over his ears, watching tensely as Bear Number One searched through the camera views of sector one without success.

"A mobile patrol is responding."

"I can hear for myself!" Rentz snapped at him.

On screen number three, a Jeep with two men inside streaked toward the scene. Rentz followed the Jeep's progress on screen number two, but then it vanished from sight.

"Patrol Two approaching coordinates," Rentz heard in his headset. *"Patrol One, do you copy?"*

Silence.

"Patrol One, do you copy?"

Rentz and the Bear behind the console looked blankly at each other.

"Er, Central, I'm having trouble raising Patrol One."

"We had Patrol One on visual just a few minutes ago," the central monitor in Paradise Village's security headquarters told Patrol Two.

"Where?"

"Returning from main entrance."

"Wait a minute, there he is! There's our downed man!"

"Where?" Rentz demanded. "Where?"

"Patrol Two, this is Central. We don't show you on-screen. State your locale."

Silence again.

"Patrol Two, this is Central. Do you copy?"

"Central, this is Rentz. Converge on and close off that area."

"Roger th—"

"Central, are you there? Central, come in."

Rentz felt something icy grip his insides. His legs felt heavy. The floor of the penthouse seemed to waver. Two Bears remained by the windows, peering outward.

"Get away from those fucking windows!" Rentz ordered them.

"Jesus fucking Christ . . ."

"What is it, Central? What do you see?"

"Bring up camera eighteen. Repeat, the view from camera eighteen!"

Rentz watched as his Bear behind the console complied. All three screens filled with a shot of a Jeep in flames against the security wall, two of his men still inside it, slumped toward the dashboard.

"That's Patrol Two!" the monitor reported, his voice panic-stricken.

"Where's Patrol One? Have you sealed off the area? . . . Central, goddamn it, is sector one sealed off? . . . *Central, where the fuck are you?"*

"They're not responding, Mr. Rentz," the Bear behind his console told him.

"I can fucking well hear that for myself. What's going on?"

"Everybody's talking to everybody else, sir. Could be the circuits are overloaded."

"Bullshit!" Rentz jammed himself against the back of the Bear's chair. "Bring up the main entrance again!"

A few clicks on the keyboard and it replaced the burning Jeep on screen, showing the shabbily dressed vagrants still in place.

"Patrol One got rid of them. That was the report. What happened?"

Rentz was still staring at the screen seconds later when one of the vagrants slumped against the other, not drunk but unconscious. The second vagrant didn't respond at all, obviously unconscious too.

"Close in!" Rentz ordered the Bear behind the console.

The Bear worked the zoom command, and the faces of the two vagrants filled the screen.

They weren't the same men he had glimpsed earlier! They were—

"Oh my God," Rentz muttered. "Those are my men!"

"Patrol One," said the Bear.

Rentz backed away from the console, straying as far as the cord of his headset allowed. "He's inside the complex! McCracken's inside the complex! Close the hurricane shutters," he ordered the Bear nearest the control panel.

The man flicked a button, and the steel-colored slats unfolded downward from the ceiling, turning the room into a well-lit vault.

"Put me on-line," he ordered the Bear behind the console. "I want to talk to everyone we've got down there."

The Bear worked his keyboard, stopped, then tried again. "I can't raise them, sir," he said tentatively.

"What do you mean, you can't raise them?"

"They're gone."

"*All* of them?"

"Or cut off. Like someone shut down the system."

"Turn it back on."

"I can't, sir. It can only be changed from the operations center."

"One of you has to head over there, then. That's all."

The Bears looked at each other.

"That wouldn't be advisable, sir," one of them said.

"It might be exactly what the intruder *wants*," added another.

"What about the guards downstairs in *this* building?" Rentz raised.

The third Bear showed him a walkie-talkie clipped to his waist. "They're the only ones on this channel."

"We could send one of them out into the complex," suggested the second. "Have him round up as many of the other guards as he can find."

"What if there aren't any others left?" Rentz shot back.

"Wait a minute," said Bear Number One, eyeing the console. "One of our Jeeps just turned onto this street."

"Christ, are those our guys inside?" another of his Bears wondered, as Rentz got close enough to study the screen.

Suddenly the Jeep picked up speed. It screeched forward, screaming toward the building lobby and crashing through the glass. The guards inside opened fire, riddling the Jeep's frame with bullets, not a speck of glass left in its windows when they finally approached the vehicle.

Bear Number One tightened the camera angle on the inside of the cab, as the guards neared it warily. "Christ, I think those are our guys. I think they just shot our own people!"

A shape popped up from the ruined husk of the Jeep and opened fire through the shot-out windshield, mowing down the three guards who strayed into his path before turning his weapon on the camera. The scene on-screen died.

Rentz stared at each of the Three Bears in turn. "One of you take the elevator, another the stairs. The third stays with me."

Bears Two and Three rushed to the door and keyed in the proper combo to activate the cobalt locks. They spun out into the hall and then rushed toward the end where the elevator and stairs were located. Rentz peered out briefly to watch them, then resealed the door. The final Bear stood protectively near him.

Seconds later, Rentz heard from one of the Bears through the walkie-talkie clipped to his belt. "The elevator's coming up."

Rentz snatched the walkie-talkie to his lips. "What about the stairs?"

"I'm right outside the door," reported the final Bear. "All's quiet."

"The elevator's stopping."

"Christ," Rentz muttered, and jammed the walkie-talkie against his face hard enough to make his ear sting.

"The door's opening. If anyone's in there, I'll—"

A noose knotted around Rentz's insides. "What is it? What's going on?"

"The compartment's empty."

"What about the roof over it?"

"No signs of alteration," the Bear reported. "Do you want me to check it?"

"No, just shut it down. What about the stairs?"

"Still nothing," came the voice of the Bear posted there.

"Lock the door. I want both of you back here!"

Rentz moved to the monitor screen and followed their progress back down the hall. As soon as they had reached the door, he moved to the pad and keyed in the proper combo to release the inner cobalt seals. Rentz heard a hollow metallic snap and then the door clicked open.

As Rentz turned to watch the two Bears enter, the hurricane shutters blew inward. It was the loudest sound he had ever heard, the percussion enough to yank his legs out and send him crashing to the thick carpet. He clutched his ears as jagged holes appeared in the space-age titanium.

The two Bears, still holding their submachine guns, had gone down too, but still managed to open up with dual sprays at the chasms where the scorched and smoking metal had been peeled away. The bullets that didn't find the chasms pinged off the steel; dull flashes spilled backwards. The night air flooded into the room, drenching the penthouse with a stiff breeze.

Ears still ringing, Rentz crawled across the debris-strewn carpet to a toppled desk for cover.

Pffffft . . . pffffft . . . pffffft . . .

The soft spits were barely audible but still enough to make Rentz twist around. His two Bears, still grasping their submachine guns, lay on the carpet with blood already pooling beneath their heads. The third Bear, closest to him behind the desk, was sitting upright against the wall, eyes glazed over and seeming to stare at the jagged hole centered in his forehead.

"So much for the ultimate in high-security complexes."

Rentz turned toward the speaker and saw the man he recognized only from a picture standing just inside the door he had neglected to seal, a still-smoking silenced pistol held dead on him. A much larger shape loomed outside on the balcony, visible only in the splashes of light filtering through the jagged holes in the hurricane shutters.

"Nice to meet you finally, Max," Blaine greeted, gazing down at him.

Rentz stumbled to his feet and backed up against the wall. He could barely breathe.

"I've got a question for you, Max. Ready?"

Rentz nodded.

"Do you want to live or die? Come on, the clock's ticking. . . ."

"Live."

"Very good. Now tell me what happened to Buck Torrey."

Rentz regarded him quizzically.

"Liz Halprin's father," Blaine continued. "I believe he paid you a visit too."

"He forced his way into my office, broke my assistant's arm."

"Then what?"

"He left."

"Alive?"

"He warned me what would happen if I didn't leave his daughter alone."

"Obviously you didn't listen."

Rentz stiffened, clenched his jaw.

"And you know what? It's all for nothing, because the gold's not under that lake."

Rentz's mouth dropped. "That can't be right. I spent tens of thousands of dollars following the trail. It's *got* to be there, I tell you!"

"You tell that to Buck Torrey?"

"He didn't care. He wanted to know about Stratton's Folly, the entire legend, the route Stratton was taking when the blizzard hit."

"Tell me what you told him," Blaine ordered.

"There was a train waiting in a small town in western Pennsylvania. I've got a map of Stratton's planned route through the center of the state—"

"*Central* Pennsylvania?" Blaine asked, something fluttering inside him. Something Hank Belgrade had said months before on the steps of the Lincoln Memorial, minutes before Blaine's life had changed forever at the Washington Monument.

Belgrade's missing tanker of Devil's Brew had been heading through central Pennsylvania too!

"From the farm that would have been the most direct route, but I'm telling you he never took it!" Rentz insisted. "He couldn't have, because he never got to the station. I've got the records. The train never departed."

"No," Blaine said softly. "Because something else happened to Stratton along the way."

THIRTY-SEVEN

ask you a question, Indian?" Blaine asked Johnny Wareagle after they had settled back into their car.

For Wareagle, that wasn't always a simple task. Car interiors weren't designed with men of seven-foot, three-hundred-pound proportions in mind. But amazingly Johnny never seemed to have to squeeze, as if he could enable his body to conform to whatever the specs allowed.

"Go ahead, Blainey."

McCracken gazed down at the ring he hadn't taken off since leaving Condor Key. "Dead Simple. You ever think about what it means?"

"Different things to different people."

"Buck told me I had it wrong."

"What did you tell him?"

"The obvious. I always took the words at face value."

"How simple it was for us to kill . . ."

"Because it had to be."

"A convenient explanation, because the times required it."

"You saying the definition changed?"

"Not changed so much as evolved, Blainey. The words were what we needed them to be in the Hellfire. They became what we needed them to be after." Johnny's owl-like eyes bored into Blaine's. "What you needed them to be recently."

"Such as?"

"In the Hellfire, it was killing that had to be simple for us. Now it's living we must make simple."

"Living," Blaine echoed, not exactly sure what Johnny meant.

"When did Buck Torrey give us the rings?"

"After our final tours were up."

"After the slogan in its most basic meaning would have no further use . . ."

"Right."

"And we were returning to a world against which we could not possibly measure the one we had left. The only way we could endure was to learn to live as simply as we had learned to kill. With the same detachment, patience, and skill. Trim all the fat aside and be left with only that which matters."

Blaine sighed. "Doesn't sound like either of us got that message."

"At least not right away. My understanding came when I finally left the world for the woods."

"And mine?"

"What did you go to Buck Torrey seeking?"

"Another chance."

"Because your life had been trimmed to the bare bones, ready to be rebuilt, remade."

"Starting from scratch—that's what it felt like."

"You went down there to face your greatest challenge: to overcome the one person who could destroy you."

"Like the warrior you told me about in the hospital, who lost to his own reflection."

"He didn't lose, Blainey; he survived and became even stronger as a result and more ready to face battle."

"You forget to tell me that part of the story?"

"I waited."

Blaine felt his mind drifting a little. "This battle's different for me."

"They are all different."

"This time I've got something to prove, Indian. Buck gave me this chance, and unless I find him I've wasted it."

"Even the greatest hunter is lost without a trail, Blainey."

"I think I've got one now."

THIRTY-EIGHT

hree hours later, just after eight A.M., Blaine rose when Hank Belgrade wearily approached his stone bench set in the center of the FDR Memorial.

"You shouldn't have," Hank said, noticing the box of doughnuts waiting by Blaine's feet.

"I brought coffee too, but it got cold. Not like you to be late."

"I forgot you said FDR. Went to the Lincoln Memorial by mistake. Out of habit."

"I figured it was time for a change."

"For both of us."

They sat down together on the bench. An elegant statue of Franklin Delano Roosevelt seemed to be studying them intently from his chair nestled comfortably in a wall formed of polished granite that matched the bench. Another granite wall directly ahead featured a fountain perpetually cascading water into a small pool. After walking up to the FDR Memorial by way of the Tidal Basin, Blaine had tossed a half-dozen pennies into the pool, but he had stopped short of making a wish. This was one of several individual displays composing the memorial, arranged chronologically, with each representing a different stage of FDR's life and presidency.

"Seven months we don't see each other, and that's all you've got to say?"

Belgrade frowned, his jowls more bulbous than ever. "You wanna check my schedule, see where I can squeeze in more social calls, be my guest."

"That what you think this is?"

"Word is you're out."

"Word also is I'm dead."

Belgrade raised the box of doughnuts to his lap and opened the box to check the selection. "No jelly?"

"Not very forgiving on the suit."

"I appreciate the consideration." Belgrade crossed his legs. "I'm glad you asked to meet here. We left too many memories on the steps of the Lincoln. All the information you asked me to get for you, all the deliveries I made."

"You sound nostalgic."

"I know how bad it was for you, that's all. Daily conference calls with your doctors. I sent specialists over there, don't forget. Candy too."

"Exactly why I want to return the favor. How'd you like your Devil's Brew back?"

"Why, you got it?" Hank smiled.

"Not yet."

Belgrade caught the look in Blaine's eyes and nearly let the doughnuts spill from his lap. "Am I hearing you right?"

"I've got a pretty good idea where to find it, Hank."

"Reminds me of the good old days back at the Lincoln. . . ."

"You have a map of your rig's planned route?"

Belgrade looked disappointed. "I got a hundred of them, complete with a detailed schema of every area we searched."

"I only need one."

"I'm telling you you're wasting your time on that count, MacNuts."

"You also told me the tanker fell off the face of the earth."

"So it seemed at the time."

"Because maybe that's exactly what happened," Blaine told him. "How much do you know about the Civil War, Hank?"

"The North won."

"There's more."

"How we gonna get that tanker out of this mine, Othell?" Jack Tyrell asked.

They both looked over as Lem Trumble slammed the hood closed. "Smooth working order," he said softly. "No damage from the fire."

"Well, we can't just drive it out of here," said Othell Vance. "Not unless we want to spend a half day digging it out."

The entrance they had found to the mine was concealed by brush and overhanging vegetation that almost totally camouflaged it. Only during a storm, with the brush and vines soaked and blowing, would the entrance be visible at all.

Based on the way the tanker's tires had sunk into the ground inside the cavern, Tyrell figured the driver must have taken refuge in there during just such a storm. But why hadn't he driven the tanker out again when the storm broke?

"What do we need?" Tyrell asked Vance.

"I don't know. A crane, I guess."

"Or a winch, maybe?"

"Yeah, that'll do."

Jack Tyrell smiled as he slid his hand down the length of the huge tanker. It was like a standard oil truck, but it had catwalks on either side and all kind of spigots and bleeder valves he couldn't quite identify. Tapping it with a rock drew a dull clang instead of a metallic ping, evidence of a heavily armored shell that could withstand anything up to a full rocket attack. That explained why the brief fire had caused no damage whatsoever and why the Devil's Brew within remained intact. The extra-wide tires, as near as he could tell, were solid rubber; no flats or blowouts to slow the rig down.

Tyrell tapped it almost tenderly and started down the tunnel toward the opening they had found that led to a plateau atop a ridge.

"Where you going?" Vance asked him.

"To get you that winch you need."

"**Y**ou wanna back up, give me this again?" Belgrade asked, fidgeting on his side of the bench now. A few tourists had arrived at the FDR Memorial and were snapping pictures. But he seemed not to notice them.

"All right," Blaine started. "Stratton's convoy waits out the blizzard on the Halprin farm and heads north the next morning when the storm breaks, to make their train. Trouble is, in Pennsylvania they run into a *second* storm, the one in which Bull Run flooded the valley and created the lake on Liz Halprin's farm. So Stratton has no choice but to look for shelter again."

"In the middle of nowhere." Belgrade nodded.

"In the middle of central Pennsylvania," Blaine corrected. "Now fast-forward a hundred and thirty-five years. An almost identical storm comes up when it's too late for your Red Dog crew in the tanker to turn back. They take a wrong turn somewhere, get lost, and end up diverting from their planned route, in the same area of Pennsylvania where Stratton's convoy found itself."

"And you're saying they'd want to find shelter too. Problem is where."

"You nod off during geography class, Hank?"

"What did I miss?"

"The lesson about this part of Pennsylvania being loaded with coal mines, specifically anthracite coal, which means deep veins that have helped turn the landscape into a wasteland. Severe storms like the ones we're talking about can cause severe erosion, enough maybe to expose the opening to one of those abandoned mines. Make a pretty inviting sight for anybody desperately in need of shelter. And all that ore mixed in with the topsoil would also explain why your satellite reconnaissance and flyovers never found a thing."

Belgrade weighed the ramifications of Blaine's theory. "The trouble with all this is that nobody ever saw Stratton again, and now the same thing has happened to my tanker of Devil's Brew. You mind telling me what happened after both came in from the rain to stop them from coming out again?"

"Get me that map of Red Dog's route," Blaine said, "and I'll find out for you."

Jack Tyrell and Othell Vance watched the trio of Pennsylvania State Police cars tear across the hillside, closely followed by a heavy-framed tow truck with a winch visible in its rear.

"I told you I'd get you one."

"I don't know. It's awful risky."

"Relax: I got everything thought out."

Tyrell had called 911 from the now camouflaged cruiser belonging to the dead trooper, claimed he was a trucker who just saw a state police car down a steep grade, all busted up. Three cruisers was one more than he expected, but still easily dealt with. The Yost brothers and Tremble could easily silence them before they could summon additional reinforcements. Tyrell intended to keep at least one of the troopers alive well into the morning, long enough to fabricate reports at the right intervals. He figured that would buy him the few hours he needed to get the tanker winched up and be on his way.

"Where'd you tell him you saw the cruiser?" Othell Vance asked him.

"Right about there," Tyrell replied, as the highway patrol cars slowed in unison, beginning a slow crawl along the edge of the road.

"Any second now," Jack said to Othell, waiting for Tremble and the Yost twins to make their move.

THIRTY-NINE

laine, Liz, and Johnny Wareagle had flown to a small airport out-side Harrisburg and then picked up the trail by car. They had left Sal Belamo back at the farm, on the chance that Maxwell Rentz would come looking for revenge.

After obtaining Red Dog's intended route from Hank Belgrade, Blaine had approximated the most likely places where the tanker could have taken a wrong turn and matched them up with the map provided by Maxwell Rentz of William Henry Stratton's planned trek through Pennsylvania. He then used an extremely detailed geological map of the region to narrow the search further by pinpointing old coal-mining veins large enough to accommodate a massive tanker and a Civil War heavy convoy.

One way or another, Buck Torrey must have done pretty much the same thing before he set out after the lost gold. Then, like Stratton and the Devil's Brew, Buck had disappeared. Find them, Blaine hoped, and he would find Buck.

But it wasn't going to be easy. The Valley and Ridge region of central Pennsylvania was unusually rugged land, dominated by lazy hills that had been stripped of their minerals. This entire piece of the world looked as though it was dying a slow, lingering death. The farther west they searched, the uglier and meaner the land became, marked by the occasional town and the dry, pockmarked surface of a landscape that might have been a foreign planet.

They had been back and forth across this area in vain, and Blaine was starting to figure all his efforts were going for naught, when Johnny Wareagle leaned forward suddenly.

"Up ahead on the right, Blainey," Johnny said. "Something's going on."

Even with the tow truck in their possession and in place, it had taken Jack Tyrell and the others several hours to clear the opening and dig the tanker out enough so it could be winched from the mine. As planned, Earl Yost had kept one of the troopers alive to issue regular reports, until he tried to escape and Weeb Yost shot him. Tyrell feared more troopers would soon be dispatched and knew he had to prepare for that eventuality.

The fact that the dead troopers were all big men had provided the germ of the idea. He, Othell, and the twins put on the dead troopers' uniforms, while Lem Trumble squeezed his huge frame into the tow truck driver's overalls. The blood from Weeb Yost's wounded shoulder kept soaking through his uniform top, and Tyrell solved this by having him wear a jacket over it, which also concealed his sling. Dressed that way now, they would seem like public servants doing no more than their jobs. Tyrell even had the two cruisers that hadn't been shot up too badly parked just down the hill to add to the illusion, hoping anyone who passed by wouldn't notice the bullet holes.

Just before noon, Jack Tyrell walked through the freshly cleared opening with the winch cable in hand and attached it to the tanker's chassis.

"Start the winch," he yelled up to Othell Vance.

"You better come up here, Jackie," Othell replied at once.

"I will. Soon as I make sure the line's secure."

"Better come up now."

Blaine drove down a narrow curving road cut out from the surrounding hillsides, pockmarked by the coal mining of years past.

"What are they doing here?" Liz asked, when the state troopers came clearly into view. They were tending to a tow truck parked on a sloped ridge that was inaccessible to anything but a four-wheel-drive vehicle.

"The better question is why did they bring a winch with them?" Blaine followed, meeting Johnny Wareagle's stare.

He pulled their car to a halt between the two police cruisers, had barely exited the car just ahead of Liz when a black trooper approached them from the ridge.

"I help you folks?" he asked, his feet kicking up clouds of dust as he slid down the last stretch of the way on his heels.

"I think we're lost," Blaine said, faking a worried expression and a lumbering gait. The way he had moved before Buck Torrey worked his magic.

"You're somewhere you don't want to be, mister."

"I'll say," Blaine agreed, clumsily unfolding a map as he extended it toward the trooper. "Last I knew, we were here."

The trooper had just started to lean forward when Blaine jabbed the pistol into his gut.

"Cops don't wear work boots," he noted, eyes half on the ridge, where he saw two other pairs of eyes, glaring down out of the sun. "And those chips in that cruiser's windshield came from bullets, not road debris. Why don't we walk up the hill? Talk about who you boys really are. Take it easy and act like you're leading us, or I'll shoot you right here." He kept hold of the map to obscure his drawn gun, as they started up toward the ridge.

"This is about to become the worst day of your lives," the trooper said, glancing at Liz and Johnny Wareagle.

"We'll see," Blaine said, and prodded him forward.

Two more men dressed as troopers were waiting when Blaine reached the top of the ridge. Liz and Johnny instinctively moved to either side of him and his prisoner. The tow truck had been backed up close to a mouth-shaped opening in the earth, its winch cable having already been swallowed, attached to something out of view.

One of the troopers, wearing a hat that sat unevenly atop his head, faked a smile and narrowed his eyes.

"Something wrong, friend?"

McCracken let him see the gun pressed into Othell Vance's ribs. "You don't make a very convincing cop."

"Shit, that's the nicest thing anyone's said to me in the longest time." Jack Tyrell swept the hat from his head and let his hair fall back to his shoulders. "I never liked pigs anyway."

Their eyes met for the first time, and Blaine felt his pulse quicken. He remembered the hate and madness in those eyes all too well. The man before him had appeared bald then, an excellent disguise that might have worked if Blaine hadn't been keeping a mental image of his eyes for what felt like a lifetime now.

"Wait a minute," the man in front of McCracken said, taking a single step forward. He stopped and rotated his right hand before him, inspecting the jagged scar that started at the back of his hand and extended through his palm. Then he fixed his gaze on Blaine again. His mad eyes seemed to glisten as he smiled. "Hey, long time no see."

"Not long enough," Blaine said to the man who had taken over the Washington Monument seven months earlier.

FORTY

got to hand it to you," said Jack Tyrell, "the way you blasted your way inside the Monument. I thought about that, you know. I just didn't think anybody besides me was crazy enough to try it."

"I'm full of surprises."

"Anyway, I owe you a favor."

"Really?"

"See, back in Washington I was ready to end things. Push that button and say hello to eternity."

"More like hell . . ."

"But thanks to you, I didn't. Without you being around then, I wouldn't be able to set things right now. That puts me in your debt, friend, which is why I'm going to let you go."

"How's your hand?"

"Not what it used to be."

"Little is."

Jack Tyrell smoothed out the ground before him with his work boot. "I guess you're not leaving."

"Nope."

"You come here for me?"

Blaine shook his head. "You're just a bonus."

"So how you wanna play this?"

"Let's start with you keeping your hands where I can see them," Blaine said, rotating his gaze from the speaker to the man on his right, who looked like an albino. "How many others, Indian?" he asked Johnny.

"Two," Wareagle responded, scrutiny of the ground in search of footsteps complete, his own gun in plain view as well now.

Tyrell laughed, slapped his thigh. "Now I've fucking seen everything. . . . Come on, what do you say? We walked away even before."

"I didn't walk away."

"You can today."

"Not until I finish what I started."

Tyrell laughed again. "Short of that, you got any idea how to work out what we got here?"

"Have the other two men with you show themselves." And Blaine edged a little closer to the opening where the winch had been lowered, dragging Othell Vance with him.

"Since you didn't come here after me, I'm thinking maybe you're here for the same reason I am," said Tyrell.

"I'm looking for someone else."

"Maybe I seen him."

"Big guy. Crew cut. Belly like he's seen his share of beers."

Tyrell nodded very slowly. "Yeah, I seen him." He cocked his gaze toward the opening. "Fucking pain in the ass is down there."

Blaine turned toward Liz, relieved that she hadn't moved. "Call him up here."

"Like to, but he's not exactly in a position to listen. He's, like, dead."

"You kill him?" Blaine asked, feeling his heart begin to hammer.

"Uh-huh. Didn't have a choice."

Blaine stole a glance at Liz, hoping she wouldn't react rashly before he and Johnny were ready. But she looked almost eerily calm, which made him fear her next move even more.

"You got one now," Blaine told the long-haired man.

"You arresting us?"

"I look like a cop?"

"No more than I do."

"There's your answer."

"Question," Jack Tyrell followed, "is where we go from here."

Blaine yanked Othell Vance in a bit closer. Just to his right, Liz held her pistol raised and ready, while Johnny's looked like a toy in his hand as he continuously swept the ridge, waiting for either of the other two men to appear.

"That's up to you at this point," Blaine told him.

"Yeah," said Jack Tyrell. "I guess you're right."

Blaine watched as the man whipped a nine-millimeter pistol from behind his back and dropped to the ground in a roll that kicked up a stubborn dust cloud. The cloud hampered even Johnny's vision as he opened fire on the albino, who ducked behind the cover of a rock slope. Blaine let go of his hostage and started shooting, angling himself toward Liz after a stray bullet clanged off her gun and stripped it from her grasp. She dropped to the ground and crawled for the pistol. But Blaine could see her path would take her square into the line of fire coming from the tow truck now.

Blaine dove atop her, firing through the open windows of the tow truck at a gunman on its far side. Then he let loose a barrage under the tow truck's cab. He heard a loud grunt, followed by the thud of something heavy falling to the ground. The black man dressed as a state trooper scurried away, leaving Blaine to focus his aim on the long-haired man. But a second albino lunged into his field of vision and began blasting away with a submachine gun. The bullets, stitching a wild path through the air, were enough to provide cover for the long-haired man's dash to cover behind a nearby rock formation.

Johnny had just gotten a bead on him when a huge man, with a face like raw meat, opened up with a shotgun as fast as he could chamber the shells. The man's ankle, bloodied from Blaine's bullet, kept him from moving fast and enabled Wareagle to dive beneath the ridgeline, small plumes of earth coughed up in his wake.

The second albino's fire, meanwhile, continued to pin Blaine down, bullets chewing up the earth around him, until Liz separated herself and groped about for her pistol. She grabbed and fired it in the same motion, chasing the gunman back.

There was a sudden blur of motion as Johnny Wareagle dashed between her and the gunmen, clacking off shot after shot, seeming to twist into the kicked-up clouds of dust to confuse their aim. Blaine seized the opportunity to dart out with Liz to the far side of the tow truck for cover.

"Who are they?" she posed, bullets chiming off the truck's frame.

"The leader's someone I was hoping to meet up with again," Blaine muttered, eyeing the winch cable, which disappeared down into the mine. He turned his gaze back to the truck and its twin tires mounted at the rear, then glanced at Liz, who had just snapped a fresh clip into her pistol.

"It looks like you got your wish," she said.

Blaine climbed into the cab, keeping low, thankful to see the keys waiting in the ignition. He guessed that whatever the winch was attached to down in the cavern must be heavy, heavy enough anyway to keep the truck from tearing forward if left in low gear.

Blaine found a mallet under the driver's seat and wedged it down against the accelerator, then turned the key. The engine raced instantly, grinding, even before he switched the truck into gear. The truck lurched but held fast, the double rear tires spinning madly, a heavy cloud of debris kicked behind them from the dusty, dried-out gravel.

McCracken snaked quickly out from the cab and joined Liz, who was firing his gun now, her own exhausted. He motioned for her to follow him downhill, toward the mouth of the cavern. They sprinted together into the cloud of dirt and stone obscuring their flight, then dropped down an elevated, leveled grade into the mine.

The two had barely regained their feet when Johnny Wareagle slid down after them.

"Jesus Christ," Blaine muttered, wide-eyed as his gaze fell on a sleek tanker truck that had been dug out of the ground.

"What is it?" Liz wondered.

"Devil's Brew," was all he had a chance to reply before gunfire poured down after them.

Wareagle jerked open the passenger door of the tanker. The decomposing body of a soldier, still in uniform, dropped toward him, and Johnny pushed it to one side out of their way, noting the anomalous absence of a corpse behind the wheel.

"Under the seat!" Blaine called to him.

Johnny had already located the pair of M-16s held tightly in slots in the cab, a standard fixture on all military transports.

"Go, Blainey!"

Wareagle drew out both rifles and fell in behind Blaine and Liz as they charged away from the cavern entrance. The light from the opening vanished quickly, leaving them with only the key-chain flashlights both Blaine and Johnny were never without. Johnny walked backwards, keeping his eyes—and the M-16s—trained on the far end of the cavern, on the chance that any of the gunmen might pursue them.

They found the bodies of what must have been the real state troopers and the tow truck driver a little farther down. Blaine ran his flashlight about the cavern, recognizing it as an old abandoned coal mine from the handcart tracks built into the floor and the way the walls had been shored up with wood. An inviting place to take refuge from a storm, just as he had told Hank Belgrade.

He had just aimed his light into the darkness before him, wondering how large this particular mine might be, when something grabbed hold of his ankle. McCracken swung his light and gun together, the beam catching a half-mad face stretched into a grin.

" 'Bout time you showed up," said Buck Torrey.

FORTY-ONE

No!" Tyrell yelled when Earl Yost started to rush from the ridge into the cavern after their adversaries.

"They're getting away, goddamn it!" Weeb yelled from his brother's side, the sling Othell had fashioned for his wounded arm dangling empty beneath his jacket.

Tyrell glanced at Lem Trumble, the biggest, toughest man he'd ever known, grimacing as he tightened a tourniquet around his leg wound. First time he'd ever seen anyone so much as give Tremble a scratch.

"Race after them into the darkness?" he challenged the Yosts. "Not a good plan, boys."

"You got a better one?"

Tyrell's gaze moved to the tanker. "As a matter of fact, I do."

I suckered them real good," Buck Torrey proclaimed proudly, grimacing.

Supported by Liz, he continued with his story as Johnny Wareagle redressed his wounds with the first-aid kit Buck had pried from the tanker's cab the night before.

"I made 'em think one of the dead soldiers from that truck was me; in the darkness, movement's movement, right, son? Their bullets got a gasoline fire going, and I figured I'd trap as many of 'em as I could in the flames. Trouble is the damn truck's extinguishers put them out too soon."

"Indian?" Blaine asked when Wareagle finished rebandaging Buck's midsection.

"His ankle's shattered. Bullet passed through his side." Johnny looked up. "He's lost a lot of blood, Blainey."

"Hell, I could've told you that much," Buck said, using Liz to prop himself up straighter as he sat on the mine floor. "Something else you need to hear instead: this place is a death trap. There's enough carbon monoxide floating around to choke a city. We're safe now, but if it rains and the lower chambers of the cavern get flooded, the carbon monoxide gets forced up to the higher ground here."

Blaine looked back at Johnny. "Explains why Hank never heard from the tanker's crew again after they pulled in here to get out of the storm."

Buck interrupted. "Will somebody explain how in the hell you found me?"

"We were searching for treasure," Liz said. "Just like you."

Blaine looked back toward the tanker's location. "Now let's make sure our friends down there don't leave with it."

Othell Vance didn't like Tyrell's idea at all. "You don't just open a valve on a rig like this. It's not an oil truck, and that's not goddamn diesel inside."

"What we got is fifty thousand gallons of liquid death sitting here for us to use." Jack's eyes glistened. "Wouldn't mind seeing it in action myself."

"I wouldn't know how much to siphon off!"

"Take a guess, Othell, and try not to blow us up too."

The sleek rig poked its dust-coated nose out of the cavern first, then rose gracefully to the ridge as the winch hoisted it upward. Its tail end was just vanishing from sight when Blaine and Johnny rounded a corner, having returned to the opening that led down into the mine, M-16s in hand.

Blaine steadied his M-16 on one side of the mine, Johnny covered the other, holding their fire in hopes of seeing a guard or guards venture up the steep grade into the light to provide a clear target. Blaine was sighting down the M-16's barrel when he spotted one of the white-faced twins, favoring one arm, backpedaling up the incline. The albino was gazing into the darkness with his pink eyes as he followed the progress of the tanker back to the surface. Blaine took a deep breath and clacked off a quick burst.

It looked as though the albino's legs had been yanked right out from under him; that's how fast he went down, the familiar spray of blood left coating the air. His twin dashed desperately up the steep grade, grabbing hold of the dead man just as Johnny added his fire to Blaine's.

✿   ✿   ✿

"Leave him!" Tyrell ordered Earl.

"The fuck you say!" Earl shouted back, opening up wildly with his submachine gun as bullets coughed dirt and rocks all around him.

He kept spraying the tunnel with fire the whole time he dragged his brother's body up from the chasm.

"What do you want me to do with this?" Othell Vance stammered nervously, liquid death sloshing around inside a pair of canteens he had filled as soon as the tanker was safely on the ridge.

"Dump it down there!" Tyrell ordered.

"Just *dump* it?"

"*Now!*"

Othell did as he was told, flinching. He spilled the Devil's Brew down into the cavern as though he were emptying stale water. It splashed lightly, and then he heard something that sounded like a hiss.

"How we gonna set it off?" Tyrell asked, as a wailing Earl Yost emptied yet another clip into the cavern's darkness to hold their advancing enemies at bay, still standing protectively over his brother's corpse.

"I don't know! Fire, I guess. We should be able to ignite it with something that's flaming."

Tyrell grabbed him by the shirt. "So what are you waiting for?"

"Can you walk?" Liz asked her father, supporting much of his weight. With her help, he had managed to heave himself to his feet.

"Gonna have to, I guess," he said, grimacing from the pain. He forced a smile. "Gave you quite a scare, didn't I?"

"I ought to shoot you myself for running off like that. Not telling anyone what you were up to."

"Better wait till I can afford to lose the blood."

"What were you thinking?"

"Not that I'd end up in a shooting war—I'll tell you that much. Just how did you find me?"

"We followed the trail."

"Mine?"

"Colonel William Henry Stratton's," she said.

The remaining twin's submachine fire was enough to keep Johnny and Blaine from advancing further toward the mouth of the mine. They waited until it stopped before they proceeded opposite each other in time-practiced hunkers.

Suddenly the ground immediately below the opening seemed to pulsate. The effect quickly turned to a rippling that spread forward, the earth turning itself over right before their eyes, creating the illusion that it was chasing them down in a foot-high wave of dirt and rock.

Devil's Brew, Blaine realized.

Johnny Wareagle had already swung back around before Blaine could warn him. They rushed away from the opening as fast as they could, neither seeing the fiery ball of paper that floated down toward the cavern's floor.

"Come on!" McCracken yelled, when he reached Buck and Liz. Barely slowing, he scooped up Buck's body and threw it over what had been his bad shoulder, just before the blast sounded, not so much an explosion as an expulsion of air from the bowels of the earth.

Liz looked back only long enough to glimpse a vast cloud of steamy darkness coming toward them. She realized in the next instant that the mine was collapsing, closing up behind them as they ran. The sound was deafening, causing a searing pain in the center of her skull. It felt like the end of the world was chasing them, about to catch up, and then the ground was pulled away and they plunged toward oblivion.

FORTY-TWO

Blaine was sprawled on a hard surface, enveloped in a cushion of earth under a soft blanket of darkness. A gagging sound snapped him alert and sent him flailing through the powdery dirt in search of Buck Torrey.

His hands closed on Buck's shape, and McCracken pushed and clawed the rubble aside until it was all behind him. He and Buck sucked in lungfuls of cold, dank air.

"I think you dropped something," Buck said. His laugh turned into a choking retch, and he coughed up a stream of dirt as he handed over Blaine's pocket flashlight.

Blaine shone the beam about, but the darkness gave back nothing.

"Johnny," he said. "Johnny!" Louder.

Wareagle appeared by his side, breathing heavily. "Here, Blainey."

"Liz," Blaine muttered, then repeated her name out loud. When there was no response, he and Johnny began to dig frantically through the piles of dirt and rubble about them.

Johnny found a leg and plunged both his hands through a wall of dirt to yank Liz's body out. He laid her across the floor of the pit, reaching down to check her vitals as she twitched and began coughing.

She opened her eyes, to find the beams of both small flashlights shining down upon her. "My father . . ." She sat up.

"Over here," Buck called weakly.

Wareagle then walked off to explore the section of mine into which they had plunged, his flashlight stopping on a dark wooden chest seconds later.

"I'll be damned," Buck said, when he recognized what Johnny's beam of light had revealed.

"One of the chests Colonel William Henry Stratton signed for," Mc-Cracken realized, moving over next to Johnny and adding his beam in a sweep about their new confines.

The other chests and strongboxes, minus the keg chest that must have been damaged when Stratton's regiment sought refuge from the blizzard, were all here as well, strewn amidst decayed and rotting wood that had been part of the wagons hauling the load. Blaine imagined the convoy taking shelter in here from a storm, just as the tanker's crew had. Sitting down to wait things out, only to be overcome by carbon monoxide fumes and never seen again—until now. Their skeletal remains were scattered about, along with the bones of the oxen that had been hitched to Culbertson's wagons. Frayed and tattered Union uniforms still clung to a number of the skeletons, coated with so much dirt and debris that they looked like extensions of the floor.

And that wasn't all. A gleaming brass radiator drew Blaine's attention to a Model T Ford, complete with a skeleton in the driver's seat, evidence of another party who had ventured into the mine, never to leave it.

Blaine's best guess was that this chamber ran partially under the one where the tanker had ended up. Its roof was thirty feet over their heads, compared to half that height in the tunnel they had fled, and that meant an even higher content of carbon monoxide was swirling through the air. And since the opening both Stratton's regiment and the tanker must have used to gain entry to the mine had been blasted closed by the Devil's Brew, they would have to find another route leading back to the surface, or face the same fate.

He moved about the cavern, cataloguing what was available for them to use in aiding their escape. Suddenly he came upon a uniform with colonel's bars pinned to the shoulders, and he crouched down. He had heard so much about William Henry Stratton lately that he felt awed to be kneeling over what must have been his corpse. Almost reverently, he dipped a hand inside the remnants of the coat and found a letter-size leather pouch sewn into the lining. Recalling his own assertions about the documents Stratton must have been carrying, he tore the pouch free and wedged it inside his own pocket.

"Blaine!" Liz called, and Blaine rushed back to her, to find Buck passed out. His breathing sounded irregular. "There isn't much time," she continued. "We've got to get him out of here."

"We've got to get *ourselves* out of here," Blaine said, looking around.

Across the cavern, Johnny Wareagle was examining the walls, finding them too unstable to climb or mount. And even if they managed that task, they would still face the challenge of digging an escape route through the roof of the mine to the surface without any tools whatsoever.

What they needed first and foremost, Blaine thought as he checked on Buck, was a stairway upward, to at least give themselves a fighting chance.

A stairway . . .

He pulled his pistol from his belt, aimed it at the latch of the nearest large strongbox, and shot off the lock. The strongbox rocked a little, then settled. Blaine lifted up the top and shone his light inside.

The neatly stacked gold bars glistened, holding their magic after one hundred thirty-five years underground. He calculated the number of strongboxes, number of bars, and then ran his eyes up the face of the wall.

"We've got work to do," he said to Johnny.

Their first task was to empty all the large strongboxes of their contents. Then they used the three keg chests that held the mysterious coins, along with the strongboxes still in decent enough condition, to form a base for the staircase Blaine intended to build. From there they worked with desperate resolve, racing the inevitable effects of the thickening carbon monoxide to erect a stairway of gold bars in the form of a half pyramid that rose toward the roof of the mine.

While Blaine and Johnny worked feverishly building the staircase, Liz toiled equally hard, emptying gunpowder from unused M-16 shells into an empty clip in the dim light from one of the tiny flashlights. Her father's breathing, meanwhile, seemed to be stable. But his features were growing increasingly pale, evidence of internal bleeding only a hospital could stanch.

Liz finished her job well before the staircase was complete and then busied herself with using the most intact boards she could find to fashion a makeshift stretcher for her father. She found rope to fasten the wood together, but most of it fell apart when she tried to knot it, and the stretcher wobbled as a result. Still, she and Johnny eased Buck onto it and tied him down with what was left of the old rope.

Starting to feel light-headed now from the effects of the carbon monoxide, Blaine climbed back up the golden stairs and wedged the magazine packed with Liz's makeshift explosive into the mine ceiling. He used a shoelace for fusing, wet down with saliva and then coated evenly in gunpowder so it would burn.

"Here goes," he said, flicking out the flame from his lighter.

He touched the flame to the shoelace, which ignited with a *poof*! in a sizzling flash. In the next instant he turned toward the wall and covered his head with both arms.

The blast shook the staircase but didn't topple it. A cascade of rubble showered over Blaine and fell to the floor of the mine. He could feel streams of light and air flooding into the cavern before he turned and looked up through the jagged hole just above him.

Blaine had to dig a little to open the hole enough to climb out. Once on the surface, he took a fast look around, sucking fresh air into his lungs. He had emerged on a plateau several hundred yards beyond the ridge where he, Johnny, and Liz had entered the cavern originally. That ridge was deserted now, no sign of the gunmen or the tanker filled with Devil's Brew.

Beneath him Blaine heard Liz and Johnny coughing as they mounted the stairway, Buck Torrey's makeshift stretcher supported between them. When Wareagle neared the surface, Blaine reached down and helped raise the stretcher to the surface. Liz and Johnny had just joined him over Buck when a helicopter swooped overhead, its rotor kicking dust into their faces.

Blaine moved instinctively to shield Buck when a dozen men in the black uniforms of SWAT commandos descended on the area from the hills above.

"Hands in the air!"

"Don't move!"

They froze while the commandos charged forward and cut their legs out with sharp rifle slashes behind their knees.

"Who's in charge?" Blaine asked from the ground.

A foot pressed into his neck. "Shut the fuck up!"

"Listen to me!" Blaine said through a mouth forced tight against the dirt. "The people you want are getting away!"

The foot pressed harder. "Where are the troopers?"

"Another part of the mine. The people who are getting away killed them."

"You son of a—"

"I'll take things from here, Captain," said a new voice.

The foot let up enough for Blaine to turn his head in the direction of a man in his fifties with a face at least twenty years older. The deepest of his wrinkles carved his face into segments of pale, liver-spotted skin. His eyes looked tired, their whites yellowed.

"I said I'd take things from here," repeated Will Thatch.

Will was at highway patrol headquarters in Johnstown when word of the missing troopers came down. A SWAT team was hastily assembled, and Will talked his way into accompanying them.

He had been waiting for hours, feeling in his gut something would happen, and knowing it had happened as soon as contact was lost with the trio of cars that had gone out after a trooper who'd been in an accident. Will had warned them about the kind of man they might be going up against, the captain's response indicating he had listened.

"I let you ride along out of courtesy, Mr. Thatch," the captain said.

"And I'd like to repay the favor, save you some time and trouble." Thatch took a long look at the man still pinned beneath the captain's foot. "These aren't the people we want."

"So you say."

"This man's right: the ones we want must be getting away."

"Ones *you* want, maybe. I'm satisfied with these folks until I've got something better. It's my men who are missing."

"Killed by the same people who shot my father," Liz said, sitting up and moving over to Buck in spite of the rifles steadying down on her. "And if we don't get him to a hospital soon, he'll die too. Difference is," she accused the captain, "it'll be your fault."

"Your choice," Will Thatch told the trooper as staunchly as he could manage. "Either I take responsibility or I assume jurisdiction."

"You better hope to God you know what you're doing," the captain sighed, and he signaled his men to lower their guns.

FORTY-THREE

Y ou're here because of the Monument," Blaine said to Will
Thatch in the highway patrol's Johnstown barracks interrogation
room.

"Monument?"

"The man you're after is the same man who nearly blew up the Washington Monument seven months ago. I figured that explains the FBI's interest."

"And what about yours?"

"For starters, I'm the one who stopped him."

"For starters," Thatch echoed. "There's more?"

"Plenty. Better explained in the presence of your superiors."

"That's going to be difficult, since, well, I haven't been with the Bureau for twenty years."

Blaine glanced at Johnny Wareagle. The three of them were alone in the room, Liz having gone with her father by helicopter to the nearest trauma center.

"We haven't got much time," Thatch added, nervously.

"Do you know this man or not?"

Thatch nodded. "I know him, all right. You may not have run into the devil today, but it's as close as you're ever going to come on this earth. . . ."

❖   ❖   ❖

Liz sat at her father's side in the hospital. According to the doctors, his condition was guarded. Surgery to repair the internal damage done by the bullet was required, once he was stable enough. But Buck was on his second blood transfusion, and his color remained sickly pale.

Liz's mind drifted back to her eleventh birthday, one of the happiest she could remember.

"You can open your eyes now," Buck had said.

Liz opened them.

"Here you go, girl." And he handed her his rifle after removing all but a single bullet.

She had already grown bored with the .22 he'd taught her how to shoot with. Ready for a real gun to aim at the cardboard target he'd wedged against the thick bales of hay.

"You know what to do," was all he said for advice, and Liz trembled excitedly, even though the big rifle was tough and heavy to hold, never mind aim.

But she got it steady enough to pretend she was aiming. Squeezed one eye closed and fired before her arms grew too tired to handle the weight.

The big gun's barrel jerked upward, the force pitching Liz backward. She staggered, trying to get her balance, but the grade of the land betrayed her. She fell right on her butt and slid downhill as if she were riding a sled.

But she clung fast to Buck's big rifle the whole time. He stood looking at her from the rise for a few seconds before, grinning, he traced her slide down.

"Not a speck of dirt on the barrel," he said, taking the rifle gently from her grasp. "I'm impressed. You wanna go back to the twenty-two?"

Grimly determined, Liz shook her head.

But it hadn't gotten much better the rest of the afternoon, Buck letting her have at it until, exhausted, she handed his rifle back to him and sank to her knees.

"Someday," he said, "this gun'll feel feather light in your hands. When the time's right, you won't believe this day ever happened, 'cause everything's about time. Waiting for the good to show up and being ready when the bad comes in its place."

Now, twenty years later, Liz gazed down at her father and thought about stormy nights spent sleeping on the farm, with his old rifle in easy reach. Seeing the shapeless form of the tentacled Bad Thing that lived in the lake sloshing up to claim her after her parents' divorce had taken Buck away from her. That old rifle wasn't all he had left Liz, but it was the most important.

Except the Bad Thing hadn't lived in the lake, after all; it had shown up amidst the ridges and valleys of Pennsylvania and had long tangled hair

instead of tentacles. Left a trail of blood behind it, not slime. And it had
come upon Buck on a night when he hadn't been ready enough.

Liz was ready. She thought about tracking down the old hunting rifle
that had spilled her down the hillside. She had never gotten the hang of
firing it, not even in later years when strength was no longer the problem.
Go find it now and finish this in fitting fashion. Aim down the gun's ancient
bore-mounted sight and get the Bad Thing centered.

All those years, Buck had protected her from all the Bad Things; the
time had come to return the favor.

Buck's eyes opened groggily. "Couldn't happen," he rasped through dry
lips.

Liz had started to lean closer to him, when Buck continued.

"No way a round-nosed hardball chews through a skull on a ricochet.
You hear me, girl?"

Liz nodded, confused.

Buck's eyes swept the room. "Get me a phone. I wanna call Ballistics
at the goddamn FBI."

Hank Belgrade arrived by helicopter from Washington an hour after Will
Thatch had finished his story. He exited the chopper and met Blaine halfway across the field adjacent to the state police barracks.

"I've already dispatched a forensics team to the area you gave me. State
police units are cordoning it off until they arrive."

"They won't find anything that can help us," Blaine told him. "The
person who took your Devil's Brew is long gone."

Belgrade's jowls wavered. "I miss something in your message?"

"Only what I didn't know yet when I left it."

"Sounds bad."

"Worse," said McCracken.

"I understand where you're coming from, Jackie, I do," said Othell Vance,
trying to sound compassionate. "But you gotta look at the bigger picture.
I'm just not sure this is so smart under the circumstances."

"She always loved the water, Othell. I owe her this much."

Othell felt the boat rock slightly as Earl, the surviving Yost twin, eased
the covered body of Queen Mary on board. "It's just that the tanker's up
there in the parking lot, where anybody could see it."

Jack Tyrell turned the key in the cabin cruiser's ignition and eased the
throttle forward. "I want her to be at peace, where the things she sees
can't hurt her anymore."

Othell swallowed hard. "On the same subject, I figure I've done my
part, Jackie. I think it's time you let me go home."

"To your family?"

"That's right."

"Good thing to have. You only get so many shots, I guess. You were smart to take yours as soon as it came."

"Jackie—"

"Let me finish, Othell. If Mary was by my side to finish this, I'd be dropping you off at your front door right now. Tell you to give your wife and kid a kiss for me. But Mary's gone, and I can't let anything get in the way of what I promised her I'd do."

Othell looked at him, saw that glint in his eyes and cringed.

"Last couple of days, I actually started thinking she and I might try getting what you got. Give this country a big kick in the ass, some payback, and then go live on a beach somewhere together. Get me one of those metal detectors to sift through the sand, looking for coins. You know the kind?"

Othell nodded.

"Man like that doesn't really expect to find anything, so he's not surprised when life fucks him. That's the problem with me, Othell: I expect too much. I tried to change things for a while, and now I see I was wasting my time. I see that waking this goddamn country up isn't going to do any good, 'cause she'll just go back to sleep. That's what I told Mary I was going to stop, Othell. That's what I promised her I was going to do, no matter how many people I've got to hurt along the way."

Satisfied they were far enough out, Tyrell slowed the cabin cruiser's speed, then cut the engine altogether.

"But—"

"Take off your cap, Othell," Tyrell said, as he leaned over Mary's covered corpse, speaking to her. "It's gonna be a helluva ride tomorrow, babe. Sorry you're gonna miss it."

"You're sure this Jack Tyrell was the one from the Monument?" Hank Belgrade asked, when they were all on board the chopper and strapped in, wearing headsets that enabled them to converse above the engine sounds.

Blaine didn't respond, didn't even nod, just pictured the messy scar on Tyrell's right hand.

His expression must have been enough for Belgrade. "All right, just how the hell did he even find out Devil's Brew existed?"

"One of his old gang is currently employed at Brookhaven National Labs," responded Will Thatch. "At least he used to be until he disappeared last week. Goes by the name of Harrison Conroy now, but used to be known as Othell Vance. An original member of Midnight Run."

"And just how many other original members has Tyrell managed to round up?"

"I can't be sure. A dozen, at least. Maybe two."

"Thing is, Hank," said Blaine, "those weren't Midnight Run people Tyrell had with him at the Monument."

"How do you know?"

"Because he was in disguise. Didn't want anyone to know he was involved."

"And now he's got my Devil's Brew. . . ."

"You started telling me about it seven months ago, Hank," said Blaine. "It's time to finish."

It took Hank Belgrade a few moments to get his thoughts settled, as the helicopter continued onward through the fading late-afternoon sunlight.

"Okay, follow me close now. Devil's Brew is manufactured in the form of an aerosol. But once it's released into the air, it changes into a foam, sucking up oxygen and using it to expand to upwards of a thousand times its normal volume."

Blaine remembered the floor of the mine rippling, as the Devil's Brew seemed to chase him and Johnny down.

"The foam is then absorbed into matter," Hank continued, "seeking out structural weaknesses."

"Where cracks form," Blaine concluded.

"Including those that aren't visible to the naked eye, all the way down to the microscopic level. Devil's Brew fills them the same way household foam insulation fills gaps in walls, or anywhere else you spray it. As a matter of fact, that's where the idea originated."

"Then once it ignites, since it has all that oxygen available to it . . ."

"You get a huge bang, on the order of a fuel-air bomb, but in a containable arena. The effects are just short of a nuke, with none of the lingering radiation problems. Nothing left of whatever the Devil's Brew soaked into."

"Active destablization," Blaine recalled from their initial discussion about it months before.

"Aimed at infrastructure. Urban arenas, MacNuts, where the entanglements of the future will be centered."

"I can't wait. How can it be detonated?"

"Same as more standard explosives: using a radio transmitter tuned to a frequency that sends a signal to a capacitor to ignite the spark."

"Tyrell used a match today."

"Crude, not quite as effective."

"Could've fooled me," Blaine said, recalling the effects the explosive had had on the old mine. "How much Devil's Brew is that tanker carrying, Hank?"

Belgrade gazed blankly out the window. "Fifty thousand gallons."

McCracken felt his mouth drop, as he recalled the madness he had seen in Jack Tyrell's eyes on the Washington Monument and then again today.

"What you're telling me is that a man who wanted to blow up the world in the sixties has what he needs to do it now."

"A big chunk anyway."

"It gets worse," said Will Thatch. "He was alone back then. He's not alone anymore."

"What are you talking about?" raised Belgrade.

"Somebody's protecting Tyrell. Somebody in the government . . ."

Thatch told them about the men who had taken the bodies from the cemetery and later appeared in his hotel room, where he had killed them when they tried to kill him. In the seat across from him, Blaine accepted the story grimly, eyes latching onto Belgrade when Thatch was finished.

"What else can you tell us about them?" McCracken asked him.

"All I've got is that license plate number, but it doesn't lead anywhere."

"Maybe not for you or your friend; Hank here's a different story," Blaine said. "We find who owns that license plate, we find who sent Tyrell to the Monument seven months ago. Right, Hank?"

Belgrade looked as if he didn't appreciate the prospects of that. "Might be something we'd be better off *not* finding."

"And why would that be?"

Belgrade fidgeted in his seat. "You don't want to know, MacNuts." And then he looked back toward Will Thatch. "You said you figured Tyrell was at that cemetery for a funeral. Any idea whose?"

Instead of his stapled set of obituaries, Will drew out the article he'd ripped from his memory wall after shooting the two strangers in his hotel room. He unfolded the tear sheet carefully and spread it out on his lap, before holding it up for Blaine and Hank to see.

"This is the last picture of Queen Mary taken prior to the Mercantile Bank bombing. It always bothered me that she wasn't around that day. I think I finally realize why." Will Thatch glanced at the clipping one more time. "I think she was pregnant."

FORTY-FOUR

Jack Tyrell moved about the windowless room, stopping before each of a dozen television monitors even though none was currently switched on.

"Sony . . . I see you went with the best, Marbles," he said to the pudgy man with thick glasses he'd found working on cable television boxes a month before.

"You give me money, Jackie, I figure you want it spent."

"We gonna be watching all those movie stations you were telling me about?"

"We're gonna be watching twelve different views, most of them courtesy of the city's traffic control bureau. Great views. You wanna check 'em out?"

"Later," Jack Tyrell said, looking in amazement at the high-tech consoles and computer equipment Marbles had managed to get completely installed in less than a month's time. "I guess you could call this the nerve center." He counted four chairs set before the display. "You been in touch with the men who'll be sitting in these?"

"One more training session and they'll be ready."

Jack smiled broadly and thought of Mary, how much she would have loved to see this. All their dreams at last about to be realized.

"You ever wonder, Marbles, what it woulda been like to have had this stuff our first time around?"

"Way I got it figured, we were ahead of our time, Jackie. Wasn't enough room in the world for all we wanted to do. Information superhighway opened up all these new roads."

"Whatever you say." Tyrell paused, his mind veering in a different direction. He walked about, surveying the remainder of their plain, dilapidated surroundings. "I don't want to sound ungrateful, Marbles, but is this place the best you could do?"

"I had my reasons."

"Sure, but I was thinking some luxury high-rise apartment. You know, watch it all happening out our window."

"Windows pose a big problem, Jackie. Percussions from the initial blasts are gonna pack a helluva wallop. Lots of glass in the city's gonna be airborne in a bad way."

Tyrell pictured thick, daggerlike shards of it flying over the city, claiming anyone in its path. His eyes glistened. "I get the point."

"There's more. Down here they won't be able to trace any of our signals. I've rigged up parabolic dishes on the surface to channel and diffuse all the electronic waves we send out of here. That includes the detonation signal codes."

"Othell was talking about going timer."

"Can't with this kind of noisemaker. No wires or fuses with this stuff. Got to use a high-frequency radio signal."

"What about the tanker itself?"

"Another reason for basing ourselves down here," Marbles told him. "Gives us easy access to it, which we may need. See, with the tanker we gotta go with timer detonation, and that might mean making some adjustments as the day goes on."

"You find the place to plant it?"

Marbles started for the door. "Next stop on the tour, Jackie."

FORTY-FIVE

First time I've ever been in your office, Hank," Blaine said, looking around.

"I got another one at State, a little bigger. Sometimes I forget where I am, have to figure out which receptionist's voice it is coming over the intercom."

"You ready to tell me who you figure Jack Tyrell was working for?"

Belgrade looked away briefly. "The phrase Black Flag mean anything to you?"

"No."

"I need to tell you how this government runs? There's light and dark; light that everybody thinks they see and dark that most can't see. Then there's operations like Black Flag that nobody's allowed to see."

"That include you?"

"That includes *everybody*, MacNuts, and with good reason. Black Flag got its start in the heyday of covert ops. We were ready to flush Vietnam down the toilet, and the Cold War was about as frigid as it ever got. Intelligence wasn't about to let us lose another war or let the Soviets expand westward through Europe one block at a time. They had a free hand to do pretty much anything they wanted, so long as participation could be easily denounced later."

"Black Flag?"

"The files of prisoners, parolees, Section Eights, and residents of the stockade with the right specialties were reviewed. The ones of special interest were flagged with a black stamp for subsequent recruitment."

"Recruitment?" Blaine repeated, feeling his pulse quicken.

Belgrade nodded. "Obviously extended further than we thought, extended to *fugitives* whose expertise they wanted to utilize. Men like Jack Tyrell."

"Proven psychos."

"And specialists."

"Explains why they're protecting him, doesn't it?"

"Protecting their own involvement with him, more likely. Trying to keep themselves covered, now that he's on the loose."

"Their specialty."

"For decades now. Strictly routine."

"And is it strictly routine for them to play terrorist on American soil?"

"Maybe he took the Monument on his own. That would explain why Black Flag decided to go after him."

"Six months after the fact?" Blaine challenged. "I don't think so."

"Why?"

"Follow the chronology. Four of Black Flag's soldiers follow Tyrell to a cemetery, end up in a grave, and all of a sudden he's putting Midnight Run back together again. Six months go by since the Monument, but he waits until three weeks ago to dip into the past? I don't think so."

Belgrade flashed Blaine an uneasy glance. "And I don't like where this is going. . . ."

"What if Thatch is right about Queen Mary being pregnant? What if she and Tyrell had a kid?"

Belgrade had no response.

"Make some calls, Hank. Get me a meeting."

"You don't want to touch these people, MacNuts."

"Maybe I'll just wait around for them to go after another American target."

"They've been in the dark too long."

"Then they'll be afraid of someone turning a light on them, especially someone who can link them to the Monument."

"Are you fucking crazy? You can't take these people on, I'm telling you!"

"Jack Tyrell pulled your tanker of Devil's Brew out of the ground because he's got big plans for it," Blaine responded quite calmly. "You want to sit around and wait to find out what they are?"

"Listen to me! The people you're talking about don't work for anyone officially, don't even *exist* officially. They're fucking ghosts, MacNuts, and they can make you disappear as easily as they can make themselves disappear."

Belgrade's phone beeped before McCracken could respond, and Hank snatched the receiver to his ear, listening without response. He replaced the receiver and looked back at Blaine.

"It's ready."

"What's ready?" Blaine wondered.

"As soon as you called me from that police station, I put out an alert on the tanker. Tollbooths, police and traffic choppers, state police, even construction crews got nothing better to do than to watch what's whizzing by them down the road. Add to that any surveillance satellites that happened to be in the area over the last few hours and, if we're lucky, we get an indication of where Tyrell's headed. First batch of material just got collated. Let's take a look."

Belgrade moved to his desk and pressed a button on a built-in control panel. Instantly the room darkened and a red-tinted, three-dimensional map of the United States appeared where a wall mural had been just seconds before.

"I'm impressed," Blaine said.

"You ain't seen nothing yet. Watch." Hank worked another series of buttons, and the three-dimensional map changed as quickly as he could press them, finally settling on a close-up of the mid-Atlantic region. "So far there've been twenty-one possible sightings." Another press of a button brought twenty-one lights flashing. "Eliminating those of low probability, we can cut that number down to eight." Just like that, thirteen of the lights disappeared. "And if we eliminate these two, we're left with a pretty clear trail."

Blaine studied the screen. With only the six lights left flashing, the direction Jack Tyrell had headed in after pulling the tanker out of the ground in central Pennsylvania was clear:

Northeast.

Blaine snatched Belgrade's phone from its cradle and thrust it across the desk.

"Make the call, Hank."

FORTY-SIX

get the feeling you're not comfortable in here," the man said, as he walked slowly next to Blaine through the reptile house in Washington's National Zoo.

"I've known my share of snakes in my time," McCracken told him.

It was hours past the zoo's closing time by the meeting's start, but as promised, a car had been parked by the front gate to take Blaine to the reptile house, where the man from Black Flag had been waiting. He was an older man, in his seventies at the very least, with silvery hair plastered to his skull and a withered, cadaverous face. But his deep-set eyes were a piercing shade of blue, a young man's eyes, as comfortable in the dark as some of the creatures lurking in the glass exhibits around them.

"Mr. Belgrade suggested you had a matter of some urgency to discuss," the man said, still having not introduced himself. "Concerning Jack Tyrell."

"He was part of Black Flag, wasn't he?"

"Yes."

"And you've lost control of him."

The man from Black Flag sighed. "In retrospect, I'd say we got greedy."

"You would've been happier if he had succeeded in blowing up the Washington Monument?"

"As a matter of fact, yes. Such an action was required in order that we retain our efficacy."

"Hell of a way to justify your own existence."

"Raising funds has become more difficult for us of late. We've found ourselves in need of new allies."

"So taking over the Monument, blowing it up if necessary, was meant to make you some new friends."

"A small price to pay, in the long run."

"Sorry I got in the way."

"No matter," said the old man. "I'm prepared to let you make up for it."

Blaine caught the implication in his words. "I get the impression you haven't exactly gone out of your way to get Tyrell back."

"Because doing so would mean risking exposure. We consider Tyrell's unexpected freedom to be an acceptable loss, under the circumstances."

"Maybe that's because you don't know what he's up to."

"So Mr. Belgrade informed us."

They stopped before an illuminated glass case where a Burmese python was slowly digesting a mouse, the last bit of a tail disappearing into the snake's mouth. Blaine studied the man from Black Flag's reflection. His slightly sallow skin had a shiny, waxlike quality to it, making it easy to view him as an exhibit every bit as dangerous as any tucked safely behind the barriers.

"During business hours, people flock to the cages where something's about to die," the man from Black Flag said suddenly. "Why is that, do you suppose?"

"Morbid fascination, I guess."

"Only in part. The truth is people are comfortable watching because they can't really see anything. Just a bulge in the snake's skin moving slowly downward. If they could see the mouse being slowly digested, nobody would last long in front of the glass."

"Except you."

The man kept his eyes on the snake. "They can't see what we do at Black Flag, either, and they're just as comfortable for the same reason. People don't want to know what the mouse looks like on the way down, and they don't want to know how we keep their little worlds safe for them." The man moved a little closer to the glass, placed his hand upon it. "You understand this meeting is most unusual, even unprecedented."

"So are the circumstances."

"Meaningless to us. The truth is I agreed because I wanted to meet you. Give you my thanks in person." He paused, studying the snake. "You didn't know that you've worked for us from time to time, did you? We retained you for the same reason we retained Tyrell: because rules don't matter, only stakes do. The higher the stakes become, the more likely we are to make up our own rules. All of us."

"Don't lump me in with men like Tyrell. Please."

"Would you like to compare your body counts to those he recorded on our behalf? Of course, in your mind the people you killed deserved it, the world is better off without them. It was no different for us."

"Yes, it was," Blaine said surely. "Otherwise, you never would have resorted to Black Flag. You couldn't ask people like me to do your dirty work for you, because you knew what our answer would be."

"Do you really think you had any more of a choice then than you do today?"

"Am I missing something?"

"You're here now because we want you to be here."

Blaine tensed slightly. "If this is a trap—"

"I know your Indian friend is in the vicinity, Mr. McCracken. I know what his course of action would be should you not leave here exactly as you came in."

"That much we agree on."

"But with you and the Indian here, you see, Mr. Belgrade and Mr. Thatch—both threats to us—are left alone, without any comparable form of protection, since I believe your Mr. Belamo is elsewhere as well."

Blaine's stomach tightened.

"But our concerns about Mr. Tyrell, regrettably, have come to mirror your own. He's become a nuisance for us that needs to be dispatched with all due haste." The man shook his head almost sadly. "I'll have to show you his active file sometime. Even you'd be impressed."

"How'd you track him down?"

"After the Mercantile Bank bombing, he needed to disappear. The people waiting to help him belonged to us."

"Providing you access to all kinds of people with reasons to disappear."

"Only the best and brightest. Otherwise, we wouldn't have employed you." Blaine could see the man's frown reflected in the glass. "Of course, unlike Mr. Tyrell, we deactivated your file some time ago."

"A lot can change in six months."

"It was considerably before that, I'm afraid. Your approach died with the Cold War, when everything was black and white, before the gray set in. How are you to define yourself in a world without enemies. That world has downsized significantly, and there's no place left for you."

"Then why am I here?"

"Because there's no place in it left for Tyrell, either."

"You want me to go after him. . . ."

The old man nodded. "But if your efforts were to somehow lead back to Black Flag, well, your friends would have to pay the price for your indiscretion."

"Then you'll answer my questions?"

"Only those pertaining to Tyrell."

"Let's start with Queen Mary. She wasn't with Tyrell at the Mercantile Bank bombing because she was pregnant: right or wrong?"

The man from Black Flag looked unmoved. "Actually, she gave birth the week before. A son."

"That's how you controlled Tyrell, isn't it? You used his son as leverage to make him work for you."

"We placed the boy in a good home, made sure he had all conceivable comforts."

"But the threat was always there, what you would do if Tyrell didn't cooperate."

"A remarkable equalizer, I must say."

"What about Mary?"

"Tyrell convinced her he had made all the arrangements himself. For the child's own good, of course. And he continued cooperating, for his son's sake, for all these years."

"Until he killed four of your men when they came to pick him up at a cemetery in New Jersey. What changed? What made him break security and come back to the world?"

The man from Black Flag finally turned away from the glass, back to McCracken. "The one thing we could not prepare for. . . ."

"Jesus Christ," Hank Belgrade muttered, looking up from the dog-eared obituary caught in the light of his computer screen. "Looks like you were right," he said to Thatch.

Will hovered over his shoulder, trembling. "I never thought . . ."

"It's all here, as close to proof as we're gonna get."

They both turned when the door started to open.

Blaine pulled the cell phone from his pocket the moment he emerged from the reptile house. Hank Belgrade had two offices but only one number, and it rang wherever he was. Blaine heard a distinctive click as the line was answered, the call already being routed.

It rang and rang, went unanswered.

Blaine tried again. After a dozen rings, he hung up and dialed a different number.

"Hello," Liz Halprin answered groggily, in her father's hospital room.

"Where's Sal?" Blaine demanded.

"He just went down to—"

"When he comes back, tell him you've got to get out of there. All of you!"

"But my father—"

"There's no choice. You're not safe. Neither is he. Sal will know what to do."

"What's happened?" she asked, the fatigue gone from her voice.

"I know now where Tyrell's headed with the Devil's Brew," McCracken told her as calmly as he could manage. "He's going back to the place where one part of his life ended, at the Mercantile Bank building twenty-five years ago, and where another finished when his son was killed after taking a classroom hostage at an elementary school last month. . . ."

Liz felt the fear pour through her like a cold rush, as Blaine finished. "New York City."

5

THE TAKING OF MANHATTAN

FORTY-SEVEN

You see what I'm talking about?"

Gus Sabella kept his hands on his hips, turning beet red as he continued to gaze at the sign affixed to the construction fence. When he'd left the job site yesterday it had read: REBUILDING NEW YORK CITY ONE BRICK AT A TIME.

But overnight somebody had painted over the B in "brick" and replaced it with a P.

"We call the cops and get squat from them," Gus moaned to his shift supervisor. "Every night it's something different. It's getting so I'm gonna start sleeping in the trailer with my shotgun. Blow the balls off any punk who messes with this site. Starting tonight."

"We make a deal with the union," said Lou Marinelli, shifting his cigar from one side of his mouth to the other, "this stops today."

"You sound like the enforcers they keep sending down. Makes me wonder whose side you're on."

"The side that wants us to come in on time and on budget. This vandalism keeps up, we'll never accomplish either. Means we can kiss any future city contracts goodbye."

"We should give up, then. . . ."

"More like in. Play the game, like I been saying."

Marinelli was big, but Gus, taking a lumbering step forward, seemed ready to swallow him. Sabella was a huge man, with a gut that sagged over his belt. He had dark skin and had managed to keep all his hair, which fell in a wild tangle whenever he took off his hard hat.

Marinelli flinched when Gus yanked something from under his jacket. It was a can of spray paint.

"Nobody scares me off," said Gus, who kept a pair of cans ready like six-guns in his trailer. As Marinelli looked on, Gus sprayed over the vandalized portion of the sign in white. Wait a while for it to dry, then do his best to trace out a fresh B in red to match the other letters.

Below in the construction pit on West Twenty-third Street, where a parking lot had been just a few months before, the monumental task of rebuilding a main junction of the city's sewer system was under way. Payloaders, bulldozers, backhoes, and cranes worked in unison to tear up old piping and install new. Huge, hangar-size entryways had been opened up to access a trio of sewer lines and storm drains, which formed part of the miles and miles of swirling tunnels that ran beneath New York City.

Gus Sabella's crew was responsible for reconstructing this main junction, which had simply collapsed over time, a job that meant first digging up and clearing the earth to remove the old pipes and conduits, and then replacing them. The company Gus was a partner in had managed to win the bid by undercutting the competition in both price and time: price by being nonunion, time by digging up one section while replacing another. That accounted for the clutter of heavy machines, which sometimes seemed to need a traffic cop to keep them from smashing each other apart. The upshot was frantic, frenzied days that didn't bother Gus nearly as much as arriving every morning wondering what had been messed with the night before.

"Hey, boss," said Marinelli, as Sabella checked if the paint was dry. "Take a look at this."

Sabella turned to see a huge black tanker truck rolling toward the ramp that led down into the block-size construction pit. Thing looked like something out of *Star Wars*. Gus had never seen anything that even remotely resembled it. The driver brought the tanker to a halt and leaned out his window toward Gus.

"What the hell you call this?"

"State-of-the-art shit removal," the driver said, producing a crumpled work order. "Got a major backup I'm supposed to pump out in tunnel 73-A."

Gus looked into the cab and gave the driver a second look. Guy had skin the color of unbaked angel cake and pink eyes that didn't seem to blink.

Gus took the work order and checked it over. "Something break?"

"Won't know until I get there."

"My reason for asking, see, if the rupture's our fault, we get docked."

The driver refolded his work order. "I go into the tunnel, find the problem, and drain it. The rest of this stuff, you're talking to the wrong guy."

Gus backed off so he had a clear route down the ramp. "Know where you're going?"

"I'll just follow the smell."

The milk-faced driver shifted and eased the tanker onto the ramp.

FORTY-EIGHT

Y ou look nervous, Othell," said Jack Tyrell.

"It's a technical thing."

"Why don't you tell me about it?"

Othell Vance seemed reluctant to speak. "I followed the parameters. I think I did everything right. It's just that not a lot is known about how Devil's Brew performs in battlefield conditions."

"That what you call this?"

"Am I wrong?"

Tyrell tapped him tenderly on the shoulder. "We know it blows shit up, Othell. That's good enough for me," he said, and turned his gaze on the latest addition Marbles had made to their command center: an electronic wall map that featured bright-red lines designating every bridge and tunnel that provided access to New York City, seventeen in all.

The night before, he and Othell had divided them up between two four-man groups disguised as DPW workers. The apparent nature of the crews' work was line striping, and in fact a pair of men in each group did precisely that to explain the lanes' being closed off. While that pair painted, though, either Othell Vance or Jack Tyrell sprayed a wide strip of Devil's Brew aerosol across the width of the targeted sites. It foamed up like shaving cream, making a slight crackling sound before sinking through the surface into the beds and superstructures, expanding to fill as many gaps and cracks as it encountered. The final man in each group was responsible for setting and tuning a tiny receiver and capacitor. A nearby safety rail provided the sites for the bridges, while in the tunnels the equipment was mounted low on a wall and a wire antenna strung upward.

Both teams had finished just before dawn. They had ditched their trucks, equipment, and uniforms and rendezvoused here in the lair Marbles had found to serve as their command center. Jack Tyrell had doughnuts waiting for them, purchased for half price since they had been left over from the previous day. For his part, Marbles hadn't stopped working yet, even now stringing coaxial cable from the dozen television monitors into the computer console. He wore a tool belt as comfortably as a gunfighter's holster, its contents equally deadly.

Of the other two dozen men in the command center, half had specific tasks to keep them busy through the day. The remaining twelve kept their distance from the machines but stayed close to the weapons, on the outside chance they would be needed. Since he was planning for the long term, Tyrell had put together as large a contingent as possible. Men who would follow him to the next target when this was over and done. None of them could be classified as young in terms of age, but the way Tyrell looked at it, the last twenty-five years hadn't been any better for them than for him. They were fugitives from the underground and ex-cons who had never made it that far. Men who had lived the best of their lives with him once before and looked forward to doing so again.

Vance still looked fidgety, so Tyrell slapped him on the shoulder and steered him toward the wall of television monitors Marbles had up and running.

"Come on, Othell, let's watch a little TV," he said, a sophisticated remote control in hand. "Maybe find a soap or one of those daytime talk shows, today's topic 'Lesbian Daughters of Women Suing Fertility Clinics.' "

Tyrell pushed a button, and one of the sets lit up with a picture of the George Washington Bridge.

"Now what have we here . . . ?"

He touched another button on the remote, and a second screen burst alive, with the scene inside the Lincoln Tunnel, traffic crawling along at the usual clip, the screen not much more than a blur of headlights and taillights.

Jackie Terror held the remote like a baton, conducting his return to the life he belonged in. He felt elated, alive again. He clicked the remote, and a shot of the Brooklyn Bridge filled screen number three.

Click, and a traffic jam inside the Holland Tunnel came alive on a fourth screen. Then the Manhattan Bridge, the Queens Midtown Tunnel, the Queensboro Bridge, the Brooklyn-Battery Tunnel, the Triborough Bridge . . . His heart was hammering against his chest so hard he was beginning to wonder seriously if he could wait until nine o'clock.

Suddenly Marbles waved to get his attention, other hand pressed against his transistorized headset.

"The tanker's in place," he reported.

Tyrell turned his attention to the red LED readout on a wall-mounted clock:

8:45

FORTY-NINE

I hate fucking traffic," Sal Belamo moaned as the car inched its way across the upper deck of the George Washington Bridge. He looked over at Blaine in the passenger seat. "I told you we should have taken the Lincoln Tunnel."

"And then you told me you hated driving through the damn things."

"All that water . . . You ever think about that?"

"No."

Sal shrugged. Moving Buck Torrey in his condition from the hospital the night before had been deemed impossible, so he had arranged the next-best thing: a half-dozen fully armed Special Forces veterans guarding Buck at all times. Sal and Liz had waited until the first group arrived before leaving to rendezvous with Blaine and Johnny.

The news when they were finally all together wasn't good. Hank Belgrade, along with Will Thatch, had utterly vanished, and with Hank went any chance of dealing with this crisis through normal channels. The only man Blaine could reach who stood a chance of helping them was the FBI assistant director in charge of counterterrorism, Sam Kirkland, who had been point man at the Washington Monument seven months before.

"This better be good," Kirkland had greeted groggily just after midnight.

"What would you say to a city about to be under siege?" Blaine queried over the phone.

"I'd say keep talking."

Kirkland listened without comment, the scratching sound Blaine heard on the other end of the line indicative of his listener's taking copious notes. But everything went silent when he mentioned the name Jack Tyrell.

"He was the one at the Monument," Blaine said. "In disguise, but it was Tyrell who got away." When Kirkland didn't respond, McCracken continued, "You fall back asleep on me, Mr. Director?"

"I only wish. Then I could be dreaming."

"Sounds like Jack Tyrell's no stranger to you, either."

"Hardly. We've met before." Kirkland took a deep breath. "I was the undercover FBI agent who infiltrated Midnight Run twenty-five years ago."

"Wait until you hear what he's been up to since. . . ."

"**W**here are you?" Kirkland had asked when Blaine was finished.

"It's better if you don't know. For obvious reasons."

"I'm the goddamn FBI!"

"If Black Flag can get to Hank Belgrade, they can get to anyone."

"Jesus Christ, what a mess . . ."

"I'll give you a cell phone number where you can reach me as soon as you've got something."

"Be patient. This is gonna take me some time to check out."

"If Tyrell's already in New York with the Devil's Brew, there might not be much time left."

"We can't close off the city."

"Why not?"

"Be serious. Look, I've got a nine A.M. meeting at New York headquarters tomorrow. I'll spend the rest of the night on the phone, if that's what it takes to get some answers."

Obviously, though, the rest of the night had not been enough; it was just past eight forty-five in the morning now, Kirkland still hadn't called back, and all of Blaine's subsequent attempts to reach him had failed. He was beginning to fear that Kirkland had gone the way of Hank Belgrade and was immensely relieved when the cell phone rang.

Blaine snatched up the phone, as Sal continued to edge the car through heavy traffic across the George Washington Bridge. "It's about time."

"Everything you gave me is a dead end," Kirkland started.

"I warned you."

"First of all, nobody my meager level of clearance could reach ever heard of this Devil's Brew, from the Pentagon to Brookhaven itself."

"The man running the project wanted it that way."

"To keep it from falling into the wrong hands."

"Yes."

"And then he decided to dump the whole supply and erase all evidence it ever existed."

"That's right, which brings us to your old friend Jack Tyrell."

"Same story, unfortunately. I can't find any record of this Black Flag project or of Tyrell spending a stretch of years in forced service to his country."

"Black Flag didn't leave records, Kirkland; that was the point."

"It's tough to sell government officials on conspiracies and shadow cadres before they've had their morning coffee. You've got to give me something more concrete."

"What about Tyrell's son? Like I told you last night, all this is happening because he was killed a month ago. In New York City."

"The problem is the man who was killed at that elementary school has since been identified as Alejandro Ortiz, a Colombian national with a long list of drug busts. His mother died in Medellín two years ago. His father is a farmer who speaks no English."

That news hit Blaine square in the gut. He thought he had everything about Jack Tyrell figured out, but obviously he didn't. At the National Zoo the night before, the man from Black Flag had confirmed that they had lost control of Tyrell after his son's death in the shootout. So what was he missing here?

"I hear traffic," Kirkland said. "Where are you?"

"Middle of the GWB."

"Couldn't stay away, could you?"

"You know me: I like to be where the action is."

"Then why don't you head toward headquarters here at Federal Plaza, so we can run this by the numbers?"

"I've never done too well working within the system."

"Make an exception."

Blaine accepted that there was no other choice open to them for now. "At the rate we're moving, don't expect us until lunch."

Behind the wheel, Sal Belamo passed by a school bus just after reaching the center of the span, and Blaine saw the source of the traffic jam: a pair of bungee jumpers who had rigged their equipment into the bridge's safety rail between the guy wires were involved in a heated exchange with a pair of cops who had just handcuffed them.

"You ask me," said Sal, "cops should just throw them off without their cords for holding up the traffic."

FIFTY

As nine o'clock drew closer, Jack Tyrell could feel his heart thudding harder against his chest. He was about to do something no man had ever done before, yet suddenly he felt a profound sense of sadness, the pain of loss never more real for him. Mary deserved to be by his side now. They should be doing this together, their son still safe and alive.

But he was dead, and now so was Mary, and with them had gone what little hope Tyrell held out for the world. He found the irony striking. Working for Black Flag had been the only way he could guarantee the boy a safe and healthy existence. Cooperate or your boy dies. So Tyrell had cooperated, and his boy had died anyway.

Tyrell closed his eyes, as he always did when sadness started to get the better of him, closed his eyes and lost himself in what gave his life its purpose:

The moment the bomb went off.

He never felt more alive than when death was at hand. Each time, his mouth went bone dry with anticipation. Flinching in the last moment before detonation, and then viewing the single flash followed by the roaring fireball that swallowed one world and coughed another back up. In that blessed moment life found meaning, a sensory feast.

From the blinding glow, to the ringing that left his ears fuzzy and hollow, to the high-pitched screams of the wounded and dying, to the wondrous stench of flesh burning amidst the acrid scent of scorched metal . . . the air cracking and popping, stubborn embers blown outward . . . pieces of the blast spewed into the air and falling back to the earth as unrecognizable husks . . .

Tyrell saw it all when he closed his eyes, opened them again to the smell of skin fried black and the sight of charred eyeballs that looked like marshmallows dropped off the stick.

He brought his transmitter up to eye level, studying the black button within easy reach of his thumb. Thought of Mary and the son he had watched from afar. He always imagined himself walking up one day and taking a close look at him, wondered if the kid would look back and know. That moment would never come now, and sadly, the closest he ever came to his son was at his funeral a month before.

The wall clock ticked to 9:00.

Jackie Terror held his breath and pushed the button.

FIFTY-ONE

On the George Washington Bridge, Sal Belamo's rental car had just crawled past a tow truck hauling an old Lincoln, even with the bungee jumpers when Blaine heard what sounded like a massive thunderclap—not just heard but *felt*, deep in the pit of his stomach. There was a flash in the rearview mirror that made him squint in the final moment before the world was yanked out from beneath the car.

He felt it being lifted off the bridge and spun violently around. His first thought was that there had been some awful chain collision that sent a hundred cars plowing into each other. But flaming vehicles were actually *hurtling* past him through the air, to be deposited back on the bridge in ragged clumps of charred, smoldering steel. His own car bounced one way, then the other, and ended up with its front tires shakily riding the bed of a four-by-four.

Shock wave . . .

The words sticking in Blaine's mind, he grabbed for the breath that had been sucked out as a burst of superheated air washed over him.

Jack Tyrell felt as though he were tripping on acid. All the times he had dropped the stuff and lived out the fantasy of the world rupturing at its core, blowing apart from the inside out. He and the other soldiers of Midnight Run alone left to witness people peeled back to the bone. Close his eyes and he could see it happen, make believe it was real.

But this time it was indeed real. The command center, though safely isolated, rumbled like a house set against an airport runway when a jet takes off. Tyrell quivered as the television screens brought his wondrous work to life.

His viewing started with the most dramatic sight of all, at the George Washington Bridge, where the force of the blast from dual spans had created a flaming vortex of air, spinning and hurling vehicles in all directions. Some crashed against each other in a domino effect, while others ended up atop one another. Still more dropped through the huge chasms in the bridge into the charcoal-broiled air, turning on their noses and rolling over before smashing into the waters below.

On the upper deck, a school bus was sent whirling like a propeller along the bridge, smashing cars from its path until it slammed into a toppled tractor-trailer. Impact sent the bus careening toward the safety rail, where it mounted a number of mashed, burning car husks and smashed through the guy wires, turning them into steel-like tentacles whipped wildly about. The bus teetered on the edge with its nose ever so close to turning downward. Flames licked at its tail before receding as if the blast had sucked them back in.

Goddamn blast was powerful enough to blow itself out, thought Jackie Terror, sweeping his eyes across the remainder of the screens. *Goddamn . . .*

The center of the Lincoln Tunnel had collapsed in a firestorm of rubble and twisted steel. Numerous secondary explosions snapped off, hurling asphalt in all directions. The smoking, crackling tunnel center looked like a barricade formed of stacked car skeletons and assorted debris.

At the Queensboro Bridge, the explosion had first blown a chasm even bigger than either of those in the GWB and then collapsed a huge portion of the center of the span onto Roosevelt Island below. Cars and trucks showered down after it, twisting against each other in the blast-baked air before landing in a mesh of ruined metal and death.

The Brooklyn-Battery Tunnel, meanwhile, did not fare nearly as well as the Holland or Lincoln. The explosion ruptured the seams layered along both its sides, exposing the walls to incredible pressure from the East River. In almost no time at all, those sides had given way to an avalanche of water as the river poured in, dousing the flames at an incredible cost.

The Williamsburg Bridge provided the biggest delight for Tyrell's eye. A smoother flow of traffic allowed the blast to catch a number of vehicles in motion, projecting them into the air, where they actually seemed to be flying. The illusion held only until they plopped back down through the flames, either atop other vehicles, still holding to the bridge, or joining the cars that had toppled through the chasm to the waters below.

What Tyrell couldn't see but pictured clearly all the same was the quartet of huge electric transformers responsible for powering Manhattan's subways, Grand Central and Penn stations exploding in a shower of sparks to more conventional explosives. Over the next few moments every train in the city came to a halt, thousands and thousands of commuters forced to hike their way fearfully out of the tunnels through the darkness.

It was all there on the screens before him, fresh shots already being captured from a greater distance by his spotter helicopter. Smoke rose in billows around the entire island of Manhattan. Tyrell invented the smells and sounds, closed his eyes and breathed deeply, letting his imagination paint the picture for him. He was an artist, and this was his mural, his landscape, the shape of his vision come to pass in one blood-soaked moment that had cut New York City off from the rest of the world.

Jack Tyrell ran his eyes over the screens again, holding on the George Washington Bridge where the blackened school bus was still teetering on the safety rail, a stiff wind away from plunging to a watery death in the river below.

"Goddamn," he said, out loud this time.

Don Imus, host of an immensely successful and nationally syndicated morning radio show originating in New York, reached for his studio phone.

"I'm calling him myself."

"He's in a meeting," his producer said again. "Something came up."

"The White House. Good morning," a voice greeted.

"Don Imus for Bubba."

"Excuse me?"

"The I-Man, lady, calling from the Big Apple, where Bubba's booked for a segment this morning. We're talking again. Now put down your doughnut, hustle your butt to his office, and tell him to pick up."

Before the receptionist could respond further, a technician knocked on the studio's glass and then barged through the door.

"Line three," he announced breathlessly. "Take the call."

Imus put the White House on hold and pressed the new line. "Is it Bubba?"

"No. Shirley, from just outside the Lincoln Tunnel."

"Is everybody all right?" Blaine's voice rose above the shrieks and panicked cries that seemed to be coming from everywhere around him.

Johnny and Liz both grunted their assents from the back seat of the car.

"Just barely, boss," Sal Belamo answered from behind the wheel.

Satisfied, Blaine turned and began kicking at the passenger door. When this produced no results, he hammered his elbow against the already spiderwebbed window until it shattered and showered to the roadbed beyond. He cautiously pulled himself outside and couldn't believe what lay before him.

The force of the blast that had launched their car airborne had carved jagged chasms through both the upper and the lower decks of the bridge. Pockets of flames pooled about the remnants of the structure, licking at the blackened shells of cars, some with the charred remains of the occupants still inside. As Blaine continued to look about, he saw that a school bus had crashed through the guy wires and was resting precariously on the bridge safety rail, starting to list ever so slowly to the front. Inside, children shifted desperately about, all their jostling quickening the inevitable tilt that would take it over the side.

One of the rear doors to their smoking car popped clean off, and Johnny Wareagle emerged to survey the scene. Liz and Sal extricated themselves from the wreck as best they could, emerging at the same time Blaine spied the tow truck they had passed just before the blast. He sprinted toward it.

McCracken tore the tow truck's door open, singeing his hands on the latch, to find the driver slumped unconscious against the wheel, then rushed to the rear. He grabbed the truck's winch cable and swung around to find Johnny Wareagle beside him.

"Work the winch on my signal, Indian."

There was no clear path to the teetering school bus, which meant negotiating an obstacle course of mangled car hulks over stubborn pockets of flames to reach it before it plummeted. So Blaine took the high road, leaping from hood to hood of some cars and hurdling across the roofs of others, the winch cable dragged behind him. He skirted clear of the flaming wrecks, which popped and crackled, coughing glass and steel into the air around him. But he felt the heat of the scorched metal right through his shoes.

Blaine reached the rear of the bus, only to see that gravity had begun pulling it over the top of the safety rail, its nose tilting ever downward. He dove and snared the cable onto the bus' exhaust manifold. The bus had just started to go over when the cable snapped taut, holding it precariously in place.

Blaine waved back to Johnny, who activated the winch. The cable began to churn, and the bus edged ever so slowly back toward the bridge.

"Oh no," McCracken muttered, his sense of triumph short-lived when he realized that the exhaust manifold was starting to bend.

"What do you mean, it's gone, Shirley?" Don Imus asked the woman calling WFAN radio from her cell phone.

"I mean somebody blew the goddamn thing up."

"You feeling all right this morning, Shirley? Didn't add a little Kahlúa to your coffee, now did you?"

"It's a mess down here," she cried. "People are going to need lots of *help*!"

Imus cupped his hand over his ear when his producer rushed through the door.

"The switchboard's jammed. It's not just the Lincoln; somebody's blowing up the whole goddamn city!"

"All right," Imus told him. "Forget the President and get me the mayor."

Mayor Lucille Corrente's conference room in City Hall featured a clear view of the Brooklyn Bridge. She had been meeting with her senior staff since eight-thirty sharp, had just initiated a discussion about price fixing in the city's garbage industry, when City Hall shook and the plate-glass window in the conference room shattered.

"Earthquake!" one of the staff members yelled.

"I don't think so," said another, who could see the fireball that had swallowed the Brooklyn Bridge through the spiderweb of cracks in the window.

"All routes confirmed down!" Marbles announced happily, his eyes trained on the electronic wall map, where the red lights denoting bridge and tunnel access to the island of Manhattan were flashing in synchronized fashion.

But Jack Tyrell didn't respond. His attention was still riveted on the scene unfolding at the George Washington Bridge, now captured on live television by a news traffic chopper.

Barely aware of the helicopter hovering overhead, Blaine looked on helplessly as clamps popped out from the bus' exhaust manifold like kernels of Jiffy Pop. Half the manifold came free, and the school bus keeled downward again, dragging the tow truck across the bridge.

Inside the bus the screaming kids were rocked forward, pitching into the aisle and sliding toward the front as though they were on ice. The rear tires had actually dropped over the edge when Blaine lunged futilely to grab hold of the cable, as if he could somehow yank the bus back up alone. Before the bus could plummet, the cable lodged firmly under its mangled frame, toppling the tow truck onto its side and leaving Blaine with the brief illusion that he *was* holding the bus up himself.

Blaine let go of the cable and pressed up against the safety rail, the hot metal burning him through his shirt. The nose of the bus was facing straight down now, the rear emergency exit about a yard away. Still intent on rescue, he climbed down onto the bus. His weight rocked it slightly and drew a chorus of yells from the kids trapped inside. He managed to work the emergency door open, hearing the raspy screech from the alarm as he leaned in toward the terrified faces gazing up at him.

"Come on!" he said. "Climb to me!"

But the sudden shifting of weight as the kids started pulling themselves toward him caused the bus to lurch downward again, the tow truck dragged with it and all of Blaine but his feet ended up inside. He would have fallen in headfirst if Johnny Wareagle hadn't reached over the rail above and latched onto his ankles. Liz Halprin and Sal Belamo then grabbed hold of Johnny's legs just in case the bus was rocked again.

But for the moment it seemed stable, and Blaine took advantage of the human chain of survivors who had braved the inferno to raise the kids up and over him so they might reach for the hands of more bystanders who had rushed to the rail to help.

"Hold it!" Blaine ordered, when the children started crowding toward him. "One at a time!"

It was an agonizingly slow process, each kid seeming to take forever. The sixth of ten in the bus had just made it over the rail when the tow truck slipped free of the cars it was wedged between and slid on its side into a toppled eighteen-wheeler. Blaine felt himself torn from Johnny's grasp, falling all the way inside the bus. Then the winch cable split from the frame, sliding free, and the bus jerked downward, with nothing to hold it.

Robert Corrothers, New York City's public safety commissioner, had been conducting his own meeting, three floors down from the mayor's office in City Hall, when the blast shook the walls. He knew instantly it was bad, but how bad would not become clear until he witnessed the bedlam that broke out in the various offices occupied by his personnel in the ensuing moments.

Within seven minutes of the initial series of blasts, he had spoken with the Traffic Control Bureau, Emergency 911 Response, and the City Engineer's Office in an attempt to get a handle on the scope and magnitude of what had occurred. Corrothers could scarcely believe what he was hearing, and it only got worse with each call.

His chief assistant, Patty Tope, found him in the "bunker" where the public safety team holed up during major storms and other natural disasters.

But there was nothing natural about this, Corrothers knew.

"We just got confirmation on the Willis Avenue Bridge," Patty Tope reported, reading from a clipboard held shakily in her hand, "the Third Avenue Bridge, the Madison Avenue Bridge, the Macombs Dam Bridge—"

"What about Transit?"

"Power's still out on all lines. They're trying to track down the problem now."

Corrothers continued scanning the various angles of New York City pictured on the screens before him, most coming courtesy of local television stations, which by now had interrupted their regular programming for continuous coverage of the unfolding crisis. Right now that crisis included one monster traffic jam that encompassed every single street in Manhattan. Corrothers had a dozen major sites that needed emergency response immediately, and he didn't have a clue as to how it was going to get there. And that, he figured, was exactly what the person or persons behind this wanted.

"The problem," Corrothers told Patty Tope, "is that somebody blew Transit up too."

The atmosphere in the Midnight Run command center had become that of a football game, with most of Jack Tyrell's men crowded around the screen that pictured the dangling school bus. Rousing cheers erupted when it dropped for what seemed like its final plunge, only to be held up yet again when the cable snared on another part of its frame.

"Well, well, well," Tyrell said, loving the scene as the traffic chopper hovered as low as possible to catch the efforts of bystanders still doing their utmost to save the children. "A bunch of heroes auditioning for the movie of the week." He yanked his wallet from his pocket. "I got ten bucks here says the kids die."

The ruckus picked up again as odds were given excitedly and money changed hands. *And this,* Tyrell thought, *this is only the beginning.* The best was yet to come.

The traffic chopper swooped in closer, catching the grimly determined visage of a bystander who had managed to work his way into the bus itself.

Jackie Terror froze, hands dropping to his sides.

"Holy shit," he muttered. His euphoria vanished as he recognized the bearded face that had been plastered on the screen for one long moment. "All bets are off," he announced suddenly, and his men went dead quiet. "I'm about to change the odds big-time. Marbles," he called to the bespectacled man who had not budged from his post at the console.

"Yeah?"

"I want to talk to the people in our chopper. I want to talk to them now."

The tires! Blaine realized. The cable had snared under the tires.

But that gave little reason for celebration. Holding on to a pair of seats to keep from falling straight through the bus's windshield, Blaine shifted his frame enough to fix his gaze upward. The bridge was twenty-five feet away now, the human chain that had helped evacuate all but four of the kids rendered useless. Blaine, meanwhile, was in no position any longer to help anyone, not even himself.

From this angle he was afforded an incredible view of the damage done by the blast. Blaine had seen the best in the business work with everything from C-4 to shape charges to fuel-air bombs, but he had never, *never*, seen anything that could shred layers of steel and asphalt as fast and cleanly as Devil's Brew.

Above him on the bridge, Johnny Wareagle had organized a group of bystanders to try to lift the tow truck back upright so he could try working the winch again.

Sal Belamo, meanwhile, rushed to the spot on the safety rail where the bungee cord remained fastened in place. He uncoiled it and pushed through the hordes of gawking onlookers directly over the swaying bus.

"Boss!"

Thirty feet below, McCracken heard the call and looked up. Sal knotted the cord onto the section of rail and then dropped it straight toward the open emergency exit. The cord fluttered through on the first try, and Blaine snatched it easily.

He had the cord knotted around his waist in the next instant, the support it provided enough to let him return to the task of getting the kids safely out. Fighting the bus' slight sway, he grabbed the girl closest to him and raised her through the emergency exit.

"Grab the cable!" he instructed. "Pull yourself up!"

The girl's feet had barely cleared the door when Blaine called for the next-closest child to climb toward him. He could feel the bus descending slowly, almost imperceptibly, just an inch or so at a time, as the winch cable ate its way through the thick tires. Trying hard not to calculate how much time he had left, Blaine pushed the second-to-last child through and then reached down for the final boy.

"Come on!" He waved.

"My foot," the boy moaned. "It's stuck."

Blaine took all the slack the bungee cord would give him to drop down even with the boy. His sneakered foot was caught in the seat. Blaine jimmied it gently until it came free. He angled himself closer to ease the boy out and saw a shape squeezed beneath the dashboard.

The bus driver! In all the chaos, he had forgotten about the driver!

"Hold on to me," Blaine ordered the terrified boy, as he began to climb back for the emergency exit. "Don't let go. Hold on tight and keep your eyes closed!"

The bus rocked harder, making Blaine's ascent to the exit even more difficult. But he reached the hatch and hoisted the boy through. Above him, a pair of kids were just being lifted over the side, back onto the bridge.

"Climb!" Blaine ordered the boy.

"I can't!"

"You *can!*" Then he lowered his voice. "Just a little at a time, until they can reach down for you from the bridge."

The boy gritted his teeth and began to shimmy himself upward. Blaine turned and slid back through the hatch, holding one hand to the bungee cord as he negotiated his way toward the bus driver, apparently unconscious.

When he reached the dashboard, he saw it was a woman, a blessing since her weight was likely considerably less than a man's. Blaine hooked a hand under her belt and hoisted her up to the shoulder Buck Torrey had fixed. This left him one arm to help retrace his path up the aisle. He pushed off the seats to quicken his ascent to the emergency exit and grabbed the cable with both hands. Then he hoisted himself and the driver up through the hatch, steadying his feet on the bus' rear just as the cable cut through what was left of the tires.

The bus plunged, and Blaine dangled in the air, supported by the bungee cord as he struggled to hold tight to the woman. Below, the school bus hit the Hudson River nose-first, the crushing impact breaking apart its front end before it sank quickly beneath the surface.

Above him, meanwhile, the last two of the kids he had guided out were struggling to climb, losing the battle to both fear and the wind, which played havoc with the cable now that the weight of the bus no longer held it steady. Blaine managed to snare the cable in his free hand and knotted it around the unconscious bus driver's waist. He looked toward the bridge and flashed a signal to Johnny, then released the cable, as Wareagle began supervising the arduous task of drawing it upward manually.

Blaine dangled from the bungee cord and watched the cable rise gradually above him, the weight of the driver anchoring its end. Blaine would have Johnny pull him up once everyone else was settled safely on the bridge. For now, he was satisfied to feel his heart thump hard every time a child was lifted over the side.

The news helicopter still hovered in camera range, capturing it all. The operator turned the lens briefly on Blaine, who flashed a thumbs-up sign in the moment before a second chopper flitted onto the scene.

FIFTY-TWO

Johnny Wareagle watched the new helicopter speeding toward the bridge's upper span as though it were angling to attack. There were still two kids dangling beneath the safety rail, being hauled up by more hands than the cable had room for. Still not enough.

Movement flashed inside the chopper as Johnny lent his own strength to the cable. The closest child soared over the safety rail, but the final boy was several yards away.

"Get the children away from here!" he ordered the bystanders, leaving only Liz Halprin leaning over the edge to help the last boy. "Get everyone away from here!"

People scurried past him, to a safer spot near the center of the span. Johnny slid sideways to grab hold of the bungee cord and, with Sal Belamo, began hoisting McCracken up, when a shape leaned out the left-hand side of the chopper's rear bay.

Blaine saw the M-203 combination M-16 and grenade launcher before he glimpsed the man wielding it.

What was happening?

The gunman pumped a grenade from the launcher slung under his barrel. The grenade hummed out and slammed into the safety rail in the center of the upper deck, sending another shower of rubble spraying through the air and hurling Sal Belamo and Johnny Wareagle backwards.

Liz Halprin managed to yank the last child over the edge. But the dangling bus driver was lost beneath her when the blast tore the rest of the cable away.

The part of the rail that had been supporting Blaine's bungee cord was destroyed as well. Severed, the cord dropped, and McCracken dropped with it, almost straight for the chopper as it swooned beneath the bridge's lower deck. The chopper banked on an angle that allowed one of its pods to snare the falling bungee cord.

Blaine felt a sudden jolt and looked up to see himself attached to the chopper as it banked agilely away.

Blood . . .

It was the first thing Liz Halprin saw and felt upon her, so much she could smell it. Her ears rang from the percussion of the grenade blast, and her insides felt as though they'd been dumped in a blender.

The blast had thrown her and the boy she had hoisted over the rail onto the hood of a car. A boy not much older than Justin, lying atop her now.

The blood! Was it hers or—

Liz shifted tentatively and saw the jagged shard of shrapnel protruding from the boy's thigh, the wound pumping blood.

Suddenly bystanders surrounded her, a few reaching for the boy.

"No!" Liz screamed. "Don't move him!"

She couldn't do anything for the bus driver or for those who had plunged to their deaths when the two spans of the bridge blew. But she could do something for this boy.

Liz eased him from her gently, as Johnny Wareagle, his coal-black hair sprinkled with chalky dust, approached through the crowd.

"I need something to stanch the—"

Wareagle was already extending his belt to her.

"This is no good," she said, after turning it into a makeshift tourniquet, the blood loss slowed but not stopped. Liz looked around, fully aware it would be quite some time before rescue personnel and their vehicles could even get close. "He'll die if we don't get him to a hospital!"

"I'll see what I can do," Johnny promised.

Blaine saw the pilot look down after the craft's nose responded sluggishly to his commands. He imagined the man's eyes bulging at the sight of him strung beneath the chopper and strained to reach the pistol holstered around his ankle.

No matter how much Blaine stretched, though, he couldn't grasp it. He noted the pilot was coming around again, slipping into a rise, and realized he intended to slam him against the structure of the upper deck or, perhaps, snare him in the suspension bridge's guy wires.

Blaine saw the upper deck coming up fast, in his mind's eye saw himself crushed against it. Two hundred feet before impact, he dropped all his weight downward to stretch the bungee cord taut. Then he let it snap back upward like a rubber band and follow the course of its momentum to spirit him up and over the span, even briefly with the chopper.

The chopper listed, then shot away, angling toward Manhattan as the gunman wielding the M-203 poked his head out again in search of a shot.

"If it isn't the mayor this time, you're fired, stupid," Don Imus snapped at his producer, who poked his head into the studio again.

"Better."

"Better than the mayor?"

"The bomber."

"Shut up."

"I'm serious."

"What line?"

"Seven."

Imus reached over and hit the button. The whole studio lapsed into an eerie silence after twenty harried minutes of juggling calls coming in from all over the city.

"What do you want?" Imus snapped into his headset.

"That's no way to greet a fan," said Jackie Terror.

"Must be a towelhead," interjected Bernard McGuirk, one of Imus' sidekicks.

"Shut up, Bernard. I want to talk to this moron," said Imus. "So you blow up our city and expect Welcome Wagon? Why don't you go somewhere else, like Baghdad?"

Jack Tyrell's laughter filled the studio through all the speakers. "Man, they told me you were good."

"*They* told you? What, you don't listen for yourself?"

"I've been indisposed for a while."

"Killing innocent people somewhere else, of course, you son of a—"

"Are we on the air?"

"Sure. And the sponsors are loving it."

"Really?"

"If you blow your own brains out while we're on, I'll pick up another ten cities by tomorrow. Providing you haven't blown them all up by then too, of course."

"Don't you want to know why I called?"

"I don't care. Do I sound like I care?"

"You're back on top."

"Have you been talking to my wife?"

"I'm being serious here. You were up, down, and now you're up again. Same thing with me. I figured that made you deserve getting an exclusive on my announcement."

"This go under the category of public service?"

"Does it ever! See, I want you to give Mayor Corrente a message for me. Tell Her Honor that I have taken all the people in this city hostage, and all five million will die when I destroy the city unless my terms are met."

"I can't wait to hear this. . . ."

"Sorry, that's for the mayor's ears only. I'll be calling her directly by eleven o'clock."

"Is that A.M. or P.M.?"

"If my terms aren't met, there won't be anybody left to take the call by P.M."

"Why don't I give you my shrink's number? You can tell him I referred you."

"Maybe tomorrow. I'm planning to have a lot of time on my hands."

Liz used a collection of shirts from equally concerned bystanders to wrap the boy's wound, pinning the shard of metal in place. She knew from experience that removing it would result in catastrophic blood loss and almost instant death. This was the best chance the boy had, but he had no chance unless Johnny Wareagle figured out a way to get him to a hospital within the next few minutes.

There was a time after she learned how to shoot when Liz sneaked out hunting with some local boys. Her father had found the two rabbits she'd shot hidden in the barn. She had never seen Buck more angry, so dismayed was he that she had not heeded his lessons about the value and sanctity of life. Liz figured that was as near as he ever came to striking her. Instead Buck had hung up the carcasses in her room, leaving them there long after they began to decompose and stink. She thought about life and death differently after that, unable to kill anything that wasn't trying to do likewise to her.

With all the carnage and horror around her, the boy was all that mattered right now to Liz. She looked at him and saw Justin, remembering how close she had been to losing him at his school a month before and how much she hated losing him to his father. Looked at the boy and saw Buck, so angry he had tears in his eyes upon finding the dead rabbits hidden in the barn. After he finally pulled their carcasses out of her room, he yanked the bullets from her .22 and left them on her dresser.

Maybe all the years since had been about making up for that one mistake. Proving that she was worthy of his training. Save this boy today and make her father proud.

Clip-clop, clip-clop, clip-clip . . .

Liz knew that sound, but it made no sense to her here and now on the bridge. She gazed ahead through the clutter of twisted, smoking vehicles and actually blinked to make sure it wasn't a concussion-induced illusion.

"You gotta be fucking kidding me," she heard Sal Belamo mutter at her side, himself bleeding from a deep scalp wound that he'd wrapped tightly in a borrowed scarf.

Johnny Wareagle was adroitly leading a pair of black horses, salvaged from a dented horse trailer, through the sea of wrecks.

Blaine's wild ride on the bungee cord continued without pause over the remaining stretch of the Hudson River toward midtown Manhattan. He quickly learned how to control his sway through the air by angling his body in various directions. Almost as quickly, the gunman inside the rear of the chopper gave up wasting bullets. Blaine felt triumphant only until it became clear what fate the pilot had in mind for him.

He was still trying to free his gun from its holster when the helicopter approached the forest of skyscrapers dotting the skyline. The pilot banked sharply to the right, throwing Blaine hard to the left directly in line with a million tons of steel and glass. He avoided the collision by straightening out and twisting his body back into the wind, steering himself close enough to the fiftieth floor to reach out and swipe the glass.

The pilot saw that his first attempt at splattering Blaine across the cityscape had failed, and he veered to try again, squeezing within a narrow space between buildings overlooking Central Park. It seemed impossible for Blaine to adjust his path quickly and frequently enough to miss all the buildings, but he dipped and darted, swerved and swirled, to avoid one after another. Coming close enough on a few occasions to actually push off with his legs.

He felt like a puppet on a string, his toughest trick being to figure a way to free his pistol from its holster. The leather safety strip that restrained it was snapped tightly in place across the trigger guard, and Blaine couldn't risk keeping still long enough to unsnap it without setting himself up for the gunman inside the chopper's rear bay.

Added to that was the problem of the buildings the pilot was directing him ever closer to. The next pair was separated by a gap little wider than he was. The chopper pulled its nose just over them, and Blaine actually had to turn sideways, the wind screaming past him as he soared with hands and legs pressed close.

No sooner had he managed that feat than the chopper went into a swoon, significantly reducing his maneuverability before it flitted sharply to the right. The result was to snap him out like a rock from a slingshot, spilled sideways on a direct path with the top floors of the Waldorf-Astoria Hotel.

Blaine had actually started unknotting the cord, ready to take his chances with a plunge to the awnings below, when the chopper banked sharply again. The loosened cord slipped down his legs and reknotted itself around his ankles, redistributing so much of his weight that he missed the Waldorf altogether but got a very good look at himself flying by its shiny windows.

He was soaring upside down. If nothing else, the pistol was now in easier reach, and he imitated the motions of a Roman Chair sit-up to snatch it. He managed to get the holster unsnapped with the first stab, and the gun freed with the second. Then he nearly lost his grip on it, as the chopper soared down a traffic-snarled Park Avenue, with Blaine swaying wildly beneath it.

Blaine first thought that the pilot intended to leave him smeared against any number of stalled trucks and buses in the street below. Instead, though, he slowed his speed considerably and left McCracken dangling almost directly beneath the chopper, a much easier target for the gunman, who immediately opened up with his M-16.

The first barrage missed him, stitching a jagged design across the tops of cars mired in the gridlock below. Blaine curled upward at the waist and steadied his pistol as best he could before clacking off a few rounds to chase the gunman back inside. His bullets clanged off the chopper's frame, but he managed to pull back up to a standing position, grasping the cord with his free hand.

The gunman lunged into the doorway again and let go a wild spray downward. But McCracken was gone, not even the bungee cord in sight.

The gunman backpedaled in the rear bay, exchanging a fresh clip for a spent one. A metallic scraping sound made him swing to the right, where he saw that Blaine had managed to crack open the other bay door and lean his upper body inside the hold.

McCracken fired before the gunman could get his weapon resteadied. His bullets punched the gunman backwards through the open door on the opposite side, and he dropped downward, to crash spread-eagled atop the roof of a bus.

The pilot pulled the chopper into a climb, angling to catch a glimpse of Blaine. Turning forward once again, he barely avoided the Helmsley building. He straightened the chopper out and, still searching for McCracken, flew over the strip that separates Park Avenue into two distinct halves. Heading south, he climbed when the huge black shape of the Grand Hyatt Hotel rose before him.

The pilot tried to swing from its path, but it was too late. The chopper crashed through a pair of windows twenty stories up from the ground, lodging there, half in and half out of the hotel over Forty-second Street.

Clinging tightly to one of the pods, Blaine had begun considering his options, when he felt the chopper yaw, ready to tumble. There was only one choice:

The bungee cord!

It had become his lifeline now, and without hesitation, he let go of the pod and dropped into the air, straightening his body into a divelike posture, pretending water was beneath him instead of concrete. The bungee cord stretched taut, then slung him back up before letting him settle fifteen feet off the ground.

Just as Blaine was figuring he would have scored a perfect ten had the judges been around, the chopper jerked downward. Its crackling descent through the glass panes forming the Grand Hyatt's side dropped Blaine before he could unfasten the cord from his ankle. He crunched against the pavement and felt his breath leave him in a rush, as the chopper fell ever faster directly above him. Blaine rolled desperately and thrust himself to one side just before it slammed into the street, scattering debris and breaking up huge slabs of concrete a mere few feet from him.

The chopper caught fire almost instantly and coughed out papers from its corpse. Blaine watched them flutter, the touch of the flames leaving them blackened at the edges. He scampered across the pavement on all fours and managed to snare a single page before the fuel tank blew in a gush of heat that slammed into him and pitched him backwards.

"What do you mean, you can't reach the chopper?" Jack Tyrell demanded of Marbles.

"I don't know. Interference, a bad signal. Give me a little more time."

In the command center, an additional four television monitors had been switched on and tuned to what CNN was calling "Manhattan Held Hostage." All four screens broadcast scenes of panic and chaos, hordes of people trying to flee the city of New York, only to realize there was no way to get off the island.

The disabled subways remained packed with people making their way out slowly through the darkness.

The streets had become parking lots.

The sidewalks were jammed with people moving futilely this way and that, because nobody was going anywhere.

Tyrell's favorite shots were aerial views of the city. He reveled in that sight the way an artist would upon recognizing the creation of his finest masterpiece. It was an even more wondrous picture than he had let himself imagine, one that almost brought tears to his eyes.

"If the media had been this cooperative in the sixties," he said aloud to no one in particular, "we just mighta won this war back then."

While he was still crowing, one of the screens cut to the scene of a fiery helicopter crash. There was a disclaimer warning that unedited footage captured by a camcorder was about to air. And there it was.

The collision with the building, the chopper falling, a man dropping ahead of it. The camera's perspective shifted wildly while its amateur operator must have backed away to safety. Then the lens steadied once more to come in for a close-up of the man who had dropped to the pavement and just managed to lurch away before the explosion ended the shot.

It was a face Jack Tyrell was coming to know all too well. It should have upset him, he knew, pissed him off royally. Instead he smiled in utter admiration.

"Whatever you're on, I wish I had some." He looked over at Marbles and Othell Vance. "I want to know who he is, and I want to know now."

Gus Sabella reached his construction site, only to see the machines abandoned in the middle of their tasks, stilled in various work-related postures. He had been hauling a truckload of pipes to the site when the world shook and New York City ended up isolated from the rest of civilization. With traffic at an absolute standstill, Gus pulled his truck into a convenient loading zone and hoofed it back to the site in a slow trot that left him dripping with sweat. Even that had been a difficult task, what with the entire daytime population of Manhattan spilling into the streets and cluttering the sidewalks. Mobs had poured out of buildings and were gathered around car radios and electronics store windows to follow the unfolding crisis, which seemed almost unreal to them, even though they were caught in the middle of it.

Gus rushed past the abandoned machines toward his trailer, swearing up a storm and cussing out his damn workers, who had apparently fled at the first opportunity. Entering the trailer, though, he found all of them gathered around his thirteen-inch television, watching the first, nearly accurate reports on what was transpiring across the city.

"What the fuck? Who gave you boys the day off?"

The men turned to him.

"Somebody's blowing up the city," one of them said, gesturing toward the screen.

"I know. That's why I came back without any pipes, goddamn it. But it doesn't mean we're gonna let it set us further behind."

"You want us to work through *this*?" another man asked, disbelievingly.

"Why not? No way you're gonna be going home anytime soon anyway."

Johnny rode alone on one of the black horses, leading the way. Liz was on the second horse with Sal Belamo, the boy wedged between them.

"Jeez," Sal kept muttering.

"You've never been on a horse before," Liz realized as they neared the Manhattan side of the George Washington Bridge.

"You noticed."

The going became easier the farther they rode from the cluttered mess of traffic near the center of the bridge. Their progress was still challenging, the gaps between vehicles sometimes impossibly narrow or virtually nonexistent. But Johnny always found them a way through, pace held to a walk to keep from jarring the wounded boy too badly.

They reached the off-ramp and clip-clopped down it, weaving their way through gridlocked traffic toward Columbia Presbyterian Medical Center a dozen blocks away, as the first rescue vehicles crawled toward the scene.

FIFTY-THREE

want you to give Mayor Corrente a message for me. Tell Her Honor that I have taken all the people in this city hostage, and all five million will die when I destroy the city unless my terms are met. . . ."

Mayor Lucille Corrente leaned across the conference table and pressed the Stop button on the tape recorder. "As I'm sure you all know," she said to those gathered before her, "that tape was made from the Imus program earlier this morning. We haven't heard from the speaker directly yet, but I expect we will be hearing from him soon."

It was ten-thirty before the department heads primarily responsible for the welfare of New York City finally gathered in Mayor Lucille Corrente's conference room. As they settled into their chairs, the shattered bay window formed the perfect backdrop, a constant reminder of what they were facing. Against the far wall adjacent to that window, a number of men with FBI photo IDs hanging from their necks were busy laying cords and wires attached to additional telephones, computers, and fax machines.

"Mr. Kirkland, we're ready to get started."

Sam Kirkland picked up his suit jacket and pulled his bulky arms uncomfortably into the sleeves as he headed back to the conference table.

Mayor Corrente, elegantly dressed and coiffed as always, adjusted the speakerphone in front of her. "Can you hear me, Governor?" she said to the state's chief executive in Albany.

"Loud and clear, Lucille. Are you on-line with Washington?"

Corrente looked at the members of Kirkland's team still stringing wires and running extension cords from the sockets spaced at regular intervals along the walls.

"Momentarily," she said.

"I'm patched in here with the state police, the national guard, and Fort Dix in New Jersey."

"What can we expect from them in the way of assistance?"

"The first deployment of troops from Fort Dix should be airborne in a matter of minutes. MPs, logistical support, and combat engineers, if I'm reading this memo correctly. They'll need a landing zone, by the way."

"Already taken care of, sir," said Kirkland, finally settling into his chair. "This is Assistant Director Sam Kirkland of the FBI. We've cleared a stretch of land in Central Park. I've been in touch with Fort Dix's people to relay the proper coordinates."

"That's a good start."

"Now," Kirkland continued, "if you'll open the folders I distributed, you'll find the dossier on the man our information suggests is responsible. Governor, I faxed it to you en route."

"I have it right before me," the governor said over the speakerphone.

Kirkland stood up again and rested his knuckles on the table. "Jack Tyrell, alias Jackie Terror, a founding member of the radical Weatherman movement of the 1960s, who later broke off to establish an even more radical and violent group called Midnight Run, responsible for a series of bombings and other terrorist actions in the early 1970s."

"Number one on the FBI's Most Wanted List for five years running," noted New York City Police Chief Daniel Logan, without reading ahead. "I was walking a beat when the Mercantile Bank blew, twenty-five years ago."

"I'm confused, Mr. Kirkland," said Mayor Corrente. "How were you able to identify Tyrell so quickly?"

Kirkland sighed. "I received information last night that placed him in the city and strongly indicated a possible threat."

"And you did nothing about it?" asked Public Safety Commissioner Corrothers.

"The information was impossible to confirm."

"And the source?" wondered Corrente.

"An ex–intelligence operative."

"Ex?" echoed Logan.

"Yes."

"And do we have his file here as well?"

"No."

"You're being evasive, Mr. Kirkland," the mayor said critically.

Kirkland looked at Corrente, then at the department heads gathered around the table. "This city is facing a crisis of unprecedented proportions, which promises to get worse before it gets better. Telling you everything I might suspect right now would only pose an unnecessary distraction. Let's stick to what we know."

"Does that include the type of explosive Tyrell used to shut off this city from the outside world?" challenged Chief Logan. "My people tell me there's no evidence at any of the blast sites of a standard bomb or incendiary device."

"Beyond that," added the city's chief fire official, Hideo Takamura, "my own experience indicates it would take an explosive device the size of a two-ton truck to blast through a bridge, and even then the results wouldn't be as catastrophic as we've seen."

"The explosive Tyrell used is an experimental one," Kirkland offered noncommittally.

"Not anymore it's not," Lucille Corrente chastised.

"It's called Devil's Brew, developed under a tight seal at Brookhaven Labs," Kirkland said, repeating the information Blaine McCracken had given him.

"Apparently not tight enough to keep it out of the hands of a terrorist," countered city Department of Transportation Director Les Carney. Carney's right arm beat the air dramatically as he spoke, while his left, a cosmetic prosthesis, rested motionless on the table.

Chief Logan was shaking his head. "If it was stolen, why weren't local law enforcement agencies notified?"

"I wasn't notified, either."

"Then how can you be sure your information is correct?"

"Same source."

"This one ex–intelligence agent?"

"Yes."

"We should get one of Brookhaven's experts on the line to explain exactly what it is we're dealing with," suggested Mayor Corrente.

"I already tried. Nobody there will confirm the existence of the explosive, never mind elaborate on its capabilities."

Corrente's features flared, the look many said exemplified the no-nonsense, draw-the-line campaign that had brought her to office. "Is that what you call a tight seal, Mr. Kirkland?"

"It was done for safety, ma'am, to keep anyone on the outside from learning of Devil's Brew's existence."

"I think it's safe to say that strategy has backfired," noted the mayor. "And for the time being we've got more pressing concerns. Bottom line:

Now that we know who we're dealing with and what he has in his possession, how can we catch him before he makes good on the threat he issued over the radio?"

Again Kirkland took the floor, relieved to have the subject changed. It was as difficult explaining McCracken's role in this as to explain why Kirkland hadn't acted preemptively. Not that he could have done anything, short of closing down the city or trying to evacuate it altogether. In fact, there had been no time to do either, even if he had wanted to.

"We've confirmed that the call Tyrell made to the radio station came in via cellular phone operating on a digital channel. We are now on-line with a tracking satellite that will enable us to pin down his precise location when he makes contact again."

"And then?" from Corrente.

Kirkland sounded more confident now, back in his element. "I've got six strike teams standing by in jets no more than one hour from any locale in the country."

A lone black telephone on the table rang.

"Goddamn it, he's early!" Chief Logan protested.

"No," Kirkland reminded. "He said 'by' eleven on the radio, not 'at' eleven!" He swung toward his technicians, who'd barely finished setting up shop against the far wall. "Talk to me!"

The men were studying the data readouts flying across their monitor screens.

"It's definitely cellular!" concluded one.

"And digital!" another added. "We've got him!"

"We're on-line here!" the governor said through the other phone.

Kirkland waited until Lucille Corrente nodded before reaching out and touching the Speaker button on the black phone.

"Hello, Mr. Tyrell," the mayor greeted.

The top officials of the city of New York heard a brief laugh before a voice resounded through the speakerphone. "My, my, my, I guess I don't have to introduce myself."

"Why are you doing this?" Corrente demanded, trying to stay on the offensive.

"Long story. Goes back a whole lotta years."

"You've made your point."

A chuckle. "Lucy, I'm just getting started. Now you got a choice to make: either you go down as the mayor who saved her city or the mayor who lost it."

"How much do you want? You said you'd tell us."

"Everything have to have a monetary value?"

"Usually, when hostages are involved."

"Well, I got plenty of them. That means we're talking *lots* of monetary value. Say, fifteen billion dollars delivered before three o'clock this afternoon, or your city is toast, Lucy."

The entire conference room seemed to quiver.

"Did you say fifteen *billion*?"

"I did, I did. You got maybe five million people trapped in Manhattan right now, which puts the price at maybe three hundred bucks a head—a bargain when you look at it that way."

"Five million and one," said Blaine McCracken from the doorway.

McCracken's clothes were shredded and smudged. He advanced grimacing, clearly in considerable pain. The first New York City policeman to arrive on the scene of the helicopter crash on Park Avenue had become his reluctant chauffeur to City Hall on an excruciatingly long drive through the gridlocked streets. The personnel standing around the conference table did a collective double take, watching him.

"I know that voice," Jack Tyrell droned through the black phone's speaker.

"We were never formally introduced, Tyrell."

"Pleased to meet you. Glad you guessed my name." Then, after a pause, "You fucked up my operation at the Monument, killed one of my men in Pennsylvania, and now you cost me a helicopter, asshole."

"I'm going to cost you a whole lot more than that before this day is over."

"This day ends at three o'clock."

"We'll see about that."

"Hey, Lucy, I'll call you back with the details. How I want the money broken up, where to deliver it—that sort of shit."

Click.

Kirkland swung from the conference table toward his team of technicians. "Talk to me!"

"We got it!" a man wearing a headset announced.

Kirkland grabbed the receiver of the phone set before his chair at the table. "Get strike teams ready to roll!"

"Damn!" said his technician, working the keyboard.

"What is it?"

"This guy's good. . . ."

"Where is he?"

The technician spoke while still punching keys. "Birmingham, Alabama. But it's the signal, not the call. He's got direct linkup with a satellite. No way we can get him."

"Can't you—"

"Wait a minute, I've got something here. Just an echo, but if it's right . . ."

"Talk!" Kirkland ordered.

The technician spun his chair around. "He's here. He's calling from somewhere in New York City."

"Like I told you last night," McCracken reminded.

That was enough for the mayor to put everything together. "This is your *source?*" she asked Kirkland, eyeing the disheveled Blaine disparagingly.

Kirkland shrugged, nodded. "Meet Blaine McCracken."

"The man from the George Washington Bridge," Corrente realized, recalling Tyrell's mention of a helicopter.

"I happened to be in the neighborhood."

"Just like he happened to be in the neighborhood of the Washington Monument when Tyrell seized that six months ago," Kirkland said by way of explanation.

"You seem to be the resident expert on this man, Mr. McCracken," noted Mayor Corrente. "We'd like to hear what you know."

"He's going to blow up this city."

"That much we're already aware of," Chief Logan said snidely.

"No, what I mean is he's going to blow up the city at three o'clock whether you pay him or not."

"Well, then," began Mayor Corrente, only half sarcastically, "if you could save the Monument, we better hope you can save New York."

"I'll see what I can do," Blaine said, producing the charred piece of paper he had salvaged from the helicopter.

"**H**ere's our boy," Marbles called to Jack Tyrell. "His name is Blaine McCracken. His file's got more seals on it than I can penetrate, but this is good enough."

"One tough fucking son of a bitch, I'd say," Tyrell said, reading over his shoulder.

"Jackie," one of his communications monitors yelled out. "We got trouble at New York Harbor."

"I was waiting for that," Tyrell said, leaving Blaine McCracken behind to move to another area of the command center.

McCracken flattened out the tattered, slightly charred page as best he could before holding it up for those around the conference table to see. At first glance it looked like the outline of a hand with a single finger pointing upward, dotted with upwards of two dozen small circles.

"It's a plan of the island of Manhattan," realized Transportation Director Carney.

"What about those circles?" wondered Chief Takamura.

Blaine shrugged. "They form an irregular line across the city, but it's not symmetrical. And if you wanted to maximize the effect of the explosives, you'd want it to be symmetrical."

"What then?" Corrente asked him.

"Why don't we start with an explanation of how this Devil's Brew works?" Logan suggested. "Mr. McCracken, you seem to be the only one here who knows anything about it. . . ."

Blaine summarized the volatile properties of the deadly substance, laying out for his audience what their city was facing.

"You're talking about a bomb that effectively has no working parts," concluded a flabbergasted Mayor Corrente.

"Then how can it be set off?" asked Corrothers.

"A number of different alternatives are possible. The most viable trigger is electronic, via a digital or transistor receiver that would respond to a preprogrammed signal. Once the signal is received, a charge is sent down a thin wire connecting the receiver or capacitor to the position of the Devil's Brew."

Chief Logan leaned forward. "This receiver be about the size of a Walkman?"

"Even smaller, maybe."

"I think we've got one. One of my squads recovered something matching that description from the explosion at the Queensboro Bridge. It's almost intact."

McCracken turned to Kirkland. "You have any communications experts at the New York office?"

"Only the best."

"Then get the receiver over to him. If he can identify the controller chip's frequency, we might be able to send a signal with enough power to burn out the rest of the capacitors Tyrell must have wired throughout the city."

"Would Devil's Brew show up in explosives sensor equipment?" asked Chief Takamura.

"Yes," Blaine replied. "In the high-end models used in airports."

"The city bomb squad just purchased four of the portable variety," Logan said, almost proudly. "And the units en route from Fort Dix are bringing three more."

"Still leaves us several short," Blaine noted.

"How about using dogs?" suggested Les Carney.

"If there's enough Devil's Brew left for them to pick up the scent, absolutely," said McCracken.

"How much would it have taken to blow each of the bridges and tunnels?" the mayor asked him.

"Twenty gallons each would be a fair estimate."

"That's all?" exclaimed a flabbergasted Logan.

"And how much is in the missing tanker that was traced to Manhattan?" the mayor added.

"The entire reserve that Brookhaven manufactured: fifty thousand gallons."

The whole room fell into shocked silence, broken finally by Corrente in a voice grim with resignation. "Tyrell really can destroy this city, can't he?"

"The question," said Blaine, "is where has he planted the tanker's contents?"

"According to you, it could be *anywhere.*"

"The sewers would be my guess," proposed Chief Logan.

"No," said Blaine. "Too much of the blast would be focused downward to achieve the effect Tyrell wants. He'd destroy a good deal of the city's infrastructure, level some buildings, and collapse a few streets, but that's not enough for a man who intends to destroy the city." Again he glanced at the tattered map. "It's got to be something else, something he wouldn't expect us to consider."

"Can I see that?" Carney asked, and Blaine slid the map down the table. Carney took it in his working hand. "This map is drawn perfectly to scale." He looked up at the mayor. "Given time, I think I can pin down the exact locations of these circles."

"How much time?"

"An hour; forty-five minutes if we're lucky."

"With dogs and the explosives sensors," started Logan, "we can come up with ten teams, possibly eleven."

"That's two sites per team at least, Chief," Blaine noted without enthusiasm.

"You got a better idea?"

"I want an update on all emergency efforts currently under way before we listen to any new ideas," broke in Lucille Corrente.

Fire Chief Takamura took the floor. "Our first priority, as you know, has been to clear routes to the blast sites in order to reach all the casualties."

"Toward that end," picked up Corrothers from Public Safety, "my crews are doing their best to clear the tunnels and bridges. I called in every tow and haul vendor in the Manhattan yellow pages, but it became clear pretty quickly even that wasn't going to be enough."

"That's where my people came in," said Carney, still holding the outline of Manhattan, as Corrothers moved to a television in the front of the room and switched it on, scanning channels for the scene he was looking for. "I had a hundred snowplows in the shop gathering dust, so I recommended we use them to shove aside the smashed cars in the roadways."

"Our biggest problem at this point is that we just don't have enough emergency personnel to treat all the wounded," Takamura explained somberly. "I've portioned out our rescue and fire forces as best I can. Then, of course, there's the added problem of getting to the wounded and then getting them to hospitals. What we've managed to do instead is to distribute hospital crews—teams of doctors and nurses with as much equipment as they can carry—to the blast sites to set up triage facilities."

"Do we have an update on the number of casualties?" Corrente asked.

"No one's had the time to sit down and tabulate all that's been reported. CNN is estimating a thousand dead and ten times that number wounded."

"Oh my God . . ."

"Here we go," said Corrothers.

The screen filled with a shot of a line of massive plows effortlessly shoving aside wrecked cars on the George Washington Bridge, mashing them against each other to create a wide channel for the emergency vehicles that kept arriving on the scene. The plows worked right up to a makeshift barrier where one of the triage units Takamura had mentioned had already been organized.

"What we've been doing on the streets where traffic was gridlocked," started Chief Logan, "is similar in strategy. Our goal is to get two lanes open on every major artery and north-south city street by forcing the traffic to one side, use the sidewalks for parking if we have to. We've blocked off every primary access route so no more nonessential traffic can enter. But our job is being substantially complicated by the crowds of people filling the streets."

"Excuse me," interrupted City Engineer Muldoon, the only man who hadn't spoken yet, in a soft voice.

Chief Logan continued speaking, not seeming to notice that Muldoon was trying to get the floor. "But it's going to take more men than I've got to do that and keep order in the city, and believe me, order in the city is going to break down pretty quick if this nut keeps broadcasting his plans over the radio."

"Excuse me," Muldoon repeated, a bit more loudly.

"You've got a full regiment on its way from Fort Dix," announced the governor through the speakerphone, "including a detachment of military police and a brigade from the Army Corps of Engineers. Get them a route into the city from New Jersey, and they can be on-site within four hours."

"Excuse me!"

All eyes in the room at last turned toward Warren Muldoon. A bookish, balding, round-faced man wearing glasses, he ruffled through a nest of papers, manuals, and binders stacked before him.

"If we can get one of the decks of the George Washington Bridge cleared, then I can have it open by three o'clock."

"Open for traffic in four hours?" posed a disbelieving Takamura.

"No way we can get an AVLB folding bridge here by then," added Kirkland.

Muldoon was unfazed. "I've got another idea of how to create one lane easily large enough to accommodate the trucks the army will be using, if the specifications in this manual here are right."

"That's assuming the city can hold out until three, of course," Chief Logan noted grimly, clearly not sure it could.

"As soon as this meeting breaks," started the mayor, "I'm going on the air. Do my best to reassure the people."

Logan looked down, hiding his skepticism.

"You worried I'm not up to the task, Chief?"

"Madam Mayor, I don't think anyone's up to that task."

The door to the conference room burst open and one of the mayor's chief aides rushed in.

"New York Harbor!" he uttered breathlessly. "Channel Five—quickly!"

FIFTY-FOUR

L iz Halprin rode her horse straight into the emergency room lobby
of Columbia Presbyterian Medical Center. She let Sal Belamo
climb off first, and then together they eased the wounded boy down
to the floor.

"This boy needs help!" she shouted through the frantic activity whirling
around her. *"Stat!"*

A nurse rushed over, inspected the wound, and then instantly summoned a doctor who was halfway out the door, on his way to join one of
the mobile triage units being dispersed throughout the city. Liz answered
what questions she could, then drifted off to join Sal Belamo, who stood
in front of a wall-mounted television, a gauze packet pressed against his
head wound in place of the scarf he had appropriated on the George
Washington Bridge.

"Hey," he said, "check this out."

Jack Tyrell had been watching Channel 5 for several minutes now. Since
the East and Hudson Rivers provided the only viable routes off the island
of Manhattan after his explosions, the frantic level of activity in New York
Harbor was hardly surprising. The piers were crammed with people seeking passage on any boat that would have them. Luxury liners that happened to be in port were besieged with desperate individuals offering to
pay anything to be ferried out. Enterprising small-boat owners had already

lined up clients and joined a massive flotilla of sailboats, speedboats, yachts, and cabin cruisers moving both north and south along the Hudson.

The result was a form of gridlock never before seen on the waters surrounding the city, as boats vied with one another to flee, the smaller craft maneuvering desperately to stay clear of the paths of the larger ones. A number of boats had already collided and were dead in the water or listing badly. The sleeker speedboat types, meanwhile, weaved through the channel, even the best pilots challenged by the obstacle course in their path.

"I think it's time we grounded the fleet," Tyrell said decisively, turning to Marbles. "Activate the mines."

"Get them out of there!" McCracken said, gesturing toward the screen.

The rest of those in the room looked at each other, unsure what he was getting at.

"Jesus Christ! This is Jackie Terror we're dealing with here. Do you think he would have left anyone a way out?"

Mayor Corrente had just snapped a telephone to her ear when, on Channel 5, explosions erupted in the harbor. Flaming chunks and refuse were hurled through the air, smashing into boats that had been fortunate enough to steer free of the mines. And in some cases, boats trying desperately to flee rammed each other, resulting in the same explosive effect.

A pair of coast guard helicopters tempted fate by dropping toward the surface, the search for survivors already beginning while another series of flaming rumbles coughed debris and black smoke into the air. Virtually no craft was spared, the harbor turned into a watery graveyard of floating oil, blood, and marine debris.

Blaine felt the rage building in him as he watched Jack Tyrell's work unfold. The drifting life jackets were the worst; McCracken knew there were bodies, or what was left of them, attached to the orange spots dotting the water. The underwater explosions seemed to stretch on forever, continuing until the hovering coast guard choppers were silhouetted by a ghostly curtain of smoke blown about by the wind.

"I say we give this bastard shit," Chief Logan muttered just loud enough for everyone to hear. "I say we call his bluff."

"Really think he's bluffing, Chief?" Blaine asked him.

"We pay him, he blows the city anyway. You said that."

"But he could be wrong," Kirkland said, aiming his words at the mayor, "in which case we use the ransom to catch him. Bills can be marked electronically now. We can disguise directional beacons as money wrappers. We can trace bearer bonds twenty seconds after they're presented for liquidation. We've got fake gold even Fort Knox couldn't tell from the real thing."

"Then I wonder what it is he's going to ask for," Blaine posed flatly.

The black phone rang again. The mayor pounded the speaker button without checking to see if the FBI technicians were ready.

"Hey, we didn't have this many channels in the sixties," Jack Tyrell greeted. "You see that boat go up on nine? Man oh man, how about that crash on five? . . ."

"We were bargaining in good faith. Why'd you do it?" Corrente demanded.

"What do you think this is, Lucy, a negotiation? I *own* your city. It's mine to do with as I choose, and what I chose was not to let anyone leave it. Didn't think that would be fair to everyone else."

"I overestimated you, Tyrell," McCracken broke in.

"Then I guess I better watch my nuts, eh, McCracken? Been reading about you. You really shoot the balls off Churchill's statue in Parliament Square?"

"You want to stand on a pedestal, see if my aim's still good?"

"McCrackenballs . . . Name's got a nice ring to it. What happened made you do that?"

"Somebody pissed me off."

"Bad as me?"

"I've been telling these people you're a pro, Jackie. Now I'm going to have to take it all back."

"You're hurting me. You really are."

"Women and children make easy targets, don't they? Especially from a distance."

"You looking at the harbor now, Mr. Balls? Their blood's as red as everybody else's."

"That what I'm gonna find inside when I cut you open, Jackie?"

"Really think you're up to that, Mr. Balls? Word is you haven't been yourself since you and I had our first run-in."

"As you saw yesterday, I've made a miraculous recovery."

"That so? Then what's it gonna be—you gonna advise the mayor to pay up so she can keep her city?"

"We don't want anyone else hurt today—no more mayhem," interrupted the mayor.

"Come on, Lucy, just imagine yourself presiding over the rebuilding of New York. No place to go but up."

"That won't be necessary."

"Might be preferable, though."

Corrente fixed her gaze on Sam Kirkland, who nodded. "Just tell us how you want the fifteen billion."

"In gem-quality diamonds."

The mayor felt her stomach sink toward her feet. Kirkland's mouth dropped. McCracken's face alone remained impassive.

"That's fifteen billion dollars *wholesale*," Tyrell added gloatingly.

"Where and when?" Corrente managed.

"Let's start with who: my friend Mr. Balls. Two o'clock."

"Where?" McCracken asked before the mayor could speak, a scowl darkening his face and the scar through his left eyebrow turning a savage red.

"You still got your television on?"

Blaine glanced at an overview of the coast guard lifting survivors out of the Hudson at New York Harbor. "Yes."

"See you right there at two, Mr. Balls."

"**I** got Kirkland on the phone for maybe five seconds," Sal Belamo reported to Johnny and Liz outside the hospital. "Apparently the boss made it safe and sound to City Hall."

Relieved, Liz climbed back on her horse. She extended a hand to Belamo. "We've got some ground to cover."

Mayor Lucille Corrente strode to the podium at the front of the City Hall pressroom without being announced. She knew it would have made a better show to have her various department heads behind her to demonstrate solidarity, but their services were urgently required elsewhere.

She ignored the onslaught of questions thrust at her and the hands flapping to grab her attention from the jam-packed room. Dozens of cameras followed her every move, the feed being carried live by all three major networks and CNN across the entire world.

She waved the reporters off again and waited for them to go quiet before beginning. "I think what I have to say will answer all of your questions as well as the city's."

Her words echoed through Times Square, where throngs viewed her on the giant Sony screen. Others watched at home, in bars, and even through the windows of the city's countless electronics stores. The few not near a television tuned their Walkmans louder or increased the radio volume in their cars, where thousands remained prisoners.

Lucille Corrente spoke without benefit of notes, leaning slightly forward over the podium.

"People of New York City . . ."

A dozen choppers painted in military green cut across the sky from the northwest. The noise as they dipped low toward the landing zone on the Great Lawn in Central Park was deafening, drowning out the mayor's words to any trying to listen nearby.

A regiment of national guardsmen was already waiting in the park, to lend whatever logistical support was required and escort the specialists from Fort Dix to the pool of waiting vehicles. A trio of guard airmen took on the task of directing the choppers in for landings in three separate zones, designated by both white spray paint and a spread of orange cones that kept getting thrown across the grass by the rotor wash.

Upon touchdown, the arriving troops flooded out, dragging their weapons and equipment. They took seats in the vehicles appropriated for them and sped away, or in some cases formed up as marching brigades and set off for their designated destinations closer by. The process went so smoothly that it looked rehearsed, when nothing could have been farther from the truth.

"Go! . . . Go! . . . Go! . . ."

That command, shouted loudly to carry over the rotor wash, was the only word to be heard.

" *. . . You all know that our city has come under attack from the most vile of criminals, one for whom innocent lives are no more than bargaining chips. He has convinced us of his capacity and capability to kill. He has demonstrated a callous disregard for everything we hold dear and demanded we pay him to preserve our homes and our lives. . . ."*

The convoy of army trucks en route north from Fort Dix stretched as far as the eye could see up Route 295, heading toward New York City. The highway had been all but shut down to accommodate it. Even so, the huge amount of heavy construction equipment and ordnance the convoy carried kept it moving at a snail's pace. The best it could manage, even with a state police escort clearing the way, was forty miles per hour, a considerable handicap given the sign that none of the convoy's members could miss: NEW YORK CITY 75 MILES.

" *. . . It has long been the policy of this city never to negotiate with criminals. However, today we must weigh that policy against the very real threat of additional casualties. . . ."*

The first reports Chief Logan received upon returning to the streets were not encouraging. Looting had broken out in certain areas of the city and was spreading. So much of his manpower had to be used to quell these disturbances before they turned into outright riots that he had little to spare toward the more pressing task of getting the streets as clear as possible.

Early into his drive-through of the city, his car was pelted with soda cans and various debris on three occasions. Both the back window and the windshield were shattered, two of the side windows as well, by mobs that were more terrified than angry. Searching to find a way out of the city when none existed.

✿　　✿　　✿

" . . . Therefore I am announcing to the people of the city of New York our intention to comply with the terms of this criminal's demands. The money, while a significant sum, pales by comparison with the preservation of even one human life. That is the difference between him and us. That is where the strength that will see us through this crisis lies."

Explosives specialists drawn from the FBI, arriving combat engineers from Fort Dix, and members of the NYPD's bomb squad were being assembled by Sam Kirkland even as Department of Transportation Director Les Carney hurried to identify the circles dotting the charred map of Manhattan that Blaine McCracken had left with him. To further expedite the process, he had made copies of the map and assigned one or two circles each to four longtime workers in the Hall of Records, specialists in either zoning or deeds who knew the city's landscape intimately.

"The best we're going to be able to do in many cases is narrow things down to a city block or so," Carney explained to McCracken, looking up from his slide rule, maps, and charts. "The scale's too small to get any more specific than that."

"It'll have to do."

Carney gazed up at the clock just as it ticked to 11:45. "You have any idea how long it takes to search a building, never mind a block? And we haven't even got enough teams to handle two apiece." He paused. "That's why I put my name in with Kirkland."

"You?"

"I did a tour as a minesweeper during the Gulf War. I know the basics."

Blaine looked at his missing arm. "That how you . . . ?"

"This? No, it was long gone before Saddam even crossed the border. Bone cancer."

"It's still a different game."

"But this is my ballpark. I figure that counts for something." Carney raised his eyebrows. "You mind if I ask you something?"

"Go ahead."

"You *want* to play delivery boy, don't you?"

"Yes."

"Why?"

"Why do you want to put all your minesweeping experience to good use?"

"Because it's my job."

Blaine's point had been made. He pointed at the map. "Do me a favor and pick two of those for us."

"Don't you have to be somewhere else?"

"Not until two o'clock I don't."

✿　　✿　　✿

The mayor's senior staff were waiting outside when a convoy of four police cars with sirens screaming led a pair of ordinary sedans off Chambers Street toward a side entrance of City Hall. Four men dressed in dark suits and sporting the trademark side curls and beards of Hasidic Jews climbed out as soon as the sedans came to a halt.

"The mayor's waiting upstairs," Lucille Corrente's chief aide said, leading the members of the Diamond Merchants Association's executive board up the steps.

The mayor hung up her phone and turned to Bob Corrothers. "They're here, Bob. Let's wrap this up."

"Just another minute."

Corrothers continued viewing the twenty-seven-inch television playing a tape his people had put together over the course of the last hour. "As you can see, we've managed to clear two lanes of traffic on all major streets running north and south," he said, as the camera panned the civilian vehicles that had been swept aside into the other two lanes.

The picture changed perfectly on cue to the West Side Highway. "On the main access arteries leading in and out of the city, like the West Side Highway here, at least two and in some cases all three lanes are being cleared." He waited for the picture to change again. "Running east and west, we're concentrating on clearing two major streets in the north, two in midtown."

Corrothers switched subjects fast when the picture changed yet again. "This is the latest footage to come in."

He didn't need to explain the massive snowplows, riding three abreast and slightly offset, clearing wrecked cars from their path to widen the channel on the George Washington Bridge.

"Muldoon still claims he can have the bridge open again by three o'clock," said Corrothers. "He just needed a little help."

On the upper span of the George Washington Bridge, City Engineer Warren Muldoon stood near the edge of the jagged chasm, setting up a tripod atop which rested a laser transit. Muldoon shifted the tripod even closer to the edge and took the readings again.

The cop holding Muldoon's laptop computer looked on in dismay. "I wouldn't get that close if I were you, sir."

Muldoon didn't look up at him. "It's the only way I can calculate the precise specifications of the missing section."

He slid the laser transit off its rest and took his computer from the cop's outstretched hand. He used a cable to connect the two devices and then switched on the laptop. Instantly, a three-dimensional representation of the gap in the upper deck appeared on-screen, complete with all necessary specifications.

"Excuse me, sir, but what exactly are you doing?"

Muldoon plugged his cellular phone into his laptop and dialed a number. "The mayor wants a route into the city, and I'm going to give it to her."

And with that he pressed SEND.

Back at City Hall, in the mayor's conference room, Lucille Corrente and her senior staff sat facing the board members of the Diamond Merchants Association. Thus far the four men had listened without comment or question to Corrente. Now that she had finished, they exchanged looks of worry and concern before the association president leaned forward to speak.

"Your Honor, we are willing to help in this crisis in any way we can. But you're talking about utilizing virtually the entire reserves of every jeweler and investor in this city. My problem is that, under the circumstances, my hands are tied until I am satisfied with what the city of New York is putting up as collateral."

"The President himself has authorized the transfer of fifteen billion dollars in government securities from the Federal Reserve Bank to any bank or banks you choose." The mayor leaned forward as well. "Now, will that be cash or check?"

FIFTY-FIVE

t's twelve forty-five already," Sam Kirkland said to McCracken, looking up from his watch. "You really want to do this?"

A helicopter sat warming in the City Hall parking lot, ready to ferry Blaine and Les Carney to a walk-in clinic near Madison Square Park, which Carney had identified as one of the circles.

"You're the one who said you needed at least one more team to get this done," Blaine explained. "We're it."

Kirkland was responsible for coordinating the teams of explosives experts with the sites Carney and his people had identified from the circles. Running the effort from City Hall took three cellular phones and a pair of walkie-talkies. After seeing the last team off, Kirkland would return to the mayor's offices on the third floor, ready to assemble whatever information came in from the field.

He gazed at the device strapped to Carney's back, which looked like an elaborate version of the metal detectors used to sweep beaches in search of lost change. "Then you better get going."

One of New York City's bomb disposal trucks, under escort by two police cruisers, pulled up in front of the Empire State Building. The truck had barely come to a halt when two members of the nation's oldest bomb squad popped out in full gear.

At the same time, one of the Humvees dispatched from Central Park with a team of combat engineers inside cruised to a halt in front of a downtown skyscraper. The engineers moved purposefully for the entrance, holding what looked like two long, extended microphones. Boxes attached to them dangled by their necks. These were sophisticated "sniffing" devices that had been programmed with residue of Devil's Brew recovered from the blast sites. As soon as any of the substance was registered, the LED readouts would flash instantly to life.

A squad equipped with dogs instead of any form of sensor equipment found itself mired in the rubble of a demolished building. The piles of debris made it hard to get anywhere very fast; the team was having trouble just keeping up with the panting dogs as they nosed their way through the mess.

Liz stopped near West Twenty-third Street to let her horse drink from a huge puddle. From Columbia Presbyterian, she and Johnny Wareagle had ridden back to the West Side Highway and headed downtown, intending to cut over to City Hall just past the Holland Tunnel.

Sal Belamo, meanwhile, had gotten much more comfortable riding behind her—almost at ease, in fact.

"You're pretty good at this," he said, as the horse snorted.

Liz remembered the first riding lesson her father had ever given her. "I had a good teacher."

And then something occurred to her, distant at first but quickly sharpening. So obvious she couldn't believe she had missed it.

"Change in plans," she said to Johnny.

"Huh?"

Liz looked behind her at Sal. "My son's elementary school is just a few blocks from here. That's where we're going."

"You ask me, it's not a good time to stop by and pick up his report card."

"I need to check something."

"Now?"

"Trust me."

The huge reserves held by member stores of the Diamond Merchants Association were kept in bank vaults throughout the city. The members of the association's board of directors personally supervised the removal of these huge caches from the vaults, as well as the subsequent weighing and tallying procedures required to attain the fifteen-billion-dollar ransom.

After being tabulated, the diamonds were loaded into specially cushioned cases and kept under heavy police guard until the time came to deliver them to New York Harbor, where the payoff was set to take place.

"How many stones we talking about here?" the police captain Chief

Logan had put in charge of the operation asked one of the board member's assistants.

"At an average of value of fifty thousand dollars per stone," the man replied patiently, "you'd need three hundred thousand stones."

"You could fill a barrel."

"Probably closer to three."

After all the bomb squad teams had been dispatched, Sam Kirkland transferred the approximate locations of the target sites to a larger, detailed map of New York City he then placed on an easel in the conference room. He had added numbers to those circles, one to twenty-four, intending to fill them in once reports from the field began coming in.

By one-fifteen he had heard from a half-dozen teams that had completed their initial sweeps and were moving on to their second sites. Not one of them had found any trace of either a receiver or the Devil's Brew, and Kirkland was beginning to fear the other teams working the field were going to encounter the same results, that their initial assessment of the circles on the map had been false.

When he received an identical report from a seventh team, he turned grimly to the mayor. "It looks like we better get McCracken ready to travel."

Blaine and Les Carney had just finished a rapid sweep of the clinic with the explosives sensor, which had turned up nothing. The only floor remaining for them to check was the basement, the door to which was marked NO ADMITTANCE.

"You mind opening this?" Blaine called to a janitor mopping a floor nearby.

The man looked at him suspiciously. "You got authorization?"

"For a boiler room?"

"Hey, don't ask me. All I know is the building inspector closed the basement off after the first-floor patients started getting sick."

"Light-headed, nauseous, headaches?" Carney jumped in, suddenly anxious.

The janitor leaned against his mop, even more suspicious now. "You a doctor or something?"

"The door!" the one-armed man yelled. "Open it *now!*"

The crisis had led to noontime dismissals at all city schools, a bad situation worsened by the thousands of frantic parents lined up at the doors, waiting for their terrified children. By the time Liz, Sal, and Johnny Wareagle got to William T. Harris Elementary, it was almost deserted. Returning to the building for the first time since the shootout brought a nervous flutter to Liz's stomach.

Maybe I shouldn't have opened fire. Maybe I should have tried to talk the gunman calm. Maybe I should have waited for backup before doing anything at all. . . .

Feelings of self-doubt plagued her until she remembered her father's words. No way Buck would lie just to make her feel better. The fact that he said he would have done the same thing meant she had acted properly.

Johnny and Sal followed her into an office, empty save for a secretary clacking away behind an ancient IBM and an older man with his shirt-sleeves rolled up, tinkering with an even older PA system's console board.

"If the two of you came to pick up your kid," the man said, looking up, "we're fresh out." His eyes sharpened, seeming to recognize her. He climbed to his feet, a dull hum in the background indicating that the power switch on the PA had been left on. "Mrs. Halprin, please forgive me. I didn't recognize you."

"Makes us even," Liz returned, realizing this was Arthur Frawley, the school principal, who had supported her in the press all along. He had his ever-present walkie-talkie clipped to his belt, even though there was no one left to speak with in the building. "I was hoping you'd let me take a look at something. A file."

Frawley cast a quick glance at Wareagle. "Should I consider this official business?"

"Yes."

"Something to do with what's happening in the city?"

"I'll let you know after I take a look," Liz told him.

"**Y**ou ready to tell me what we're looking for?" Blaine asked, sweeping his flashlight about the dark and dreary basement as Les Carney rummaged around.

Carney stopped and looked at him. "Smell it?"

"Smell what?"

"The odor comes and goes," Carney said, shifting some boxes aside near the center of the floor. "That's why we always have trouble pinning down the source."

The clinic's boiler room was lined with ancient pipes running haphazardly in all directions. The frothy thunk of blowers pushing air and the clacking of an occasional baffle opening and closing added to the eeriness of the scene. Puzzled, Blaine watched as Carney crouched down over a relatively clear patch of the asphalt floor, near the center of the basement.

"Just what I thought . . ."

That section of the floor was lined by small hairline cracks in the shape of a spiderweb, some too small even to wedge a fingernail through. Carney moved toward a sink, and Blaine heard water running as he knelt to make his own inspection. He was still tracing the cracks with his finger when Carney returned with a rusted steel bucket full of water. He poured the water out into a wide pool and then watched it bubble slightly while it drained through the hairline cracks into the floor.

"This is where the gas is coming from," Carney announced. "This is why the patients upstairs were getting sick."

"Where *what* was coming from?"

"Methane," Carney announced, with a flatness Blaine quickly realized came from fear. "That's how Tyrell's going to blow up the city."

Liz held the folder in her hand, almost hypnotized by it. The answers were right before her, in the birth certificate clipped to the file Mr. Frawley had provided: why Jack Tyrell had come back, why he had targeted New York City. McCracken had told her about Tyrell's son. Only he had been wrong, wrong and right at the same time.

She dialed Sam Kirkland's cell phone number. He answered on the first ring, obviously expecting it to be someone else.

"I thought you were McCracken."

"I figured it out," Liz told him. "Why Tyrell's doing this."

"I really need to keep this—"

"Tyrell's son *was* killed in the shootout at the school, but it wasn't the gunman." She steadied herself with a deep breath. "It was *the teacher*, goddamn it! Tell McCracken that Tyrell's son was the teacher!"

"McCracken, where the hell—"

"Your line was busy," Blaine told Kirkland.

"I was talking to your friend Halprin."

"Where was she?"

"The damn school. She says the teacher killed in the shootout was *Tyrell's son*! According to his birth certificate, he was born *one week* before the Mercantile Bank bombing."

"Just like the man from Black Flag said . . ."

Blaine felt a brief surge of static pass through him, as he was struck by the irony that the offspring of Jack Tyrell had grown into an upstanding citizen, only to suffer the violent fate his father had managed to avoid against all odds for so long.

"We've struck out across the whole city," Kirkland told him. "We've got to get you to New York Harbor and pay this asshole. It's over."

"No, it's not. Listen to me, Kirkland. Those circles on the map represent pockets of methane gas that have collected beneath the sewers and storm drains. Tyrell's going to set off the Devil's Brew in close enough vicinity to these pockets to create a ripple of explosions that will collapse the entire city."

Silence.

"You hear me, Kirkland?"

"Shit . . ."

"You can do better than that. . . ."

"No, it's Tyrell. He's calling with your final instructions."

Still standing in the office of her son's former elementary school, Liz thought she finally understood why Jack Tyrell was doing this. She thought of him watching his son grow up from afar, never making contact with him as a boy or a man, accepting that as a necessary sacrifice of the life he had chosen. It wasn't hard to imagine his son's senseless death being enough to push him back over the edge, considering the gut-splitting terror she had felt when bullets had whizzed dangerously close to Justin.

If only her aim had been better . . . If only that ricochet hadn't—

"Mr. Balls on his way?"

The voice echoing scratchily over the PA snapped her alert again. Mr. Frawley, the principal, jerked away from the console, banging his head.

"En route now, Tyrell."

"Here's what he's got to do. . . ."

She was listening to *Jack Tyrell*! His latest phone call to City Hall had somehow been picked up by the walkie-talkie clipped to Mr. Frawley's belt and then broadcast over the school PA system.

"He must be on the same frequency," said Johnny Wareagle.

Liz stared at Frawley's walkie-talkie. "What's the range of that thing?"

"A few blocks," Sal Belamo answered. "At the most."

"The manhole cover! Hurry!"

Blaine lifted it off and set it down to one side, while Les Carney nervously checked the map yet again, seeing it in a whole new way. Blaine watched him trace the circles with his finger.

"He must have planted the Devil's Brew along this line. Like playing connect the dots."

McCracken was still waiting for Kirkland to come back on the line. "And what are our chances of disconnecting the charges?"

"Not very good."

"Even knowing the locations?"

"Knowing the general sites doesn't help much underground. There are five thousand miles of sewer lines and interconnected storm drains beneath the city. Our teams could be down there for days, weeks even, and never come across the Devil's Brew."

"They've got seventy-five minutes," said McCracken.

The chopper slid through the sky, angling for the center of Madison Square Park as Blaine waited with the cell phone pressed against his ear.

"Tyrell's orders are for us to place all the gems in airtight hazardous waste containers," Kirkland explained. "After that we load the containers—and you—onto a boat at Pier Sixty-six."

"Then what?"

"He hasn't said yet."

The chopper was coming in for a landing, its rotor wash spraying Blaine with dirt and debris. "Try this out: He strands me in the harbor and sets the rest of his underwater mines to go off."

"I'm working on that."

"Work fast."

And, crouching, Blaine rushed for the chopper.

FIFTY-SIX

Les Carney swept his flashlight before him, stopping occasionally to shine it upon his explosives sensor, in the hope it might register some sign of Devil's Brew. The sewer tunnel dipped sharply, and Carney picked up his pace. He realized he was under the city's West Side sector, slated to be the first to undergo drastic repairs and upgrades, needed to bring the system into the twenty-first century. This particular tunnel, cut off for years, ended in a mass of rubble where backflow had caused lines to rupture and collapse, the damage so great that the section had been bypassed instead of rebuilt. The resulting effect was that of a cavern or cave.

Carney was under no illusions that the other bomb squad teams would be as successful in their explorations. Before taking over the Department of Transportation, he had been a top assistant with the Department of Environmental Protection, responsible for drafting a twenty-year plan to rebuild New York City's crumbling sewer system. During those months, this multilevel maze of sewers, storm drains, and abandoned railroad tunnels had become his world—one he knew not only from firsthand experience but also from an exhaustive study of schemas, maps, and blueprints.

Still, New York City's system of sewers and storm drains had been revamped, renewed, restored, and renovated so often that no map was totally accurate. Some parts of the oldest piping were actually made of wood, and this section of the West Side, not far from the main laterals, was in the worst disrepair of any. The labyrinthine tunnels ended without warning, having been bypassed or abandoned years before, the levels built atop one another. Somehow Jack Tyrell had managed to find the same mothballed series of train tunnels running beneath the main sewer lines that Carney had selected to house the first stage of the new sanitation infrastructure. No way could Kirkland's teams ever come to the same conclusion knee-deep in muck with no idea of what lay beneath them. And down here there was no way he could use his cell phone or walkie-talkie to alert them. Their searches for Devil's Brew, almost certainly, would yield nothing in the few minutes that remained.

Suddenly an acrid stench assaulted Carney's nostrils. He proceeded until he nearly gagged. Water was dripping nearby, pooling en route to a slow drop through a fissure in the floor to the cavernous sublayers of Manhattan. Carney lit a match and extended it toward the crack, jumping back when a blue flame sparked and surged upward before he tossed it aside.

He steadied himself, trying not to breathe too deeply, aware he had found one of Tyrell's methane pockets. He stepped back and started on again, sweeping his explosives sensor, rigged to the specific signature of Devil's Brew, from side to side across the width of the tunnel.

Sam Kirkland dashed out of the elevator on the ninth floor of the FBI's New York headquarters at 26 Federal Plaza. His knees ached and cracked, punishment for the pounding they had taken through years of football. They had begun to hurt so much the last few years that he'd had to give up jogging, and now a dash even halfway down the hall left him gasping and damp with sweat by the time he reached the office he was looking for.

The spacious office was wall-to-wall machines, so many, arranged so haphazardly, that they looked as though they'd been tossed in and left where they landed. Sitting on the floor amidst them, with his blue-jeaned legs crossed and a charred piece of steel balanced upon them, was a bearded man with a long ponytail. Kirkland didn't know his real name; like everyone else in the building, he knew him only as "Mr. Peabody," after the little dog who operated the Wayback Machine with a boy named Sherman on *The Bullwinkle Show.*

Mr. Peabody was an expert at deciphering codes and frequencies, at linking a bomb to its makers by the unique signature it gave off. He had been a key player in the World Trade Center bombing investigation and the subsequent capture of the terrorist team responsible, thereby pre-empting far more catastrophic attacks. Some people in the building swore he hadn't left his office since.

Mr. Peabody looked up nonchalantly from his scrutiny of the chip from the receiver recovered near the Queensboro Bridge. "This is a hell of a piece of work, let me tell ya. I'd like to dance with the dude who made it."

"I think I can arrange that," Kirkland told him.

Chief Logan personally led one of the three convoys speeding toward New York Harbor under massive police security. The diamonds had been loaded into armored cars at each of the banks where they'd been stored and then had been provided with a visible and ominous escort.

According to Logan's specifications, along all three routes police cruisers covered both flanks, as well as the fronts and rears of the armored cars. Additionally, all side streets had been blocked off and mounted patrol officers stationed at regular intervals to keep bystanders back. Though traffic lights continued to function, as they had all day, the streets had been cleared of all other vehicles, allowing the convoys to streak without delay to their destination at New York Harbor.

Mr. Peabody had taken a seat in one of the chairs now, shoving everything he didn't need from one of his work stations to the floor.

"Well?" Kirkland asked him, after explaining what they were up against.

"Okay, what I got to do is identify the frequency Sherman's using to talk to his mines in the harbor and then insert another signal into the code to confuse the son of a bitch."

Kirkland glanced forlornly at the chip Mr. Peabody had had no luck with yet. "Slim odds at best, in other words."

Peabody wheeled his desk chair sideways to a different computer. "Hell, no, 'cause the difference this time is I'm gonna be waiting when he sends the signal itself."

"Then you're saying you *can* do it?"

Peabody smirked. "Last time I couldn't crack a code of any kind was 'cause my Johnny Quest decoder ring came broke out of a cereal box."

McCracken spotted the three armored cars as his helicopter descended toward New York Harbor. Their collective cargo of fifteen billion dollars in diamonds was presumably now inside the concrete storage hangar extending down the slip. There the diamonds would be placed in the toxic waste containers, which would in turn be loaded onto a boat he was prepared to pilot in keeping with Jack Tyrell's instructions.

Blaine knew he would be safe so long as those containers were on board, the mines switched off until he got to wherever he was instructed to go. But he also knew that as soon as delivery was complete, Tyrell would be free to switch the mines back on, leaving Blaine in the middle of the Hudson River to face the same fate as the flotilla sunk just a few hours before.

It was one fifty-five by the time the chopper touched down and Blaine rushed out toward Chief Logan, who was waving at him from the head of the pier.

On the George Washington Bridge, Public Safety Commissioner Bob Corrothers joined Warren Muldoon near the edge of the huge chasm blown in the upper deck. He stopped slightly behind the balding, bespectacled city engineer, who was called "Mr. Magoo" behind his back. Corrothers was astounded to see Muldoon standing fearlessly a shoe length away from the giant hole, while Corrothers himself had all he could do to stop his stomach from quivering as he stood five feet back.

"I see you've been busy," he said lamely.

Muldoon kept his eyes on the sky, as if waiting for something to appear over the horizon. "I E-mailed the specifications to my counterpart in Jersey. He managed to locate everything we need, and three freight helicopters have already been loaded." He checked his watch briefly. "They should be here any minute."

"Freight helicopters?"

"You'll see."

Corrothers grasped a nearby steel support and turned his gaze in the same direction.

Blaine climbed down the short ladder onto the deck of the harbormaster's patrol boat, a converted cabin cruiser. Along the pier, a platoon of police led by Chief Logan escorted the huge drums filled with diamonds toward the boat.

McCracken's cellular phone rang.

"It's one fifty-seven. We've got to make this fast," said Sam Kirkland. "One of my men, dressed as a cop, is going to hand you a homing beacon when the containers of diamonds are lowered onto your boat."

"Homing beacon?"

"Whatever happens," Kirkland told him, "this son of a bitch isn't going to get away."

"What about the mines?"

"Tyrell's got to turn them off before he can send you anywhere. We'll have the frequency jammed from this end before he turns them back on. My man's also going to give you a second cell phone, programmed with the number I gave Tyrell. Keep the line open on the phone you've got now, and put on that earpiece I gave you back at City Hall."

"Already in place."

"Okay. I'll be able to hear what Tyrell says and talk to you the whole time."

A trio of cops under heavy guard climbed down the ladder and joined Blaine in the boat. The airtight toxic waste barrels, gleaming in the sun, were placed one at a time on a mechanical platform built into the pier, then they were lowered. The officers reached upward to guide the barrels and then carefully hoisted each of them down to the deck in the boat's stern. The stern settled a bit. One of the cops extended a hand.

"Good luck," the man said.

Blaine took his hand and felt the homing beacon, encased in a tiny Ziploc bag, pressed into his palm.

"Just stick it on like a stamp," he instructed, then gave McCracken a second cell phone, which rang as if on cue.

"I was just thinking," greeted Jack Tyrell.

"That supposed to be some kind of first?"

"Don't be rude, Mr. Balls. Here we are, a couple old warriors from another generation. You off fighting the same war I was fighting to stop."

"What's your point?"

"That we both had our time and now we're back."

"Some of us never left."

"That was my other point," said Tyrell. "How for a lot of the years in between we were working for the same boss, doing lots of the same shit. Then we run into each other at the Monument. Now here we are, together again. Must be fate."

"Maybe just bad luck."

"Question is whose? Kinda funny when you think of it that way."

"Too many people have died today for me to laugh."

"I killed more than this in one day before. Difference is today I did it for myself."

"I know about your son, Jack."

"You know he's dead?"

"I know he was a teacher, got killed for no good reason at all."

"Life sucks, don't it? Kid plays by the rules, only wants to do good. And some crazy with a machine gun walks into a classroom, *a fucking classroom*, and he takes a bullet in the head. But men like you and me, who never played by the rules, we're still at it. Makes you wonder."

"Don't compare him to us."

"Old soldiers who shoulda been put down—that's what we are. We stick around 'cause we don't know anything else. My kid tries to do some good and gets dead because of it. Dies with a piece of chalk in his hand, not a gun. I goddamn had to do something."

"The guy who killed him's already dead, Jack," Blaine said, realizing Tyrell must have bought the story given to the press that mentioned nothing about Liz Halprin's culpability.

"But not the society that spawned him. That's where you and I part ways, Mr. Balls. You're part of the system that's gotten all fucked up. We're both outcasts, fuck-ups in our own way. We're from the same time, created by the same war, except on different sides. It's like we're twins. I'm just willing to go farther to set things right again."

"How does blowing up a city set things right again?"

"Gotta make people take notice before they take action, 'cause no one believes in anything anymore. Well . . ."

In the command center, Jack Tyrell stopped long enough to glance at the men working their posts, every single eye upon him. They had all traveled with him and Midnight Run for some period after time served in the SDS, the Weatherman movement, or the Black Panthers. Restless men who had gone into hiding but never stopped missing the life that set them apart.

". . . we believed," he continued, "and it cost us our identities, sometimes even our names and faces. But we stopped a war. Today nobody out there can even stop a clock."

"There's no war to stop today, Tyrell."

"Yes, there is, Mr. Balls, and I'm declaring it. I'm declaring war on this whole damn country. You think it ends here, today? Bullshit. This is just the beginning. I'm gonna be visiting plenty of other cities. Put the whole damn country on notice, make everyone wonder where I'm headed next. Gonna get so people barricade their own doors until I get what I want."

"And what's that?"

"Satisfaction."

"Tough to pack that into a toxic waste canister."

"Guess I'll have to settle for what you've got packed into that container now."

"Fifteen billion the price tag you're putting on your satisfaction?"

"Got to hit people where it hurts, my friend. Money's all anyone pays attention to these days."

"And maybe it's all you're really after. No better than anyone else who takes hostages. Same as the scumbag that killed your son . . . and the scumbags from Black Flag who sent you to ice the Monument."

"I see you've done your homework."

"They wanted me to go after you. You've become a nuisance to them, a piece of shit."

"And they sent you to flush the toilet, that it? My, my, they're just sending the both of us all over the place, aren't they? From where I'm standing, that makes us the same."

A long pause followed, Blaine wondering what Tyrell would say next.

"Trouble is you're on the wrong side, Mr. Balls."

"Facing off against you suits me just fine."

"Then take your boat out to the center of the harbor and do it from there."

McCracken turned on the engine of the harbor patrol boat, gazing back at the biohazard canisters stashed in the stern before inching away from the dock. He used only one hand on the wheel, keeping the cell phone pressed against his ear with the other one, and heard Jack Tyrell issue a single command.

"Deactivate the mines."

The instant the mines were deactivated, information began flying across Mr. Peabody's screen, his bar grids and wave indicators fluctuating madly. His headphones were on, frequencies dialed up on the screen before him. Two other machines laden with grids and wave flows held steady within easy view.

"Come on," he said to himself, working the keyboard, "where are you? Where the fuck are you?"

Blaine eased the boat to a halt in what he judged to be the center of the harbor, halfway to New Jersey. The Statue of Liberty watched his every move now, along with the dozens of police back on the pier, who were mere specks from this distance.

McCracken brought the cell phone back to his ear. "What now, Jack?"

"Pop open the canisters and dump the diamonds overboard."

"*What?*"

"You're right, Mr. Balls, this isn't about money; it never was. I just wanted to hit 'em where it hurt. Hey, people might tend to think I was crazy if I took a whole city hostage and didn't ask for anything."

"Because you planned to blow it up all along."

"Do as I say and maybe I won't. You seem to have a way of changing my mind."

Blaine left the cell phone on a ledge in front of the wheel and moved to the boat's stern. He unfastened the first canister's sealed top and pried it off. With considerable effort, he tilted the canister over the gunwale and let the diamonds spill into the water. They clinked against each other, sounding almost like bells jangling as a few of them skittered across the currents. They hung on the surface briefly, then disappeared slowly beneath it toward the bottom of New York Harbor.

It was closing on two-fifteen when Liz and Johnny met Sal Belamo at a construction site on West Twenty-third Street a few blocks from William T. Harris Elementary School, where workers were rebuilding a section of sewers beneath an unusual motto: REBUILDING NEW YORK ONE   RICK AT A TIME.

Her own efforts had so far been fruitless. The strength and duration of the signal the school PA system had accidentally picked up indicated clearly that Tyrell was in a three-or-four-block vicinity. But those blocks encompassed countless buildings, and all Tyrell needed was a single room from which to run his operation. Accordingly, she held little hope that either Johnny or Sal would have fared any better than she had.

But Sal, much to her surprise, approached her eagerly and gestured toward the construction pit. "Foreman down there remembers a tanker truck pulling into one of those tunnels this morning. Pretty close match for the rig you and the big fella here described from Pennsylvania. We better check it out."

Liz frowned as she gazed into the darkness of the tunnels. "If the Devil's Brew is down there, Tyrell won't be far behind."

"Good point," Sal agreed. "The two of you take a walk. I'll cover your backs."

"How?"

Sal looked down into the construction pit. "Leave that to me."

You need to take this call," Marbles told Jack Tyrell, handing him the headset he kept depositing around the command center. "It's from the spotter watching the entrance to the sewers."

"What is it?" Tyrell asked the spotter.

"A woman and an Indian just entered the tunnel via the Twenty-third Street construction site."

"*A woman and an Indian?*" Tyrell asked incredulously, recalling the shootout yesterday in Pennsylvania.

"Less than a minute ago."

Tyrell yanked off the headset and laid it atop the table before him. He considered the hulking shape of Lem Trumble, then fixed his gaze instead on the surviving Yost twin, Earl.

"I've got a job for you."

Mr. Peabody swung round excitedly to face Sam Kirkland.

"I got it, man!"

A single unvarying wave modulation had locked onto the center of his three screens, looking like the blueprint for the path of a roller coaster. He reached to his right and pressed a red button, causing a red light flashing over it to switch to green.

"Take that, asshole."

Tell me you're not impressed, Mr. Balls," Tyrell said to Blaine on the phone seconds after he had finished dumping the diamonds into the Hudson River.

"Nothing about you impresses me."

"How 'bout how easy it's going to be for me to kill you?" With that, Tyrell turned toward Marbles. "Reactivate the mines."

Marbles worked his keyboard rapidly, then hit EXECUTE. He narrowed his gaze on the screen, scowling, then repeated the sequence.

"Er, something's wrong here."

Tyrell leaned over Marbles' shoulder in disbelief. "Switch to a different frequency!"

"I'm trying!"

"It's jammed!" Kirkland screeched into Blaine's ear.

Across the office from him, Mr. Peabody was reclining comfortably, smoking an imaginary celebratory cigar. Suddenly long bands of figures began to fly across his computer screen. A noise like a bird chirping sounded at regular intervals, and the green light turned back to red.

Peabody rocked forward and squeezed his chair back under his desk.

"You're better than I thought, Sherman," he said out loud.

In the harbor, Blaine was racing for the pier, weaving through the mire of floating hulks and chunks of other craft, when an exploding mine blew the aft side of his boat apart. It spun out of control, directly into the path of another mine, which blew out its stern, hurling Blaine into the air. He hit the water hard and clawed back for the surface.

What was left of his boat drifted into another mine and exploded, a shower of fragments hurtling straight for him. Blaine dove, feeling the heavy shards plop against the surface of the water he'd occupied an instant before. Holding his breath as he maneuvered, he felt he was back at Buck Torrey's stilt house, testing his lungs a little more each morning.

But the depths provided no respite. He saw he was surrounded by dozens of mines that looked like floating balls attached to thin strings. The unpredictable currents were pushing the mines in all directions, some straight for him.

Blaine tried to dive deeper, but his lungs burned and the thirst for air quickly overcame him. He swam up cautiously and broke the surface, drinking in breath. He tried swimming toward the pier, using carefully measured strokes to avoid any of the deadly balls that fluttered on the surface, while at the same time trying to keep track of those just below. But the mines kept appearing everywhere he turned. The tension caused his legs to tighten, and he could feel the beginning of a cramp coming on.

Then he heard the voice of Buck Torrey in his ear.

Gonna let these things beat ya, son? Come on, show some guts. Minefields on land never bothered you. Why should these?

Blaine began swimming again, his hands like knives digging just under the surface of the water as if it were soft dirt. One of the deadly bobbing balls caught in his grasp and he froze in place, knowing what would happen if he removed the pressure, while the currents pushed more of the mines straight at him.

✧   ✧   ✧

"Blaine, come in! Blaine, can you hear me?"

Before Kirkland, Mr. Peabody was pounding the keys, his hands a virtual blur. A hard crackling sound had replaced the soft rattle of the strikes.

"Oh, you're good, Sherman. You're very good. But I'm better."

He slammed his last stroke down.

When the pair of mines brushed up against him, McCracken flinched, squeezing his eyes closed, only to open them again when no blast followed. He held his breath and released his hold on the mine trapped in his hand, sighing deeply as it floated harmlessly away. A harbor patrol boat sped toward him, and a pair of cops helped him on board.

The men who had accompanied Earl Yost to the construction site enjoyed this kind of work as much as he did and, like him, had been chosen by Tyrell for their expertise. They had loaded a pair of stolen Department of Transportation vans with weapons and readied them while Earl laid out the plan just out of view of the construction site, accessing the section of tunnels they had come here to secure.

"What happens if the workers get in our way?" one of the gunmen asked him.

"Shoot 'em," Yost replied.

But when they finally walked down the ramp into the construction pit, there wasn't a single worker in sight. The place had been humming with activity just minutes before. A few of the heavy machines were still turned on, but there was no one behind their controls or inside their cabs. It looked as though the drivers had just quit in the middle of the job or, more likely, had gone on break.

Yost and his men had barely reached the center of the site when the machines shifted like great beasts stirring, shapes suddenly reappearing behind their controls.

"What the . . ."

Yost realized then that the machines had them surrounded, and he hoisted his M-16, ready to fire.

Bob Corrothers and Warren Muldoon gazed up at the third freight helicopter descending for the upper deck of the George Washington Bridge. The huge steel I-beams, located at a New Jersey construction site, easily spanned the gap wrought by the explosion.

"What now?" Corrothers screamed over the rotor wash, shielding his face with a hand.

"We use flash powder to join the beams together," Muldoon yelled back, "then weld deck plate over them to simulate the road surface."

And Corrothers watched as another trio of I-beams settled into place with a satisfying clunk, effectively joining the two ruptured sides of the bridge back together.

"Well, I'll be damned. . . ."

Chief Logan was waiting for McCracken back on the dock, his face red and the veins near his temples pulsing.

"You dumped the diamonds overboard. The son of a bitch had you dump the diamonds overboard. . . ."

"Gonna be a lot of rich fish in these waters, let me tell you," Blaine said, stripping off his soaked shirt and accepting a dry one from a nearby cop, who had made a fortuitous stop at a dry cleaner's first thing that morning.

He was about to repeat the process with his pants, when Logan's cellular phone rang. The police chief listened briefly, then turned to Blaine.

"What is it?" McCracken asked him, holding a fresh pair of pants in his hand. "Is it Liz?"

"No," Logan said, his face ashen now. "It's a war."

FIFTY-SEVEN

The loaders, shovels, trucks, and backhoes rolled forward through the construction pit, converging on the gunmen they had surrounded. Gus Sabella took the lead, driving a loader called a "stacker," with fully articulated grasping arms for hauling heavy pipe and hands formed of viselike pincers.

Sal Belamo had quickly laid out the situation for Gus, and the big man had not looked pleased with the prospects.

"You telling me the men behind the bombings are about to head into my tunnels?"

"Some of them."

"And you want *me* to stop them?"

"That's what I was hoping, yeah."

"I don't know. . . ."

"What if they were the shitheads who fucked with your sign?"

Gus' features flared; Sal watched his mind changing right before him. "I do this, you put a word in for me?"

"Word?"

"City's gonna need an awful lot of repairs. I'd like to think my crew deserves one of the contracts."

"I'll see what I can do."

"You're not with the union, though, right?"

"Nope."

"It's just that I thought I recognized you from somewhere."

Gus had taken volunteers, Sal Belamo insisting on driving one of the shovels himself. He and the other drivers kept rolling on, shovel extremities placed so the gunmen couldn't see into the cabs, never mind shoot those inside. The initial rounds of desperate fire from the trapped gunmen clanged wildly off steel. Then a rail-thin wild man, who looked as though his skin had been painted white, began shouting at them to aim for the tires and engines instead.

A pair of payloaders, one of them Sal's, closed on two of the gunmen from either side, trapping them in the middle until their teethlike steel prongs sliced through flesh instead of rubble. But the maneuver exposed the loaders' cabs to machine-gun fire from several angles. Sal ducked as glass blew in all around him. He grasped the pistol from the seat where he'd stowed it between his legs, then lost it when fresh bursts showered more glass upon him.

Sal was fumbling for his pistol again when a pair of gunmen charged him, firing furiously. At that, Gus Sabella, driving the stacker, roared in from the side. Gus fastened the stacker's left pincer extremity on one man's neck and jerked him off the ground, while he smashed the other man aside with the right.

"That's what you get for messing with my city!" Gus screamed at them, continuing on.

Les Carney had covered another quarter mile when his sensor's LED readout jumped into the red. He lifted the sensor away from the liquid washing over his feet, and the needle instantly dipped back into the black. Then he lowered the sensor almost even with the water's surface, and the needle jumped off the scale. The water running along this tunnel actually had an ebb and flow to it as it followed the natural curve of the city to the northeast.

If Carney had his bearings right, he was fairly close to the start of the circled areas on the map McCracken had recovered. He withdrew a copy of that map from his pocket and followed the jagged line starting under the West Side with his flashlight. Then he looked back, aiming his beam far down the tunnel's length. This interconnected series of abandoned tunnels, he recalled, cut a nearly straight path beneath the center of Manhattan—the same path the currents were now leisurely following.

Currents ...

Carney trembled a little. He started walking against the flow, following the direction the currents were coming from as he resteadied his sensor.

The LED readout continued to flash bright red, and Carney picked up his pace through the water roiling about his feet.

❂   ❂   ❂

"Pack up. It's time to move," Jack Tyrell said to the remaining soldiers of the reborn Midnight Run. "You all know the drill. It's two twenty-five. We want to be out of Manhattan in thirty minutes."

Tyrell trained his eyes on a television monitor picturing the third of three massive cargo helicopters hovering over the George Washington Bridge.

"And it looks like our escape route is just about ready."

Warren Muldoon watched his crew working feverishly to lay the deck plate over the steel I-beams and weld them into place. The resulting make-shift bridge had been fashioned to his precise specifications, slightly wider than a single lane, enough to accommodate the convoy from Fort Dix that would be arriving on the Jersey side in a matter of minutes now.

He found he'd been sweating from the tension of the operation and mopped his damp face. But he remained amazed at the rapid progress being made by his men, who were energized by the desperation fueling their every move. Keeping his eyes on their work, Muldoon pocketed his handkerchief and lifted his cell phone to his lips.

"This is City Engineer Muldoon," he said, over the loud bangs of his crew bolting the deck plates down prior to welding them into place. "Patch me through to the mayor." Then, to himself while he waited, "Muldoon, you've done it again."

"How could the tanker possibly be down here?" Liz Halprin said to Johnny Wareagle.

"It came this way several hours ago and continued down the tunnel," Johnny said, crouching again. He brushed aside some of the pooling water their feet had been sloshing through ever since they'd entered the tunnels and inspected the mushy layer of debris beneath it.

He rose again, his knees embedded with dirt and grime now, and continued on the tanker's trail.

"We're almost there," he said, stopping suddenly.

"Then what are we waiting for?" Liz asked him.

"Someone's coming," Johnny said.

Les Carney was thinking of his missing arm. He always felt the phantom limb throb when he was nervous or anxious and he was both of those right now. He continued moving against the soft, all but unnoticeable current, certain he was onto at least a portion of Jack Tyrell's plan and realizing the utter brilliance of it. Suddenly, though, he came to what appeared to be a dead end, the grimy water lapping in a pool against a wall.

He had just noted that the LED readout on his sensor was still firmly in the red, when a huge arm closed around his throat, a motion away from snapping it like a twig.

"Who are you?" a voice asked.

"I work for the city! Department of Transportation," Carney gasped, feeling the arm relax and release him. He turned and found himself looking up into the flaming eyes of a giant Indian. An attractive woman was standing just beyond him. "Who are *you*?"

"I think we're looking for the same thing," said the woman.

"But where is it?" Carney wondered, stretching his arms out to see if the entire wall was wet.

The wall shifted slightly under his touch. Johnny Wareagle moved up even with him and swung a heavy boot against it. The wall cracked and splintered along its entire length. All three of them proceeded to smash and batter their way through the opening.

"Sheetrock," Carney realized, shining his flashlight to reveal the huge black tanker parked directly before them.

"Looking good, people!" Jack Tyrell complimented, as the remainder of his men finished pulling DOT uniforms over their clothes.

Lem Trumble opened the heavy bunker door and checked the tunnel beyond to make sure their initial escape route through the sewers where the command center was located was clear. His flashlight glowed off the dark, wet walls, and he advanced slightly, like a dog sniffing at the air. Only when he turned and nodded did Tyrell start forward.

"Let's move," he ordered.

"Chief, where are you?" a desperate voice screeched over the car radio.

Blaine watched Logan pry the mike off its stand. "Coming down Sixth Avenue for the construction site. ETA two minutes."

"For Christ's sake, hurry up!"

As if to punctuate the cop's plea, Blaine and Logan heard the staccato bursts of machine-gun fire and the rumble of a blast in the background, loud enough to make them flinch. McCracken punched the accelerator all the way to the floor, and the chief's car shot forward, an armada of police vehicles following close behind.

The bullets had hit the backhoe's engine block just right. When it exploded, chunks of yellow steel flew in all directions, scattering the letters that spelled out CATERPILLAR all over the site, leaving a flaming husk in its place and a driver scampering desperately away.

Sal Belamo watched a shovel operator spin his massive machine around, changing its angle. He caught the shooter reloading, the man looking up just before the operator yanked back on the control rod. The shovel dropped straight down and flattened the man to the ground.

At the same time, a monstrous bulldozer, its leveled front section looking like a gaping mouth of orange fangs, rolled its treads toward a retreating group of gunmen who were firing at it nonstop. The gunmen ended up pinning themselves against the wall between two of the open tunnel entrances and the huge dozer drove them straight through the asphalt, leaving them buried in the resulting pile of rubble.

Fifty yards away, Gus Sabella spun his stacker around again. Gus worked it like the expert he was, having made his bones on this machine years before. The pincer extremities seemed like extensions of his own arms, and he used them to attack any of the gunmen offering serious resistance.

He saw a trio of gunmen who had regrouped make a dash for a tunnel entrance. No way he could cover that much ground in the stacker before they got there, so Gus whirled the machine sideways toward a massive pile of black sewer pipes waiting to be laid into the ground. He captured a dozen in the stacker's articulated arms and twisted the machine away as the rest of the pile collapsed.

Gus aligned the stacker with the gunmen rushing for the tunnel and then pushed the button marked RELEASE on his control panel. The arms snapped open, thrusting the pipes from their grasp. Gus watched them roll under the gunmen's legs and drop them like bowling pins, an instant before a burst of gunfire sliced into his cab.

"Just like I thought," Carney said, backing away from the gauge he had located at the rear of the tanker.

"What?" Liz prodded, as Johnny Wareagle looked on.

"This tanker is actually composed of four inner tanks. Two of them are empty, drained clean." He turned and pointed in the direction he had come from. "Dumped here to be swept away with the currents that flow beneath a good portion of Manhattan."

"That doesn't sound good," muttered Liz.

"I'll say," followed Carney, picturing the two dozen methane dumps that lay stretched beneath the center of the city. The currents would sweep thousands of gallons of Devil's Brew down the tunnels past them, to soak into the ground and ignite all the pockets in an unfathomable underground firestorm when it exploded.

"Set off how?" Johnny Wareagle wondered.

"The methane dumps are too far underground to reach with standard fusing. You'd need something big." Then, after finding what he was looking for beneath one of the sleek rig's twin catwalks, Carney continued, "Like this. Come see for yourself."

Johnny and Liz dropped to their knees beside him. An elaborate timing device had been attached to the rig. Wires ran out from it in several directions, connecting up to a long band of plastic explosives that would undoubtedly serve as the trigger.

"It's set for three o'clock," Carney said, inspecting the device closely.

"Twenty-six minutes from now," Liz muttered.

"I've got to disarm it," Carney insisted. "If this goes up, the whole city comes down."

He could see it happening in his mind, the effects like those of a giant earthquake swallowing all of Manhattan at once, as the methane dumps ignited one after another. Roads and streets crumbling, the buildings built upon them folding up and collapsing. Millions of lives lost in the rubble, New York City left with barely any structures standing or streets intact.

When Carney started to reach for the wires, Johnny Wareagle fastened a powerful hand on his wrist.

"Wait. Booby trap."

"Where?"

"Somewhere we can't see," Johnny said confidently.

"You got a better idea what we're supposed to do with this thing?"

Wareagle looked the truck over and smiled ever so slightly. "Yes."

The gunfire had bled the stacker's radiator dry, spilling blinding hot steam, which didn't stop Gus Sabella from fighting to turn the engine over one last time. It ground, sputtered, wouldn't catch.

More glass showered inward, and Gus tumbled out the cab door, dropping hard to the ground behind the machine's cover. He could hear the crunch of footsteps advancing toward him, longed for a weapon he could use, *any* weapon. He could see he was bleeding in a couple of places and didn't honestly know whether he'd been pricked by glass or hit by bullets.

Gus peered around the rear of the stacker and was chased back by a burst of automatic fire. He had caught enough of a glimpse to recognize the tall, rail-thin gunman with milk-white skin advancing purposefully toward him. Recognized the bastard as the man who had driven the tanker into the tunnels that morning. Take away the machine gun, and Gus figured he could break him in two over his knee. He took a deep breath and spun away from the stacker, ready to launch into a desperation charge, when out of nowhere a wrecking ball swooped into his line of vision. It slammed into the albino with a bone-crunching thud and hurled him effortlessly through the air.

Gus looked toward the wrecking ball's control cab and saw Sal Belamo flashing him the thumbs-up sign.

"Little Sally B!" Gus yelled, finally recalling where he'd seen this man before. Tough little fighter with bad technique who'd been decked twice by Carlos Monzon. Gus remembered his nose got mashed to pulp both times.

Good thing for me he works a wrecking ball better than he fights, Gus thought to himself, as the first of the police cars screamed onto the scene.

Jack Tyrell had made sure their exit route through the mazelike construction of sewer tunnels was clearly marked. He led his remaining fifteen men in their DOT uniforms along the route himself, stopping at a ladder and beckoning them to go up ahead of him.

They climbed rapidly to ground level and reached a floodlit construction site enclosed by walls of hastily erected plywood that was surrounded by plastic flapping in the wind. The jeeps, cars, and trucks the members of Midnight Run had used to get here were parked everywhere, but they didn't plan to use them now. Instead they clustered around a single large truck colored royal blue, with raised white letters reading: NEW YORK CITY EMERGENCY SERVICES.

It was their ticket out of Manhattan, guaranteed to assure them passage across the temporarily repaired upper deck of the George Washington Bridge. The city planners had cooperated brilliantly by responding exactly as Tyrell had expected they would, right down to the minute.

"Let's rock and roll," he announced.

Tyrell heard a beeper going off as he moved up to the truck's cab, and he swung to see Marbles lifting the device from his belt.

"Shit," Marbles muttered.

"What's wrong?"

"The tanker . . ."

"You gonna tell me what you're talking about?"

"It's moving."

"I feel like you after one of your fights," a banged-up Gus Sabella said, as Sal Belamo helped him toward the rescue vehicles that had just thumped down into the construction pit.

"I had some good nights."

"Not when I bet on you."

They looked up to see Blaine McCracken charging down the access ramp ahead of a horde of well-armed police officers. McCracken surveyed the surroundings, assessing in an instant what had happened here.

"You've been busy," he said to Sal Belamo.

"Me and my friend here," Sal corrected. "He remembers me from my fighting days."

"Any sign of Liz and Johnny?"

Blaine had barely finished the question when a deep-throated rumble shook one of the nearby tunnels. He peered into the darkness just as the black tanker appeared, snorting and bellowing, Johnny Wareagle behind the wheel, with Liz Halprin seated beside him.

Blaine turned toward Belamo. "You up for a drive, Sal?"

FIFTY-EIGHT

M aybe you didn't hear me," Blaine said to Liz Halprin. She looked up from her inspection of the shotgun Chief Logan had just passed up through the window. "It's not a Mossberg, but it'll do."

He threw open the door. "Climb down. You can keep it as a souvenir."

Liz didn't budge. "If my father were here now, what would you say to him?"

"Welcome aboard."

"Well, I'm the next-best thing."

Blaine shrugged and leaned out the window toward Logan. "We're gonna need another set of guns, Chief."

Jack Tyrell's remaining men doubled up in a number of the vehicles that had originally brought them here, nine in all including Tyrell's own truck, with Tremble behind the wheel. The escape plan utilizing the Emergency Services truck had been abandoned once the tanker was found to be on the move. Tyrell knew that whoever was behind the wheel would have to drive it out through the same construction tunnel Earl Yost had driven it in, just four blocks away.

Not that he had much doubt who that person was.

A set of camouflaged doors leading in and out of the bogus construction site were yanked open, revealing a ramp that bridged the short distance to the street. The vehicles rolled along it in convoy fashion toward daylight, past Jack Tyrell, who waved them on before climbing into the passenger seat of the truck Tremble was driving, Othell Vance squeezed between the two of them.

Blaine leaned out the open cab door toward Logan, while Liz and Johnny inspected the weapons the chief had requisitioned for them from the trunks of four squad cars.

"Let me get this straight," Logan said, puzzled. "You don't want an escort."

"You have to use every man you've got to evacuate as much of the West Side as possible, in case we don't make it. The whole city may no longer be in jeopardy, but we still could be looking at lots of damage, blocks and blocks of it."

"Okay, what else can I do for you?"

"Clear the West Side Highway all the way to the George Washington Bridge. And make sure it happens before three o'clock, so we can dump this rig in the Hudson before the rest of the Devil's Brew blows."

Logan froze. "Did you say 'dump'?"

"Yes."

"Er, we've got a problem there. . . ."

On the upper deck of the George Washington Bridge, the cell phone trembled in Warren Muldoon's hand.

"You want me to do *what*?" he posed in total disbelief.

"Mayor's orders," Logan told him.

Muldoon gazed out over the final stages of the deck plate's being fastened to the I-beams that spanned the chasm.

"She told me to get the damn thing open!"

"And now," said Logan, "she's ordering you to close it down again."

Muldoon considered the prospects. "It may not be that easy. . . ."

Snowplows that had already done yeomen's work throughout the day swung onto the West Side Highway from various through streets, lining up in staggered groups of three. At least two lanes had been cleared almost the whole way to the GWB, and now the plows had to finish the arduous task of widening the remaining stretches to that same width.

But the improvement was not without costs, as cars, some only slightly damaged or unmarred, were crashed from the plows' path, shoved aside to create twin jagged barriers of twisted steel.

Blaine and Liz huddled in the rear of the truck's cab, while Johnny Wareagle rode in the front passenger seat, next to Sal Belamo.

"Handles like a dream," offered Sal, picking up speed on West Twenty-third Street. "You wanna go over the plan again, boss?"

"Simple. We get to the GWB and drop this baby in the drink before three o'clock."

Sal checked the dashboard clock:

2:40

"That'll be cutting things close."

"I don't think we'll hit much traffic."

As Blaine spoke, he spotted a number of vehicles on the various cross streets, angling to cut the tanker off before it reached the West Side Highway.

"Tyrell," he muttered.

A four-by-four tried blocking the tanker at the intersection of Ninth Avenue, but Sal slammed right through it, the occupants of the cab barely receiving a jolt for the effort. They looked back to see the four-by-four smashed against a light pole.

"You think that's a good idea?" Liz wondered.

"This baby's got three extra inches of titanium around it," Blaine told her. "That makes it a fine idea."

The tanker continued speeding across Twenty-third, with four of Tyrell's vehicles closing and another three curling onto the street to join the pursuit. In his own truck, Tyrell himself was holding his head out the window, letting the wind whip past him.

"Had a German shepherd once," he said to Othell Vance. "Now I know why he enjoyed this so much."

"I'm no soldier, Jackie," Vance said to him.

"What? I can't hear you, Othell!"

Vance leaned a little closer to the open window. "I said I'm no soldier! I was hoping you could just drop me off!"

Jack Tyrell pulled himself back inside the cab. "Absolutely, Othell, whatever you want. Next time we stop."

Sal Belamo screeched in a right turn off Twenty-third onto the West Side Highway, directly across from the Chelsea Piers. Just one lane was open for a brief stretch here, but up ahead he could see that the snowplows had cleared all lanes along the twisting route past the Thirtieth Street Heliport to the Javits Center. They had squeezed a line of wrecks against both sides, creating the effect of a tunnel the tanker roared through, with Tyrell's vehicles gaining ground quickly.

"Smile, boss. I think we're on television," Sal remarked as a news chopper hovered overhead.

What he didn't know was that the feed was being picked up by CNN, enabling the entire country to follow the chase live. In greater New York City this meant in bars, through electronics store windows, even on the huge Sony screen in Times Square, where it looked like New Year's Eve, except for the very visible presence of patrolling army MP squads, who had arrived from Fort Dix by helicopter earlier in the day.

Gus Sabella's entire crew, exhilarated by their recent battle, had squeezed into his trailer to watch the proceedings on his small television, listening in frustration as a newscaster attempted to explain what was going on.

"I'm turning the sound off," Gus said, and nobody argued with him.

On the West Side Highway, a pair of Jeeps carrying Tyrell's men accelerated, drawing up along either side of the tanker as it reached the awesome sight of the Intrepid Museum, built on the water around the aircraft carrier of the same name. Blaine leaned out the cab window on one side with a shotgun, Liz on the other with a submachine gun. Both heard the high-pitched wail of the wind whistling past the rows of car wrecks as they opened fire before the gunmen inside the Jeeps had gotten off a shot. The windshield of the Jeep on Blaine's side exploded, sending the vehicle careening into the smashed cars, which it rode in a shower of sparks before lodging amidst the wreckage. The second Jeep skidded out of control, forcing Tyrell's remaining vehicles into evasive maneuvers just to avoid it, as the tanker curled past the assembly of concrete piers lining the Hudson River.

Three pickup trucks whirled around the Jeep and took up pursuit of the tanker abreast of each other, just to its rear. A pair of gunmen opened fire from the rear cargo beds, while a third man fired from behind the wheel of the center truck. Their bullets clanged off the tanker but managed to shatter the outside mirror on the rig's driver's side.

"Shit!" yelled Sal Belamo, his view of the battle gone.

Blaine and Liz exchanged a flurry of gunfire with their pursuers, then popped back inside to reload, while Johnny Wareagle took their place leaning out the window. Johnny was wielding both a shotgun and a submachine gun, the latter just to hold the gunmen at bay while he fired off low rounds from the shotgun.

The middle pickup's front tire exploded, and the vehicle swerved violently from left to right, forcing one companion truck and then the other against the line of wrecks on either side. Showers of sparks sprayed outward on both sides of the road, the trucks' drivers unable to extricate themselves from the steel while still, incredibly, offering pursuit as the vehicles shredded themselves apart.

The two pickups had run up the length of the tanker, almost even with the cab, when Sal Belamo twisted the wheel hard to the left, ramming the one on that side into the line of wrecks, where it embedded itself. Impact slowed the rig enough for the truck on the right to draw even with its cab, pouring such a nonstop fusillade through the windows that Blaine, Johnny, and Liz were prevented from returning the fire.

"Son of a bitch!" Sal wailed, his face bleeding from flying glass, as the tanker roared past the Seventy-ninth Street Boat Basin, where the West Side Highway had become the Henry Hudson Parkway. "Now I'm fucking pissed!"

And he worked the brake just enough to let the pickup shoot ahead of the tanker. Before the driver could respond, Sal clutched and shifted, accelerating again straight for the truck. The tanker rammed its back end and sent it spinning across the road.

"Hold on," Sal warned, tensing as he gave the rig still more gas, slamming into the truck broadside and hurling it into the air and over the guardrail, to the other side of the highway. It spun onto its side on impact and skidded wildly across the road.

In the construction trailer, the flames and smoke rising from the wreckage drew hoots and hollers from Gus Sabella and all his men, while in the mayor's office Lucille Corrente shot a fist into the air with a triumphant "Yes!"

"I wouldn't celebrate yet," Sam Kirkland warned grimly, eyeing the clock resting on the conference table:

2:48

As he passed the flaming remnants of the truck, Jack Tyrell pressed a walkie-talkie against his lips.

"Fly Boy, you out there?"

"Read you, loud and clear."

"Fuck reading me, just listen. Where are you?"

"Waiting for evac at the rendezvous point."

"There's been a change in plans," Tyrell told him.

Only three vehicles were trailing the rig as Sal picked up speed past Riverside Park. They kept a cautious distance, reluctant to face odds that had now shifted against them. The gunmen inside continued to shoot from a distance, their bullets clanging off the cab as Blaine, Johnny, and Liz alternated returning the fire.

"Sal, how far from the bridge are we?"

"You can see it from here, boss," Belamo said.

Blaine took a quick glance at the George Washington Bridge, looming in the distance.

"I'm thinking seven minutes," Sal advanced, as the trees and grass of Riverside Park gave way to an assemblage of softball fields, tennis and basketball courts.

Blaine lifted the radio Logan had given him. "You there, Chief?"

"Read you."

"We're ap—"

"I know where you are. This whole thing is on television."

"Don't tell anyone Sal had his license suspended."

"What charge?"

"Driving to endanger. How are things going on the bridge?"

From his police helicopter, Logan took a long look at the welders burning through the seals that affixed the I-beams and deck plate to the bridge. Warren Muldoon was frantically supervising the effort to reattach the hovering chopper's heavy steel cables and lift off the entire assembly as a single unit. Logan wasn't sure one chopper could manage that task, even if Muldoon's crew managed to get all the cables locked down.

"You just get that rig here," Chief Logan told Blaine. "We'll take care of the rest."

Blaine returned the microphone to its stand as they continued past Riverbank State Park, where a throng of skateboarders in shapeless shirts and jeans stood at the fence of their skating court with boards in hand, cheering them on.

"Company, Blainey," Johnny warned, snapping Blaine alert again.

Before he could ask where from, he heard the familiar *wop-wop-wop*. A helicopter, a heavy transport, was angling on a direct course for them, flying over the Department of Sanitation's primary storage facility on the other side of the parkway. The chopper banked, tilting slightly on what looked like a thinly disguised attack run.

At least one and maybe two gunmen opened up with heavy machine-gun fire from inside the chopper as it soared overhead. The bullets, thankfully off the mark, left pockmark-like dings in the thick steel skin of the tanker itself and lodged in the vehicle carcasses lining the highway. Beyond them, meanwhile, the chopper spun around for another pass, at the same time the rig reached a part of the highway to which the snowplows had never paid a return visit. Just a single wide lane weaved amidst the wrecks on both sides.

Sal Belamo did his best to negotiate what had become an obstacle course. But the maneuvering forced him to ease back on the accelerator, making them an even easier target for the chopper as it surged forward again.

"Keep to the left!" Blaine said, needing space so he and Johnny could offer return fire from the rig's right side. Liz, on the left, handled the reloading chores.

"Easy for you to say . . ."

Blaine leaned out the window, close enough to touch the cars alongside him, and pumped shell after shell at the chopper from the shotgun.

"Indian!" he signaled when his ammo was gone.

Wareagle followed with an equally futile barrage of submachine-gun fire, drawing sparks from contact against the chopper's frame and nothing more. The pilot knew combat, that much was obvious. He had chosen the perfect attack angle, meant to minimize the target his craft offered in return.

Johnny lurched back inside just before the next round of fire splintered the cab. One of the bullets drew a gasp from Liz, as the chopper overflew them with another burst, which stitched a jagged design across the rig's hood.

"Liz!" Blaine screamed, and slid across the seat to her.

The right side of Liz's back was leaking blood through her jacket. Impossible to tell the severity of the wound now, never mind dress it in these conditions. After easing her gently back against the seat and clipping the shoulder harness in place to keep her restrained, Blaine turned to Johnny Wareagle.

"Cover me."

With that he angled himself out the shattered back window, stretching toward the tanker. Johnny Wareagle's covering fire consisted of a submachine gun in either hand clacking away at the chopper, which suffered a minor hit and veered away, belching black smoke.

The hit gave Blaine the time he needed to grab the spool of black hose affixed to the head of the tanker near the cab. He yanked it loose and drew it back inside the cab with him.

"Tremble, get us up even with them! Othell, you get ready to take the wheel!" Tyrell ordered.

"Huh?"

"You heard me. When we're close enough, Tremble's going to jump across and climb onto the tanker. That's when you grab the wheel."

Lem Trumble waited for the road to widen again before he shot past the two remaining pursuers just ahead of them. The truck bucked as he floored it, flying past their two vehicles and tearing apart the passenger side of the truck in the process. Tremble got the truck so close to the tanker the two were almost touching. Before he allowed Othell Vance to take the wheel, he wanted to be sure of reaching the ladder that extended down at the rear of the tanker's right side.

The transition on the accelerator pedal was made easily, though not the steering wheel. Until Othell gained control, the truck rode the tanker steel to steel, shedding its driver's side now. Finally Tremble managed to grasp the ladder with both hands and jerk himself through the window, pushing off with his feet and holding fast as the truck slowed.

"Don't fall back, Othell," Tyrell ordered, starting to pull himself out the passenger window for the hood. "Keep us up against it."

"What are you doing?"

"Going for a walk."

° ° °

Still belching smoke and flitting through the air, the chopper banked around and angled for another attack.

Inside the cab, Blaine grabbed the twelve-gauge, chambered a shell, and stuffed the end of the hose down the length of the barrel until it rested square against the firing chamber, wedged in tight.

The chopper attacked low and almost sideways, seeming to defy gravity. Bullets blazed toward the cab relentlessly, as Blaine squeezed himself back out the right-hand window, dragging the unspooling hose with him. The chopper's nose was angled down, machine-gun fire clacking in a constant burst, when Blaine aimed the shotgun upward and fired.

The hose jetted out the barrel, powered by the force of the shotgun shell, rising into the air dead on line with the helicopter's churning rotor blade. The hose caught near the base and was reeled in by the rotor's churn. The chopper started to spin out of control, while the rotor coughed and spit, still sucking hose.

The chopper turned onto its side and soared straight over the tanker, one of its landing pods actually scraping the cab's roof as it dropped. Still twirling madly, it crashed onto the highway, right in the tanker's path.

"Hold on!" Sal Belamo warned, flinching, in the instant before he barreled into the smoking chopper. What was left of the rig's windshield disintegrated, spraying the cab with thick glass shards that made Sal, Blaine, and Johnny turn away to protect their faces. McCracken threw his body over Liz to shield her from the flying fragments, as well as from the black hosing that had whiplashed back when the chopper crashed into the pavement.

Impact with the tanker, meanwhile, hurled the helicopter's carcass up and over the rig, where it slammed into the last of Tyrell's pursuing vehicles near West 158th Street. The resulting explosion was so dizzyingly bright that the crowd squeezed into Gus Sabella's trailer winced before exchanging high fives and passing around cans of beer Gus had been saving for his stakeout of the site that night.

Tremble had just pulled Jack Tyrell from the truck's hood onto the tanker when the flaming chopper carcass soared over them.

"Just us now, Tremble," Tyrell said, after the crash that had claimed Othell Vance too. "Just us to finish this right."

"Trouble, boss," Sal Belamo said in the cab. The truck had begun vibrating and shimmying madly, and Blaine could tell Sal could barely control it. "I think we lost a tie rod. We don't do something, I won't be able to turn this baby onto the bridge."

The dashboard clock read 2:53.

"Let me see what I can do," Blaine said.

FIFTY-NINE

The wind was playing havoc with the efforts of Muldoon's crew to get the temporary bridge span secured and raised. Only three of the six cables extending down from the largest of the three freight helicopters had been threaded through the hooks. The other three dangled stubbornly, resisting all efforts of the workers to fasten them into place. Muldoon watched as a pair of men finally grasped one and looped it home. Another worker, meanwhile, leaned over the edge of the deck plate, while a partner held fast to his belt. He snared the fifth cable, the effort nearly pulling both of them over the edge before he recovered his balance and shoved its hooked end into the bolt.

Even with all the cables in place, there was the very real possibility that this single chopper would lack the load capacity to hoist the entire assemblage back upward. After all, it had taken *three* helicopters to ferry just the I-beams here, before the weight of the deck plate had been added to the equation. But there was no way two choppers could manage the task together, which left Muldoon with this one chance he had no choice but to rely on.

Come on, he thought, eyes on the lone remaining cable. *Just one more to go . . .*

Muldoon turned his gaze briefly toward the Henry Hudson Parkway and could now see the tanker charging for the bridge. He swung back to the trio of men trying frantically to secure the final cable long enough to work its massive curved hook through the waiting eyebolt. Then, to the shock of Public Safety Commissioner Robert Corrothers, Muldoon stepped out atop the deck plate, which glowed bright beneath the sun.

"Everyone get out of here now!"

The volunteer crew looked at him.

"I said *now!*"

No one on the bridge or off it could remember Muldoon's ever raising his voice before. The mere sound was enough to send the remaining workers scurrying away toward New Jersey, while he sidestepped gingerly and reached up and out to snare the final cable.

Johnny Wareagle grasped Blaine's legs at the ankles as McCracken slid across the hood and lowered himself in line with the rig's right front tire.

Sal Belamo, meanwhile, struggled with all his strength to keep the steering wheel pinned to the left, the only way to keep the tanker steady. He had no choice but to downshift and slow the rig, afraid of reaching the GWB's entrance at 178th Street before he could manage the sharp curl up the on-ramp.

Blaine could feel the heat of the engine through the badly damaged grille; the hood itself was still charred and smoking from the crushing impact with the chopper. He probed ahead with his hands, hearing the grinding sound that emanated from the right wheel well. Another foot down and he could actually see the dislocated tie rod scraping against the pavement, the noise reminding him distressingly of fingernails on a blackboard.

Aware the slightest jolt in any direction would result in his being sucked under by the wheel, Blaine stretched his hand down to grab hold of the tie rod.

The slowing of the tanker helped Tremble ease forward, clinging to the catwalk for support while creeping along the tanker's passenger side. Before him, he could see two of the familiar figures that had been inside the cab extended over the hood now, one of them having dropped totally out of sight.

He looked back, waved Jack Tyrell on, then pulled a grenade from his belt.

Johnny Wareagle had just readjusted his own position to keep a better grasp on McCracken, when he glimpsed the massive shape of Tyrell's henchman moving toward the cab. Knowing Blaine couldn't hear if he shouted out, Johnny tugged hard on his ankles, hoping to alert him to danger before the Indian released his grasp and slid away. Tremble had just reached the cab and was looking backward for Tyrell, when Johnny twisted his body around and thrust himself over the roof.

Tremble saw only a blur as he reached a hand up to draw the pin from the grenade. Impact drove the grenade from his grasp and sent it skittering across the tanker's surface.

✤ ✤ ✤

Blaine knew something was wrong as soon as he felt Johnny tug on his ankles. He grabbed firm hold of the rig's reinforced grille, ready when Johnny released his grasp. McCracken's legs instantly slipped forward, sliding across the hood. He managed to keep them directly above his body, which was facedown above the road surface speeding by barely a yard from his eyes.

Awkwardly, Blaine began shimmying to the right, toward the snapped tie rod. The exit for the on-ramp to the bridge's upper deck was less than two hundred yards away on the left now; no way Sal Belamo could possibly swing onto it unless the tie rod was jammed back into place. But the grille was steaming hot, and Blaine's flesh began to sting. Hot air from the engine blasted his face, and the flying sparks stung his eyes. On top of everything else, dangling upside down from the truck with the road rushing by beneath him made him dizzy, almost nauseous, and he came up short when he groped for the tie rod.

You gonna quit, you son of a bitch? You gonna let all my hard work go to waste?

Blaine was certain he heard Buck Torrey's voice badgering him again. He figured if he glanced up at the hood, old Buck would be leaning over it, shaking an angry fist.

What the hell did I bother for?

Not to worry, Blaine wanted to tell him, as he inched a bit farther sideways and this time managed to lock a hand onto the broken tie rod.

But he needed a better angle to get it back into place and let his left leg slide all the way off the hood. It banged against the grille, nearly tearing his precarious grasp free and spilling him beneath the truck. He gritted his teeth and managed to maintain his one-armed hold, and finally he succeeded in pushing the tie rod back into its slot.

Sal Belamo suddenly felt the rig's steering wheel stop fighting him. He still didn't have total control, but he had enough to twist the tanker sharply to the left onto the swirling ramp. Holding the wheel steady as the ramp gradually straightened, he breathed a sigh of relief at the feel of the bridge's smooth whistling surface beneath him.

Then he caught his first clear glimpse of the freight helicopter that hovered uneasily above the upper deck, with heavy steel cables sprouting from beneath it.

"What the hell is that?" he was asking himself out loud, when a hand reached in through the window and grabbed hold of the wheel.

Johnny Wareagle had seen Jack Tyrell dash past him along the far catwalk, but kept his focus on the grenade. He dove through the air, landing atop the tanker and sliding across it. The grenade had plopped over onto the catwalk, where it rolled slightly back and forth. Johnny reached it and saw the handle was miraculously still in place, enabling him to snare the grenade in his grasp and keep the handle pinned.

He heard the thuds of heavy footsteps rushing toward him across the tanker. Tyrell's giant henchmen slammed kick after kick into him, before stooping to shove him over the edge.

Johnny felt his legs tip over the side and grabbed the catwalk at the last moment with his single hand, the other continuing to clutch the grenade. When the giant leaned farther over to finish the job, Johnny hurled both his legs upward and caught him with a glancing blow that staggered him backwards. Enough time stolen for Johnny to hurdle back onto the deck, as the rig began to waver madly from side to side.

Having done what he set out to accomplish, Blaine thrust himself back atop the hood and was almost instantly thrown off, left to cling to anything he could find. Holding on desperately to the lip of the hood, he saw Jack Tyrell lying across the cab's roof, a hand snaked inside through the window, trying to wrest control of the wheel from Sal Belamo. Blaine watched Tyrell yank a pistol from his belt with his free hand and aim it toward the window.

Blaine dove across the hood, lunging for the roof. He grabbed hold of Tyrell's arm and jerked it away as he pulled the trigger. The bullet sliced sideways, just missing McCracken's leg. Tyrell groped for Blaine, and the two of them slid down onto the hood with Tyrell on top, the gun still in his hand.

The cable had fought him, the wind had fought him, even the steel plate had fought him, but Warren Muldoon stubbornly managed to grab firm hold of the hook and then wedge it through the eyebolt. He turned to see the tanker coming fast and began signaling upward for the chopper to hoist his creation up and away.

Muldoon lurched forward as the steel patch tore free of its bonds. He lunged to the pavement and landed clumsily, turning his ankle. He staggered back to his feet and stumbled off toward New Jersey, eyes cheating back to find the tanker surging into the final stretch.

As Muldoon watched, the helicopter lifted the steel plate free of the span, opening the chasm once more.

Tremble's scarred and pitted face had turned angry red. The huge Indian stood between him and the cab. He was about to fail Jackie, let him down, lose the trust of the one man who had ever made him feel good about himself. He continued savagely attacking, but the Indian deftly avoided his blows and lunges, parrying Tremble's attacks and forcing him onto the defensive.

Finally, out of sheer frustration, Tremble launched himself into a headlong charge. He rammed his shoulder into the Indian's midsection and forced him back hard against the cab, impact enough to snap the spine of a normal man.

But Johnny Wareagle was hardly a normal man. He felt the powerful and scarred hands, which looked like mangled slabs of beef, close on his throat and remembered the grenade still clutched in his right hand.

The giant's hot, rancid mouth was open wide enough for Johnny to jam the grenade between his teeth and yank the handle free. He then joined both his hands under the giant's shoulders.

Tremble had started to gag, hands flailing to yank the grenade out, when Johnny hurled him off the side of the tanker. His head and face exploded as he hit the line of wrecks on the bridge, the entire pile shifting in the blast.

Blaine's head had ended up inside the cab while the rest of him shifted from side to side upon the hood. Tyrell had locked one hand on his throat, while the other angled a pistol for Blaine's face. Blaine thrust a single hand out and snared Tyrell's wrist before he could fire.

Jackie Terror was grinning madly, slowly righting his aim upon the man who had fucked up his plans for the last time.

But Sal Belamo felt for the brake pedal and jammed it down. Tyrell was thrown backwards onto the hood, grasp lost on his pistol, which came to a clanking halt just beyond his reach.

Blaine smashed him in the back of the head with one hand, while the other snared the black hose that was slithering like a snake through the cab. When Tyrell lunged to reach for his pistol, Blaine twirled the hose around his chest and torso, wrapping it tight. Instead of trying to free himself, Tyrell desperately kept going for his gun and coming up just short.

"Fifty yards, boss!" Sal warned, opening the driver's door as Blaine steadied himself on the hood.

Inside the cab, Johnny Wareagle eased Liz through the windshield, into Blaine's waiting grasp.

"It's coming up!" Sal screamed.

"Jump!" Blaine ordered.

He could see the familiar jagged chasm in the bridge clearly ahead, as Johnny lunged from a shattered window and Sal Belamo pushed himself out the driver's door. On the hood, Tyrell finally snared his pistol and turned to fire. But Blaine had already tumbled off the tanker's side, with Liz squeezed against him. The tanker sped forward on its own, Jack Tyrell still struggling to right his gun back at McCracken, the hose wrapped around him like a tentacle.

Blaine hit the pavement hard, cushioning the impact for Liz.

Tyrell pulled free of the tangle of hosing, rising atop the hood with gun in hand and turning, just as the tanker crested over the chasm. His eyes bulged, his hands stretched outward as if to grasp for the wind.

"Ahhhhhhhhhhhhhhhhhhhh!"

Blaine heard Tyrell's banshee-like scream as the tanker toppled through the air. He was close enough to watch it drop through the gap in the lower deck, with Jackie Terror riding it like a surfboard until the last moment before it splashed into the Hudson River.

The explosion came seconds later, in a massive air burst that sent a bubble of flames shrouded by water up out of the Hudson. The incredible percussion dragged a stack of vehicles from both spans into the churning waters below.

Blaine was hugging Liz tight against him when he felt the shock wave hit him, sucking all the oxygen it could from the air. He jammed both his hands through a ruined van's door handle, pinning Liz between the van and his body. Piles of cars were shifting everywhere, vehicles spinning free and darting wildly in all directions. Blaine could feel the van straining, but it held, wreckage jamming tightly against it.

A piece of flying debris caught McCracken in the wrist, tearing Liz from his grasp. He managed to grab her, but now they were in danger of being sucked over the edge. His grip on the van gave finally, and both of them were dragged across the pavement, Blaine groping desperately for a handhold on something, *anything*, as the chasm in the upper span loomed dangerously close.

His fingers had scraped across the wrecked husk of a BMW, when a hand shot down from its open sunroof and clamped like a vise upon his shoulder. Blaine looked up into the determined eyes of Johnny Wareagle and focused entirely on holding on to Liz.

The wave dissipated as quickly as it had come, leaving Blaine and Liz sitting on the debris-strewn pavement a mere ten feet from the jagged edge of the gap. Sal Belamo, whose leap had ended between a pair of heavy trucks that effectively shielded him, limped gingerly past them and peered down at the frothy, bubbling water, which had turned smoky black.

"Anybody for a swim?"

On the New Jersey side of the bridge, the huge convoy from Fort Dix was lined up as far as the eye could see, awaiting permission to cross into New York City.

"Just tell them to stand by," instructed the governor, as he spoke with Mayor Lucille Corrente on another line.

And on the upper span, Warren Muldoon, his face blackened with soot, his clothes torn and splattered with grime, rose between a pair of car wrecks, holding his cellular phone tight to his ear.

"Put it *back* again?" he asked disbelievingly. "Can't you people make up your minds?"

EPILOGUE

Blaine walked with Liz along the hospital corridors, her IV hookup keeping their pace slow.

"What about the Devil's Brew still underneath New York City?" she asked him.

"Apparently, it begins to dissipate after twenty-four hours. But, just to be on the safe side, they flooded the tunnels with overflow from the Hudson River."

"Even Devil's Brew won't be able to survive that."

"There's something else," Blain told her. He had visited her daily since the day New York City almost perished, but this was the first time she had been allowed out of her room. "According to Kirkland, the FBI lab has tried to re-create what your bullet supposedly did in that classroom and hasn't even been able to come close. You're being exonerated in the death of Tyrell's son."

"My father was right. They made me the scapegoat."

"And now they're prepared to reinstate you, with the Hostage and Rescue Team, if that's what you want."

"As a favor to you?"

"Payback's a bitch."

Liz shrugged. "Right now, all I want is my son back. I think he'd like growing up on the family farm."

Blaine stopped and faced her. "That doesn't sound like a Torrey to me."

"Not Buck, because I can't be like him."

"There are plenty worse things."

"But I've watched him and I've watched you, and from what I've seen, well, it just seems like you can never walk away from that kind of life. It sticks with you like gum on a shoe. Like it or not."

"I like it; I was afraid I had lost it."

"So you went to my father to get it back."

"And you know what I learned? That I had never lost it. That's what your father was trying to get across to me in Condor Key. That's what this means," Blaine said, holding up his hand so Liz could see his *DS* ring prominently displayed. "Dead Simple wasn't about the ease with which we killed; it was about the attitude that kept us alive. It's a mind-set that defines the level where I, the Indian, and your father play out our lives. . . . You too, if that's what you want."

Her gaze fell on Blaine's finger. "You notice Buck never gave me one of those rings."

"Maybe he was waiting for you to ask for it, hoping you never would."

"Why?"

"Because he didn't want you to pay the same price for wearing it he had."

"Is that why he ran away and hid in Condor Key?"

"No more than the Indian or I hid in other places, other ways. That's what your father didn't want to happen to you. I don't think he realized it had happened to him as well, until I found him down there. But he got it back, Liz. That's what brought him up here. That's what sent him after Stratton's gold, because he realized how goddamn much he missed the kind of life he turned his back on when he moved to Condor Key."

"Thanks to you going down there and reminding him," Liz said, not bothering to hide the bitterness in her voice. "I'm sorry. I shouldn't have said that."

"Why not? It's true."

"I already lost him for five years. I don't want to lose him again."

"You won't," Blaine promised.

Will Thatch was waiting upstairs when Bob Snelling got to his office.

"I told you I didn't want to see you ever again," Snelling told him.

"There's something I need you to do," Will said flatly.

"I'm not messing with those people again. Christ, not ever."

"That's all in the past, believe me."

Snelling looked him over. "So what is it you want?"

"My family. I want you to find them for me."

They met at a roadside diner, Farley Stratton into his second cup of coffee by the time McCracken walked through the door. He laid the leather pouch he had recovered from the corpse of William Henry Stratton on the table and eased it toward the colonel's great-great-grandson.

"I think you'll find the documents you're looking for inside," Blaine said. "I figured I'd leave the rest to you."

Stratton grasped the pouch tightly. "I've got a safe-deposit box just waiting for them."

"You're not going to open it?"

"You already told me what was inside."

"Doesn't mean I was right."

"But this way I'll never know if you were wrong."

"So history remains unchanged," Blaine concluded.

"The colonel was a hero. He helped win the Civil War. That's enough for me."

"What about the monster under the lake?"

Farley Stratton leaned back. "I think it's time it became extinct."

"Last of his kind. Too bad."

"It happens. Like dinosaurs."

"Be careful," Blaine warned, a smile tucked behind his lips. "They've been known to come back."

"This is as far as I can take ya," the sheriff said, stopping the old squad car where the dirt road ended. "But I reckon this time he knows you're coming."

Blaine McCracken nodded his thanks and slid out of the car, focusing on the tangled growth of vegetation and dark waters ahead.

"Don't forget your bag, now," the sheriff reminded, shifting it across the back seat.

Blaine reached inside and hoisted his duffel bag out effortlessly. The sheriff made no motion to join him outside the car, pointed straight ahead through the windshield instead.

"Looks like he's waiting for ya."

For the first time, Blaine noticed Buck Torrey's figure seated on the edge of the dock. He heard the sheriff pull away as he made his way over. Buck sat staring straight ahead. His legs dangled over the side. A pair of crutches lay dampening next to him. The familiar skiff was tied up to a mooring.

Buck kept his eyes on the water. "I heard what you did for Liz."

"I just told the FBI what you said. They took it from there."

Buck looked at him. "Good thing too, 'cause I got a bone to pick with you: what the hell you doing down here when those sons of bitches from Black Flag are still running around free?"

"They let Hank Belgrade and Will Thatch go, both unharmed. I figure that's as close as they can come to a show of good faith. Declaring a truce."

"They kept them alive just in case they needed them. Knew what would happen if they didn't."

"I can live with that."

"Can you live with playing their game?"

"It's our game too."

Buck gazed at his still heavily bandaged ankle. "Yours, maybe."

Blaine sat down so the crutches were between them. "That's why I came down."

"And me hoping you just wanted to buy a place in the neighborhood," Buck said, and hobbled gingerly to his feet.

"No vacancies, remember?" Blaine rose, bringing Buck's crutches with him. "You ready to get started?"

"I'm beginning to think I taught you too well, son."

"That's Captain to you, Sergeant Major."

They started the day after Blaine's arrival, Buck wearing old fatigues that made him hot but kept the bugs from eating him alive. They took the skiff past all the stilt houses into the shallow muck that made Blaine remember this was the Everglades. . . .